The Grail and the Ring

Ace Books by Teresa Edgerton

THE GREEN LION TRILOGY

CHILD OF SATURN
THE MOON IN HIDING
THE WORK OF THE SUN

GOBLIN MOON
THE GNOME'S ENGINE
THE CASTLE OF THE SILVER WHEEL
THE GRAIL AND THE RING

THE GRAIL
and the
RING

TERESA EDGERTON

ACE BOOKS, NEW YORK

This book is an Ace original edition,
and has never been previously published.

THE GRAIL AND THE RING

An Ace Book / published by arrangement with
the author

PRINTING HISTORY
Ace edition / January 1994

All rights reserved.
Copyright © 1994 by Teresa Edgerton.
Cover art by Dorian Vallejo.
Interior art by Ann Meyer Maglinte.
This book may not be reproduced in whole or in part,
by mimeograph or any other means, without permission.
For information address: The Berkley Publishing Group,
200 Madison Avenue, New York, New York 10016.

ISBN: 0-441-30157-6

ACE®
Ace Books are published by The Berkley Publishing Group,
200 Madison Avenue, New York, New York 10016.
ACE and the "A" design
are trademarks belonging to Charter Communications, Inc.

PRINTED IN THE UNITED STATES OF AMERICA

10   9   8   7   6   5   4   3   2   1

. . . so they carried the corpse to a distant place and they buried him deep in an unmarked grave, where the earth would not know him, where there were no priests or holy men to speak words over the bones of the dead, and the unhallowed men were powerless to reject him.

—*From* The Nine Sorrowful Tales of
the Misfortunes of Mochdreff

1.

Where the Dead Men Lost Their Bones

When Gwenlliant first came to live in the witch's house, she was almost fourteen, a fey child, pale and composed, who said little and thought much, growing slowly into her power. Dame Ceinwen, on the other hand, was . . . well, it was doubtful that even the wise-woman herself knew precisely how old she was. Some people said that she was the most ancient living thing on Ynys Celydonn, and she looked every bit of it, a gaunt old woman with parchment-colored skin drawn tight over crooked bones. Her dress was a collection of rags, black on black, layer upon layer, like strips of rough bark on a gnarled old tree. Indeed, Gwenlliant sometimes wondered if Ceinwen had produced these garments by any *ordinary* craft—the work of spindle, shuttle, and needle—or did the witch simply grow a new gown underneath for every ragged layer that wore away? There were so many remarkable things about Dame Ceinwen that growing and shedding a skin of black dresses seemed scarcely beyond her.

For instance, the stone hut where the girl and the wise-woman lived was truly extraordinary. If you stood in the center of the house, it appeared to be an ordinary circular one-room cottage—though there was something misty and indistinct about the edges

1

that might have warned you that things were not exactly as they seemed—a humble dwelling built of smooth white stones with a dirt floor and a single hearth, and a few sticks of furniture woven out of branches. But as soon as you ventured into the darkness at the edge of the room, you began to discover the many large cupboards and closets, the doors leading off into unexpected rooms, which the shadows and the fog so artfully concealed.

The winter that Gwenlliant lived there, the cottage was situated at the edge of a morass, the marshes of the Marches-Between-Here-and-There. That was a nebulous region belonging to no particular time or place, though day existed there and nighttime, too, and an orderly progression of seasons. When Gwenlliant stood on the doorstep looking east, it was all bulrushes and reeds and brackish water for mile upon mile, a vast, uninhabited stretch of black fenland and reeking bogs. But great wars had once been waged in that region, in days long past when the borders of reality were thinner, and the marsh concealed considerable booty from those ancient battles, as well as the remains of unfortunate refugees fleeing from one world to the next, who had lost their way and been claimed by the bog.

On days when the weather was mild, the girl and the wise-woman fared far across the fens, taking turns to hold the baby, Grifflet Og, whose steps were still unsteady, and whose short legs tired easily. Ceinwen went first, with an iron-shod staff clutched in one clawlike hand, poking experimentally at mud holes, while Gwenlliant followed after with a net and a long hook, waiting to fish out whatever the crone discovered beneath the surface. In this manner, they brought up a number of interesting items: homely objects like soup pots and ladles covered with rust and verdigris, several fine skulls and a large collection of assorted bones turned the color of polished ivory, and a fair amount of treasure—gold coins, jeweled daggers, silver circlets, and the like, which came out of the mud tarnished but more or less intact. There was some quality in the black soil and the brackish water of the marsh—whether natural or magical the girl did not know—that preserved things for centuries and centuries.

All of these items, the crowns and the coins and the bones and the soup pots, Gwenlliant and the witch returned to the marsh. "We have not come to rob the dead," said Dame Ceinwen, as they tipped a chest full of bottles and scrolls back into the bog, allowing it to sink down into the water and the mud until it was completely covered, "but to reclaim something that I lost here long, long ago.

"It is true that I was happy enough to be rid of it at the time," she added, with a shrug, "yet I have been thinking, lately, that it might be of use some day very soon."

But one day, with much tugging and pulling, much heaving and huffing, the witch and her apprentice brought an entire mummified body out of the deepest hole in the bog. The winding sheet was just beginning to rot, and through a rent in the fabric, against the leathery brown skin, Gwenlliant caught a glimpse of fine scarlet linen and glimmer of pure, bright gold. It could only be the gold of Tir Gwyngelli, which never tarnished under any conditions.

Without thinking what she was doing, Gwenlliant knelt on the grassy embankment beside the mummy, and removed the ring from its shriveled finger. "This is for me, I think." Then, blushing at her own boldness, puzzled by the odd impulse, she looked to Ceinwen for approval.

"Yes," said the witch, shifting the baby from one hip to the other. "This jewel you may keep. For they say all things of Gwyngelli, be they earth, metal, stone, or wood, desire to return there."

Gwenlliant slipped the heavy golden band onto her finger. It was a strange design, inscribed with symbols she could not decipher and set with a great rough cloudy crystal, yet its workmanship was every bit as fine as that of the bracelet she wore on her left arm, under the sleeve of her homespun gown.

They rolled the corpse down the embankment and back into the quagmire, which boiled and made sucking noises as if eager to receive it. "A king or a wizard or a great and powerful nobleman, perhaps . . . buried in secret in an unmarked grave," guessed Gwenlliant, watching the last bubbles rise to the surface. She could picture a midnight procession, all in black, with covered lanterns, threading a careful path across the bog.

And she wondered a little about his history. Perhaps he was still the subject of songs and legends in some distant place, one of those undying heroes expected to return at any moment and lead his countrymen into battle in their hour of direst need. She wondered, too, about the men who had brought him into the marsh for burial. Murderers and regicides, stealthy and subtle, seeking to conceal all evidence of their horrid crime? Or the last tattered remnants of some lost cause, trying to protect the bones of their fallen hero from desecration at the blood-soaked hands of his victorious enemies?

Do you *know?* she asked the dark water, the wind that rattled the dry bulrushes and lifted the hem of her brown wool cloak. But there was no answer. Above the surface it was all ephemeral, water, wind, and reed, and a history that extended no further back than the summer and autumn just past; whatever secrets lay hidden down in the depths, the marsh guarded them well. As for the ring, it spoke only of molten gold and careful craftsmanship, of the deep, cool silence of mines . . . and one phrase over and over: *I must and will go home.*

It was growing late, so Gwenlliant gathered up her net and her hook, and followed Dame Ceinwen back toward the cottage. Already, she scarcely noticed the weight of the golden ring; it felt quite natural there on her hand, as though she had worn it for years and years.

That evening after supper, when they were back in the hut, sitting by the hearth, Gwenlliant on a stool with Grifflet in her lap, the witch in her chair of woven branches, Dame Ceinwen asked to examine the ring. She kept the jewel for many minutes, turning it over in her hand, poking at the gold with a skinny finger, holding the ring up and peering through the golden circle with one beady black eye.

"I am minded to tell you a story," she said at last. "One that you may wish to repeat to your cousin Prince Tryffin, when you next meet him."

Gwenlliant settled Grifflet more comfortably on her lap, dropped an absentminded kiss on his soft auburn curls. (Not white-gold hair like her hair, or sun-gold like Tryffin's, but the rusty red he had inherited from his treacherous father.) He was growing so quickly, it was harder and harder for her to carry him about—especially on cold days when he was so heavy and awkward, bundled up in innumerable small coats and tunics, as well as his woolen leggings and lambskin boots—yet she liked to feel his strong little arms around her neck, his head resting sleepily against her shoulder.

"There was a great ruling prince, once, in the land of Mochdreff," Dame Ceinwen began her story. "And his name was Cerddin Wledig."

Gwenlliant gave a start. "The Prince of Mochdreff? But I always believed—that is, I was always taught . . . "

"You were taught that no man ruled in the land of Mochdreff, that it was all chaos and clan against clan, until your High King in Camboglanna invaded Mochdreff and chose one of the petty lords to be greater than the rest, to govern from the High Seat at Caer Ysgithr," said the witch.

Gwenlliant nodded. "But isn't it true, then, the story I was told?"

"It is true," said Ceinwen. "Or at least it is true so far as it goes. When the Emperor Cynfelyn led his men into Mochdreff and conquered the land, there was no native prince to swear fealty, to pass on the sovereignty. That is why the Wild Magic remains untamed, why it cannot be bound to the soil. But long years before that, perhaps a thousand years ago, there was a line of ruling princes. Not grand men who lived in castles, who dressed in rich brocade when at home and encased themselves in shining armor when they went into battle . . . these were men of a humbler sort, who lived in wooden halls, who possessed perhaps a single garment of silk, yet they led the clans in time of war, and they exercised true sovereignty.

"Cerddin Wledig was the last of that line," the witch continued, handing the ring back to Gwenlliant. It slid easily and comfortably onto her finger. "He did something so wicked that the people deposed him, so base and treacherous that his own kinsmen felt the shame so keenly that none was willing to succeed him afterward. Indeed, the entire clan dispersed to the four winds, and it is said that every single one of them changed his name and renounced his lineage, rather than carry the taint of Cerddin's crime. There may be men living in Mochdreff now who are descended from princes—perhaps in the old, proud clans like Guillyn and Machain—but no one knows who they are, nor would any man boast of the fact, even if he knew it."

"But what did Cerddin *do* that was so monstrous?" Gwenlliant asked, shivering a little in spite of the fire, as she tried to imagine a crime so heinous that every single one of the Prince's clansmen would renounce a crown and a royal heritage, rather than share in the infamy of the traitor's name.

"No one knows," Ceinwen answered. "Yet it must have been some unnatural act, a deed so wicked that the land itself cried out against it, and the innocent were punished along with the guilty."

Gwenlliant cuddled the baby a little closer. This shocking story had more to do with Grifflet than it had with her, because some day *he* might be Lord of Mochdreff . . . and he also carried the taint of his father's and mother's treachery. "Do you think—do you suppose, Dame Ceinwen, that people will hate Grifflet simply because Rhys and Essylt were so very bad?" she asked, with a frown.

The old woman hunched a narrow shoulder under her ragged black cloak. "That I cannot say, but there is some hope they will not do so. When your cousin claimed him, by that act he remade the child's destiny—nor should we forget the power of naming. Rhys the son of Rhys the traitor must be viewed with suspicion . . . but Grifflet fab Tryffin may some day grow up to be a great and honorable man."

Even on days when the weather was harsh and it was impossible to leave the cottage, the girl and the wise-woman never sat idle, they had so many tasks to occupy them. There was bread to be baked, and herbs to be steeped, pots and plates and cups to be scrubbed, spells to be learned then practiced and practiced. *To weave Ropes out of Sand*—that was one of the spells that Gwenlliant copied in her little grimoire, using a goose-quill pen she had made for herself, and a dish of ink made of oak galls and bark. *For enchanting an Apple. To induce a Serpent to divulge his Secrets. To capture an Image within a Mirror.* These were but a few of the spells that Gwenlliant wrote in her book.

And when all of these things were accomplished and done, there was the weaving, the mending, and the spinning, sitting long hours by a smoking peat fire. Gwenlliant was learning to spin flax into a fine linen thread, but it was a puzzle to her what Dame Ceinwen was spinning. The crone would reach into a little basket that she held on her lap and pull out the oddest things: bits of eiderdown and dandelion fluff . . . lambswool and clusters of mayblossom . . . what looked like it might be a piece of fur from Achushla the red vixen . . . enough straw and twigs to build a bird's nest . . . all of which went into the wise-woman's thread, along with hanks of her own white hair.

"What are you making?" Gwenlliant finally asked, one long, dull, rainy afternoon, when Grifflet was napping in his wicker cradle and it seemed like the day would never end.

Dame Ceinwen glanced up from her work. "Silk for your wedding gown." In fact, the thread was not nearly so coarse as one might suppose, considering some of the things it was made of; it emerged from the witch's crooked fingers as a fine, light, sky-colored thread.

But at Ceinwen's words, Gwenlliant felt her stomach lurch, a cold sensation creep up from her toes to her neck. "But I am already married to my cousin Tryffin."

The wise-woman shrugged a bony shoulder. "That was in Perfudd," she said—just as though nothing that happened in the wilds of Perfudd was of any account at all. "And the ceremony was conducted with unseemly haste. Prince Tryffin must marry you all over again, in the presence of his father and his family in Tir Gwyngelli. And *that*, we may be certain, will be an altogether grander affair, for which you must be suitably gowned."

Of course Gwenlliant knew all these things. She had, after all, been an active participant at that precipitous wedding in Perfudd, about to be wed against her will to a perfectly loathsome bridegroom, when her big golden cousin arrived at the very last minute to banish Gwenlliant's unwelcome suitor and marry her himself. She *was* Tryffin's wife, and that second ceremony was not really necessary, though she supposed inevitable.

And that was what troubled her . . . because why should Dame Ceinwen be spinning her spells to assure an event that was already decided and fated to be?

With that thought, the thread snapped. The witch put the broken length aside and calmly continued spinning, apparently unruffled by the unfortunate omen—even when the thread snapped a second time. But Gwenlliant waited breathlessly to see if it happened again.

All afternoon and into the evening, the thread continued to grow on the witch's spindle, longer and longer . . . while Gwenlliant grew colder and colder, watching with a kind of fascinated horror as Dame Ceinwen spun. Because she knew it would take a great deal of thread, the work of many rainy afternoons, of long nights spinning beside the hearth, to weave a length of silk sufficient for her wedding gown—which would provide plenty of time for the strand to break again.

And Gwenlliant was not certain that even Ceinwen, as ancient and wise and powerful as she was, could mend a spell that was three times broken.

It was a town of crooked streets and overhanging second stories, a town of slate and granite, of limestone and mortar gone soft with erosion, built on the flinty bones of an even more ancient city. It was a town where age lent little dignity, for everything had a decaying, impermanent air, and there was something inexpressibly oppressive in the way the shops and the taverns all leaned inward, in the tumble of stifling little drystone huts built up against the outer walls, in the faded grandeur of the crumbling mansions of the petty lords. Why anyone had chosen to build a city there to begin with was something of a mystery, except for its proximity to the sea, because the wells all steamed faintly, and the air and the water carried more than a hint of brimstone.

It was also, strangely, a town with an uncommon number of churches and graveyards. From his vantage point at the tower window, facing westward, Tryffin could see at least a dozen spires, and riding into Anoeth from the south on his big roan gelding, earlier that day, he had passed a number of ruinous small chapels surrounded by overgrown cemeteries.

He turned away from the open casement, returning his attention to the petty noblemen who had gathered together in the round tower chamber to plead for his assistance. Tryffin had come to Anoeth in answer to an urgent summons by these same minor lords, but the letter they sent him had been garbled and confused, and the stories which greeted him on his arrival had been no easier to follow, for they were all as wild as they were inconsistent.

"A curse more fearful than the plague or murrain." That was Rhonabwy, Lord of Llech Obrwy. He was the oldest man there in the room, bent and grey, with a shining dome of a skull encircled by a thin fringe of hair. "And if the Governor will not aid us . . . if Your Grace should deny us . . . I do not know what will become of us."

Tryffin sighed and shook his head. "If I thought I might be of use, I would be entirely at your service. But I hardly see what I or my troop could possibly accomplish that your own men-at-arms, even your ordinary able-bodied townsmen, could not manage equally well. This is no country village, the men of this place are armed with better weapons than scythes and staves and skinning knives, and you certainly don't require my help to organize a party to hunt down and kill this—this animal roaming your streets."

"No animal, Lord Prince . . . no natural creature, anyway," said one of the other men—Tryffin had failed to catch his name. As with most of the others present, he appeared pale and strained, and was somberly dressed in dull, heavy fabrics, like a man on his way to a wake or a funeral. "Say rather a ghost or—or a shadow, for no one living has actually seen it, though a few have seemed to sense its approach like some foul premonition. Women dream, sometimes, a night or two before an attack, of an immense grey cat, yet it enters into rooms where no animal could go, for it lifts latches and turns keys in their locks."

His hand played nervously with the hilt of a jeweled dagger as he continued. "Yet, unlike a ghost, it leaves a trail of sorts behind, though faint and ambiguous. It is true that dogs and horses can scent the creature, but there is not a hound in Anoeth that can be coaxed or brutalized into following that scent. What we need—"

"—what we need," said Lord Rhonabwy, "are more men to watch and to guard, until by luck or persistence someone actually surprises the creature feeding."

Tryffin turned back toward the window. The nearest church was but two streets away, close enough that it was possible for him to make out the transfixed martyrs in the stained-glass windows, the gargoyle waterspouts, and the curious ornaments adorning the bell tower. There were a great number of these iron castings, which seemed to be imps or minor devils, crawling about on the peaked roof of the belfry. One of those imps, a bat-winged monstrosity, even had the audacity to dangle by its tail from the cross at the top.

Tryffin found that one more disturbing than the rest, the ones that gaped and leered and groveled on the roof; from its neck to its toes it was clearly a devil, but it had the face of an innocent, dreaming child. He thought the craftsmen who made those ornaments must have possessed some hidden streak of cruelty, to attach that head to such a hideous body.

"But surely the whole of Anoeth is already watching." Moving lightly and silently in his riding leathers, despite his size, Tryffin left the window and took a seat in a carved oak chair. "What difference could twenty men make? As you already know, I was on my way to Cormelyn when your letter found me. Three clans teeter on the verge of blood feud, and though the principal men of all three families have pledged to allow me to settle their dispute, I fear they can't restrain their folk much longer, since emotions are running high. If I delay here for a week or ten days, many men . . . perhaps women and children, too . . . will almost certainly die."

"Many have died in Anoeth already." That was the Lord of Llech Obrwy again. "There have been dozens of victims in the poorer parts of town, as well as many mysterious disappearances, old people and small children, who were perhaps devoured whole. Perhaps no one told you, Prince Tryffin . . . " Here, his voice broke, and Rhonabwy needed several moments to regain his composure. ". . . that the beast preys mostly on children and nursing infants."

Tryffin felt the blood drain from his heart. This might, of course, be a story invented for his benefit, this slaughter of the innocents, meant to appeal to his particular sensibilities, the outrageous (by Mochdreffi standards) sentimentality of their foreign Governor. The Mochdreffi, as he well knew, were a pragmatic race—silent, aloof, and callous by southern standards—so it was difficult for him to believe that these petty lords felt genuine distress simply because children were dying "in the poorer parts of the town."

He glanced across the room at the one man who was out of place there: a spare, cold man, elegantly dressed, who far from bearing the marks of strain and tension, looked nothing so much as unutterably bored. "Lord Cernach, you were against my meeting with these men, so I am told . . . and you seem not to take this tragedy so much to heart." Tryffin watched carefully, gauging the man's reaction as he spoke.

Cernach fab Clydno turned a ruby ring around on his finger, made a slight adjustment to the fall of a purple velvet sleeve. "Rather, let us say, I was against bringing the Governor so far, merely to involve him in our trivial misfortunes," he replied smoothly.

The Governor raised a sandy eyebrow, shrugged a broad shoulder. "I was in Penhalloc, only a few hours away. And the death of so many children . . . I hardly count that as a trivial misfortune. I wonder, Lord Cernach, why you seem to regard this matter so lightly."

Cernach smiled, made an airy gesture. "The children of the poor are always dying for no apparent cause . . . why should anyone suspect some supernatural agency, merely because they are doing so now in unusual numbers?"

Someone made a sound of protest beside and a little behind him, and Tryffin turned in his chair to face the lean, dark Captain who had been silently guarding him all this while. "Well, Meligraunce? It seems you have something to say about that."

"Your Grace, I do," said Meligraunce, clenching those big knobbly peasant's hands of his. With Tryffin's help, he had educated himself far above his natural station, he spoke and dressed and handled a sword as well as any nobleman in the land, but those hands which had tilled the soil, which had been gnarled and broken by weather and hard work, invariably betrayed his humble origins. "With all due respect to Lord Cernach, the children of the poor do not often die of *unknown* causes. They are unfortunately susceptible to disease, it is true, and great numbers die of hunger or of cold . . . but not in March, not when the weather is mild and food is no longer so scarce."

Lord Cernach made another dismissive gesture. "Say then some mysterious disease which robs them of breath. And all this talk of nightmares and ghostly grey cats a hysterical reaction by ignorant men and women, simply because they do not understand the true cause. It is all an old wives' tale, you know, that cats steal the breath of sleeping infants."

There were murmured protests around the room, a rustle of heavy cloth. "I never heard it said that cats subsist on the blood of infants," exclaimed Rhonabwy. "I never heard any such tale before this."

"They *say* the dead children are pale and bloodless when they are found, but I never spoke with anyone yet who thought to open a vein and make absolutely certain," said Cernach. "I repeat what I told you before, Prince Tryffin, it is all ignorance and superstition. You would do better to continue on to Cormelyn, where you may do some good, rather than linger on here."

Tryffin frowned, drumming his fingers on the arm of the chair. Someone in this room was lying—perhaps all these petty noblemen were lying. There was an edginess, a tension in the way these men of Anoeth held themselves and spoke and moved, even in the very pattern of their breathing, that suggested someone was hiding something, and that every one of them knew it. The only exception was Lord Cernach—and while his callous air of indifference was certainly more convincing, in its way, than anything the others had told him so far, that, too, might be carefully calculated. "These other noble gentlemen don't agree with you," said Tryffin. "Now, why do you suppose that is?"

"But they *did* agree with me," said Cernach. "Until three days since, when Lord Garwy's little granddaughter was found dead in her cradle, apparently suffocated, and they all began to fear that their own children were in danger."

Tryffin continued to regard him suspiciously. "But you do not? Or perhaps it is just that you have no children of your own and so have nothing to lose if this plague continues?"

Lord Cernach inclined his head slightly; a cynical smile played about the corners of his mouth. "It is true that I am not a married man . . . and if I have children, their mothers have been admirably discreet. But as to the matter in question: If the death of a dozen infants did not convince me there was some supernatural creature stalking our streets, why should the death of one more? And I see no reason to connect the one incident with any of the others. The child was a miserable sickly thing to begin with, and there was no talk of nightmares or premonitions before she died."

There was a long silence after that, during which the other men shifted uncomfortably in place, waiting for the Governor to proclaim his intentions.

Tryffin rubbed a hand over his brow. There was a sharp pain behind his eyes, and his temples were beginning to throb. And that was another thing that made him uneasy, these uncharacteristic headaches—an insult to his accustomed robust good health, his sober and practical turn of mind—which had recently begun to assault him whenever he had to make some particularly agonizing decision. Like the choice that faced him now: whether to rush off to Cormelyn, in the hope he might avert the bloodshed and the horror of a feud that might continue for . . . ah God, there was no way of telling how many generations! . . . or to stay in Anoeth and attempt to confront and defeat the horror there.

"I will stay in Anoeth tonight, at least, send out my men, ask a few questions of the families of the murdered children, before I decide whether it is possible for me to help you," he said at last. "And if—in all good conscience—I can delay my journey into Cormelyn for the length of time it might take me to do so."

But he knew that unless the ordinary citizens of the town told him a story that was substantially different from that of the petty lords, he was going to stay. As he knew also that whatever he decided, someone, somewhere, was going to suffer for it.

*But when Cynfarch grew weary with age and the burdens of
power, being at that time more than a century old, he took on the
shape and the nature of one of his ancient ravens . . . but what
became of him afterward no man can say.*

*Yet it is said that those who were later born of his line felt a
deep kinship with the birds of the air, but particularly the ravens
and the crows, which they were wont to regard as their brothers
and sisters, cousins, uncles, and aunts.*

—From the Oral Tradition of Rhianedd

2.

The Breathing Mist

When spring came, the rivers feeding the fenlands rose, and
the marsh flooded. No longer a sea of mud and reeds, it became
instead a vast silver watery ocean, with here and there an
island-hillock, and the tips of the very tallest cattails and
bulrushes raising their heads above the surface.

The witch's house, though it stood on a rise, was entirely
surrounded by water; on days when it rained, the water lapped as
high as the doorsill. For weeks upon weeks, Gwenlliant felt
restless and caged. It was impossible to go out on foot; the crone
owned a little boat made out of rushes, but where would it take
them? It seemed to her that the worlds were unmade, that nothing
existed, any longer, but the house, the muddy islands, and the
great, featureless face of the deep. Even if they still existed
beneath the waters, it would be impossible to locate the mud
holes where the girl and the witch did their dredging.
There could be no more hunting for treasure, not until the deluge
subsided.

Yet there came a grey, blustery day, as Gwenlliant was pacing
the floor, moving with quick impatient steps from one window to
the other, peering gloomily out at the rain and the flood, when
Dame Ceinwen announced they would soon take a journey.

The girl whirled to face her. "A journey . . . where? Are you going to move the house again?"

Ceinwen sat by the fire, in her chair of woven branches, mending one of Grifflet's lambskin tunics. "Far out in the marsh, further than we have ever ventured together, is a ruined tower." She continued to stitch as she spoke. "An old man lives there, a wizard who wandered into the Marches out of the distant past and decided to stay. I say he is a wizard, but in fact he is one of the great Adepts: wizard, warlock, and priest in one. There are certain questions I would pose this wizard, riddles too complex for me to unravel."

"But you . . ." said Gwenlliant, moving swiftly to kneel on the packed-earth floor beside the old woman's chair. ". . . you are also a great Adept."

The witch cackled and shook her head. "You are kind to say so. It is true that I once held certain ambitions, when I was young and I lived in my brother's house, but the Science of Wizardry was dry and unsatisfying, and of course I had no great burning desire to become a holy sister . . . and the Old Religion had passed from the land. I decided, instead, to become one with the earth and the seasons, to learn the old magics more deeply than any witch ever had learned them before, and in that ambition I eventually succeeded.

"Had I not learned early the wisdom of restraint, the folly of too much meddling in the destinies of others, I might have become the greatest curse, the most horrifying plague the land of Mochdreff has ever known." The old woman sighed and shook her head, gazing into the fire with unseeing eyes. "With immense power, so long as it be coupled with a similar amount of wisdom, comes a certain impotence. I soon discovered that it was not for me to rule in majesty, or to sit in judgment in the halls of kings and princes. I became like the bad fairy instead, appearing at weddings and christenings with blessings and curses . . . the tattered old crone that one meets in the forest or crossing a lonely moor . . . the asker of riddles, the imposer of solitary tests. Every now and again there was a child to care for and raise in seclusion: the infant hero, the lost heir, the witch-born princess found wandering the dusty roads like a beggar, in search of a teacher . . ."

"You are speaking of me," said Gwenlliant, a smile quirking her lips. "Of Grifflet and, I suppose, Mahaffy."

"I speak of making decisions, which is sometimes very hard," the witch replied. Outside the cottage, the wind howled and the rain continued to fall on the roof in a slow, depressing drizzle. "For every choice that we make, we turn our backs on some other course of action, often not knowing what it is we are rejecting. My knowledge is deep, as deep as hidden springs and underground rivers, but it avails me nothing in trying to solve a certain charming little riddle the fates have posed for me."

She put out a gnarled hand, caught a strand of Gwenlliant's white-gold hair. "I found you wandering the roads with the dwarf Brangwengwen, your head full of evil spells which you had gleaned from the books of the Princess Diaspad. Your powers then were wild and terrifying, for you had studied your craft with only that foolish and wicked dwarf to guide you, and had learned only the worst sort of magics. I brought you to this cottage, erased those spells from your mind, and began the slow and painstaking task of teaching you all over again. You are an apt pupil, for Witchcraft comes naturally, but as for me, I am often baffled . . ."

She went back to her mending, threading the needle with a strand of her own white hair. "It is the way that witches and wizards receive their educations. A Mochdreffi wise-woman begins her education very early, often as soon as her gift becomes known. It is very different with wizards. They gain their power not through inborn talent but through a harsh discipline which trains the mind and the will. For this reason, only those with a strong vocation are initiated into their mysteries, and they do not begin to train their apprentices before they are ten or twelve—and often much older. They know very well the ways and the means for teaching young men and young women, but they know very little of our own Earth magics. Unless, of course, they happen to be Adepts."

"Yes, I see," said Gwenlliant, with a sinking feeling. "I came here too late. You will ask this wizard to let me stay with him, and be his student instead of yours."

Outside, the wind had died, and inside the cottage, there was a long moment of silence. The room was so still that Gwenlliant could hear the mice up inside the roof, nibbling away at the thatch.

"Perhaps I didn't mention that he is your distant kinsman—or so I believe," the witch said at last. "He is tall and fair like most Rhianeddi, and that castle of his is like a great rookery, filled with the sight and the sound of dark wings. Not only rooks live there, but blackbirds, magpies . . . and a flock of ravens, almost as ancient as he is himself, who sit on his shoulder and eat from his plate, and occasionally whisper their secrets into his ear. If he is still alive, and in full possession of his senses, I think he will make you an admirable teacher."

Gwenlliant rose to her feet, picked up a poker, and stirred up the fire. She did not want to leave Ceinwen—not unless she was going home to Tryffin—she did not wish to be uprooted again from a place where she was comfortable and happy, to live, instead, with a mysterious old wizard she had never even heard of before. Yet she understood what the witch was telling her, and realized there was no use protesting.

In the predawn chill, they dressed and began to prepare for their journey, moving quietly about the cottage so as not to disturb the baby.

"It is likely to take us the better part of the day," said the crone. "We must make certain to take plenty of food and water with us." By the light of a single candle, she put black bread and cheese, a flask of sweet water, and a handful of oat cakes into a wicker basket. She added some dried berries and a hard winter apple, then covered it all with a rough linen cloth.

Gwenlliant bundled together her clothes, the book of spells, and a number of smaller items, before waking Grifflet and beginning to dress him. A sudden painful doubt struck at her heart. "Is Grifflet to stay with me . . . or return with you?"

"The child is yours to raise," said the witch. "Have I not said so?"

The pain subsided a little, yet she still felt shaken and more than a little homesick, not only for this place she was about to leave, but for her big, broad-shouldered cousin, and for Caer Ysgithr, where they had lived together, and for their household of squires and pages . . .

Except that Cei, who had been her page, would be somebody's squire by now, she reflected gloomily. And little Elffin would be serving another lady, not waiting about for her to return, his education in the courtly graces entirely neglected. In fact they would all be changed, one way or another. Garth and Mahaffy would have been knighted, with suitable pomp and ceremony. And if Conn had not been knighted as yet, he soon would be. She had missed a great many important occasions, already, and would likely go right on missing them, because who knew when she would be going home? Tryffin had promised to come and claim her at Midsummer—but how many months, how many seasons or years, would pass here on the Marches Between the Worlds before summer arrived in Mochdreff?

But I have Grifflet now, she told herself, cradling him close. He was warm and solid in her arms, his auburn curls still damp with sleep. She wrapped him up in his cloak and a blanket, and carried him out to the boat.

Soon they were skimming across the silver water, the rising sun warm on their backs. The baby was curled up fast asleep at the bottom of the canoe, so Gwenlliant paddled. Where the water was shallow, the old woman used her staff like a pole to steer them.

The marsh had been empty the day before, but now great nations of migrating waterfowl had settled on the muddy islands: cranes, wild swans, ducks, and grey geese. As the crimson sun climbed higher in the sky, the birds began to wake and to move about, and soon they were wheeling in enormous flocks overhead. It was difficult to talk over the clamor they made, so Gwenlliant continued to paddle in silence.

After about an hour, Ceinwen opened her basket, and they ate their breakfast. Grifflet woke up and demanded his share. He was such a downright, decided little person, for all he was just beginning to talk—he could only say "please" and something that sounded like Gwenlliant's name.

"I wonder that you never taught him to call you Mother," said Ceinwen.

The girl thought about that, as she broke an oat cake into tiny bits and fed it to Grifflet. It was true she had taken care of him ever since the wet nurse left. She had fed and cuddled him, washed and dressed him. When he was frightened or ill, she held him; when he could not sleep, she sang him lullabies. The wicked Lady Essylt had done none of those things. But did that make Gwenlliant his *mother* . . . or only his nurse? Nursemaids were fond of their charges, she knew, so loving him dearly had nothing to do with it. And when she was a princess again, and had children of her own, she would not be the one charged with their care; there would be plenty of servants for that.

But my own little ones will sleep under my heart for nine long months, and so I will learn to love them.

"I will teach him to call me his mother when I have earned that right," she finally decided. "When I have fed him and cared for him just as long as Essylt did before he was born."

The crone nodded approvingly. "You know something of binding and making. To become a father, there is not much to it: a little thrusting and groaning at the beginning, then nothing to do but wait and acknowledge the child after it is born. To become a mother is a longer and far more wearisome task."

They paddled and poled until they reached a place where the ground was higher. "We will leave the boat and walk from here," said Ceinwen, as they pulled the canoe up onto the muddy embankment.

"But what if it is flooded, further on?" asked Gwenlliant.

"There are reeds enough, and rushes for binding. We can make a new one if we must," said the witch. She indicated Grifflet, who was sitting in the grass and sucking on his fist. "You must carry the young one the rest of the way—being that you are still gestating him," she said, with a cackle.

As it was growing quite warm, Gwenlliant removed her brown wool cloak and the top two layers of the baby's clothing, and made it all into a bundle which she slung over her back. Then she picked up Grifflet, balancing him on her hip, and followed the old woman as she beat a trail through the cattails and the high marsh grasses with her staff.

They had not progressed far when a mist came creeping over the ground to meet them, swirling around their ankles, then climbing to their waists in a matter of minutes. It was such a thick, damp, clinging fog that moving through it actually felt harder than pushing through the grass.

The ground shuddered beneath Gwenlliant's feet, and the air seemed to shudder as well. "It is the Breathing Mist," she exclaimed, coming to a sudden halt. "Dame Ceinwen . . . did you call it here?"

The Mist was a natural phenomenon, there in the marsh, but it could also be summoned, with a pot of boiling water, a handful of herbs, and the proper incantation. Arriving unbidden, it could be terribly dangerous.

"I did not call it," said the witch. "Yet it is certainly the Breathing Mist. We must go back to the house; we must go swiftly and try to arrive before the fog does. Otherwise, the cottage will be in one world and we in another, and it will be no easy task trying to find it again."

They turned back the way they had come, Ceinwen in the lead. But they could not outdistance the blanket of fog, which moved as quickly as they did. The Mist was over their heads now, blotting out the sun, but the fog had its own luminosity, so it was like moving through a sea full of light. The most difficult thing for Gwenlliant was keeping up with Ceinwen, burdened with the baby as she was. She had never realized the crone could move so quickly.

For a moment, the girl thought she had lost the old woman entirely . . . then Ceinwen's voice came through the enveloping Mist, thin with distance. "The ring, you must take it off at once. It is drawing you away from me."

That was not how it felt to Gwenlliant. She thought that the crone was moving away, and she was the one forced to stand still, unable to make way against the curtain of vapor. Yet she tried to obey at once, tugging at the ring. The golden band would not budge—Gwenlliant could actually feel the metal contract on her finger.

"It won't come off . . . Ceinwen, don't leave me," she cried in a panic, still struggling to free herself.

"You are going where I dare not follow," the old woman answered, her voice continuing to dwindle. "Into the Shadow Lands, to a time and place forbidden to me. Only remember what I have taught you: Do not reveal your name to anyone."

By now, it was impossible to even guess which direction Ceinwen was speaking from. "I will send help, as soon as I may, to bring you back again," said that faint voice, lost somewhere in the fog and the grass and the cattails.

Gwenlliant cried out again, but this time there was no answer, only the harsh breath of the Mist, the quaking ground beneath her feet. Except for Grifflet, whimpering in her arms and hiding his cold little face against her neck, she was completely alone.

After a time, the fog quit pushing at her and she was able to move again. She began to walk, though with no real sense of direction, yet it was important to keep moving. The Mist was cold and penetrating for all its luminosity, and Gwenlliant was chilled to the bone. Worse, she could feel Grifflet shivering, and his clothes all heavy with damp. She was horribly afraid he would take ill; he was much too little to withstand the cold. But her cloak was wrapped up in the bundle at her back, and she did not dare put him down in order to get at it, for fear the Breathing Mist would snatch the baby away, as it had just stolen Ceinwen. She could only hold Grifflet closer, hoping to lend him a little heat, and try to find a way out of the fog. She could only keep plodding on, for hour after weary hour, carrying the baby, no matter that her arms were aching and she was already stumbling with cold and exhaustion.

After what seemed an eternity of walking, the Mist began to thin. Gwenlliant realized she had left the marsh behind some time back, and was now walking across what appeared to be a vast stretch of moorland. The grass was still high, but there were bushes as well: heather, gorse, broom, and wild thyme. As the Mist continued to dissipate, the sky overhead turned blue, and the air was filled with a vast buzzing . . . which Gwenlliant soon realized was the humming of bees. The bushes were full of them: fat gold and black honeybees, gathering nectar from the blossoming thyme and heather.

The air was a good deal warmer—deliciously so, in fact—but the baby was still shivering, and she could feel him coughing against her neck. She set Grifflet down on the grass and unwrapped her bundle. Then, kneeling down beside him, she proceeded to strip off his damp outer garments and replace them with the others she had carried on her back.

"But how am I going to feed you?" she asked. "Ceinwen had the basket—and all of my things." Grifflet, at least, had been wearing practically every stitch that he owned. He would not lack for clothing, but was likely to grow hungry and thirsty before very long.

"And how to get back again? Even if I had a pot to boil water in, and the proper herbs, I don't suppose it would do any good to summon the Mist, not while this beastly ring remains on my hand. I wonder what it meant to accomplish by bringing me here?" She tried to tug it off again, but the gold band was just as stubbornly determined to cling to her finger as ever. "Dame Ceinwen said that she would send help . . . but who could help us where she could not? It really seems hopeless."

Gwenlliant sat back on her heels and glanced around her. She knew that she was in the Shadow Lands, the Inner Celydonn, and that she and the baby had arrived in some ghost, some blurred mirror image, of the island kingdom, past or present. She had ventured into that country before, but only with Ceinwen along to guide her, and they had been careful never to meet up with any of the inhabitants, because dealing with the people who lived in that realm could be very dangerous. Some were quite powerful, and if they knew anything about magic at all, they had dozens of ways of finding you out and then taking advantage.

"Wherever we are, it is high summer, though I don't see anything that we can eat, no berries or nuts or mushrooms. But I do see a thicket of trees up ahead—an oak wood by the look of it—and what appears to be smoke rising above the trees. That means there is probably a house and some people, people who might provide the things that we need."

Grifflet, of course, gave her no council. He just lay blinking up at her, waving his chubby little hands and coughing weakly. She was relieved to see that he had finally stopped shivering. And the cough, she supposed, might even be feigned—now he had discovered a way to gain her instant and complete attention—yet he was likely to grow genuinely and dangerously ill if forced to spend the night out-of-doors, after all he had endured already. If she had only herself to think and contrive for, Gwenlliant might have attempted to live off the land for a day or two at least. But with the baby to care for . . .

"If dealing with the inhabitants should happen to be dangerous . . . well, at least I know all of the rules," she decided at last, climbing wearily back to her feet.

She could picture Dame Ceinwen in her mind, sitting before the fire, reciting those rules, one by one, in her creaking old voice:

"Never tell your name to anyone, for if you do, you will be in their power.

"You cannot change the true past—the people you meet will be ghosts, shadows. Their actions you may subtly alter, though history will struggle to follow its accustomed course, and if you set yourself in opposition, you will be the one who is destroyed.

"Besides these ghosts there are other creatures, not quite human . . . giants and goblins, and of course the Sidhe. Whether such folk ever truly existed in our own world, I cannot say. But this much I can tell you: Some of them are noble and good, others most terribly wicked, but even the best are perilous to know, and you had best not cross them if you can possibly help it.

"Try not to meet yourself coming or going, neither the ghost of your past, nor any shadow of your present self, for that way lies madness and maybe even death."

Gwenlliant shook her head at the memory. "Well," she said, looking down at Grifflet, "I know that *I* never passed this way before, and there is not much chance that *you* have, so we need not worry about that. As for the other dangers, we will just have to face them . . . because I am afraid we are going to be here for a very long time."

With that thought to bolster her resolve, she draped her cloak over one arm, picked up the baby out of the grass, and began to walk toward the thicket of oak trees.

It was an hour after daybreak when Tryffin entered the inn, dismissed his men, sent his squire to the kitchen to see what was available for breakfast, then trudged upstairs to his bedchamber. Though the stories he had collected patrolling the stony streets of Anoeth during the dark hours just past had scarcely been appetizing, it had been a long, cold, wearisome night, and he thought a hot meal would go a long way toward reviving his spirits.

It was a typical Mochdreffi inn, with the sleeping chambers up under the eaves. At night (thought Tryffin) you could probably lie awake in bed and listen to the wind rattling the slates. Because it was an inn of the better sort, the room was clean and spacious, with wide casement windows, the bed linens freshly washed, but the ceiling was still oppressively low and the fireplace tiny, which kept things dim in spite of the windows. Yet he was pleased to note that candles were still burning from the night before, two big wax ones standing in pools of their own drippings, and someone had kindled a fire on the miniature hearth.

He doffed his cloak, ducked under a blackened beam, and took a seat by the fire, waiting for Conn to arrive with the food. Though the wait was not long, he was already deep in thought, and he reacted with a start when the door opened up and the boy came in balancing a wooden tray.

"Did I come too soon? I thought you wanted your breakfast at once. I can—" Conn started backing toward the door.

"No, you don't interrupt . . . not anything of value." Tryffin waved his squire into the room and examined the tray with reviving interest. "What did you bring me?"

Like the Governor, Conn wore armor, a combination of mail and plate—though Tryffin's had been treated with linseed oil to turn it black, and the vambraces and gorget inlaid with a thin tracery of gold.

"They only had tripes and boiled eggs, some coarse bread and a bit of beef . . . and the usual very poor wine." The boy spoke as he placed his tray on a table by the hearth and began to set out the plates and cups.

"Good enough," said Tryffin, and set to work at once. He was halfway through his second helpings of tripe and eggs, when Meligraunce knocked and entered the room.

"Have you eaten yet, Captain? If not, serve yourself, and take a seat by young Conn." He indicated a bench by the open window, where the boy had retired with a laden trencher.

"Thank you, Prince Tryffin, but I had a bite at dawn. That should suffice for the moment."

The Governor gave him a wry look. Though Meligraunce occasionally unbent in private—enough, at least, to accept a seat and a cup of wine or ale—he was the very soul of rigid propriety when any third party was present. "Very well then. Make your report."

"This is an unfriendly town for strangers—as no doubt you noticed," said the Captain, removing his dark wool cloak and taking a few steps into the room. The burnished metal of his own light armor glinted softly in the pale candlelight. "But this much I was able to learn: The Lord of Llech Obrwy and the rest did not exaggerate the danger. If anything, things are far worse than any of them guess. More than a hundred children have died of this . . . plague."

"More than a hundred? I had reckoned the dead at half that number, but I suppose you have reports from Ciag's party as well?" Meligraunce nodded, and the Governor pushed away his plate, his appetite suddenly gone. "I hadn't thought there were that many children in a town this size."

"The numbers of the children of the poor are far vaster than you may realize. As Lord Cernach implied, few survive long enough to intrude on anyone's notice," said Meligraunce, with a shrug.

Tryffin balled his hand into a big fist. "If this were Tir Gwyngelli, you may be certain that even the children of the very poorest would intrude on my father's notice . . . and if they were dying in unusual numbers, Maelgwyn fab Menai would be the first to realize it."

"Your father is a remarkable man; even among kings and princes he is remarkable. But with all due respect to Lord Maelgwyn, he has been ruling Gwyngelli since before you were born and he has the love of his people to make that task easier.

You have worked wonders here in less than two years, but you could not make Mochdreff into Tir Gwyngelli in an entire lifetime." Meligraunce frowned. "You have never been the man to torture yourself with unrealistic expectations. Are you aware of something happening in Anoeth that I don't know about?"

But Tryffin waved that question away. "Continue with your story. The ghostly grey cat, the babies found smothered in locked rooms . . . these all conform to the general report?"

"They do. And I am sure you noticed, when Lord Rhonabwy and the rest were speaking, they seemed to be withholding something. If anything, that impression was even stronger when I spoke to the common people. There was often . . . a sudden halt in a conversation, a word left hanging, a sentence begun but never finished. In truth, I believe there was some natural suspicion of me as a stranger, and yet it went deeper than that. I felt they were afraid that someone might overhear what they said, and that they were in mortal terror of the consequences. Not of Lord Rhonabwy or the other lords, but of something greater . . . something more pervasive."

Meligraunce moved toward the cherrywood fire smoking on the hearth. He put his hands out over the blaze, but as usual the flames offered little heat; there was something in the wood that grew in Mochdreff that starved a fire. "At first, I thought it might be the creature itself, stopping their tongues. But the truth is, they hardly spoke of anything else. Their grief is terrible; not a family among them has not been touched—even Lord Cernach, for all he spoke so coldly. The child he mentioned, the infant that died . . . she was his niece, his sister's little daughter."

Tryffin pushed back his chair. "That I did not know. He is a good deal harder than I had suspected. But I wonder if you noticed: Nothing has been said of the witches of Anoeth. I would think that hardly a house in the town would not be surrounded by their spells of protection. You will remember last year, when we were riding through Mochdreff hunting Lord Cado's monsters, and whenever we came into a village, no one would tell us what we wanted to know, not unless we spoke to their wise-women first."

"It is not like that in the streets and the taverns of Anoeth," Meligraunce agreed. "No one said anything about wise-women or warding spells. I had the impression, wherever I went, that I had suddenly been magically transported out of Mochdreff and into some other place—Rhianedd or Perfudd, perhaps—to a town where nobody practiced Witchcraft at all."

Conn looked up from his wooden plate. "But I have heard of the witches of Anoeth; they are said to be very haughty and powerful. They could hardly have disappeared from the town, and no one willing to speak of it."

"So I think also," said the Governor. "Yet it is certainly very puzzling."

Meligraunce gave up on the fire and turned to face him. "There is something else . . . perhaps I should have mentioned it earlier. There was another child killed during the night."

The room was very still. Tryffin felt his stomach contract into a knot; Conn stopped chewing and swallowed hard.

"Mother of God! So much for any good we had hoped to accomplish with our patrols last night." The Governor left his seat and began to pace the floor.

"Yes," said Meligraunce. "It is particularly unfortunate, because the little lad died only a few streets from the tavern where I spent half the night asking questions."

Tryffin rubbed his forehead; the pain was beginning again, just behind his eyes. "Captain, could you arrange for me to see the body? I mean, can the thing be done quietly and without intruding on the grief of his family?"

"Naturally, Your Grace, anything you wish can be arranged." Meligraunce hesitated. "But there is no need for you to distress yourself. I have already examined the body, and there was nothing—"

"Nevertheless, I would like to see for myself," said Tryffin. On a sudden impulse toward action, he left his chair, threw his cloak over his shoulders, and strode purposefully to the door. "And if, as you say, the sight of one dead child should happen to distress me, then so much the better. When there is so much sorrow in this town of Anoeth, the least I can do is share their grief."

The house where Meligraunce took him was narrow and dingy, with a shop below and a dwelling above, squeezed in between houses of a similar sort. As he meant to go quietly and draw little attention, the Governor had decided to take only a minimal escort. Besides Conn and Meligraunce, who walked ahead of him, two guardsmen followed him up the steep staircase and into the stifling upper room. Tryffin ducked his head as he passed over the threshold, to avoid a collision with the door frame.

The small body was lying on a wooden table, and someone had placed tallow dips and wooden bowls of burning grease in a circle around the corpse; the family was too poor to afford candles. A linen shroud was on him, and except for the coins on his eyes, his waxy pallor, it would have seemed from a distance that the little boy was only sleeping. His expression was peaceful and his limbs had been arranged in a lifelike manner.

"They never cry out," Meligraunce said in Tryffin's ear. "Even the infant snatched from the breast of his sleeping mother never makes a sound."

Tryffin nodded and moved closer. For all the body appeared so fresh, there was a cold stink rising up from the corpse, a rank odor so thick and so cloying, it took all his control to keep from reeling back. "When did this happen?" he asked softly, so as not to disturb the mother, a worn-looking woman who sat in a chair in a corner, with two ragged children in her lap. She was clinging to her two remaining babies and weeping quietly.

The room was so tiny and crowded, Tryffin was all too keenly aware that any awkward movement of his outsize limbs would knock something over and cause a disturbance.

"They found him at daybreak, perhaps three hours after he was first missed." The Captain stepped toward the table, moved one of the tallow dips closer to the child's head. "Why do you ask? Have you seen something that I did not?" And it was clear to Tryffin, in that moment, that he was the only one who smelled anything, anything but sweating bodies and burning grease.

"No . . . I see nothing worth mentioning." He forced himself to look again at that pitiful small body, the deceptive peace of that waxen countenance, the auburn curls lying on the forehead. "Beyond the fact that the murdered child bears a certain resemblance to my adopted son."

Tryffin moved abruptly away from the table. He turned to one of the guards who had followed him into the room. "You, Garreg, will stay here in this house and help the parents to keep watch over their surviving children. God knows, they have already suffered enough."

Turning on his heel, he left the room and went down the stairs to the street, two steps at a time. Once outside, he leaned up against the rough stone wall of the house, lifted the damp blond hair from his sweating brow, and took several deep breaths, filling his lungs with the sulphurous air. After the reek in the room up above, the scent of brimstone was actually welcome.

"Lord Prince, are you well?" The voice seemed to come from such a great distance, it was a moment before Tryffin realized that Meligraunce was speaking.

With an effort, Tryffin answered him. "The room was too close; I am better now."

Meligraunce was frowning, clearly perturbed by something he saw in his master's countenance. "It is not like you to grow faint because the air is stale."

Reviving a little, Tryffin moved away from the wall. "Could you take me to the place where they found the . . . ah God, I suppose he had a name. Do you know what it was?"

Meligraunce spent a long moment staring down at the cobblestones at his feet. "The boy's name was Rhys," he said, and Tryffin felt his heart sink. "An unfortunate coincidence that it should happen to be the name of the child you adopted in Clynnoc. But I believe it is one often bestowed—"

"—often bestowed by Mochdreffi mothers," the Governor finished for him. Out in the light and air, his head was clearing, his stomach beginning to settle. "And if someone wanted to send me a particular message, they would have no difficulty finding a child with that particular name . . . much easier than the one I gave him later."

He squared his shoulders, under the crimson cloak. "Rhys . . . then. Where did they find him? Do you know that, Captain?"

"I will show you the way," Meligraunce answered.

In those times, they had the hearth in the center of the house, and the people slept on the floor around the fire. And the reason why they began to build chimneys in the corner was because the Hag had a habit of reaching in through the smokehole with her terrible long arms, snatching up a child, and carrying it away to be eaten.

—*From* The Black Book of Tregalen

3.

A Handful of Dust

The place was a narrow, climbing lane, lined with flinty little shops and houses. Where two streets met, there was a sort of lopsided market square, with a pair of weathered statues at the center: a ragged man in a posture of abject supplication, and a mighty winged figure with a fiery sword, rising up like a whirlwind to smite him.

Rain and wind had done their work, the faces were blind and nearly featureless. Dark patches of damp against the pale stone lent both a leprous appearance.

"This is where they found him. When I arrived, he was still lying in a pitiful little heap on the lower step . . . rather as though someone had carelessly dropped him there, then hurried off on some other business," said Meligraunce. "As you can see, there is no blood, nor any sign of violence. The boy was still dressed in his little nightshirt, which appeared to be recently washed and mended, nor was there anything about the body itself to indicate the child had been dragged all this distance by a large animal.

"He must have been carried—" the Captain began, stepping back from the pedestal. Then his eyes widened and he drew in his breath sharply. "This is very strange—there are only two figures. Yet I am certain there were three, earlier this morning."

He circled the statues, shaking his head in wonderment. "It makes no sense. Why would anyone go to the trouble of dislodging one of these statues and hauling it away?"

Tryffin glanced around him. "There is nothing here to say that a statue was moved . . . no chipped stone, no straw from a cart, no sign that a team of horses was here only an hour or two since. Conn, you and the Sergeant go down the street and see if you find any fresh droppings."

He moved forward to examine the foot of the pedestal. Here, too, were ugly patches of damp. A faint scent of corruption lingered on the air, as it had in the vicinity of the corpse, but this time he was prepared for it.

He looked over his shoulder at Meligraunce. "That third statue—if there was a third—it didn't happen to be the figure of a large cat? A lion, perhaps . . . or a manticore, tearing that poor fellow to pieces?"

"It was not, Your Grace. I remember it well, because it was so different from the others. Her features were not weathered but clear and distinct, and her face had a terrible beauty."

"A woman, by God!" Tryffin sat down on the crumbling granite base, below the angel with the sword. "You are absolutely certain that it was a woman?"

"A young woman wrought in marble; I could hardly be mistaken about a thing like that. But though she was very beautiful, as I have said, her face was stern and her posture was somehow . . . threatening."

Further down the lane, where the street became narrower, the houses more crowded, Conn and the guard had crouched low to the ground, which they seemed to be examining with intense interest. A moment later, the boy sprang to his feet and came jogging back to the square.

"We found something," Conn said breathlessly. "A trail of dust or very fine sand, and it goes on for a considerable distance."

They followed Conn between the leaning houses, the tumble of stone and slate and rotting wood. And there, sure enough, down the middle of the street was a faint trail, like a thin trickle of sand, across the cobblestones. Tryffin sat down on his heels, scooped up a handful of dust, and weighed it thoughtfully. As it had been at the base of the decaying statues, the odor was faint but sickening.

"Your Grace . . . my men searched these streets. I blame

myself that they were not more thorough." Meligraunce appeared intensely mortified.

The Governor rose slowly from his crouch. "This may have been here earlier, it may not. You have no reason to reproach yourself, anyway. The light was poor and the shadows were long just after daybreak—and even now, with the sun so high, it took a sharp pair of eyes to spot this trail."

"But who moved the statue . . . and why?" Conn wondered, hazel eyes wide, his expression troubled.

"It may be that the statue walked off the pedestal of her own accord." Tryffin bent to dust off his cloak. "I never did believe those tales of a great grey cat. The child, after all, was carried, not dragged. How large would a cat have to be, to carry a child so far in its mouth and not even the hem of his shirt touch the ground?

"I thought all along it was probably a woman doing these terrible things," he added, under his breath.

"A woman—not a statue?" said Meligraunce. "It was not so dark I would mistake a living woman for a piece of stone."

Tryffin released a long sigh. "There is no large animal stalking the streets of Anoeth, but a slender woman in a long brown cloak . . . who enters locked rooms without a key . . . who moves so quickly and quietly, she can steal small children right out of the arms of their sleeping parents, carry them away by dark of night . . . and then drink their blood without even breaking or bruising the skin.

"She is also," he added grimly, "sufficiently skilled in dreams and illusions, and whether or not she can turn herself into stone she could certainly assume that appearance."

Meligraunce cleared his throat. "You mean to say that a witch, a Mochdreffi wise-woman, is killing the children?"

"I am all but certain that's what is happening," said Tryffin, turning on his heel and beginning to follow the trail of dust, wherever it might lead him.

"What is more," he continued, as the others hurried to keep up with him, "I am convinced that half of Anoeth suspects the very same thing. That is the reason they are all so reluctant to speak what they know: They fear a witch-hunt."

Their way led uphill, the streets of Anoeth twisted and turned. By now, Tryffin was longing for the sight of wattle-and-daub . . . a half-timber cottage . . . a thatched roof . . . even a house built of mellow bricks . . . but there was nothing like that in the town of Anoeth, only stone, stone, a dry, depressing wilderness of stone—and silent crowds of the dark-eyed Mochdreffi, cloaked and veiled in dull black like a city in mourning.

"That doesn't make sense," said Conn, attempting to match his stride to Tryffin's. "What I mean to say is that it makes too *much* sense. Their children are mysteriously dying, everyone is terrified—it would seem that a witch-hunt is just what they do want."

"This is not Gorwynnion," said Tryffin. "Not Rhianedd, Draighen, Perfudd, or any other place where as soon as people grow confused and apprehensive they search out some suitable scapegoats—a miserable old woman living alone on the edge of the forest, an equally miserable vagabond beggar—and burn them for witches and warlocks.

"This is Mochdreff, where the magic is strangely accessible yet still wild and dangerous, where many are born with a gift for Witchcraft, where no family could long survive in this hard, hard land without its matriarch, its woman of power."

"Yes, I see," said Conn, with a sympathetic shudder. "It would not be tinkers or wandering beggars, but their very own mothers and sisters, aunts and grandmothers, who would be dragged out of their homes, tied to a stake, and set on fire."

Meligraunce frowned. "But why—why does this woman you describe feed on children? And what does she hope to gain by terrorizing an entire town?"

The Governor paused, so that his companions could catch their breath. "Why else, but to lure me here, to send me a message I cannot and will not ignore: a challenge written in the blood of a hundred innocent children."

"Lure you here . . . to what end?" said Meligraunce.

"To the same end, and perhaps for the same reasons, that Lord Cado defied me last year," replied Tryffin. "She sees me, or anyone else who seeks to bring order to Mochdreff, as an obstacle to her ambition.

"She means to destroy me, Captain, and is not above using the most ruthless methods possible in order to accomplish that."

The street was paved with flags now, the way grew broader, the houses on either side grander. These were the great grey mansions of the petty lords, stepped and fortified, towered and turreted, with iron bars on all the windows, gargoyles and waterspouts higher up.

The trail ended at a fence of iron pickets surrounding one of the overgrown graveyards. All this time, Tryffin had followed his nose as much as the signs he could see with his eyes, except when he passed near to a well and the odor of sulphur proved stronger than the stench of Black Magic. Indeed, his sense of smell had kept him going in places where the trickle of dust had been entirely scuffed away by passing feet or carts.

But when he reached the iron fence and the trail terminated in a dry little pool of dust, the scent was cold as well. He turned around and around, sniffing the air, but the only odors he detected were horses and middens, and somebody boiling laundry.

"Lord Prince, what is this?" said Meligraunce, bending to scoop up something. He held out his hand; in the palm lay a flat piece of stone, rough on one side, smooth on the other, and gently rounded, like a bit of carving—or a piece knocked off a statue. "I found it by the fence . . . there where that iron picket is bent."

The Governor ground his teeth, cursing himself for a short-sighted fool. "We have been following the trail in the wrong direction. This is not where the statue went, but the place that it came from."

Meligraunce quirked an inquiring eyebrow. "You are far too quick for the rest of us, I am afraid."

"If a statue could move and could bleed, what sort of sign would it leave behind but a trail of dust?" asked Tryffin.

The Captain pondered a moment, weighing the piece of stone in his hand. "You mean that the thing was injured and bled all the way to the lane where we started? But then . . . it was only by chance that we happened to stumble across the trail, because she was not bleeding when she entered the house where the boy was taken."

"Yes," said Tryffin, turning, so that his cloak swirled around him, crimson, against the dull black of his armor. He stared thoughtfully back the way they had just come. "Perhaps by chance, perhaps because she is somehow attracted to that particular pair of decaying statues. She may stand there with them and listen to conversations as people walk by.

"She may," he added, "even choose her victims from there on her pedestal, marking their names and the places they live."

Meligraunce nodded slowly. "This morning she may have been forced to drop the boy and stand with the other statues . . . and had to remain there while my men searched the square and the streets all around. And then, perhaps, became flesh once more as soon as we left. As a woman, she could walk through Anoeth quite freely, could go anywhere that she wished . . . even back here."

"Before God," breathed Tryffin, "she might at that." He looked over the iron pickets, out across the graveyard. Beyond the fence was a tangle of woody vines which all but obscured the nearer headstones. Further on, there were great tombs and mausoleums, rising out of the thicket, and what appeared to be the ruin of a church and the remains of a bell tower. Starting near the fence and heading toward the ruin was a sort of a path, a place where the vines were broken and trampled, as though something heavy had passed that way.

Putting one broad hand on the iron rail and the toe of his boot between two pickets, Tryffin vaulted over the fence. As he pushed through the thicket, thorns caught at his cloak, but thanks to his armor, he reached the ruin with no worse injury than some scratches on his hands.

"Let us hope that these vines are not poisonous." Meligraunce had followed him over the fence and through the tangle of vines, and arrived nursing a jagged gash on his hand. "Some of these thorns are as long as iron spikes."

Conn and the Sergeant were working their way through the thicket more cautiously and stopping to examine gravestones as they passed. Tryffin and Meligraunce drew their swords and began to circle the bell tower. It was made of irregular pieces of rock—limestone, granite, and flint—carefully fitted and mortared together, the bones of the ancient city of Anoeth. Beyond the tower, in what must have been the sanctuary, were a raised platform of two steps, and a block of stone resembling an altar. Tryffin bent down to examine the carvings on the face of the stone. They were so weathered, it was hard to make out the figures of men and angels, yet he thought there was something in the posture of all of them that seemed to denote great suffering.

"This was never a proper church." That was Conn, coming up behind him. And Tryffin realized, suddenly, that the boy was right.

It was not just that the plan of the church, as it could be seen from the remaining walls, was not cruciform—he had been in very old churches before, and some of them were square and some rectangular—no, there was something else, something in the arches and the pillars and the bays. It was a moment before he recognized that everything was jumbled and asymmetrical.

But that would explain why the church stood in ruins. The history of Mochdreff was one long tale of schisms and heresies, of one sect gaining power while another declined, usually followed by a purge of the losing sect. The countryside was dotted with the burned-out remains of churches, convents, and monasteries.

Conn had turned white under his shock of unruly brown hair, and actually looked as though he were about to be physically ill. His own people, the Gorwynnach, were orthodox to the point of fanaticism. In his case, travel had broadened him, made him more tolerant. But the old habits were still very strong; something deep inside was always telling him that sin was contagious and heresy a disease that a man might contract by mere proximity.

In the present instance, Tryffin could sympathize with him. There was something indescribably horrible in the thought that the statue might have come from this church. It was, he decided, like stumbling into a nightmare, into a strange, inverted world where angels walked in the guise of devils, and images of the Holy Virgin stepped down from their pedestals and roamed through the town like ravening beasts.

"For the love of God," he said, "I would never ask you to do anything against your own conscience. If you feel you can look over those tombs in the far corner without imperiling your immortal soul, then do so. If not, go back to the inn and order my dinner, and no one will blame you."

But Conn shook his head grimly and trudged off with the guardsman to search among the tombs.

"You do not care for this place any more than he does," Meligraunce guessed shrewdly.

"No, I do not, though I can't think why," said Tryffin. "What right have I to turn up my nose at the rituals and practices of fellow Christians, when I was raised in Tir Gwyngelli and counted pagans among my friends and neighbors? And very good people most of them were, too—for all they espoused the Old Religion. It is nothing to me what another man might choose to believe. Or at least, it has never seemed to matter before." He gave up trying to make out the figures on the altar and began to move down the length of the ruin.

"But that was before your lady fell under the influence of the Black Canons," Meligraunce reminded him.

The Governor nodded, remembering the sinister Father Idris and his unholy relics, with which he had tempted and tormented Gwenlliant almost to the point of madness. If it had not been for Dame Ceinwen . . .

But the thought of Gwenlliant was so painful, his desire to see her again so intense and frustrating, that he forcibly pushed it out of his mind.

"I wonder if the people who worshipped here belonged to a similar sect. Or were they gentle and inoffensive, as such folk usually are?" Tryffin stepped over some shards of glass from a stained-glass window: viper green, midnight black, and a deep, disturbing purple.

"They could hardly have been gentle *or* inoffensive—not if they worshipped a bloodsucking Madonna," Meligraunce pointed out.

"Ah well," Tryffin said. "It may not be so bad as that. I still believe that we are following a woman of flesh made stone, not the other way around."

But for all that, he drew his sword and ordered the Captain to do the same.

After an hour of fruitless searching, they gave up combing the graveyard and returned to the inn. Conn was the first to speak as they entered the smoky common room. "Will we stay in Anoeth to hunt and slay this . . . monster?"

"Most of us will," said the Governor, as they climbed the stairs to the upper floor. "But you I shall send on to Cormelyn."

"Your Grace!" Conn's voice rose high in distress. "My place is here with you. And it is not as though *I* were in any special danger."

Meligraunce, uncharacteristically, sided with Conn. "If you are concerned for his safety, there has not been a single report of an attack on an able-bodied youth."

They entered the bedchamber, Tryffin shaking his head. "I know that it doesn't sound nearly so exciting, carrying messages on to Cormelyn, when you think you might be here slaying supernatural monsters—it's not so long since I was your age myself, so I do sympathize. And it is true that you missed out on most of the excitement last spring . . ."

The boy had opened his mouth to protest but closed it with a snap, reminded that, instead of adventuring with Tryffin, Garth, and Mahaffy, *he* had been charged with the safety of the Lady Gwenlliant, which task he had failed miserably, at least in his own estimation.

". . . but someone must carry a message to Cormelyn explaining the delay, and it would look better if I sent someone close to me, rather than one of the common men-at-arms," the Governor continued. "Also, you will recall that Mahaffy Guillyn and his men were to meet us there, after he has completed his business in Ochren—though what business even Mahaffy could have in that blasted wasteland I fail to understand—and he is likely to suspect the worst has happened when we don't arrive as planned. Seeing you there will reassure him, and so he will stay in Cormelyn and try to keep the peace there, instead of riding back here in a mistaken attempt to rescue us.

"In truth, Conn," he added, as he took a seat and stretched out his long legs, "I am depending on you as well as Mahaffy. No, don't look so frightened. I am not asking the pair of you to resolve the quarrel, only to keep things quiet and to avert bloodshed, if you possibly can. That responsibility will fall mostly on Mahaffy. He is young and but newly knighted, but he has been Lord of Ochren since Lord Cado's death, and Lord Gilfaethwy and the other clan chieftains should respect him as their equal. You are merely there to aid him in any way possible."

"Yes, I see," said Conn, trying very hard to conceal his disappointment. He helped Tryffin to remove his armor and then slipped quietly out of the room, to go downstairs and order the Governor's dinner.

After the boy had left the room, Meligraunce cleared his throat. "If you will pardon me, Lord Prince . . . I am sure that you have good reasons for being so secretive, yet I cannot help thinking that I would be better able to serve you if I knew a bit more. For instance, how you came to guess before the rest of us did that it was a woman killing the children."

Tryffin permitted himself a faint smile. "I do not mean to be secretive. But the truth is, I am a little embarrassed to tell you how I knew. It is because I have been meeting that woman in my dreams for several months now."

Meligraunce strolled over to the fireplace, picked up a poker to stir up the embers, then threw a few more sticks on the fire. "Now, that is very curious indeed. I do not know how I gained the impression—perhaps it was something you said a long time ago—but I did believe that of all the men I knew, only you slept too deeply for dreams."

"I believe I have always dreamed, though seldom so vividly that I remembered anything afterward," said Tryffin. Moving easily without the weight of armor, feeling lighter and freer in his red velvet tunic, parti-colored hose, and boots of soft black leather, he crossed the room and took the same chair by the hearth that he had occupied earlier. "Even now, now that I dream with such amazing clarity, the nightmares come only one night out of every three or four, and the rest of the time I sleep as well as I ever did."

Reaching over toward the table, he picked up a flagon and poured himself a cup of thin purple wine. "I dreamed of this city, and of that attic room with the dead child on the table, a month or two back. Though I thought the child was Grifflet at the time." He tasted the wine, winced, and put down the cup. It was flavored with honey and orris root like all Mochdreffi wines, but even that did little to mask the bitter vintage.

"More recently, there is a new dream that comes again and again: I am traveling down a long dusty road, with you and ten guardsmen. From time to time, I catch a glimpse of someone walking at my side—someone I can never see clearly, just a long brown cloak with the hood drawn low to conceal the face. The figure is light and graceful, however, and moves like a woman. But when I stop to look, the brown cloak is gone. And when I count myself and the rest of the party, the number is always twelve . . . yet again, as I turn and begin to walk on, the figure in brown returns, treading with the softest step imaginable, moving on my left but a pace behind."

"I still do not understand why you expected to meet this woman in Anoeth . . . and not, for instance, in Cormelyn, where you were headed," said Meligraunce, throwing another stick on the fire.

"Sometimes, when I dream, it seems to me that she is carrying an infant, that lies very still and small in her arms. I cannot see clearly, of course. But there is always a breath of evil, a kind of horror hovering about the woman, that makes me fear for the child that she carries." What he did not say was that the "breath of evil" was the same vile, smothering odor he had detected earlier . . . the one that no one could scent except for him, though he suspected it might have had something to do with frightening the dogs and the horses.

"Even accepting, as I do, that you have suddenly been gifted with prophetic dreams, I fail to see what any of this has to do with sending your squire away," said the Captain.

Tryffin sighed. "You implied earlier that you felt responsible, because the child had been killed in spite of the fact that you spent most of the night only a few streets away. But I think that young Rhys was murdered precisely *because* I am here in Anoeth. Oh . . . another would have died in his place, there is no doubt of that, but I think that the death of this particular child, like the random slaughter of the others before him, was meant to send a message to me."

"Yes, I see," said Meligraunce. "When you said it would be easy for someone to find a child by the name of Rhys, you meant that the boy had been killed for his name and the color of his hair."

Tryffin left his chair, began to pace the floor. "I fear that the next step, now that this evil creature has lured me to Anoeth, may be to strike at me personally by destroying someone close to me. The youngest members of my household would naturally be the most vulnerable. I can only thank God that Gwenlliant and Grifflet are safe with Dame Ceinwen, while Garth, Cei, and Elffin are almost equally well protected at Caer Ysgithr."

"But Conn and Mahaffy would only serve to distract you here in Anoeth," the Captain finished for him. "While if you make certain they are safe in Cormelyn, they may even be of use."

"Yes. I hope it may be enough to protect them. I know no better way to accomplish it, under the present circumstances." The door opened, and Conn came in to report that dinner would be served in half an hour.

"As you wish, then, Your Grace," said Meligraunce, moving toward the open door. "What time are we to begin the evening patrols?"

"At sundown," answered Tryffin. "But there is one thing more before you go." Meligraunce paused on the threshold, awaiting further orders.

"For the love of God, Captain, watch your back at all times. I value your friendship and would not care to lose you."

*All manner of Strange Folk and even more Terrible Creatures
may be found in the Mochdreffi Woods: Witches, Bears, Basilisks, Giants, Outlaws, Ogres, Werewolves, Demons . . .*
> —*From* A Natural History of the Isle of Celydonn,
> *variously attributed*

4.

The House in the Wildwood

The sun was still high when Gwenlliant entered the eaves of
the wood. At first sparse, the trees began to crowd together,
shouldering up against each other, restless and a little bumptious,
while the leafy canopy over her head became steadily denser and
greener. Yet she was able to find a well-worn pathway, winding
toward the heart of the wood, and followed it into the deepening
shade.

Besides the oaks she had spotted from a distance, there were
towering elms and stately limes, and down in the underwood,
maple, silvery hornbeam, fruiting hazel and elder. And though
Gwenlliant had been in wooded country before, in tamed and
domesticated little forests maintained for the King's pleasure in
Camboglanna, she had never ventured into the true wildwood.
The undergrowth here was more tangled and exuberant than
anything she had ever imagined: holly, bramble, and bracken;
ivy and honeysuckle twining around the trees; and now and then
a patch of brightness where some toppling forest giant had made
a clearing and the ground was covered with briars and stinging
nettles, grasses and willow herb.

The path branched, and branched again and again. The forest,
she realized, was a maze of pathways. After perhaps an hour, she
became very tired, her breath labored and her arms and legs
aching with the strain. She was not sure how much longer she
could continue, it had been such a long walk already, and Grifflet

39

felt heavier and heavier, dozing with his damp little head resting against her shoulder. Gwenlliant thought it might be nice to settle down in the shade and take a nap, too, but she was afraid she might not wake again before nightfall. And though the forest was very beautiful and disarming during the day, she thought it might be another matter at night, when the trees shut out the stars. The air would be alive with owls, and there would be mysterious rustlings down in the undergrowth: foxes, and bears, and wolves, probably, come out of their dens to hunt. Gwenlliant shuddered to think what it would be like to suddenly wake in the smothering darkness, to all that ominous unseen activity.

Better to keep moving now, she told herself, to keep on walking while the light was still good and the air was warm, smelling of pollen, mulch, violets . . . and a faint whiff of woodsmoke leading her on, to what surely must be some house hidden deep in the woods.

The way ahead became brighter and brighter, the trees were thinning, as though she had walked right through the forest and was now approaching the other side, or else was coming to a large clearing. And there was something else that was different: Where before there had only been trees and squirrels and the occasional deer bounding through the thicket, now there were birds, hundreds of birds—perhaps even thousands—up in the trees. Blackbirds, mostly, and ravens, rooks, magpies, wrens, and a few with brighter plumage, robins, blue jays, cardinals, and all of them chattering, singing, chirping, trilling . . .

A few minutes later, Gwenlliant came out of the trees and into a grassy clearing. At the center of the clearing stood a large wooden house with a well, like no house she had ever seen: cruck-built, with all the posts and beams elaborately carved and painted, and the roof, strange to say, was thatched with turf, on which grass and wildflowers grew luxuriantly. As she soon discovered by circling around, the house was a great deal longer than it was wide, and higher at one end than it was at the other. It had few windows and only one door, but that was a large one, nine feet high and built of solid oak, with decorative hinges made of brass, and it was further adorned with bands of copper and disks of tin nailed to the wood.

It looked, Gwenlliant decided, exactly like a house in a dream or a fairy tale, and therefore dangerous, the home perhaps of ogres or wicked fairies. And considering what realm she was wandering in now, it might well be.

She disliked the look of the door in particular; it seemed a great weight, all that wood and metal, for ordinary folk to open and close. Yet she saw there were two or three steps leading up to the door, and a little porch, and the proportions there were not very ogreish. It was hard to imagine a pair of great horny feet climbing such narrow stairs, shuffling about on that ledge of a porch.

Most likely, Gwenlliant thought as she crossed the clearing, the large and decorated door was meant to convey the importance of the people inside, and not their physical stature. But why were people so grand and important living so deep in the woods? *Still, if they* are *very grand, they will probably be hospitable . . . too proud to turn away a footsore young woman and a hungry child.*

With that thought to bolster her courage, she climbed the steps, walked boldly up to the gigantic door, made her hand into a fist, and rapped on the timbers.

Unfortunately, after several minutes had passed, Gwenlliant realized that no one was going to answer. Perhaps no one inside had heard her knocking, with that heavy wooden door muffling the sound. So she shook the pale hair out of her eyes, settled Grifflet more securely on her hip, and pounded again, this time much louder.

Again she waited, but still there was no reply. She looked over her shoulder, a longing glance at the well. By now, she was getting very thirsty.

And really, she thought, as she descended the steps, *it is hardly stealing to drink water from a well. No worse than sipping from a stream or a natural pool, because the water comes up out of the earth and belongs to everyone.*

She put her free hand on the windlass and loosened the catch, then watched the pail go spinning down and down at the end of its rope, until it landed somewhere in the darkness below with a faint splash.

It was then that Gwenlliant realized that something was wrong, that something had changed in the forest or the clearing. Glancing around her, she realized that the birds had all flown, the wood was silent.

There was a flash of foxy red under the trees, and suddenly, on the near side of the clearing, a woman was standing and watching her, a beautiful woman with night-black hair tumbling over her shoulders and down her back in a mass of shining ringlets. She had moved so swiftly and quietly that Gwenlliant had not even seen her come out of the forest.

She wore a plain gown of scarlet linen, which left her white arms completely bare and only extended as far as her ankles. Yet along with this simple costume, she wore a great deal of jewelry: brooches to fasten her gown at the shoulders, bracelets, rings, a torc, and a wide leather girdle cinching her waist, that was studded with metal and semiprecious stones—agate and moonstone, quartz and amethyst. It was all very gaudy, but the designs were primitive, and the metal was mostly bronze, decorated with spirals and delicate lacings of copper and silver wire. She looked as though she had raided a barrow and come out laden with all the treasure.

The woman lifted an arm, pointing at the girl and the baby. "What are you doing here? Where have you come from?"

Again, Gwenlliant was startled. She knew that language but had never expected to hear it spoken out loud. It was the language of deserted places, of standing stones and ancient causeways, of monuments scrolled with knotwork and spirals carved into the rock. It was the language of places where men had lived in the distant past, which still resounded with their passionate voices . . . echoes so faint that only a gift like Gwenlliant's could detect them. She had whispered those words herself, in conversations with burial mounds, ruins, and graveyards, but she had never before met another person who spoke that tongue.

She took a deep breath and replied uncertainly, clutching Grifflet protectively close. "I have come a long way and I am very tired. Also, my little boy needs something to eat, and I have nothing to give him."

As she spoke there was a rustling in the bushes, and a number of other women appeared at the edge of the clearing, all of them dressed in the same strange fashion, though some wore grey and some wore saffron. Gwenlliant was a little frightened; they could only be women of power to arrive so suddenly, without the forest announcing them first. And though she was very powerful herself, there seemed to be a great many of them, and she had no way of knowing whether they were friendly to strangers or not. Certainly, they did not look pleased to find her wandering in their forest or drinking from their well.

"This wood is sacred," said a tall, fiery-haired woman in a

saffron gown and a heavy necklace set with cairngorms. "We do not encourage visitors."

"I am sorry," Gwenlliant began. "I did not know the wood was forbidden, and—"

"The wood is not forbidden, only restricted." That was the first one, the dark-haired beauty, interrupting her. "Nor are you answerable to Caithne, whatever she might choose to believe. I am Maelinn, the Lady of the Wood and the Well, and I am the one who will determine whether you are welcome here or not. What is your name, and how do you call your little boy?"

Gwenlliant hesitated. It seemed she had landed right in the middle of some quarrel between these two powerful women, and that was a dangerous place to be. Yet glancing around her, she noticed that no one protested what Maelinn said, not even Caithne.

"My name is Gwenhwyach," she said, mindful of Dame Ceinwen's warning. But Grifflet's name she gave quite freely. He would answer to no other—and besides, he was a baby, and already in the power of every adult he chanced to meet.

"I suppose," said Maelinn, "you have come here to ask for sanctuary. That we may freely offer, if we choose to do so, but the boy is another matter. If a father comes seeking his son, we cannot deny him."

Gwenlliant shook her head. "His father is dead," she answered truthfully.

The others came gathering around, murmuring sympathetically, no doubt mistaking her for a very young widow. Gwenlliant said nothing to deny it. It was better, she had decided, they should not know too much about her. And just then, Grifflet woke up, hungry and thirsty, and started to fuss, which softened the women even further. They clicked their tongues, crooned soft words of comfort under their breath.

"He ought to be fed," said someone, and the others agreed.

At a word from Maelinn, the door opened wide, leading Gwenlliant to believe there was some sort of spell on it. The women hustled her and Grifflet up the steps and inside the house, and before Gwenlliant knew it she was seated on a bench by a central hearth, in a long room with a lofty ceiling.

Someone brought her a plate of tiny cakes made with berries and hazelnuts, someone else offered a bowl full of goat's milk. Gwenlliant helped Grifflet to drink from the wooden bowl, yet for all her assistance he still acquired a milky mustache and dribbled a little on his clothing as well. When he had finished eating, she cleaned him up with a rag that someone handed to her, then put him down on the floor to amuse himself. Maelinn offered him a handful of nuts, strung like beads on a piece of twine, a plaything he eagerly accepted.

While Gwenlliant sipped water from a copper beaker and ate one of the cakes, the women hovered around her, touching her pale Rhianeddi hair, fascinated by the way that her dress was made and by the texture of the wool cloth. It was the best gown that Gwenlliant owned, put on to favorably impress the wizard— the plainest and the most practical of the gowns she had worn as a princess at Caer Ysgithr, in a terrible state by the time Dame Ceinwen discovered her wandering the dusty road with Brangwengwen the dwarf. But the crone had mended the gown and dyed it, and the dress had emerged from the witch's cauldron a deep blue-violet, exactly the shade of Gwenlliant's eyes. The young women commented on the rare color, but after a bit they lost interest in her clothes and wanted to learn more about her.

"Why have you come here, and why are you traveling without an escort—for it is very clear that you are not a peasant," said a woman with chestnut hair and leaf-green eyes.

She wore a belt set with opals and a torc set with moonstones, and her gown was as grey as ashes. The others called her Sceith, and there was a strong resemblance between her and Caithne— Gwenlliant thought they might be Draighenach, because of their height and coloring.

The other women were like Maelinn, small and delicate, with hair so dark it was nearly black, and great brown eyes dominating their faces. She thought they must be pure-blooded Mochdreffi, or else Gwyngellach, and that she had landed in the distant past, long before her own northern ancestors had begun to marry and mix their blood with the southern nobility.

Gwenlliant tried to think how she should answer their questions. For all their kindness, she was still very much aware that these were women of power and possibly dangerous. And though it seemed wrong to lie to them, she had not lived most of her life at court without learning it was possible to be utterly deceptive while never speaking a single false word.

"My father wished me to marry a man that I hated, a wicked old man with evil habits. He took me away from the house of my kinsman, away from any friends who might have prevented the wedding, and I feared I would be forced to give my consent."

There were shocked looks on every side, where Gwenlliant had expected only sympathetic interest and perhaps a little mild censure for her disobedience. It seemed that the customs here were very much different from the ones that she knew.

"That was very wrong of your father," said Maelinn, sitting down on the bench by Gwenlliant. "It is one thing for virgins to marry in order to oblige their parents. Indeed, it is their duty to do so. But a woman who has married, borne a child, and been widowed can be expected to know her own mind, and she has every right to choose a second husband to suit herself. Your father appears to have no idea of the way that things should be properly done!

"You must have come a very long way to get here," she added. "For I have never seen anyone like you before."

"I was going to visit a kinsman and ask him to help me," Gwenlliant answered truthfully. "But the Breathing Mist came down and took me away." According to Dame Ceinwen, the Mist was as natural to the Shadow Lands and their shifting boundaries as it was to the Marches, so it was perfectly safe for her to say this.

"That was very unfortunate," said Caithne. "For you might have come from *anywhere* . . . and you will almost certainly have a difficult time returning."

And this time, when the others made sympathetic noises, Gwenlliant did not feel the least bit guilty. She *was* lost and she had no idea how she was going to get home again—or how she and Grifflet were to live in the meantime.

But Maelinn drew herself up and proclaimed grandly, "You may stay here just as long as you please. Or at least, until your boy is a little older. Men are not allowed here, but babies are another matter, and the Green Lady forbid we should ever refuse our assistance to a woman and a mother in her time of need."

The air was turning violet with the coming of night, a faint mist was creeping in from the sea, when the Governor and six of his men left the inn and began their nightly patrol. The streets were empty and silent. The great fortified stone mansions, the flinty little shops and houses, appeared blind and dumb, their doors locked tight, their windows shuttered. After a time, the sound of his own echoing footsteps, the faint rattle of armor following behind him, began to wear on Tryffin's nerves.

He stopped by one of the sulphurous wells, staring down into the steaming depths. The moon was already high in the sky; he could see its haggard reflection drowning at the bottom of the well. For no reason that he could think of, a chill crawled down his spine.

No wonder these people are demon-plagued, he thought. *They have dozens of gateways straight into Hell right here in the town.* "I wonder," he said out loud, "if the water is actually wholesome to drink."

"One may drink small quantities without any harm, where the water smells of brimstone," said a voice behind him. Startled, he turned to see a dark young woman in a drab wool cloak standing not twenty feet distant. "But it is mostly used for bathing and scrubbing. There are other wells, where the water is sweeter, where we draw up water for cooking and drinking."

As she moved a little closer he caught a glimpse of sapphire velvet and sparkling jewels beneath the plain cloak, a hint of expensive oils and rare perfumes. She was clearly the daughter of some noble house—and just as clearly a witch. Who but a woman of power would be out unescorted, wandering the streets at this dangerous hour? As she moved, his men moved also to intercept her, but Tryffin stopped them by raising his hand.

He spent a long time studying her face, which was handsome rather than beautiful, and her posture, which was exceedingly arrogant, before he spoke. "Why sink wells where the water is bad?"

"These wells," she said, with a shrug, "are very old. And legend has it there was a time long ago when the springs of Anoeth were known throughout the land, and there was no water more pure or beneficial."

As she finished speaking, a hail of large pebbles came hurtling out of the shadows at the edge of the square and landed at their feet, scattering across the cobblestones—followed by the sound of running footsteps. Tryffin's men would have given chase, but he stopped them with another command. "You will never catch up to them, and they've done no harm. Just keep your eyes and your ears open after this, so that no one surprises us a second time."

"I believe, Lord Prince," said the woman, "that those stones were meant for me."

Tryffin raised an inquiring eyebrow. "For you, Lady? But how is that? Are not wise-women highly regarded in the land of Mochdreff? Who would dare to molest a woman of power?"

"None dare to do so openly, not as yet. As you have seen, they are content to throw stones from the shadows," she replied calmly. "But the day may come very soon when they grow bolder."

Tryffin drew in his breath. So he had guessed correctly, and Anoeth was turning against her witches. This was not a circumstance where he enjoyed being right; in truth, he had been hoping all day that he would be proved wrong. It was another burden, another wearisome but unavoidable responsibility for him to shoulder, because now he must do everything in his power to see that the contagion did not spread outside the city walls, throughout Mochdreff. Being married to a woman of power, he had a certain interest in keeping this one last corner of Celydonn safe for witches.

"Perhaps," he said, for lack of anything better he could offer, "you would allow my men and me to escort you home."

"Indeed, I approached you, Prince Tryffin, hoping you would offer me your protection," she answered. "Also . . . I think you would be very happy to visit my home. There is a great lady who lives there, and she is eager to tell you a number of things that you may not know."

Tryffin considered that. Walking with her through the streets of Anoeth was one thing, entering an unknown house was another. Not that he was about to sink to the general level of superstitious panic by distrusting every wise-woman that he chanced to meet—but neither was he going to do anything foolish.

Yet he would be hardly alone, having six men to guard him, and he and they were armed with cold iron, which ought to be effective against most kinds of magic. Besides, he would be aware of any spells before she finished casting them; that was one advantage he had over ordinary folk. And the truth was, she had piqued the curiosity which was his greatest failing. He realized he was willing to take a few calculated risks, to discover just what the witches of Anoeth might have to tell him.

"Very well," he said. "You lead the way, and we will follow."

And the maiden led Finarfon into that house, which appeared to be larger on the inside than it was on the outside, and through many corridors and passageways and exceedingly fair chambers, each more magnificent and more richly furnished than the last. Following behind her, marveling at all that he saw, Finarfon began to wonder if all these things were real, or only the result of a pishogue the young woman was working on him.
—*From* The Book of the White Cockerel

5.

Strange Perfumes

She took him to one of the fortified mansions—more like a prison than a house for all its faded grandeur. And more like a tomb than a prison, thought Tryffin, with its stonework of lizards and skulls, its iron bars, its somber stained-glass windows on the stories up above, and an indefinable suggestion of hidden vaults where things lay rotting. And yet, it was no worse than any of the other great houses he might have visited; they were all exactly the same—which was one among many reasons that Tryffin was staying at the inn instead.

Staring up at the looming stone structure, he wondered what the petty lords of Anoeth had feared, in the days before the present horror, that had caused them to immure themselves alive, when the walls of the city ought to have served to protect them. But then he shrugged—far be it from him to understand the workings of the suspicious Mochdreffi mind. He supposed they had entombed themselves on general principles.

There was a decoration graven in stone over the double doors, two wild cats in the midst of a skirmish. Tryffin hesitated, for he knew whose badge that was. "This is the house of Cernach fab Clydno."

"Dame Brangwaine is Lord Cernach's grandmother," said the

48

lady. "They share the same roof but little more. She lives in private apartments at the back of the house. And even if she did not, her power and influence are sufficient to forbid interference by Cernach . . . or by any man."

The Governor frowned at her. "I wonder, since I am already acquainted with her grandson, Dame Brangwaine didn't come to *me* if she wished an audience."

There was a high stone wall surrounding the house except on the side by the street, and a little door set into that wall. The young woman produced a key and unlocked that door, which opened to reveal a torchlit garden on the other side. "My great-grandmother is an old, old woman; she is carried in a chair wherever she goes, and requires a physician and a number of attendants whenever she goes abroad. She might have visited you only at great inconvenience. Also . . . I don't think she wished to attract attention, which would be impossible to avoid under the circumstances."

She stepped through into the garden. After a moment of thought Tryffin followed her in and his men did likewise. The last one through closed the door, but moved to block the young woman when she would have locked it again.

The Governor nodded his approval. "The Sergeant is correct. I will go no further unless the door remains unlocked, and I will station two men here in order to make certain the way remains open."

The woman made a careless gesture, and again there was a glimpse of jewels and rich fabric—and also some very tempting feminine curves. "As you will, then, Prince Tryffin. It is not important. I made to lock it as a matter of habit only."

The garden was not much to look at. A plot of dry grass, some fruit trees with twisted limbs, and the inevitable scrambling growth of thorny vines. Briars seemed to thrive in Mochdreff, though Tryffin had never been able to determine why. At the back of the garden was a flight of crumbling stone steps winding up the side of one of the towers. With the lady leading the way, Tryffin and his four remaining men climbed the stairs, then passed through another oak door into a brilliantly lighted chamber.

The room was illuminated by a hundred wax candles, standing in wrought-iron holders, which formed an aisle down the center of the hall, leading up to a low dais where a crooked old woman in purple velvet was seated on a marble throne. Besides the candles, there was a fire blazing on the hearth, and a brazier of smoking incense.

The air was so heavy, each breath that Tryffin took was a labor as he walked down the aisle. The room reeked of spices, oils, unguents, and exotic perfumes, and if there were any windows to let in a breath of fresher air, they were all concealed behind the glowing tapestries and other rich hangings that lined the walls.

Also . . . there were cats, seemingly dozens of them, in every imaginable color from black to cinnamon tabby, perched on tables or sleeping on velvet cushions, or rubbing their backs against the freestanding candle holders or the elaborately carved dark oak furnishings. Little wonder the atmosphere was well nigh suffocating.

"My apologies, Lord Prince," said the ancient dame, as Tryffin approached. "I cannot rise to greet you as I ought, but perhaps you will pardon my age and infirmity." Though her words were gracious, there was more of challenge than apology in her tone. Strangely enough, that served to reassure him. If she had meant to disarm and then entrap him, her manner was likely to be far more conciliating.

"If you can't stand, then I will sit," he replied, taking up a stool, placing it on the lowest step of the dais, and sitting down. Which act of courtesy—choosing a seat that was so much lower than hers, for all he outranked her—had the expected effect. Her expression softened ever so slightly.

He glanced around him. The heavy perfumes were obviously meant to conceal something . . . but he could detect no spells at work in the room. No chill of Wizardry, no humming in his bones, no quicksilver fire in his blood, which was his inevitable reaction in the presence of Witchcraft.

"Are you growing light-headed?" she asked, with a sweeping gesture of one frail hand. The skin was so thin, it was nearly translucent, and he could see the veins and the shape of the bones quite clearly. "Do these fumes make you swoon? Perhaps you suppose I am working some subtle enchantment over you and your men."

"No," he replied. That movement had revealed perhaps more than she intended: Above her wrist, where the purple velvet sleeve fell away, her arm was discolored and the skin appeared to be separating from the flesh in tiny silvery scales. He realized the old woman was dying of some loathsome progressive disease, and the perfumes, the spices, and the incense were only meant to disguise the sickroom odor. "I think that since it is difficult for you to go down to the garden, you have chosen to bring the garden up to you."

At that she began to laugh soundlessly. "Very prettily phrased," she said, when her mirth had subsided. "Your wits are as sharp as your eyes, I see." She gestured toward the younger woman, who had remained by the door all this while. "Luned . . . send one of my grandson's servants to bring up some wine."

Dame Brangwaine turned her attention back to Tryffin, studying him with her bright dark eyes. "I wonder how far your courtesy extends. It's not often that I entertain such exalted company. Will you stay awhile and play a game of Chess with me?" She indicated a golden board and some jeweled chessmen laid out on a table near the dais.

When Tryffin hesitated, she smiled craftily. "Is it because I am a woman that you will not play with me? You think I would make an unworthy opponent."

"No doubt you were playing the game long before I was born," he replied politely, evading her question rather than lie to her. That she was a woman had nothing to do with it; it had been so long since he faced a worthy opponent of either sex, he had lost all pleasure in the contest. Unless he was handicapped by several pieces or used dice to add an element of chance, he invariably won. Nevertheless, he would have been perfectly willing to sacrifice an hour to the amusement of a sick old woman, were it not that he had such pressing responsibilities just at that moment.

"Lady," he said, "you seem to be testing me—either my courtesy, as you have said, or else my patience. Under ordinary circumstances I think you would find that my patience is vast, but tonight I would prefer that our dealings were direct: Why have you invited me here, and what do you want of me?"

She tucked up a wisp of white hair which had fallen out of her jeweled hairnet. "But you are the one who wished to see me, or at least, someone very much like me. Sensing your desire, I summoned you here in order to satisfy your curiosity. Ask your questions, Prince Tryffin, and I will attempt to answer them."

Tryffin blew out a long breath. He certainly had questions . . . so many of them, indeed, that it was difficult to know where he ought to begin. "Lady," he said at last, "I wish to know why the witches of Anoeth have done so little. I know that it is possible to draw a magic circle, to ward a house, so that nothing supernatural can enter inside without first being invited. Yet the houses in this town, those I have passed and those I have visited, are all unwarded."

The wise-woman sniffed. "And do you suppose, young man, that we leave signs above the door to show which houses enjoy our protection?"

Tryffin smiled and shook his head. "Not signs for ordinary folk to see. But anyone with even a touch of the gift can tell whether a house or a room is protected or not. Unless your spells are amazingly subtle, like nothing I have ever met with before."

She stared at him for a long moment. "So . . . the rumors are true. The Governor of Mochdreff has certain powers of his own."

"I am no warlock, nor wizard either," said Tryffin. "I have no power to do or to make; only sometimes, I sense things."

"Yes of course," said the old woman. "The ancient Earth magics were once strong in your line. That is how your ancestors came to rule in Ynys Celydonn. And though those gifts are somewhat debased, they do reappear occasionally. I am told that your bride—your kinswoman, isn't she?—is quite remarkable."

Tryffin sighed. Dame Brangwaine seemed sharp enough, but she showed a distressing tendency to wander from the subject. And he wanted to finish up here and go back to patrolling the streets, for whatever good that might accomplish.

"We were speaking of wards and magic circles, and not of the Lady Gwenlliant," he reminded her.

"Aye," said Dame Brangwaine. "We were, at that. Well . . . after the first children died we worked spells enough. But the wards did no good. Indeed, they seemed to attract the creature rather than repel it. No less than a dozen children were killed during that first terrible week, in rooms that ought to have been magically protected. Also, there are the nightmares that often precede an attack, and I am not the only witch in this town with a house full of cats.

"Of course there were ugly suspicions, stories indicating that *we* were somehow to blame, that the wise-women of Anoeth had created the monster, or were in league with the beast, or else enslaved by it. That last, in its way, is the most pernicious," the old woman continued. "The other stories were too incredible with our own children dying, and they did not continue to circulate long. But the tale of our enslavement is still repeated, if only in whispers behind locked doors."

She sat back in her chair, put a hand over her eyes—an involuntary gesture of weariness. "Since those stories began, the wise-women of Anoeth have dared to do very little, except to remove those wards we had already set."

The door opened, and in flowed Luned with a boy behind her, a page in black and purple livery, carrying a tray, a flagon, and two silver goblets. The youth knelt at the foot of the dais, and the young woman poured, handing the first cup to Tryffin, the second to her great-grandmother.

"I beg your pardon," said Tryffin, gesturing to one of his men, then handing the goblet over to be tasted when the Sergeant approached. That task was usually performed by one of the Governor's squires, as inobtrusively as possible. But with Cei in the south and Conn in Cormelyn, Tryffin knew better than to neglect the formality. If he did, that failure would probably come to the attention of Meligraunce, and there would follow reproaches and repercussions . . . like the Captain continually dogging his footsteps and politely refusing to allow his master a moment's respite, since he was clearly unable to look after himself.

The Sergeant swallowed a mouthful of wine and wordlessly passed the cup back to Tryffin.

"But how could such a thing happen?" The Governor took up the discussion where Dame Brangwaine had left off. "Wards do not fail. As I understand it, the more powerful the person or creature attempting to enter, the more the warding spell—the sidhe-stone or magic circle—ought to repel it."

"That is so," said the old woman. "But what if one were to entirely avoid passing the wards, and yet still enter the house or the room in question?"

Tryffin frowned at her, over the silver goblet. "Enter a warded house *without* passing the wards? I don't understand how that could be done."

"By the use of a pattern spell," said the witch.

Tryffin sat up a little straighter. "By the use of a *pattern spell*? Do you mean that this creature . . . this woman, rather . . . is able to create such spells wherever she pleases?"

His own experience of the mysterious pattern spells was somewhat limited, although there were at least a dozen in place at Caer Ysgithr. These spells were activated by walking certain invisible patterns, usually involving recognizable stationary objects—arches, doorways, fountains, stairways, even the corners of buildings—which then transported you, without any recognizable moment of transition, to another location entirely. Once you had arrived there and finished whatever business had brought you, you had only to walk through a specific door or gate to complete the final part of the spell and be transported back.

It was rather, so Tryffin understood, like chanting a verse to cast a spell, only the rooms, courtyards, and other locations involved in the pattern took the place of words. At Caer Ysgithr, these spells were rarely used except as convenient shortcuts, since few of them led anyplace that was not readily accessible, and anyone who knew the patterns could use them. But some of the spells were different: They could not be used by just anyone, and they only worked on certain days, or at certain hours.

"There would be no need for her to create new patterns," said Dame Brangwaine. "There are at least a hundred such patterns in Anoeth already. No one knows precisely how many, only that our ancestors, in their pride and their arrogance, were amazingly profligate in creating them. Did you never detect any as you walked through the streets of Anoeth?"

He took a sip of the wine. It was surprisingly good, being light and dry, and was therefore probably a foreign vintage. "I know when I am in the presence of magic and something of its nature, whether Witchcraft or Wizardry. And there is a certain stench to the blacker arts, which sometimes remains as a residue after a spell is performed. But as for recognizing a specific spell, much less seeing or sensing the patterns, I cannot do it."

"No more can I or any other witch that I know," said Dame Brangwaine. "Yet I believe that the child-killer can."

His fingers tightened on the stem of the goblet. "Before God . . . that would explain her ability to enter otherwise inaccessible rooms! But what made you suspect that she is able to do so?"

"Many of the houses where children were murdered—or stolen and then found dead—may be reached by known pattern spells," Dame Brangwaine replied. "It therefore seems likely that the other houses are similarly accessible. And once the woman or creature is inside, then she lulls the parents with a simple sleep spell. Such spells are easy enough to learn and perform; indeed, they are hardly beyond anyone with a trace of the gift. Yet they are difficult for any but the strongest mind to resist."

Tryffin absorbed that slowly. "A certain rare talent and a

simple sleep spell—enough to explain how the children are stolen. But not how they die without a mark on them, or these dreams of a great grey cat.

"Tell me," he said, "is it possible for a Mochdreffi wise-woman to alter her shape, to become a cat, a wolf, or a bird, as I have heard that witches sometimes do in the far north?" He was not ready to confide all that he knew or guessed, or to mention the woman who knew how to turn her flesh into stone.

"You are speaking of shapeshifters and skinchangers," said the old woman. "The stuff of legends. It is said that the wise-women of Mochdreff had that power in ages past, when they lived in closer harmony with the land. How that may be I do not know. As for the witches and warlocks of the north, they may have powers unknown to us, but they are mostly ignorant. What they *might* do and what they *can* do are two different things."

Absently, Tryffin held out the cup for Luned to refill. An unpleasant idea was swimming up from the depths of his mind. He pushed it firmly down, only to have it resurface. "But what," he asked softly, "what if a young witch should come into Mochdreff from another place . . . Rhianedd, for instance—no, let us say Gorwynnion . . . and be taken in and taught by Mochdreffi wise-women? As she came into full possession of her powers, would the ability to change her shape be among them?"

Once he had said those words, he wished them back again, but there was no recalling them, or anything they implied—anything they *might* imply about someone very much like Gwenlliant.

But Dame Brangwaine only shrugged, as though she found the idea entirely fantastic. "I suppose such a thing might be possible," said the old woman. "But in truth, I cannot say."

"Lord Prince," said Meligraunce, when Tryffin returned to the inn early the next morning and relayed to him all he had learned from Dame Brangwaine, "if you will pardon my saying so, it was most unwise to go into that house without a sufficient escort. You didn't know anything about these women, and I know very well that you distrust Lord Cernach."

As they crossed the firelit common room, then paused at the foot of the stairs leading up to the bedchambers, the Captain continued, "In truth, our adventure yesterday morning was also ill advised, and had I been thinking, I would have suggested we come back here for more men before following that trail of dust . . . which might have led us anywhere and into far worse circumstances than it actually did. Your Grace, you are far too important to too many people, to continually risk yourself in this way."

Tryffin sighed. "Meligraunce, why do you suppose my cousin the High King chose *me* of all people to administer justice in Mochdreff, to pave the way for one of Morcant's possible heirs to ascend to the High Seat at Caer Ysgithr? Why me as Governor, and not one of his own councilors, an older and wiser man?"

"Because," said Meligraunce, as they climbed the stairs, "the situation here was extremely delicate, and the Mochdreffi knew you and were inclined to trust you as they would trust no other foreigner. Because—"

"Because they trust me, yes," replied Tryffin. "I am only effective so long as I can maintain their confidence, and I can't do that by mistrusting them."

As that was irrefutable, Meligraunce was silent as they continued up the stairs. But when they reached the door of Tryffin's bedchamber, he spoke again. "Your Grace, while Conn is in Cormelyn, I wondered if you might permit me to sleep on the pallet beside your bed. You should not spend your hours of rest unattended. Indeed, you would not do so under ordinary circumstances if either of your squires were here in Anoeth, and the circumstances here are hardly ordinary."

Tryffin smiled and shook his head. Meligraunce appeared to be anticipating a protest, but he had none to offer. "I expected something like this, Captain. Very well. Go downstairs and bring up your things. It seems that privacy is one luxury the Governor of Mochdreff can ill afford."

Meligraunce bowed and turned on his heel. Tryffin pushed open the door of his bedchamber and walked inside.

The room was dim: the ashes on the hearth cold, the candles out, and the windows shuttered, all but one tiny window at the far end of the room—though Tryffin thought he remembered the shutters had been open when he left the inn. When he closed the door behind him, there was a rustling in the shadows by the fireplace. As he moved to see what it was, a cold stench assaulted his senses.

A slender figure in a trailing brown cloak stepped silently out of the shadows and stood defiantly in the center of the room.

"By God," said Tryffin, drawing his sword, reaching for the door with the other.

The brown cloak drifted empty to the floor, but instead of the woman that he had expected, he was facing a snarling cat, larger than a lion, with tufted ears and tail . . . not a creature of flesh and blood at all, but a stone gargoyle. Instinctively, Tryffin threw up his sword to ward off the monster's attack.

There was a clatter of steel against granite, of sword against stone. The blade bounced back in a rain of sparks, and as the Governor swung again for another blow, the gargoyle leaped faster than thought, hitting him squarely in the chest with the full force of its weight. Tryffin went over backward, and his head hit the floor with a loud crack.

By sheer force of will, he did not lose consciousness . . . though the room spun madly around him, and he was too stunned to move. Then there was a grinding sensation of bone against metal, as the stony jaws of the cat seized him by the shoulder and bore down.

The shock was too much. Tryffin cried out, and the world went utterly black.

The hour was late and the nursery fire was burning low, but the little boy with the dark curls sat nodding on a stool at his nurse's feet, trying with all of his might to stay awake, that he might listen to her relate all the terrible deeds of his deplorable ancestors.

"It was pride," said the old woman, "that was ever the downfall of all the Guillyns. And though some of them struggled to be good and valiant men, it was said there was some dark secret, some taint of the blood which they all shared, that made them inclined to be more wicked and arrogant than ordinary men."

6.

A Nest of Hornets

When Conn arrived at the steel gates of Castell Gauvain, the guards were reluctant to admit him. Even when the boy from Gorwynnion reached into his saddlebag and presented a letter bearing Prince Tryffin's seal, slipping it in through the grating of the portcullis so that one of the men might examine it more closely, the guards in the gatehouse, their fellows gazing down from the parapet, all continued to glare at him with black suspicion.

Jesus, Mary, and Joseph! the boy said to himself. *Just what sort of mischief do they suppose I am plotting?*

Out loud, he asked: "Is Mahaffy Guillyn inside? Then, as you are reasonable men, send for him at once. He will tell you that I am who I claim to be. Also, that I mean you no harm."

This, after a long whispered consultation, some of them eventually agreed to do. A man was sent off, and a short while later an unmistakable graceful figure appeared on the wall above.

"It is Conn mac Matholwch, Prince Tryffin's squire," said Mahaffy. He wore light armor, a grey cloak, and a harried expression on his handsome face that said as plainly as words: Here was a young man who had suffered as many fools as any one man *could*. "Before God, show a little common sense and admit him at once. He may bring an important message from the Governor."

The portcullis rose with a creaking of gears, and Conn and his horse passed through. By the time he dismounted by the stables, the young Lord of Ochren had descended from the wallwalk and was striding across the courtyard to greet him.

"Where is Prince Tryffin? Will he be following soon? When may we expect him?"

Conn shook his head. "You can't expect him at all. I mean to say . . . he may not arrive for a good long time."

Mahaffy stopped where he stood, his great dark eyes growing wide with apprehension. "He's in some sort of danger. He must be or he would never—"

"Does it make any kind of sense that *I* would be here if Prince Tryffin were in any serious danger?" asked Conn, as he handed his chestnut mare over to one of the Castell Gauvain grooms. "It is just that he has other, more pressing matters to attend to."

And he went on to explain the situation in Anoeth, while keeping a keen eye on the stableboy, who unsaddled the mare and rubbed her down, before leading her off to a stall.

"It sounds perfectly ghastly," said Mahaffy, with a shudder. "But I tell you truly, Conn, it is like Purgatory here. Well, you know that Lord Balin invited the chieftains of all three clans here for a parley, and promised them and their attendants safe conduct—which he and his clan have been desperately trying to enforce until Prince Tryffin arrives. To do that, he made sure that the numbers were exactly equal: that neither Lord Galfaethwy and his household, nor the representatives of clans Killian and Chenoweth (who are allied in this matter), had the advantage. And beyond that, when all these visitors were combined together, they should not exceed the number of Lord Balin's men-at-arms, who have to keep them under control."

"It seems like a very good plan to me," said Conn, taking his saddlebags from the groom and tossing them over his shoulder.

"I have to admit that it is," answered Mahaffy. "But it can also be most damnably inconvenient at times. Because it is also the reason the guards are reluctant to let anyone in . . . anyone who might claim to be a messenger, or to have urgent business at Castell Gauvain, but who is actually a member of one clan or the other, trying to unbalance the numbers."

Mahaffy ran a hand through his wild dark curls. "But you know, the men who are already here are just *spoiling* for trouble. Every single day, it seems, there are quarrels and insults and challenges. I've already been forced to break up two separate duels, single-handed, and I have only been here for five days."

The two young men started across the courtyard, Mahaffy leading the way. "But did you tell me who the Governor was sending, to talk sense to these people and keep the peace until he arrives?"

Conn hesitated a moment, not quite knowing how to break the news. Then he blurted it out. "He is counting on you to do that. Well, I am to help, but it mostly falls on you, because you are the Lord of Ochren, and the other men should listen when you speak."

Mahaffy, who was pale to begin with, turned as white as a ghost. "He is relying on *me?* You must be jesting. Conn, tell me that you only said that to make me jump. Lord of Ochren, that means nothing. I am Lord of no one and nothing, but one foolish old giant who happens to live in the ruins at Castell Ochren. And I have no experience of statecraft or diplomacy. God Almighty, I would not even know where or how to begin."

"You seem to have already begun," said Conn, "if you broke up two duels. And you've had plenty of time to observe how Prince Tryffin does these things. Besides, there was nobody else for him to send."

They circled around the lists, and stopped for a moment to watch two of Balin's men practicing with blunted swords and wooden shields. "He might have sent Meligraunce," said Mahaffy.

"Meligraunce is the son of a man who herds sheep back in Camboglanna and scratches his living out of the soil," Conn retorted. "Difficult to remember, sometimes, but true nevertheless."

Mahaffy turned pink with indignation. "Meligraunce is the best man I know, after Prince Tryffin." He lifted his chin, the old arrogant gesture that Conn remembered so well. "If a Guillyn is not too proud to show him respect, then lesser clans like Killian, Lochein, and Chenoweth have no cause to turn up their noses."

"You only say that because he helped Prince Tryffin save your life at Castell Peryf," Conn pointed out, as they started on their way again. "No, don't glare at me so. I agree that Captain Meligraunce is a fine fellow; I just wonder if *you* would think so, any more than these other petty lords, if you did not have cause to be grateful to him."

Mahaffy's flush deepened. "He saved my life twice, as it just happens. But that has nothing . . . well, perhaps it does," he admitted. "And the men here know nothing about him. Damn and blast, I suppose they would even account it an insult, if the Governor sent Meligraunce here in his place, no matter how temporarily."

They passed through an inner gate and entered another courtyard. "Not that they are likely to take anything that I say seriously. Most people treat me as though I hadn't a brain in my—"

Mahaffy's complaint was cut short as he spotted two young boys on the other side of the yard, engaged in a fierce scuffle. "By God," he said, "Lord Gilfaethwy's page and that boy of Killian."

He and Conn were across the yard in an instant, pulling the young combatants apart and forcibly restraining them. Something flashed in the sunlight, and Conn saw that the boy he was holding, the boy in Gilfaethwy's livery, had drawn a short jeweled dagger. A hand clamped firmly around the wrist and a vicious twist were enough to make the page loose his grip, and the dagger fell to the flagstone pavement.

Conn's mind whirled with all the possible implications of the boy's reckless act. He looked around to see if anyone else had noticed. Fortunately, Mahaffy was still wrestling with the lad from clan Killian, so Conn placed one booted foot over the dagger, effectively concealing it—though he kept a firm hold on the boy who had dropped it, anyway.

When the two pages were finally subdued, a round of angry reproaches and excuses followed:

"Ifan started it."

"No, I did not. You were the one who gave me a shove as I walked by."

"Lord Mahaffy, I swear, I never touched him. Neither did I do anything else to provoke him. Cadllyn was the one who said that my sister—"

"Your sister has stronger arms to defend her," said Mahaffy. "Supposing she even cares what a grubby-faced brat like Cadllyn says of her . . . or would not be shamed nearly to death if she knew that her younger brother was brawling like a churl in Lord Balin's courtyard."

Both pages blushed, exchanged accusatory glances, and then looked down at their feet.

"No doubt you are both playing truant, anyway," he continued scolding them. "This time of day, you ought to be usefully employed. Go on with you both and polish some armor—or see that the grooms are properly tending your master's horse, or whatever else you can find to do."

With a few muttered words—of apology or defiance it was impossible to tell—the boys shuffled off in opposite directions.

But Conn called one of them back. "Cadllyn Lochein . . . that is your name, I think?" He removed his foot and bent to pick up the dagger. "You dropped your dirk."

Lord Gilfaethwy's page came back, with a swagger this time, though Conn suspected the swagger was meant to disguise a sudden panic.

"No," said Conn, as Cadllyn held out his hand. "I think I will keep it—and you—out of trouble for a time."

Young Lochein responded with a hot glare of resentment. He was a typical Mochdreffi, slight and dark, and Conn stood head and shoulders above him. "Then you had better take Ifan's dirk as well," he said, wiping the sweat from his brow with a silken sleeve. "It would only be fair. If he is armed and I am not, then Killian and Chenoweth will have the advantage. I am sure Lord Balin—"

"Ifan was not the one who drew steel," Conn interrupted him. "And as he is not aware of your dishonorable act, he is not very likely to retaliate in kind. Mother of God! Do you not realize that if you had killed him, you would be guilty of murder, and probably be hanged right here in Lord Balin's courtyard?"

"I never intended to kill him," said Cadllyn, beginning to look frightened. "I only meant . . . I don't know what I meant."

Conn continued to regard him sternly, gazing down, not only from his greater height, but from the lofty vantage point of his seventeen years. "I know very well that if you were determined to be wicked and foolish, you could find another blade. I am ready to believe that you acted in the heat of the moment. The more reason to keep your dagger safe, so that you are not tempted to do the same thing again."

"You are not . . . " The boy drew a tremulous breath, looked from Mahaffy to Conn and then back again. "You are not going to tell anyone what I did?"

Mahaffy shook his head. "We will tell no one this time, though perhaps we ought to. God help you if you make us regret it."

"Yes," said Conn, showing his teeth. "God help you if you make us regret it. Because I tell you right now, if any harm comes to Ifan after this, no matter how confused or clouded the circumstances, I will make it my task to seek you out and personally break your neck."

"I won't—I won't do anything to make you regret it," said Cadllyn, backing away. "Thank you, Lord Mahaffy. Thank you . . . sir."

When the page had gone, Conn and Mahaffy exchanged a harried glance. "That was quick thinking to cover the dirk," said Mahaffy. "If Ifan had seen it and gone running to Nefn Chenoweth or Morgan Killian . . . "

Conn blew out his breath, a long sigh of mingled relief and exasperation. "I see that you spoke the truth. These people *are* spoiling for trouble. I hope Prince Tryffin finishes his business in Anoeth quickly and arrives here before all the squires and pages cut out each other's hearts."

"Aye," said Mahaffy, with a deep sigh of his own. "Though I have to admit, you handled that boy rather well."

Conn was shown to a tower bedchamber and given a basin of water, that he might wash up, change out of his boots and riding leathers, and don the velvet tunic, parti-colored hose, and soft leather shoes with elongated toes deemed suitable for serving a petty lord at the table.

He had finished dressing and was just buckling on his swordbelt again, when Mahaffy entered the chamber carrying a branch of candles, followed by one of the men-at-arms he had brought to Cormelyn with him.

"I said you were to share my room," said the young Lord of Ochren. "Otherwise, you would be in the dormitory with the other squires, and I tell you there is little peace to be had in that place."

"My thanks," said Conn. "And I have been thinking: I ought to serve as your squire while we are here. Prince Tryffin would not mind, and the others will treat you with more respect, if you are properly attended."

Mahaffy dismissed the man-at-arms, set the branched candlestick down on a table. "I was thinking much the same, though I hated to ask."

Since only a few months had passed since Mahaffy's elevation, the two were still on familiar terms and it was hard to remember they were no longer equals. Besides that, Conn would be knighted in a year or so himself, and then they would stand on much the same footing as they had as squires.

"You ought to have your own squire—no, your own household," said Conn. "I wonder you haven't seen to it already. It is no more than you deserve, as the Lord of Ochren."

Mahaffy made a gesture of disgust. "Do you think I don't know that? Can you really not guess why I have neglected to do so?"

Conn moved over to the fire and threw on some logs. "I haven't the least idea. I always thought . . . well, I assumed you would want all the pomp and ceremony that was coming to you."

The treacherous color rose in Mahaffy's face. "Of course you did. You know me well enough to reckon just how far my damnable arrogance is likely to take me. But the truth is, I cannot *afford* to keep a household of my own," he said softly. "Before God, Conn, I am practically a pauper."

"That can't be so," protested Conn, standing with one foot on the fender. "You inherited Lord Cado's lands and estates, and he had a vast number of servants. In fact, he lived like a king. Far more splendidly than Prince Tryffin does, and *he* is so wealthy that it hardly bears thinking about."

"My uncle," said Mahaffy, "lived mainly by the favor of great men . . . men like Lord Morcant, and Goronwy before him. And he was always borrowing money, which he seldom repaid, because no one likes to dun a wizard—it just seems too dangerous. He spent what little substance he had there at the end, hiring mercenary soldiers in order to overthrow Prince Tryffin."

Mahaffy began to shed his armor, and Conn moved swiftly across the chamber to assist him. "All that I inherited from Lord Cado was a ruined castle, some barren acres, and the house in Trewynyn. I might sell that, but then I would have no place to live when Prince Tryffin returns to the court of his cousin the King. That is, if he goes to Camboglanna and not straight home to Tir Gwyngelli."

Conn scratched his head. "I rather thought you would go with us."

Mahaffy laughed ruefully. "Go to Camboglanna or Tir Gwyngelli? I know very well what they think of the Mochdreffi in that part of the world. Warlocks, heretics, thieves, and murderers. What sort of welcome do you suppose I would receive there?"

"Well," said Conn, measuring his words, "I have no idea how it is at Lord Maelgwyn's court in Gwyngelli, but nobody *knows* any Mochdreffi at Caer Cadwy. That is, they knew the Princess Diaspad, but she was Mochdreffi only by marriage, and they knew Calchas, who was raised Mochdreffi but wasn't really, as it turns out. Calchas was a wretched little toad by anyone's standards—so it is no wonder if people have the wrong impression.

"You might," he added, as he unbuckled Mahaffy's vambraces, "do a great deal to correct that false impression. You would make a splendid emissary on behalf of your people."

"No, I would not," said Mahaffy emphatically. "Nor will I go there only to be continually patronized, treated as a foreigner and a spy, insulted and . . . Ah God, I have no right to say any of this to you. You have endured as much and probably a great deal worse, right here in Mochdreff."

Conn grinned good-naturedly. "Very true . . . but then, I haven't your famed Guillyn pride to contend with."

"And that," said Mahaffy, perfectly serious, "is a greater advantage than you may ever know."

As Lord Balin of Cormelyn had grown weary of quarrels along with his meals, he had adopted the prudent custom of inviting only one faction to dinner at a time. Since tonight was the turn of clan Lochein, Lord Gilfaethwy was already there in the lofty, banner-draped dining hall when Mahaffy and Conn arrived—and also young Cadllyn, serving as Gilfaethwy's taster.

When Mahaffy entered, there was a rustle and a flutter among the ladies, a resentful glitter of masculine teeth. He set his jaw and went straight to the table without acknowledging anyone. Mahaffy was drearily accustomed to women who caught their breath suddenly when he walked by, to men who instinctively despised him for no better reason than his damnable face. But tonight it was somehow particularly annoying.

In truth, he was still out of sorts, after his conversation with Conn, the humiliating revelation of his reduced circumstances, as well as wishing fervently that he were in Anoeth with the Governor, where he might just possibly acquit himself with some distinction . . . rather than at Castell Gauvain breaking up fistfights among pages, and causing the hearts of the local maidens to beat just a little faster.

"It is good of you to join us," said Lord Balin, as Mahaffy took a seat according to his rank near the head of the table, under a crimson banner suspended from the rafters. Lord Gilfaethwy, who was seated directly across from him, greeted the young Lord of Ochren with his usual rough courtesy.

Mahaffy felt a twinge of guilt. Gilfaethwy Lochein was a bad-tempered old man, true enough, but his clan stood precariously poised at the brink of disaster. Beside the fearsome possibilities of a blood feud, Mahaffy's own difficulties seemed trivial indeed.

And there were some advantages, he mused, glaring moodily down at his pewter plate, to having no family to worry about. Now that Lord Cado was gone, Mahaffy had but two living relatives. His cousin Dahaut he utterly despised, and as for Dame Ceinwen . . . worrying about that remarkable old woman was a little like worrying over the stars in the firmament. She had preceded everyone else that he knew into the world, and she was almost certain to outlast them all.

"Perhaps young Guillyn will oblige us, by telling what Prince Tryffin might say if he were here in this company tonight." That was Lord Gilfaethwy, breaking into his thoughts. Taken by surprise, Mahaffy could only stammer a response.

"I don't—I don't understand why you are asking me."

"I understood," said Lord Gilfaethwy, gazing at him over a tankard of ale, "that you were in the Governor's confidence. But perhaps I was mistaken."

Mahaffy looked to Conn for support, but his friend was offering a dish of saffroned eels to Lord Balin, and neither of them seemed to be paying any attention to the conversation.

"No," said Mahaffy. "No, you were not mistaken." He tried to think what Prince Tryffin would say, and when he decided that he knew, he blurted it out without pausing to consider how it might sound. "I believe, Lord Gilfaethwy, if Prince Tryffin were here, he would ask you first to examine your conscience."

A shocked silence settled over the room. Lord Gilfaethwy turned white and then very red before he spoke. "I believe that you must be mistaken. My conscience is clear. I am the wronged party, and have done nothing but what was necessary for the honor and safety of my clan."

As he had proceeded too far to back out now, Mahaffy plunged ahead. "No doubt Morgan Killian and Nefn Chenoweth would say the same, and mean it just as sincerely as you do now. It is a rare circumstance when anyone *means* to start a blood feud. Someone is careless, or greedy, or just intractable, which leads to a disproportionate retaliation . . . and soon everyone feels he is in too deep, it is impossible to withdraw without appearing a coward, or displaying some other fatal weakness."

Lord Gilfaethwy growled something under his breath, and Mahaffy felt a sinking sensation, sure that he had somehow made matters worse than they were before. "I beg your pardon," he said meekly. "I am afraid that I spoke out of turn."

"You speak," said Lord Gilfaethwy, waving away Conn and his dish of eels, "without knnowing anything at all of the matters involved in this particular dispute."

Fortunately—or unfortunately, Mahaffy was not sure which— Lord Balin chose that moment to enter the conversation. "As it happens, Lord Gilfaethwy, he does know something," said Balin, stroking his beard. "We discussed the situation quite thoroughly the day he arrived."

Lord Gilfaethwy muttered something into his ale. Then he fixed Mahaffy with a piercing gaze. "And would you say, young man, that *I* was the one who was . . . careless, or greedy, or just intractable . . . or do you merely accuse me of *grossly disproportionate* retaliation?"

Mahaffy shook his head. "It is not for me to say. That would be for you to determine, if you followed Prince Tryffin's advice. But I ask you this: If you had considered all the possible consequences when this quarrel began, if you had even imagined that things would proceed as far as they have, would you not have behaved a great deal differently? Would you not have yielded those worthless acres . . . accepted compensation for any insults, real or imagined . . . tempered your words when you confronted clan Killian . . . would you not have done all those things and done them *gladly*, rather than plunge your clan into the horror of a blood feud which may involve them in ruin for a hundred generations? I pay you the compliment, Lord Gilfaethwy, of believing that you would—just as I believe the same of the other chieftains involved."

For just a moment, Mahaffy thought that Lord Gilfaethwy was really listening to him, that he had said the right things, and that something good might actually come of it. But then the old man clenched his fist and pounded it on the table, causing the pewter plates to dance and rattle. "Even if what you say is true, it makes no difference now. A fatal weakness you said, and that is precisely what I should display by backing down now. I will not expose my clan to ridicule and contempt. If other clans do not respect us, they will take advantage of our supposed weakness, they will band together to wipe us out. And that I will never permit to happen."

"No," said Mahaffy wearily, "you would rather see your clansmen perish just as certainly for the sake of your pride."

Lord Gilfaethwy stiffened. "You are a young man, a very young man, and so I will pardon you. You know nothing at all about pride, or family honor, or—"

"On the contrary," Mahaffy interrupted him. By now, his own temper was wearing thin, and he spoke in anger, reckless of the consequences. "You seem to be forgetting, Lord Gilfaethwy, to whom you are speaking. I know everything about pride and family honor; I come of a clan far older and prouder and purer in blood than any in Mochdreff. And I tell you this: If you wish to see Lochein, Killian, and Chenoweth reduced to the same pitiful numbers as clan Guillyn, then you cannot do better than continue on the course you have already chosen."

The meal proceeded in icy silence. Mahaffy picked at his food, his appetite gone, while Conn silently waited on him and the other petty lords. As soon as the plates were cleared away, the young knight rose from his seat, asked the Lord of Cormelyn's leave to depart, and walked stiffly out of the hall.

When his friend caught up to him in the passageway, he was pounding his fist into a wall. Conn caught the bleeding hand and held it to his chest, before Mahaffy could reduce it to a bloody pulp.

"Oh, Conn, Conn, what have I *done*? I wish I were dead . . . I deserve to be dead. I only made everything worse than it was before. Will I never master my wicked pride and my even more wicked temper?"

"You spoke what was in your heart," Conn said soothingly. "You only said what was perfectly true, what the Governor would have said for himself, if he were here."

Mahaffy leaned back against the cold stone wall. "But don't you see? I am not Prince Tryffin and I should never have spoken. I lack his—his way of explaining things. You know very well that he often carries the day by the sheer force of his personality."

As he spoke, the image came vividly into his mind: Prince Tryffin as he might have looked and acted confronting Lord Gilfaethwy. The placid air of calm authority (which was somewhat deceptive), the expression of patient, compassionate interest (which was not). The almost overwhelming physical presence. And the musical Gwyngellach lilt that made everything he said fall so pleasantly on the ear that who could refuse to listen?

"It is true," Conn said slowly. "It is not just what he says, but the way that he says it. He is always so good and so sensible that he *shames* other people—the ones who are leaping about and shouting and waving their fists—into sitting down calmly and discussing things rationally."

"But now, on top of everything else, he will have to come up with another argument," said Mahaffy. "Lord Gilfaethwy has heard it all and already rejected it. He will only grow bored and angry if he hears it again."

He shuddered and closed his eyes. "I should have held my tongue . . . or just babbled any nonsense that came into my head. What made me think, even for a moment, that anything I said would do any good?"

In those days, the People of Celydonn were exceedingly wicked. They worshipped trees, stones, rivers, wells, tempests, and whirlwinds. They built great temples dedicated to the Sun and the Moon, but they also worshipped in forest glades and on rocky heaths, under the stars at night.

—*From* The Sermons of St. Teilo

7.

The Bonds of Destiny

On her second day in the house in the woods, Caithne took Gwenlliant to the low end of the long room, where the women did their spinning and weaving. There was a tall standing loom, as beautifully carved and painted as the beams and the doorposts, and a basket full of wooden spindles . . . another of wool, another of flax, and a great many more, containing petals and dried flowers, nutshells, berries, feathers, and other things besides, which Gwenlliant assumed must be used for dyeing. Because the ceiling was so low at that end, someone had pounded wooden pegs into the beams, and hanks of bright yarn and skeins of thread hung from those pegs like a multi-colored web. When she looked up to examine those threads more closely, Gwenlliant could actually see roots coming in through the roof, great ivory taproots with fine white hairs, pushing down from the turf thatch up above.

"Can you spin flax?" asked Caithne, taking a seat on a stool, arranging the skirt of her saffron gown.

"Yes," said Gwenlliant, kneeling down on the wooden floor, sitting back on her heels. "And wool, too." Not surprisingly, there was an odor of earth and of growing things at that end of the house, which Gwenlliant found rather pleasant.

The redhead lowered her voice. "Did you ever spin *grass and twigs*?"

Gwenlliant shook her head, affecting astonishment. She knew

70

perfectly well how the thing was done, after watching Dame Ceinwen dozens of times, but she had never tried it herself.

"Then I will show you," said Caithne, taking up a spindle, then reaching into one of the baskets and pulling out a handful of dried grass.

The thread she produced was coarse but serviceable. Gwenlliant longed to tell her that hair and thistledown would make it both stronger and finer, but she held her tongue. Caithne did not seem like the sort of young woman who took advice, and besides, Gwenlliant wanted no one here to guess that she was a witch.

"Caithne!" said Maelinn, sitting down by the loom and taking up the shuttle. "You must not frighten Gwenhwyach. Remember that she is a stranger and new to our ways."

But Gwenlliant guessed that Caithne was showing off . . . *not* to frighten her, but to impress Maelinn, because of some rivalry existing between them.

Several days passed, and Gwenlliant remained at the house in the wood, sharing the rustic life of the women who lived there. Their land, they told her, was known as Achren, because of its many trees and forests. It extended from their own pleasant woodland, all the way to the hall of the High Prince, a two days' ride distant . . . and for many miles beyond.

The house in the wood was so pretty and tidy—and so cleverly arranged, with its great room for eating and working and visiting, and a loft at the high end where everyone slept in deep feathery beds, with lovely carved bedposts all in a row—that Gwenlliant found it pleasant to live there. And it was a peaceful life as well as a simple one: spinning, brewing, and baking, milking the goats that lived in a pen under the trees—not very different from the life she had shared with Dame Ceinwen, and it was very easy to slip into the patterns and the rhythms of the days and the nights.

Yet it did not take Gwenlliant long to come to the daunting conclusion that her newfound friends—Maelinn, Pethboc, Ceri, Pali, Caithne, Sceith, Mai, Morfa, Ettare, Regan, Tiffaine, and Gleis—were not witches, as she had first supposed, or wizards either (though their spells were mainly of the domestic sort, for making bread to rise or milk to stay sweet no matter how long it remained in a bowl, there was a high windy feel to some of their magic that reminded Gwenlliant of wizards), but were pagan priestesses of the Old Religion, their home a sort of temple or cloister in the deep woods.

To be sure, they had a great many odd and disquieting habits. The well in the clearing, for instance—everyone behaved as though there were *someone* living at the bottom, and they all lowered their voices when they walked by. And they had any number of chants and rituals, which they performed every day, and sometimes late at night, dancing outdoors in the moonlight without any clothes. Yes, it was all rather difficult and even quite shocking, for someone like Gwenlliant with her strict Rhianeddi upbringing. But she thought to herself: *These women are gentle and kindly, and Grifflet and I are safer with them than wandering abroad—where we might meet people equally pagan, but perhaps more violently disposed.*

So, when Ettare poured a dish of grain onto the fire, Gwenlliant simply looked the other way. When Sceith sprinkled wine on the ground, she made no comment. When Maelinn invoked her goddess and her many consorts, Gwenlliant made the sign of the cross and whispered a prayer of her own. No one seemed to notice or to care what she did—in fact, they seemed to take it for granted she would not worship in the same way they did.

Gradually she realized the nature of their community: twelve priestesses, each dedicated to a different divinity, each one observing her separate rites. Though Maelinn was, in effect, the High Priestess, and ordered the others about quite freely.

For all that, everyone did the same work, and even the dirtiest and most boring tasks were shared equally.

One day, when Grifflet was napping by the fire, all wrapped up in the brown wool cloak, and Gwenlliant and Maelinn were scrubbing the floor around the hearth, the priestess asked about Gwenlliant's ring. "It is very unusual . . . the strange symbols engraved on the band, and that great cloudy crystal. I have only seen one that was anything like it, and that ring was almost identical."

Gwenlliant dipped her scrub rag into a bucket of soapy water, then twisted the cloth to wring it out. "Was it truly? But who did it belong to?"

"It belongs to Caerthinn, the High Prince," replied Maelinn. They were both kneeling on the wooden planks, with the bucket between them. Gwenlliant had borrowed a cast-off garment belonging to Sceith, in order to save her gown, and Maelinn had stripped off her bracelets and rings, and was similarly attired in brown sackcloth.

It was a little difficult to figure out Maelinn, who could be quite haughty and disagreeable, especially when it seemed that one of the others did not pay her sufficient respect. Caithne and Sceith were the worst offenders, and with them she could be amazingly spiteful. But Gwenlliant she appeared to regard as an equal, perhaps because she had arrived so richly dressed, and to her she was invariably kind and affectionate.

Even in sackcloth, even up to her elbows in dirty wash water, Maelinn maintained her dignity. "The ring was a gift to Caerthinn from his friend Mabonograin."

Gwenlliant glanced up sharply as the name was repeated. "Cerddin—you did say Cerddin? That is the name of your High Prince?"

Maelinn shrugged. "Well, you pronounce it strangely, but that is his name. I know Prince Caerthinn very well; at one time there was even talk of our marrying, but that came to nothing. I did not mind very much, because he is rather plain and not very amusing. But my brothers stand high in his favor. The Sons of the Boar are very powerful, so naturally Caerthinn maintains an alliance."

Gwenlliant's heart was beating very swiftly. She thought this Caerthinn must be the same man who had figured in Dame Ceinwen's tale, the Prince who had lived a thousand years before her own time, and disgraced himself so badly that none of his kinsmen would acknowledge the relationship or claim his crown. She thought she might be about to learn something very important. "And the other name you mentioned . . . Mabonograin, you said. Who is he?"

"He is the son of the King of the far Hill Country," said Maelinn. "Mabonograin and Caerthinn are great friends and visit each other as frequently as possible. Of course, it was a little thing so far as Mabonograin was concerned. His father is the wealthiest man in all the world, and Mabonograin is very free with his gifts to everyone. He gave *me* a gown of green silk, when I lived in my father's house, and a white stallion to my brother Gereint, and something much better to the Princess Tinne. The Hill Country is riddled with gold mines and silver mines, and places where precious gems may be found. Or so I have heard—I have never actually been there myself."

"It all sounds rather familiar," said Gwenlliant, twisting the golden band around and around. It all sounded *very* familiar. "Perhaps my ring comes from the same place."

"Mabonograin says that the stone in Caerthinn's ring is a fragment of bone from a great dragon." Maelinn wiped off her hands and moved a little closer to examine the ring.

"No," said Gwenlliant, shaking her head. She knew nothing of dragons but had a fair acquaintance with precious stones. "I am certain that mine is a sidhe-stone."

The larger sidhe-stones sometimes had magical powers, though finding out what those powers were could be rather difficult, even for a witch or a wizard. The gem in Gwenlliant's ring seemed to have no special qualities of its own—unless you counted pulling her into the past and keeping her there.

"That is very plain to see," replied Maelinn. "But Mabonograin says the dragons that live under the earth have bones made of crystal, and that is the origin of sidhe-stones. He is full of pretty fancies, Prince Mabonograin, and he tells the most remarkable stories."

Gwenlliant considered that, absently drawing patterns with soapy water on the planks of the floor, while Maelinn went on with the scrubbing. The name Mabonograin was certainly a strange one, but everything else about him sounded exactly like Tir Gwyngelli: the hills riddled with gold mines, the careless generosity, the irresistible urge to improve on reality by spinning fanciful tales. Only one thing was wrong and that was his friendship with Cerddin.

Because the Gwyngellach and the Mochdreffi had been feuding for . . . well, nobody knew exactly how long, though a thousand years seemed like a good round number. Until Tryffin came along, the Mochdreffi had despised anyone with even a drop of Gwyngellach blood. Yet long, long ago, said the legends, the two feuding tribes had lived like brothers, until a foolish quarrel had forever divided them.

Perhaps they are somehow connected, those two stories, thought Gwenlliant. *Cerddin's disgrace and the beginning of the feud. I never believed that nonsense about wild pigs, anyway.*

Only one thing was certain: The ring had drawn her back in time to this shadow of the distant past for a particular *reason.* And she thought she might be very close to discovering what that reason was.

When Tryffin opened his eyes, the room was ablaze with candles. His head was so heavy, it was a great effort to raise it up off the pillow, and when he was finally able to lift it a very few inches, everything spun so madly around him that he was forced to lie back again.

"Where is Meligraunce?" he whispered weakly. Tryffin had a dim memory that he had been in some sort of peril, and another memory of a long period of confusion, during which he had heard the Captain's voice pleading with him to respond. Now that he had finally struggled up out of the well of blackness which had threatened to engulf him, it did not make sense that Meligraunce was no longer there.

There was a light step, a cool hand on his brow, and a soft voice answering his question. "The Captain is sleeping now, after spending three days and two nights watching by your bed. But if it is *very* important, I will wake him for you."

"No," said Tryffin. "No, don't disturb him." The room began to settle, and he recognized the pale, handsome face of the woman standing over him. "Luned . . . it is Luned, is it not? Why are you here?"

"When word came that you were lying close to death, my great-grandmother insisted on being carried here in her chair, and naturally I came with her," said the young woman. "We have nursed you all this time, Dame Brangwaine and I."

"Dame Brangwaine . . ." he murmured. "That would explain all the candles, I suppose."

Luned permitted herself a brief smile. "My great-grandmother is a great believer in the power of light to banish any evil presence. Had she arrived with her candles earlier, the contest between you and the powers of darkness might have been more equal."

Tryffin tried to move again, but found that his arms and legs were as heavy as his head. "May I speak with her? There is something . . . something . . ." His thoughts clouded over, and he could not remember what he had wanted to ask her. Yet a dull sense of horror nagged at the back of his mind, and he had a strong impression that he was not yet out of danger.

"She, too, is resting," replied Luned, adjusting his pillow, smoothing the blankets covering him.

"You have nothing to fear, Lord Prince," she added. He wondered what he had done to betray that emotion—it was hard to school his face, modulate his voice, when he felt so weak and so ill. "You are as well protected as any man in Celydonn. Also, your fever is much less than it was, thanks to Dame Brangwaine's healing spells. Now there is nothing for you to do but sleep, for when all is said and done, sleep is the greatest healer of all."

Tryffin wanted to say that he knew that already, but that three days and two nights ought to be enough sleep for anyone. He wanted to say that, but he could not, because the room was growing darker around the edges and he was sliding into confusion once more.

When Tryffin opened his eyes again, Meligraunce was seated in a chair beside his bed. When he tried to speak, his voice came out stronger than it had before. "Ah, Captain . . . there you are."

"I heard that you asked for me earlier, Lord Prince. I am sorry that I was not here."

Tryffin shook his head, and was pleased to discover that he could do so without growing dizzy. "You would have been little use to me in the condition I was in at the time. I have a number of questions to ask you now. But first . . . I wonder if you would mind helping me to sit up?"

Meligraunce was instantly out of his chair and across the room, moving toward the door. "I will ask the ladies if that can be safely done." Before Tryffin could protest, he had opened the door and was speaking to someone out in the corridor.

When Tryffin tried to lift his arms this time, he discovered that movement was possible—but that any motion of his left arm caused a sharp, sickening pain to lance through his chest. "Never mind, Captain," he said, when the pain subsided. "Just prop me up on these pillows a bit. I feel too helpless flat on my back."

Meligraunce closed the door softly and did as he had requested. With his head at a better angle for observation, Tryffin discovered that someone had moved him out of his room at the inn. This room was smaller and lower, and there was only one window—a small window up near the ceiling—that was tightly shuttered. With all the candles burning, it was almost unbearably close. "For God's sake, can we please have some air?"

"I suppose there is no great danger opening the shutters this time of the day," said the Captain, suiting his actions to his words. "As you can see, we moved you to another bed on the same floor, as the other room no longer seemed safe."

"Tell me," said Tryffin, "everything that happened after the stone gargoyle attacked me."

Meligraunce returned to his seat. "The stone . . . ? Perhaps you will explain that when I have finished." He cleared his throat and began his story. "When I heard you cry out, I was still on the stairs. I ran to your room but it was very dark, so I rushed out again to bring in a light. When I returned with a branch of candles, you were lying on the floor and a woman in a long brown cloak was kneeling there beside you."

"And?" Tryffin prompted him, when the Captain gave no sign that he was not about to continue.

Meligraunce shuddered. "It is rather difficult to describe what I saw. It was like some obscene act of love, if you will pardon my saying so. You were bleeding quite heavily from the shoulder . . . it was pooling on the floor, and she had apparently put one hand right down into it, because her fingers were red and sticky, and her palm left an imprint afterward . . . but you appeared to be conscious because you were making, well, making what I can only describe as sounds of pleasure. All this time, while I was observing this, she had her mouth over yours and both hands *pressing* down on your chest in such a way . . . that it seemed she was forcing the air right out of your lungs and swallowing it herself.

"It all happened very quickly, and I had no time to study the situation or to correct my first impressions, for it was clearly the time for action," Meligraunce added apologetically.

"And what did you do?" said Tryffin, finding nothing to quarrel with in any of that.

"I drew my sword and stuck it right through her. It went through quite easily and came out the same way, as though—as though she were not entirely substantial at the time. Yet she seemed to feel it sorely, for all that. She convulsed, cried out, and then fell to the floor. I thought I had killed her.

"Naturally, I turned my attention to you. You were so pale and still that I thought for a moment . . . well, the wound was still bleeding copiously, so I realized you could not be dead, after all, and did what I could to staunch the flow of blood. While I was doing that, she apparently crawled on her belly over to the window, where she heaved herself up, leaving a trail of blood to mark her passage, and . . . and was gone, Lord Prince."

Tryffin sighed, and closed his eyes. "Either she turned herself into some winged creature and flew away, or the window was the last portal in a pattern spell."

Meligraunce cleared his throat again. "Dame Brangwaine

seemed to think there was a pattern spell. That is why we moved you to this room, immediately after the old woman arrived."

"You don't think that the creature is dead," said Tryffin, opening his eyes again.

The Captain appeared to consider that. "I would like to believe that I had killed her. But she made it to the window so quickly, she must have retained a certain vitality. And once she had shifted her shape . . ."

Tryffin nodded. "Once she had shifted her shape, the wound would immediately heal, of course. If you are going to alter the substance of your entire body, why leave a gaping hole in your flesh?"

"Nevertheless, Lord Prince," said Meligraunce, "you may rest easy. I do not think she will return anytime soon. There is a whole coven of witches watching this inn and you."

Tryffin smiled faintly. Mochdreffi witches did not meet in covens—a fact that Meligraunce knew as well as he did. "And how might that be?"

"When she came here to tend to your wound, Dame Brang-waine brought her great-granddaughter with her . . . but also, it seems, her sisters, cousins, and more distant connections, including a great-grandnephew who appears to be that rarest of creatures, a Mochdreffi warlock. Some of them, I might add, are quite formidable old women. Indeed, were it not so, I should never have been so weak as to allow them to see you."

Tryffin was surprised. "More formidable than Dame Brang-waine herself?"

Meligraunce shook his head emphatically. "That hardly seems possible. But haughty and powerful, for all that. I fear it has quite destroyed the innkeeper's business, for nobody wishes to enter the common room with all those stern old women stalking about in their dark gowns and their immense headdresses. I was privileged to see one of them warn off Lord Cernach and the other petty lords, when they came to inquire after your condition. She reduced them all to the status of erring page boys with a few brief sentences, and they left in a terrible hurry, that I can assure you.

"The story we are spreading about," the Captain continued, "is that you are still burning with fever and are not expected to live. And you will be glad to know that these last three days not a single child has been attacked."

Tryffin shook his head. "I am happy to know that the children of Anoeth have been safe all this time. But it only confirms my suspicions: She killed all those other children to attract my attention. And knowing that she may begin the slaughter once more, just as soon as I rise from my bed . . . that doesn't provide much incentive for me to get well again."

Meligraunce stood up, began to pace the floor. "But it should, Prince Tryffin. I believe that she only waivers because she remains uncertain of your survival. But if you were dead, she would not be long in committing—well, it would be difficult to imagine a crime more heinous than any she has committed before. Let us say that she would soon be up to more widespread mischief. Why else, indeed, should she go to such lengths to lure you here and then destroy you?"

"Certainly, she must intend something of the sort eventually," said Tryffin. "A rebellion, a bid for power. And though she may not know whether I am healing or dying, she knows very well that I am alive."

Meligraunce paused in his pacing. "The woman—the creature—has continued to send you dreams?"

"Yes," said Tryffin, closing his eyes, "but don't ask me to tell you about them. They were . . . somewhat confused."

And also, he seemed to recall, faintly sexual, though he had not thought of that until Meligraunce described what he had seen, the woman hovering over his body and drawing the breath out through his mouth.

His eyes opened wide. "You said that you saw her, possibly in her own form. What did she look like?"

Meligraunce began to move around the room again. "Things happened so swiftly. Then, too, her face was so close to yours . . . all I recall is that she wore her hair in a kind of knot at the back of her neck, and there seemed to be a great deal of it. Her hair was very fine and light, Your Grace, and that surprised me."

Tryffin tried to sit up, and again the pain shot through him, forcing him to lie back on the pillows with a low moan. "Before God, what is wrong with me?" he whispered.

"Your collarbone was broken; I do not think you should try to move about until we put your arm into a sling. Also, you lost a great deal of blood through the wound in your shoulder, and contracted some sort of contagion which made you burn steadily with fever for two days and a night."

Meligraunce frowned, as the Governor continued his attempts

to sit up. "I wouldn't say that you are entirely out of danger even yet, so I beg you to lie still until your nurses say otherwise."

"Nonsense," said Tryffin, though not as loudly as he might have wished. "If I were dying, I would know it. But my heart is beating strongly, I am not in the least feverish, and I breathe quite easily."

"If you will pardon my saying so," replied Meligraunce, taking the unprecedented action of laying hands on the Governor's person and physically restraining him, "that your heart is pounding so loudly that you can hear it is a very bad sign. Your Grace, if my conversation continues to inspire such imprudent behavior, I will be forced to leave the room and answer no more questions."

Tryffin attempted to glare at him, but had an idea he was not doing a very good job of it. "By God, Captain, I have never before known you to be guilty of insubordination."

"Nor have I ever known you, Prince Tryffin, to ignore good advice, except where it involves your own well-being. I wish you would stop being so abominably selfish and only consider how important you are to the people of Mochdreff, and what would happen to them all if you died."

Tryffin went suddenly still, too stunned to fight any more. The one sin he had never been accused of in his brief generous life was selfishness. "Abominably . . . *what* did you call me, Captain?"

"My apologies," said Meligraunce, relaxing his grip a bit. "Perhaps I should have said heedless and self-centered. Because you are normally so strong and vigorous, you have this remarkable notion the angels have chosen to make you immortal.

"Or if not the angels, then perhaps the fairies," he added, referring to a certain tendency, among the common folk especially, to confuse the Gwyngellach with those other People of the Hills, the Sidhe. "Or in any case, you *behave* as though you imagined yourself immortal, and that is just as bad. I know you will not deny that or blame me for speaking freely, because you are far too honest."

Which set Tryffin to thinking, whether he had violated any of his geasa lately, which might serve to explain his recent brush with death. By far the most inconvenient of these supernatural prohibitions was the one that Meligraunce referred to indirectly, the one that forbade Tryffin to ever knowingly speak an outright lie.

"I ask you to forgive me," he said after a while. "I fear that I make an ungrateful and difficult patient."

The Captain stifled a smile. "I believe that is often so when those who are rarely ill find themselves ailing. Naturally, I will not regard it."

Tryffin tried to think what they had been talking about before. "Ah yes . . . you were saying, I think, that the woman was blonde and that surprised you. But why? Fair-haired women are not unknown in Mochdreff, except among the very oldest and most pure-blooded families."

"It surprised me," said Meligraunce, settling back in his chair, "because I had been thinking, up until that moment, that Dahaut might be the woman in question."

"Dahaut?" Tryffin remembered, just in time, not to make another attempt to sit up. "Do you honestly think Dahaut is capable of these terrible things?"

"That would depend on what you mean by capable," said Meligraunce. "That her wickedness, her pride, her ambition, and her personal resentment toward you are sufficient, I cannot doubt. That she would be powerful enough to do any of these things seems unlikely, but not impossible, since she was so nearly related to Lord Cado and in his confidence. Why should not the wizard's niece have learned some of his magic? Or if not from him, from the Black Canons, with whom they were both hand in glove."

"But Dahaut has been in Trewynyn all this time—or at least she was there when the first children were killed in Anoeth," said Tryffin.

Meligraunce shrugged. "She was certainly rumored to be in Trewynyn, being kept by a minor lord. But I don't recall that I saw her there, after her uncle died."

"I did," said Tryffin. "I passed her in the streets of the town, the day before we began our journey north, and she gave me a venomous glance. But I doubt very much that she has the discipline necessary to become a wizard . . . or that the Black Canons vest much power in women."

"If you saw her in Trewynyn, then I see my suspicions were entirely misplaced. And of course, when I saw the creature bending over you, I instantly thought of the Lady Essylt instead."

Tryffin gave his henchman a look of amused inquiry, for all the subject matter was so grim. "Foolish and wicked, but no woman of power, that I will vouch for. But is every woman I ever slept with going to suffer your suspicion before we are done here?"

"No, Lord Prince. But you must admit that this particular woman answers very well. Essylt has a quantity of fine golden hair, and she must certainly hate you with an implacable resentment exceeding even Dahaut's. Also, it might seem an appropriate act of revenge, on account of the child you took from her, to kill a number of children under your protection, and finally . . ."

He hesitated, and a faint blush came into his cheeks. "As you know, I heard rather more than I might have wished, guarding the door on the night you slept with her. I gained an impression that the lady's tastes were somewhat perverse."

"As well say that mine are," said Tryffin, fair-minded as always. "I was a willing participant. But we were both excited that night, half crazed if the truth were told, after all the bloodshed. Our lovemaking was . . . not so tender or kindly as it might have been. I don't know if you would call it perverse, but I can tell you I would not gladly spend another such night, not if I wished to retain my self-respect."

"Then you see why I found it advisable to make inquiries at the convent where you had her confined," said Meligraunce.

"And you learned?"

"That she has not set foot beyond the gates this entire year. You will recall there was a wasting sickness in Eildonn at the time that her son was born. It seems that she contracted the disease but was slow to develop the symptoms. You can congratulate yourself," said Meligraunce, "for removing the infant before he succumbed to the same contagion."

Tryffin lay gazing up at the beamed ceiling, turning these things over in his mind. "Then all we have been able to do so far is determine that Essylt and Dahaut are both innocent . . . which leaves all the other women in Mochdreff as possibly guilty."

"Not Dame Brangwaine or any of her relations, I think," said Meligraunce. "Somehow, they all strike me as extremely trust-worthy, though I cannot tell you exactly why."

"I am inclined to agree with you, at least so far as Dame Brangwaine and Luned are concerned," Tryffin admitted. "For one thing, they both have the look of pure-blooded Mochdreffi, and I am willing to believe the old woman when she says that no true Mochdreffi witch can alter her shape. Perhaps an illusory rearrangement of her facial features in the way of a disguise, but no more than that . . . perhaps not so much."

Meligraunce considered briefly, his fingers drumming on the arm of the chair. "But unless you trust the old woman to begin with, why should you take her word for that?"

"Because," said Tryffin, "in all the years I have lived in Mochdreff, I have never seen any of them *do* it, though I have witnessed a great many other remarkable things during that time."

He sighed and continued. "What I think we may have encountered is a woman of the half-blood nobility, perhaps from the region of Loch Gorm, up near the Rhianeddi border—that would explain the light hair. I want you to send some men up there to ask some questions. If there is a woman with the power, a family with the ambition . . . you will know what is needed."

"Yes, Lord Prince, I know what is needed," said Meligraunce, rising from his seat and heading toward the door, his cloak swirling around him. "And I will see to it at once."

. . . Unicorns, Satyrs, Manticores, and vile Hairy Woodwoses.
—*From* A Natural History of the Isle of Celydonn

8.

Of Hearts and Daggers

Mahaffy came out through the door of the Castell Gauvain chapel, blinking a little in the bright morning sunlight. The chapel was hardly more than a stone cell at the bottom of the garden, a dark little cave where the family lit candles and gabbled their prayers, without even a priest in the castle to say a proper Mass. And the only carvings or statues were some particularly hideous foliate masks on the arch above the altar and two vine-shrouded wild men, worked in high relief, guarding the door. *Who could find consolation in such dreary surroundings?* thought Mahaffy. Indeed, he had spent the entire morning down on his knees, with no such result.

The first thing he saw as he left the garden was Lord Gilfaethwy, pacing the flagstone pavement in the outer courtyard with an impatient step, as though he had been waiting for someone a great while already and was not in the mood for further delay.

That someone, it developed, was Mahaffy himself. "By God, I had no idea you were such a man for religion!" said Gilfaethwy, falling into step with the young knight. "Nearly two hours at your prayers . . . it seems excessive. I had heard Prince Tryffin had connections in the north, but I wonder he should be so remarkably strict with his household!"

Mahaffy stiffened, as he always did at any implied criticism of the Governor, and his hand instinctively went to the hilt of his sword. Yet he managed to keep his temper. "Prince Tryffin regards religion as a private matter—though he is, I believe, extremely devout in his own way. It was the Lady Gwenlliant

84

who set a more public example when she was there. An example that I rarely follow, I am ashamed to say, except when I feel particularly troubled in my mind."

Lord Gilfaethwy cleared his throat. Although the day was bright and warm, he was attired as usual in leather and furs, which along with his unkempt hair and his bristling beard lent him a close resemblance to the woodwoses down in the chapel. So close that Mahaffy could almost believe he saw thorns sprouting from the old man's beard. He roared like a wild man on most occasions, so the young knight steeled himself, expecting the worst.

"I hope," said Lord Gilfaethwy, "that it is not on account of anything that was said last night that you are feeling so troubled."

Mahaffy stopped in his tracks. "No? I was under the impression I had insulted you deeply, being proud, impertinent, thoughtless, and most abominably dis—"

"I shall certainly think the less of your manners if you will not allow me to continue without interruption," Gilfaethwy retorted, though not so roughly as he might. "No, there is no need for you to apologize. It seems to me that I am the one who spoke rashly and . . . perhaps discourteously, before. You are very young, Lord Mahaffy, and I believe there are aspects of the present situation which are as far past your understanding as they are beyond your experience. You are also, if you do not mind my saying so, a great deal too handsome and too facile in your speech for your own good. A young man like you should learn to cultivate silence and humility if he wishes to get on well with his elders and betters. However, there was some value in what you said to me. I spent the night pondering your words and . . . yes, examining my conscience as you advised. I am not blameless, that I will admit, yet I still contend that Morgan and Nefn harmed me worse than I ever harmed them."

"I never said otherwise," said Mahaffy contritely. "I am sorry if I gave any such impression."

Gilfaethwy ran his fingers through the bristling beard. "Yet I remember that you *did* say that a man like myself should be great enough, and generous enough, to leave the precise reckoning of petty hurts and slights to lesser men and concern himself with larger matters instead."

Now, Mahaffy did not recall that he had said anything quite so conciliating, but as things seemed to be proceeding so amazingly well, he saw no good reason to point that out.

"And you were right," Lord Gilfaethwy went on, clapping him on the shoulder. "For the sake of my clansmen, for the sake of future generations, I can be forgiving, I can be magnanimous. Indeed, my personal injuries are as nothing, nothing. I am willing to forget them, and if fair compensation were offered for the more material suffering of my clan, I would be more than happy to accept it and consider the matter entirely settled."

"I don't . . . I hardly know what to say," said Mahaffy. In fact, he was so surprised by this unexpected turn of events that he could barely breathe.

Lord Gilfaethwy smiled, displaying a great many strong, ivory-colored teeth. "You were eloquent enough last night. And I hope you will find it possible to be so again, for I am depending on you to bring Morgan and Nefn around to a reasonable state of mind."

"I . . . you wish *me* to speak to Morgan Killian and Nefn Chenoweth?" Mahaffy's mind was whirling, and he was afraid that he was babbling.

"And who else is there to do it?" Gilfaethwy replied impatiently. "Prince Tryffin is a hundred miles distant, and Lord Balin has accomplished nothing at all this entire fortnight, for all his well-meaning efforts. Or do you think you cannot convince the pair of them as well as you convinced me?"

In fact, Mahaffy was certain that he *could* convince the two of them, since it had been his opinion from the very start that Morgan and Nefn were inclined to be far more reasonable than Lord Gilfaethwy. The thing that he found so difficult to grasp was that he, personally, seemed about to bring the situation in Cormelyn to a peaceful conclusion.

"I will speak with them both immediately," said Mahaffy, with all the dignity and presence that he could muster. "Or at least . . . as soon as I can arrange a suitable opportunity."

"I did tell you," said Conn, when he heard the news later that day, "that you said nothing, last night, absolutely nothing amiss. But I have to admit that I had no idea that it would come to this!"

Mahaffy had stopped him on the winding staircase leading up to their tower bedchamber, and they had sat right down on the steps to discuss the matter.

"He was perfectly amazing," said Mahaffy. "Lord Gilfaethwy has somehow taken it into his mind that the man who is the most generous, the most forbearing, will somehow emerge victorious at the parley tomorrow. From a war of pride and greed, it has become a war of nobility, and the man who gives the most will carry away the laurel. How this may be, I do not know, but by our sweet Lord, I am exceedingly grateful."

"And Killian and Chenoweth agreed to meet with him in the same spirit?" Conn shook his head in amazement. "What did you say to the pair of them?"

"That was largely Lord Balin's doing. I said very little. Though my words did seem to carry a great deal of weight, simply because they knew I had been able to sway Lord Gilfaethwy." Mahaffy paused, staring thoughtfully down at his boots. "But you know . . . it never occurred to me before, but I am beginning to think now: If I could just learn to control my temper, I might have a certain turn for diplomacy. God knows, I've had opportunities enough to learn how these things ought to be managed, just by listening. First as Lord Morcant's squire and then as Prince Tryffin's. And it would be a great shame if I allowed those opportunities to come to nothing."

"I don't doubt the Governor will be exceedingly proud of you," said Conn, rising to his feet. The steps were cold, and besides, he had business elsewhere. "And surprised to see us both in Anoeth, when we finally arrive."

Mahaffy made a swift mental calculation. "Tomorrow they meet, and Lord Balin will need another day to draw up an agreement for everyone to sign. Say another day while people quibble, then a two days' ride, if we travel swiftly. We should be with Prince Tryffin in less than a week.

"And you acquitted yourself very well, with that boy Cadllyn," he added graciously. He stood up and smoothed the wrinkles out of his grey cloak. "I think Prince Tryffin should be very proud and happy to see us both."

Conn shook his head, remembering how the Governor had hustled him out of Anoeth on such very short notice. Proud, Prince Tryffin would certainly be, when he learned what Conn and Mahaffy had accomplished in Cormelyn. But happy to see them—that was not nearly so certain.

The Governor was sitting surrounded by pillows in a chair by the fire, when Dame Brangwaine came into the room. She did not walk so much as allow herself to be carried, for she was supported by Luned and her page (who was apparently the great-grandnephew Meligraunce had mentioned a few days before, the boy who was training to become a warlock), and leaned heavily on both of them with every step she took.

The old woman favored Tryffin with a sharp-eyed glance, as her attendants carefully lowered her into the only other chair in the tiny bedchamber.

"Out of your bed so soon? I do not recall that I gave you leave, or that we even discussed the idea the last time I visited you." She was wearing a dark gown with daggered sleeves, a jeweled girdle, and an immense horned headdress with a spangled veil, which, as Tryffin had gathered from observing her habits, was her idea of a simple costume appropriate to a sickroom.

He adjusted the sling which held his left arm against his chest. "That was two days ago. I am much stronger now, and saw no reason to remain flat on my back a moment longer."

Dame Braingwaine waved her attendants away. The page left the room, but Luned took up her accustomed position beside the old woman's chair. Luned was also in black with a jeweled bodice, and her dark hair unbound, falling nearly to the floor. Though she smiled at him, Tryffin thought she looked weary, with two demanding invalids to look after instead of the usual one.

Dame Brangwaine leaned forward in her chair. "I am told by my great-granddaughter and by Captain Meligraunce that you have an inflated opinion of your own powers of recuperation . . . an opinion which causes them endless worry and inconvenience."

In his place by the door, Meligraunce coughed softly. Tryffin gave him an amused glance. "Don't concern yourself, Captain. I know very well that you would never complain of me . . . not for any ears but my own. She reads your face and your posture, I suppose. But Lady Brangwaine, who should know better than I whether my health is improving or not?"

The old woman regarded him with a superior smile. "You do not know how close you came to dying. We, for our sins, know a great deal more. You were a ghastly sight when I arrived here to save your life, and I regret to say that you are a dismal spectacle even now, though you were a fine-looking man the first time I met you."

Since Tryffin had caught a glimpse of himself in a mirror

earlier that day, when Meligraunce shaved him and trimmed his hair, he knew very well that the old woman exaggerated. "If I am a little pale, so much more reason to allow me air and exercise," he said.

Dame Brangwaine sniffed loudly. "I wonder, Your Grace, if you think it convenient for me to stay at this inn? I tell you that it is not. Yet I endure the discomfort simply because you refuse to obey your other nurses and they plead with me daily to visit you here and attempt to talk some sense into that hard head of yours."

This mode of attack was as successful as it was unexpected. "May God forgive me, I never even considered that," said Tryffin, moving uneasily in his chair. He was shocked to realize he had never given a single thought to the old woman's convenience, and that he had caused her so much trouble already. "If you like, I will return to my bed right now."

"And be out of it again in another hour," she replied tartly. "There is no reason why you should not remain in that chair a little longer, now you are already there."

The door opened again, and the young warlock returned, carrying a small wooden chest banded in iron. He looked about ten or twelve years old—though perhaps his long hair and satin livery made him look younger than he actually was—and Tryffin wondered idly what illness or injury had made him a warlock, since only women were born with an obvious gift and males developed relatively late, usually in response to some traumatic experience.

"As it happens," said Brangwaine, "I didn't come here in order to scold you, Prince Tryffin . . . not this time, anyway. I came to give you a gift."

The Governor sat up a little straighter. "A gift? That is very generous, but I don't see why—"

"A gift which you may find of great practical use," continued Dame Brangwaine, ignoring the interruption. "You know, of course, that many evil things may be destroyed by the mere touch of cold iron. Unfortunately, that is not the case with the creature that attacked you."

Tryffin frowned. "Meligraunce is certain she cried out when his sword passed through her."

"Not entirely impervious to iron, then, yet she retained sufficient life and strength to escape the room." Dame Brangwaine gestured with one frail hand, and the boy opened the wooden chest. "But where iron fails, silver often suffices."

Tryffin saw that the box contained two silver daggers, resting on a bed of black velvet. The blades were silver and of curious design, but the hilts were gold and very finely made.

Again Tryffin moved uncomfortably in his chair, repressing a strong urge to reject the gift. Because he had so much himself, he was rarely happy accepting expensive presents, but he had learned to put his own feelings aside at times like this, and accept graciously whatever was offered with sincere good will.

"You are very kind," he said softly. "But why two?"

"One is for you, the other is for Captain Meligraunce," Dame Brangwaine replied. "As he did cause the creature some hurt, she may bear him a grudge. Also, he seems to be of great value to you, Prince Tryffin, and therefore to the people of Mochdreff.

"I wonder," she added, with a speculative glance in the Captain's direction, "whether the fellow has been perfectly open with you concerning his antecedents. He seems a good deal too intelligent, fair-spoken, and courageous to come of peasant stock. I suspect a backhanded connection with some better family."

Over by the door, there was the audible sound of grinding teeth. Tryffin smiled. "You are not the first person to ask that, and I am afraid it is rather a sore point with the Captain. I am slightly acquainted with his family, and have every reason to suppose that his mother is an honest woman. No, Meligraunce is a remarkable man, but I fear we must ascribe his talents to an accident of nature, rather than to any moral lapse on the part of his female relations."

There was a long moment of silence before the old woman spoke. "In that case," she said irritably, making some fussy movements to adjust the spangled veil, "I would advise you to invent something . . . perhaps a connection with your own family. He is very nearly as tall and broad as you are, so that story would serve. Otherwise, you are likely to lose his valuable services. For I tell you quite frankly: I know many men who would regard a man of his birth and his talents as a great danger; nor would they be slow to remove that danger if the opportunity arose."

She gestured to the boy and to Luned. The page put the box on the table, and then he and his cousin assisted the ancient wise-woman out of the room. That was a slow and painful process, and took several minutes. But when Tryffin and his Captain were alone together, he smiled sympathetically and said to Meligraunce: "I hope that you realize she meant that as a compliment."

"That is evident, though peasant as I am, I fear that I do not appreciate that compliment as perhaps I should," Meligraunce replied stiffly. But then his expression softened.

"Nevertheless, I am grateful for her high opinion . . . and for the warning. Of whom was she speaking, do you think? Lord Cernach?"

"Of Cernach and Rhonabwy and half the petty lords in Anoeth, I should imagine, but of her grandson in particular," said Tryffin. "Meligraunce, no one knows your mother here, and even if they did, they would not think less of her for bearing a nobleman's bastard . . . much less a royal one. I would never ask you to lie about your birth, but if Dame Brangwaine should take it on herself to voice her suspicions elsewhere, do you think you could manage *not* to deny it? It would be a great pity if I were to lose your valuable services simply because some damned petty nobleman imagines a threat to his entire way of life when he meets a single educated peasant.

"Not," he added, leaning back in his chair, for the old woman's visit had exhausted him more than he cared to admit, "that the fact you can read and write is the real issue. It is the way that you speak and the way you hold yourself that terrifies them, I suppose."

Meligraunce clenched his fists. "Are you telling me, Your Grace, that I should comport myself more lowly? If my manner offends you—"

"If your manner offended me, I think I might have mentioned the fact a great deal sooner," said Tryffin soothingly. "Before God, Captain, you ought to know that everything about you suits my purpose admirably; a meek or a groveling man could not accomplish nearly so much on my behalf. Only think how inconvenient it would be if I was forced to send you away, as I did Conn, for your own protection?"

"You need not worry," said Meligraunce, taking up one of the silver-bladed daggers and slipping it into his belt, next to the knife he already kept there. "I am quite capable of defending myself . . . particularly now that I am armed with this."

Two days later, Tryffin was up again, this time pacing the floor, when Luned slipped unattended into the room. "Lady," he said, "how much longer do you suppose I must remain confined here?"

She closed the door softly behind her. "A few days more, I think. You know how important it is that your enemy should not realize you are out of danger . . . not until you are strong enough to renew your efforts to track the creature down.

"I would offer to play a game of Chess," she added, with a toss of her head, "but I remember that you were reluctant to play with Dame Brangwaine when she asked you."

The Governor sighed. "Yet I think the lack of exercise will make my recovery that much slower." He made a restless gesture with his good hand. "And can we not at least be rid of some of these candles?"

"Certainly," she replied, and proceeded to snuff a number of them out, one by one. "Now that you are armed with the silver dagger, I doubt that so many are really necessary."

As she continued to bustle about the room, Tryffin felt increasingly uncomfortable. She was not wearing very much, only a thin gown of wine-colored silk, cut very low at the neck and shoulders—perhaps because the burning candles and the shuttered windows made the room so unbearably hot. He, on the other hand, expecting her visit, was fully and a great deal too warmly dressed.

"Perhaps," he said uncomfortably, "now that I am no longer bedridden, it would be better if you did not spend so much time alone with me here."

She smiled faintly, as she moved to smooth out the covers on his bed. The rich hue of her gown, the sparkling jewels she wore in her dark hair, lent an exotic touch to that simple chamber. "Would that be for your protection, Prince Tryffin, or for mine?"

He felt himself flushing, the palms of his hands beginning to sweat. He was not usually awkward with women, but he found the present situation particularly disconcerting. "I am concerned for your reputation, Luned, as you should be also."

She shrugged a bare white shoulder. "Are your own men so indiscreet, then? I can assure you that nobody else who knows of my visits—none of my kinswomen here at the inn, certainly not my great-grandmother or my young cousin, who departed yesterday—would be inclined to bandy my name about."

She turned away from the bed, took a step in his direction. As usual, a wave of heavy perfume accompanied her. "Perhaps you are less concerned for my reputation than for your own. Perhaps . . ." Luned smiled sweetly. She had very white teeth, which only served to make her mouth that more enticingly pink and soft looking. ". . . perhaps you would like to make love to me, but fear I might refuse if you asked, and then boast of it afterward. I promise you, Lord Prince, that would never happen."

Tryffin cleared his throat. He knew better than to ask what she meant . . . whether it was the possibility of rejection or boasting afterward she was denying. The truth was, it had been such a very long time since he was last with a woman, he did not trust himself to speak at all.

"Be plain with me, Prince Tryffin," she said archly. "Don't try to spare my feelings. It is simply that you are not attracted?"

That annoyed him just enough to spark a reply. "Be honest with *me,* Lady. Since you appeared here to nurse me back to health, we both know that you have been by me at times when . . . when I was unfortunately unable to conceal any attraction I might feel."

She took another step in his direction. "Then why?" she whispered. "Why attempt to deny that attraction, now that you know that I am equally attracted to you?"

Tryffin turned away, since looking at her made refusal so difficult. "You know that I am a married man. And I will do nothing to injure the Lady Gwenlliant."

She laughed softly and scornfully. "That child you have not even lived with for nearly a year . . . oh yes, that fact is widely reported. Do you think she even knows what you do . . . or that she cares?"

He sat down in the chair, pressed a fist to his forehead. "What she knows I cannot predict; she is a very powerful witch. That she cares what I do and whose bed I sleep in . . . I believe that she does, I hope that she does." He made himself look at her. "By my confession to God, I don't know what should become of me if Gwenlliant ceased to love me."

"Well, that is very pretty," said Luned, taking a seat on the bed. "Yes, your devotion is very pretty . . . and I believe sincere. At least you act it well enough to remove any possibility of an insult to me, and I am willing to settle for that since I can't have more." Her eyes were very bright and the color in her face was high.

It had not occurred to him that she felt anything more than a physical attraction, that her heart was in any way involved. Now that it did, he felt unaccountably guilty.

Yet the memory of Gwenlliant made him ache horribly—and not for this other woman, as attractive as she was. Instead, it served to strengthen his resolve. "My cousin and I have been deeply attached to one another for many, many years. Long before we thought of marriage. I cannot explain the nature of the bond between us, but it is very strong."

"Yet everyone says that you never consummated your marriage," said Luned, smoothing out the wine-colored silk of her gown.

"That was not, if you will believe me, because she felt . . . felt any personal distaste for me," he answered painfully. "It was only because she was very young, and another man—no, a wicked willful boy—wanted her once and frightened her badly. If it had not been for that, I think she would have come to me willingly."

Luned smiled. "That I can readily believe. But perhaps you will satisfy my curiosity: You have been married, I hear, for almost two years. Have you really gone all that time without a woman?"

"Near enough," said Tryffin, with a touch of embarrassment. In truth, he found his own situation most damnably humiliating, and he was not certain which part of the truth made him look weaker or less of a man: the fact that he had not been entirely faithful, or the fact that he had lived celibate for so many months. "At least I take no mistresses. And I have an idea, Lady, that you wish for something more than a single night's pleasure."

Her chin lifted defiantly, and the color in her face came and went. "Are you so very certain, Prince Tryffin, that a single night would be enough for *you*?"

"Perhaps not," he said, with a smile and a shrug. "But this much I can promise you: If I was *not* convinced that a single night would satisfy me, you would never lure me into bed to begin with."

I am the nightmare, I am madness
I am all things to all men
  Let them beware me
I am passion, pain, betrayal, despair
  And my touch is death.
                    —*From* The Song of Donwy

9.

The Terror That Walks by Night

The sun was sinking below the horizon when Mahaffy and Conn, with the men-at-arms under Mahaffy's command trailing behind them, rode into Anoeth. They had stopped earlier that day in a village about fifteen miles distant, where they were greeted by news of the attack on Prince Tryffin and the grim communication that he was not expected to live. With that story to spur them on, they had not stopped again except when the horses absolutely required it, and they had arrived in Anoeth exhausted, dusty, and fearing the worst.

As they dismounted outside the inn, one of Meligraunce's men came out to greet them, and Conn was profoundly relieved to note that the man did *not* have the look of someone with tragic tidings to relate.

"Is the Governor expecting you? We had no word that you were to arrive, here below," said the Sergeant, and was taken by surprise when Conn suddenly embraced him, and Mahaffy (who was ordinarily very proud and reserved among the guardsmen) clapped him enthusiastically on the back.

The two young men went in through the common room and up the stairs, where a guard directed them to a chamber at the end of the corridor. The sound of familiar voices encouraged them to open the door without first knocking.

There were a great many people inside the room, so many it

95

hardly seemed that the crowded bedchamber could hold them: the Lord of Llech Obrwy, Rhonabwy's pages and personal attendants, Lord Cernach and his squires, and two other noblemen Conn was unable to identify by name. The petty lords had gathered around the Governor and Meligraunce, and a spirited discussion appeared to be taking place.

As soon as Conn and Mahaffy entered the room, there was a sudden silence, during which Meligraunce put a hand to his forehead, and Prince Tryffin sank wearily down into a chair.

"Before God," said the Governor. "It needed only that."

Hesitating near the door, Mahaffy drew a deep breath. "I take it you did not receive the message I sent you two days past. Your Grace, the feud is *over* in Cormelyn. I . . . Lord Balin and I convinced all three clans to negotiate a truce. There is no need for you to go to Castell Gauvain, after all."

Prince Tryffin rose from his chair and stepped past his visitors. "Your letter arrived this morning, along with a message sent by Lord Balin. You did a fine job in Cormelyn, Mahaffy . . . and you, too, Conn. I am sorry to give you such a very poor welcome." He gave each of them an awkward one-armed embrace; the other arm was held to his chest by a black satin sling. "The truth is, I did not expect to see you this soon."

He was so much thinner than he had been nine days ago, when Conn saw him last, that the boy felt a lump rise in his throat. "You have been ill, and we were not here to help look after you."

"Aye . . . well. I did not lack for attention, that I can promise you," the Governor replied, cheerfully enough. He indicated the petty lords, with a sweeping gesture of his good arm. "As you can see, these very noble gentlemen hurried to attend me as soon as they learned I was well enough to receive visitors. They are, however, on their way out. So if you will open that door a little wider, Mahaffy . . . "

Lord Rhonabwy made a sound of protest, and Lord Cernach scowled, but Prince Tryffin continued to beam on them with such a perfect combination of bland geniality and blank disinterest that the petty lords could do nothing but gather their attendants around them and file out of the room.

Conn and Mahaffy exchanged an uneasy glance. They both knew perfectly that when the Governor smiled like *that*, someone had seriously annoyed him.

But when the door closed behind Lord Cernach, the smile disappeared, and the warm brown eyes took on a livelier expression. "As for the pair of you," he said, glancing from one exhausted and apprehensive face to the other, "you look to be in need of a good night's rest, but I am afraid you will find me a hard taskmaster. After you've had something to eat and to drink down below, I want you to join Meligraunce and me on our nightly patrol."

"Your Grace . . . " began Meligraunce, but did not continue.

Prince Tryffin gave him a challenging glance. "You were about to say, Captain?"

Meligraunce shook his head. "I was only going to say, Lord Prince, that if you are indeed planning to resume the patrols, it would be a very good idea to take Conn and Mahaffy with us."

When the boys had descended to the floor below, Tryffin returned to his chair. "Why does it always happen that everything happens at once?"

"My apologies," said Meligraunce. "Those men should never have been allowed inside the house."

Tryffin shook his head, "You can hardly blame yourself for that, since you weren't even here when they arrived . . . being off on *my* business, if you recall. Besides, I am genuinely surprised we were able to keep them out as long as we did. They had every reason to feel concerned and wish to see me. Especially considering the news Lord Rhonabwy brought me, which was hardly welcome but certainly important.

"I hope," he added, "that I have made it perfectly clear that I mean to go out tonight, and that no good purpose could possibly be served by debating the matter further."

"So it would seem, Your Grace," said the Captain. "And of course it must be as you wish. But as you go out so lightly armored, I hope you will at least allow me to remain at your side."

The armor in question consisted of a black leather tunic studded with brass, and wide golden wristguards. Tryffin's shoulder and collarbone had not yet sufficiently healed to sustain the weight of his mail and steel plate.

"I see no reason to divide our forces, since we know very well which house we ought to be guarding," said Tryffin. "That much we gained from our unwelcome visitors."

Meligraunce folded his arms across his chest. "You are convinced that this woman, this cobbler's wife who dreamed of the great grey cat, had a true presentiment? That the story was not some invention of the petty lords, an excuse for them to demand to see you?"

The Governor sat for a long moment, staring into the fire. "I am convinced the dream was a true presentiment," he said at last. "The more so, because I had a similar dream last night."

Meligraunce could not repress a cry of protest. "Your Grace! You never told me of this, and it changes the outlook of things entirely. It is clear the shapechanger has decided that if you were going to die of your wounds you would have already done so, and is therefore ready to move against you. And while I know you are eager to extend the children in that house every possible protection, you surely must see that a trap has been set and baited, a trap meant specifically for you."

Tryffin shrugged. "Have you never heard of a huntsman so careless that he chanced to fall into his own trap? That, I hope, is what will happen to the child-killer tonight. Also, we did send a man to tell the cobbler and his wife to expect us, and I won't go back on my word.

"Besides," he added, "supposing the dreams were meant to warn me away, at the same time they drew the rest of you out of the inn and into the streets of Anoeth? Will I be safer here with a handful of men . . . or at the cobbler's shop, with you, Mahaffy, Conn, and a dozen guardsmen to protect me?"

As the answer to that seemed obvious, Meligraunce said no more. Tryffin reached into his belt and drew out the gold-hilted dagger Dame Brangwaine had given him. "Also, I have a keen desire to put this blade to work, and I reckon that you have also. I do not think this evil creature knows that we are armed with silver."

"The design of these blades is very unusual." Meligraunce scrutinized his own dagger. "To say nothing of the words and signs I see engraved on mine. I think there must be some strong magic about them, beyond the power of silver."

Tryffin rose from his chair and reached for his cloak. "Does that trouble you?" he asked, as he threw the scarlet cloak over one shoulder, pulled it around to the other side, and fastened the clasp. He knew that Meligraunce had never used any form of magic before . . . nothing beyond the ordinary magic of cold iron. For that matter, neither had he, at least not intentionally.

"Not in the least," said Meligraunce. "I have been in Mochdreff long enough to put any prejudice of that sort aside. If you wish to know the truth, the only magic I fear tonight—on our side, at least—is that *you* may be provoked into a battle madness, as you were the last time a child was threatened in your sight. I hope you will be able to restrain any such impulse, for I doubt you could endure the reaction afterward."

"I feel very far from the battle madness tonight," said Tryffin, looking out the window. The street below was growing dark, and the moon had yet to rise above the houses. "Though I am conscious of a certain impatience to be out and about."

He knew that the creature never attacked much before midnight, but he decided that unless Mahaffy and Conn finished their supper and appeared very soon, he would be obliged to collect them on his way out.

It was a short uphill walk from the inn to the lane where the cobbler lived. As Tryffin's first experience of freedom in nine days it was not much, the streets were so narrow, the sheer weight of granite and slate and black oak timbers on either side still seemed oppressive, but he was glad of the chance to stretch his legs. The others had difficulty matching his stride and keeping up with him.

Except that halfway there, the Governor discovered that his heart was pounding, his vision blurring. He stopped and pretended to check the clasp on one of his wristguards, so that none of his men should guess his weakness.

"Your Grace—is something amiss?" That was Meligraunce, of course, a look of concern on his lean, intelligent face.

But Tryffin's vision had already cleared, so it was possible to smile grimly and reply quite truthfully. "Nothing that won't be a great deal better when we run the shapechanger to earth and put an end to her." And he set off again, at a more moderate pace.

Outside the shop, he deployed his men, sending most of them to hide in the shadows of houses all down the street. Then with a half dozen still in attendance, he climbed the steps to the shop and knocked softly on the door.

The cobbler opened the door himself, a gaunt man with a wild-eyed look. Tryffin could only imagine the terror this man and his wife must feel, knowing that one of their little ones had been marked for destruction, knowing how helpless other mothers and fathers had been to protect their children under the same terrible circumstances. To make matters worse, they did not even know which child was in danger, which one they ought to be holding close . . . perhaps for the very last time.

Tryffin put a comforting hand on the cobbler's shoulder. "I wish I could promise that your children would come to no harm, but I will tell you no lies. Still, I do truly believe that I am the only one that the creature intends to kill this night."

He left Meligraunce, the Sergeant, and Ciag in the shop, while he, the boys, and Garreg, the remaining man-at-arms, followed the cobbler up a steep ladder staircase to the half-floor above. There was a short passage and two tiny rooms. In the further room lay three sleeping children, so thin and so small it was difficult to guess at their age. A boy and a girl had curled up together on a narrow pallet and the baby was dozing in his mother's arm. The woman sat wide-eyed and sleepless in a chair by the bed, clutching the infant to her.

Tryffin said nothing—what could he say in the face of such horror, to make this woman feel any better?—but silently lowered himself to the floor to wait.

The hours until midnight passed slowly. No one wanted to talk, to disturb the children or upset the mother. Mahaffy and Conn, exhausted after their day in the saddle, sat with their knees drawn up to their chests, each taking it in turns to drift off . . . only to be roused by a friendly jab from the other, at the exact moment his head touched his knees. Tryffin paid them scant heed; he had brought the boys along to keep them safe, not the other way around. For his own protection, he was relying on the silver-bladed dagger . . . and at need, on Meligraunce, well within shouting distance at the bottom of the stairs.

The single candle lighting the room burned low. At the Governor's bidding, the guard rose to his feet and lit another one. It must be midnight by now. Tryffin thought he heard church bells tolling in the distance, but the house was wrapped in a nearly palpable silence which seemed to muffle all sounds from without.

A sudden drowsiness assailed him. The room spun wildly around him, his head became heavy, his eyelids drooped. It was all he could do to blink his eyes, to keep his head up. He remembered Dame Brangwaine had mentioned the possibility of a sleep spell, and that a strong-minded person could fight off the effects.

He also remembered something else: a night long past when he sat by a campfire with his brother Fflergant, his cousin Ceilyn mac Cuel, and Teleri ni Pendaren, listening to the young sorceress speak. *"If you ever have warning that someone is trying to tamper with your mind, you must concentrate as hard as you can on something else. It needn't be a spell—a song or a bit of poetry or a verse from the Bible will serve nearly as well, so long as you repeat it over and over and think of nothing else."*

A line from the ninety-first psalm came into his mind:

Thou shalt not be afraid for the terror by night; nor for the arrow that flieth by day; nor for the pestilence that walketh in darkness; nor for the destruction that wasteth at noonday.

His head cleared almost at once, but the moment he stopped reciting, the drowsiness returned.

And all around him, the others had fallen into a restless doze: the mother in her chair, Conn, Mahaffy, and Garreg, all three sprawled gracelessly across the floor.

He reached out and shook the guard by the shoulder, because he was the nearest, and Garreg opened his eyes and fixed the Governor with a glassy stare. Tryffin was about to get up and go over to the place where the boys were lying . . . when he heard a small sound, the merest rustling, followed by a light footstep out in the passage. A faint, sickening odor crept into the room, under the door.

No one had barred that door, taking it for granted that the creature could enter whenever she wanted to, afraid they might only put up a barrier between themselves and the men below. Tryffin rose silently to his feet and waited to see what would happen, taking the hilt of the silver dagger into his hand and reciting the psalm in his mind.

> A thousand shall fall at thy side, and ten thousand at thy right hand; but it shall not come nigh thee. . . . Thou shalt tread upon the lion and adder: the young lion and the dragon thou shalt trample under thy feet.

The handle of the door rattled, then the door slowly opened. Tryffin's mind was perfectly clear, but the sleep spell continued to weight his limbs.

A slender figure, in a trailing cloak of thick brown wool and a deep, concealing hood, slipped in past the door. Tryffin lunged in her direction, brought the dagger down in a slashing motion . . . but the movement was so slow and so awkward that his stroke went wide, catching in cloth and ripping through it, then sliding across bare skin.

As the silver blade touched her, the shapechanger shrieked and pulled away. She was out of the room in less than a second, and scrambling down the ladder staircase before Tryffin had time to stumble as far as the passage.

Two deep breaths and he had recovered enough to follow her, descending the stairs in a rush, and dodging just in time to avoid a collision with Meligraunce.

"May God forgive me, I actually had her," the Captain exclaimed. "She ran right into my arms but—"

"But you were asleep on your feet," said Tryffin, throwing open the door to the street. "For the love of God, if you feel the urge again, start reciting verses from the Bible. In the meantime, rouse these men and follow after me as quickly as you can."

As he burst out the door and leaped down the steps to the street, he caught a glimpse of something sleek and shadowy disappearing around a corner. It was not a woman but it was some sort of large animal, so Tryffin gave chase.

Down a short lane . . . around another corner . . . then up a steep winding street, he continued to pursue. He had already recognized the street, which led up to the ruined church and the ancient cemetery. His head began to spin and it became nearly impossible to get enough air into his lungs . . . but he was losing her, he could hear the rapid footsteps of his own men gaining on him, so Tryffin lengthened his stride.

By the time he reached the iron railing and his strength gave out, she was nowhere in sight. He reached for the fence with his good right hand in order to support himself, and he somehow managed to keep himself from sliding to the ground, just as Meligraunce arrived. "Your Grace, did she hurt you?"

Tryffin shook his head. "It is just this damnable weakness," he panted. "For God's sake, go after her." The Captain waited for no more questions, but was over the rail in an instant, and pounding down the path to the ruined church.

The rest of his men appeared a minute later, so Tryffin sent them over the fence, too.

In truth, he was glad to see the last of them, because he thought he was about to pass out—and he did not want anyone there watching him do it.

When Meligraunce returned to report that the shapechanger had eluded them all once more, Tryffin was back on his feet and had recovered sufficiently to receive the news with his accustomed air of quiet authority. "The moon is setting. Send some men to bring torches. We will search every inch of the graveyard and the ruins."

Six men went off and returned soon after with enough flaming brands for all. Tryffin took one for himself and led the way, around the fence of iron pickets, through a gate on the other side of the cemetery, and then through the thorny thicket.

"Your Grace, I believe I spotted the shapechanger just before it disappeared," said Mahaffy, coming up behind him. "It seemed to be one of my men, standing there in the fading moonlight and staring at me with such a look on his face, such fury and loathing, I can't describe it. Naturally, I stepped forward to ask him what was amiss . . . but then I stumbled over one of the gravestones. When I righted myself, there was no one there, and a moment later the same fellow hailed me from the opposite direction. I just spoke with him, and he insists he was never anywhere near the spot where I thought I saw him."

"And where was this?" asked Tryffin. It was chilling to think of the shapechanger wearing the face and the form of someone he knew. How long and how intimately, he wondered, would she have to observe someone in order to mimic that person exactly? She had apparently feared a closer inspection by Mahaffy, and that was at least reassuring. "Show me, if you can, the exact spot where the creature was standing."

Mahaffy led him to the ruined church. "Here in the sanctuary, standing a little apart from the steps to the altar."

Tryffin might have found his own way by following his nose. As it was, the stench was waiting there for him when he arrived at the spot Mahaffy had indicated. He knelt down to examine the ground more carefully. There was grass and some scrubby-looking weeds growing in the cracks of what had once been a very fine floor made of stone slabs. Some of the weeds looked like they had been partly uprooted.

"I think," said the Governor, "that this larger stone has been recently lifted and moved aside. Yes . . . see here where there are clods of earth and the grass is crushed down. This is where the stone rested. It must cover the entrance to some underground vault."

"A tomb," said Meligraunce, when Tryffin summoned him over and explained what he had found. "An ancient crypt belonging to the ruined church."

The guards set to work, with their daggers and some pieces of splintered timbers they found in the ruins, to pry the stone loose again. They found it was very easily moved, being lighter than anyone had supposed, and there was some sort of mechanism which Tryffin did not take the time to examine. He was much more interested in the crypt down below.

He held his torch high, to shed more light on the set of narrow steps leading down into the pit. They seemed to go down a long way and ended somewhere beyond the light.

"The air may be poisonous," said Meligraunce. So it was necessary for someone to go after a rope to lower a torch, which made for another delay while the Captain sent two men back to the streets to knock on doors.

By the time they had performed all these operations and determined that the air was good, dawn was staining the eastern sky. "I will go first," said Tryffin, using his left hand to loosen the silver dagger in his belt. "Since I seem best able to resist her sleep spells."

The steps went down and down in a long curve. The stairs were so steep and narrow, so slick with moisture, that it was necessary for Tryffin to proceed very carefully, with his back to the wall, one step at a time, concentrating on the exact placement of his feet. He had no chance to look around him until he reached the bottom.

He had entered what appeared an immense tomb, a great underground vault supported by pillars of stone, the chamber in which he stood opening into several others, perhaps equally vast. "Not a single tomb," he said to Meligraunce, who was descending the stairs. "But a series of catacombs." His voice echoed weirdly as he spoke.

"There are underground tombs and passages beneath Castell Maelduin, where I was born," he added. "My brother and I had a fine time exploring them when we were boys!"

He glanced back at his companion. In the golden torchlight, Meligraunce looked oddly pale and shaken. "What is it, Captain? Have you sensed something here to disturb you?"

"I don't much care for cellars or dungeons or . . . or underground places," said Meligraunce. "It is nothing, Your Grace. No doubt I will soon become accustomed to the notion of so much earth and stone hanging over my head."

As the other men were beginning to arrive, Tryffin struck boldly out into the darkness. For one thing, the place piqued his curiosity, and for another, he felt perfectly at home under the earth. It was something in the blood, he supposed, a natural affinity, which all the Gwyngellach shared, for cavernous places.

Conn, Mahaffy, Meligraunce, and the others followed him, with a certain hesitation in their steps. Whether it was the dark or the underground or the fact they were walking in places meant for the dead . . . they all seemed less eager than he was to explore the catacombs thoroughly.

At the arch leading into the next chamber there was a short flight of steps, and with each succeeding chamber Tryffin and his men descended deeper and deeper into the earth. There were stone coffins arranged in precise rows around all the walls, and an occasional raised marble slab on which the bones of the dead lay neatly arranged, some of them still in the rags of their burial finery. The pillars, the arches, and the coffins were marvelously carved, with knotwork vines, and solar spirals, and graven apostles and angels, mendicants, martyrs, and mighty kings. There were, however, no statues or effigies.

As Tryffin led the way from chamber to chamber, down one flight of stairs after another, admiring the stonework, raising his torch high that he might get a better look at the vaulted and groined ceilings and fully appreciate the amazing construction of this mighty sepulchre, he felt a deep vibration, a faint but pleasant humming in his bones, which told him that he was in the presence of some benign form of magic. A pattern spell, he guessed, though it was impossible for him to discern the pattern. Whatever had possessed the ancient Anoethi witches to make so many of them, he wondered. Even down here in the darkness, where few men would desire to go?

It was partly due to the fact that the Earth magic was so dangerously accessible, here in Mochdreff. Instead of residing deep in the soil—as the Wild Magic did elsewhere in Celydonn—providing needed fertility, it seemed to lie around on the surface, float about in the air, making it all too easy for the Mochdreffi witches and warlocks to snatch it up and bend it to their own purposes. So far as he knew, the pattern spells and certain other Mochdreffi magics did not even exist anywhere else.

And along comes this evil thing with her terrible powers and uses their own apparently harmless spells against them, to enter their houses and slaughter their children . . . and now to escape my vengeance, down here in the darkness.

After an hour or two of fruitless searching, he and his men returned to the long staircase leading up to the surface.

"We will watch this place in shifts, until she returns," said Tryffin. Even he had to admit that he was very near the end of his strength, the limit of his endurance. He needed food and he needed rest.

"Something seems to keep drawing her back . . . and even if I cannot be here myself, I mean to have someone waiting here with a silver dagger, the next time she appears."

There was a momentary silence in the tower laboratory, while the young knight absorbed what the wizard's apprentice had just told him.

"But the old gifts disappeared long ago," Ceilyn protested. "I'm not the only man in Celydonn who can claim Blood Royal on both sides of the family. I could name you several others: Fflergant fab Maelgwyn and his brother, Tryffin; their uncle, Manogan fab Menai; my cousins Garanwyn and Gwenlliant . . . but they are all quite ordinary."

"Are you quite ordinary?" Teleri asked him. What she thought of those others he had named, she kept to herself.

Ceilyn sighed and shook his head. "My own peculiarity is not one of those lost gifts. The Kings of Celydonn were never shapechangers."

Now it was Teleri's turn to think before she answered. And when she did, she chose her words carefully. "Your ancestors had many extraordinary abilities," she said. "No one knows their full extent."

10.

Of Changes and Pattern Spells

The weeks passed swiftly in the land known as Achren. Summer gave way to autumn, the maple and the hazel put on their most brilliant colors, the ash dropped its leaves, the bramble grew heavy with fruit, and the rowan bright with berries. The days were clear and cool, the mornings frosty, so the twelve young priestesses and their new young friend donned squirrel-skin cloaks and ventured out into the forest: gathering nuts and mushrooms to store in the root cellar under the house, berries for wine, honey for sweetening, willow for weaving, and ivy to brew their sacred ale.

For Gwenlliant, the wooden house with the turf-thatched roof was beginning to feel like home. Yet, every now and again, without any warning, she felt a rising sense of panic, wondering why Dame Ceinwen did nothing to help her, why no one arrived to rescue her out of the past. It frightened her even more to think what might happen if Tryffin arrived at the house on the Marches for his promised visit . . . and Gwenlliant was not even there.

The first time she thought that, she was milking one of the goats. She stopped and leaned her head against one hairy flank, waiting for the painful pounding in her chest to subside.

Of course, time moved at a different pace in the Inner Celydonn, just as it did on the Marches, and it was possible to twist time a little, moving from one world to the next. It might only be Christmas, or Twelfth Night, or Lady Day, at Caer Ysgithr, and months to go before Midsummer's Day.

Gwenlliant finished the milking. She fished Grifflet out of the pile of straw where he was burrowing, stood him on his feet, picked up her stool and wooden bucket, and headed back to the house. Grifflet—no longer a baby but a sturdy little boy who insisted on walking and not being carried—caught hold of her skirt and stumped along at her side.

But what if summer is already over? she asked herself. Tryffin would always keep his promises, that she knew, but supposing that *she* was the one who failed to keep her part of the bargain? She had reached the porch, and because no one was there to see what she did, Gwenlliant spoke the work which opened the massive decorated door. But she paused on the threshold without going in, turning the matter over in her mind.

Tryffin might . . . he might decide he was better without her, might even be glad she had broken her word, because then he would be free to do as he chose. If Midsummer passed without reuniting them, they would not even be married anymore.

The very thought left her breathless and ill. Gwenlliant knew she had caused her cousin a great deal of trouble, and it could hardly be easy being married to a witch . . . and worse than that, to a *virgin* witch, after two whole years of marriage.

But there was no use brooding about it, she told herself, as she took the little boy into the house and went on with the rest of her daily tasks. Indeed, she had to be brave and she had to be hopeful, for Grifflet's sake if not for her own.

He was talking all the time now, in one- and two-word sentences—mostly phrases he picked up from Maelinn and the other young women. Which was going to be embarrassing when he and Gwenlliant found their way back home. If things continued on as they were, he would be perfectly conversable with ruins and barrows but not with any of the people at Caer Ysgithr, and they might think him fey, or they might think him slow, but either way he would never be able to pass for an ordinary little boy.

So whenever she and Grifflet happened to be alone together, Gwenlliant would speak her own language, telling him the names of birds and animals and trees. And when she was lying on her feathery bed, with his warm little body tucked up against her, she would whisper stories into his ear, fairy tales mostly, of the Princess Gwenlliant who lived with her handsome young husband in a castle by the sea. She knew that he made but little sense of any of her stories, but she wanted the *sound* of the language to be familiar.

Because they *were* going home. Gwenlliant had given up trying to remove the ring from her hand, the golden band and the cloudy sidhe-stone, but if no one came to escort her and Grifflet back, then she was determined to find the way for herself . . . just as soon as she discovered whatever it was the ring meant her to learn here in the past.

One fine day, a great deal warmer than the days which had preceded it, Gwenlliant dressed Grifflet in the new wool tunic she had woven and stitched and dyed a deep scarlet there in the wooden house, picked up a basket, gave him her hand, and went out with Morfa, Caithne, Regan, and Gleis, to gather oak galls. The galls, of course, were quite inedible, but were useful for brewing medicines, tanning leather, and dyeing cloth.

Because the day was so fair and so fine, the young women were all in high spirits. They chattered and laughed as they gathered the hard little knobs—which were really the nests of wasps inside the bark—from the branches of oak trees. Gwenlliant knew that their lack of constraint was at least due in part to the absence of Maelinn, whose feud with Caithne and Sceith was growing particularly bitter.

After about an hour, the baskets were nearly full. Taking Grifflet by the hand, Gwenlliant moved further down the path, to a place where the trail divided on either side of an enormous oak. "No, Gwenhwyach, that is the path to the other house," Morfa called out. "You really don't want to go there."

Gwenlliant turned and looked at her. "The other house? No one told me there was another house here in the woods." Morfa had sounded—well, not frightened, exactly, but troubled and urgent. Gwenlliant remembered how she had been afraid, that first day in the wood, that the forest might be occupied by ogres and bad fairies. "Does something . . . unpleasant live in that house? Something dangerous?"

"Dangerous, no—not unless you count Maelinn's brother Gwythyr, who is certainly unpleasant," said Caithne, and the others tittered, as though they were ashamed of themselves for laughing but could not help it.

"It is only the temple of the goddess Cerridwen, where her High Priest lives with the oracular swine," the redhead continued, "and with the three beautiful young priestesses, sworn to silence, who are his wives."

Regan moved closer and said in Gwenlliant's ear, "You had better not walk that way, Gwenhwyach. They say that Gwythyr is looking for another wife, even younger than the rest. And if he saw you and decided that you were the one that he wanted, you would have no choice but to marry him."

Gwenlliant stared at her, eyes growing wide, not certain whether to take this seriously. "Could he . . . could he really do that?"

"She is only teasing," said Caithne briskly, taking Grifflet's other hand and leading the way down a different pathway, to another stand of gnarled oaks. "Of course he could not take you into the temple or marry you against your will, because you are a widow. Besides, he wants one of Prince Caerthinn's sisters, the Princess Tinne . . . Tinne, and the gifts she will bring to the temple with her."

When they had gathered enough galls to fill their baskets, they all sat down in a grassy clearing, and Gleis opened another wicker basket that she had been carrying and brought out a skin full of mead, a wedge of goat cheese, and a round loaf of bread, which she passed around to the others.

Gwenlliant sat with Grifflet in her lap, feeding him a handful of berries she had gathered along the way. Caithne and Morfa sat with their heads close together, speaking very low, though now and again it was possible to pick up a word or a phrase, which made it clear they were discussing Maelinn. Gwenlliant tried not to listen; she wanted no part in that quarrel. But it was difficult *not* to pay attention when Regan called out a warning.

"Be careful what you say. Maelinn is here." Regan pointed

toward a tangle of bushes, where something a foxy shade of red could be seen through the branches. In a moment, it was gone, but Gwenlliant had seen enough to be certain that it had been a small, fleet, furry animal, and not a woman in a scarlet gown.

Caithne tossed her head. "I say nothing here that I would not say as readily to Maelinn's face. She knows very well what I think of her. Besides," she added, taking the wineskin from Gleis, "it wasn't Maelinn, but Sceith. She only does it to annoy Maelinn, who regards the fox as her own special beast—and I think that it serves her right for being so proud and selfish."

The others looked slightly embarrassed. "Well . . . but you know, Caithne, it *is* her own special beast," said Morfa consideringly. "The Lady of the Wood and the Well always takes the fox as her second—"

She stopped speaking suddenly when Gleis cleared her throat, as if in warning. And everyone turned and stared at Gwenlliant, who tried to look utterly unconscious, sitting there in the grass with the little boy in her lap, feeding him bread and blackberries.

That these women were able to take on the shapes of birds and of beasts, she had long since guessed—they were always dropping hints and exchanging glances, and they were not very good at keeping secrets—but now she was sure of it. And she thought to herself: *if I can only catch one of them in the midst of the shapechange, if I can only* see *one of them taking on fur or scales or feathers, I might learn the spell . . . in the exact same way I have been learning their magic from the very beginning.*

For that was the nature of Gwenlliant's gift: to see and to know. Even the most difficult spell, once she had seen it performed all the way through, was hers forever. So far, she had learned nothing here of real value, only the very simplest spells, not so very different from the very first charms and tricks of illusion that Dame Ceinwen had taught her. But this one she wanted; this one she desired with such intensity, she was a little bit frightened by the strength of her own desire.

It was one of the Great Spells, but more than that, Gwenlliant knew that the gift was there in her blood, her own Rhianeddi ancestors had worked this magic of transformation: Cynfarch of the Ravens, Selgi of the Iron Crown, and a hundred other great warlocks and warriors, who had run with the wolves and the wild deer, and soared with the mountain eagles, in the days before Witchcraft was banned in the north.

If I can go on pretending to be so stupidly unobservant, if I can pretend not to see what I see, or hear what I hear, these women will continue to be careless when and how they perform their magic.

So Gwenlliant sat in the grass and pretended just as hard as she could. It seemed that she had been deceiving people in just that way for all of her life—a lesson she had been forced to learn as a strange, fey child among powerful adults.

At sunset, the Governor returned to the graveyard and the crypt, with the Captain, a handful of men, and Mahaffy and Conn. They brought fresh torches with them, blankets to sit on, and some jars of wine to see them through the night, and set up a sort of camp in the furthest chamber, where Tryffin thought he had detected the pattern spell.

Tryffin spread a blanket across a limestone sarcophagus and sat down to wait. Meligraunce placed a single lighted torch in an iron ring on one of the pillars. Tryffin meant to see the shapechanger if and when she arrived, but had decided it would be foolish to light up the entire tomb and warn her off, should she happen to approach by some other means than a pattern spell.

The air smelled damp and earthy—though fresher now than it had earlier—and a chill draft came down the staircase and swept through the vaults. Meligraunce sat down on the ground at Tryffin's feet, and the others disposed themselves in pairs around the chamber.

The night crept past slowly—more slowly by far than the night before, because then there had been the constant expectation that something was about to happen and tonight there was no way of telling if anything would. As a result, Tryffin found it increasingly difficult to remain alert, and his thoughts kept wandering off in unexpected directions.

He thought of the heavy tasks still awaiting him as Governor of Mochdreff; and of the web of circumstances which had brought him into that harsh land in the first place; of the many months he had spent unraveling the tangled skein of history and destiny, in order to better understand why he had been chosen— and exactly what he had been chosen to do. He thought of the two young heirs, Math and Peredur, one of whom the High King would select to be Lord of Mochdreff, just as soon as Tryffin had transformed that troubled land into the sort of place where a young boy might rule safely; and of Peredur's half-brother, now known as Grifflet, whose birth had very nearly precipitated a rebellion. But most of all, he thought of Gwenlliant.

In truth, he was only just beginning to acknowledge that the seductive Luned had stirred up some painful memories, awakened a great many suppressed emotions. He was remembering the first tumultuous year of marriage to a twelve-year-old bride—before Gwenlliant had run away and found the witch Ceinwen to be her teacher. Who but a brute or a fool would take so young a wife, especially one who had already been subjected . . . not to an actual rape, but to something almost equally atrocious. He had known when he married Gwenlliant that the effects of Calchas fab Corfil's wicked spells and vile whisperings might still linger, that they might color her emotions toward Tryffin himself and cause her to shrink from every strong feeling he was able to inspire in her. Who could consummate a marriage under those conditions? Particularly when their relationship had always been perilously close to that of brother and sister, and there was always that faint lingering suggestion of incest standing between them.

Tryffin shook his head; the answers to these questions were all too obvious. Yet what choice *had* he but to marry Gwenlliant, with her father standing by ready to marry her off, if Tryffin faltered, to an even less suitable bridegroom? His innocent little cousin in the hands of the brutal and lascivious Rhun of Yrgoll was simply unthinkable! And besides all that and against all reason, he knew that he wanted her for himself . . . and that the years ahead would be bleak indeed if Gwenlliant did not eventually return to him.

So deeply did these thoughts occupy him that he barely took notice when the woman started to materialize about a dozen feet in front of him. He had never seen anyone arrive by means of a pattern spell, and as the brown-cloaked figure shimmered into existence, he sat for a moment staring at the pale blur of the face inside the hood before he realized what had happened.

Her own reactions were considerably swifter. Seeing that she had transported herself directly into the jaws of a trap, the shapechanger turned to flee, even before Tryffin sprang to his feet and drew the silver-bladed dagger.

Yet rather than flee directly, she ran an erratic course: from one pillar to the next, then a sharp turn round, and from there across the shadowy chamber and up the short flight of steps leading to the next vault.

Realizing that she was using a pattern in order to escape him, Tryffin pulled out the torch and followed in her footsteps exactly. He could hear the startled exclamations of the others, and someone—almost certainly Meligraunce—running lightly behind him. They arrived in the other chamber almost simultaneously, in time to see the brown cloak pause by one of the marble biers, and then flicker out like a dying candle.

Without stopping to consider if the boys and the guards would be able to follow them, Tryffin and the Captain leaped across the chamber and toward the place they had last seen her. Tryffin had only a momentary glimpse of the bier and the bones, before the spell took him, casting him out of the shadowy crypt, into a green leafy dimness.

"Holy Mother of God . . . what *is* this place?" breathed Meligraunce, gazing in wonder at the forest of ancient oaks and venerable elms which seemed to surround him on all sides. His sudden transition to such an unexpected location had rattled him considerably.

"There *is* no forest within a single day's ride of Anoeth. Is it possible that a pattern spell could transport us such a distance as that?"

"It seems that it can," replied Tryffin, considerably more accustomed to these strange adventures, yet still rather shaken. Like Meligraunce, he had expected the spell to take him no further than the outskirts of the town, to some hidden cellar or bricked-in chamber perhaps . . . someplace, that is, even less accessible than the underground vault, but at no great distance.

Now, as he gazed around him, at the elm trees choked in ivy, the oaks festooned in whiskery grey moss, the deep drifts of leaves piled up on the forest floor, as he listened to the branches creaking overhead, he felt a sinking sensation.

"Ah God . . . I know where we are, Captain. We have traveled much further than you imagine, for this is the Bearded Wood."

"And what place is *that*?" asked Meligraunce, turning to look at him.

Tryffin shook his head; he did not know much about the wood, but what he knew was not reassuring. "I cannot say exactly what it is, but it seems to exist outside the world that we know, and its paths are like the pattern spells, only many times more powerful. Also, it twists time. Not just by hours, but by whole days. Perhaps, if one were to wander here long enough, for a week or a month maybe, whole years and decades might pass in the world out—"

Just then there was a crashing in the bushes, and whirling around to look, he caught a glimpse of the shapechanger—the stone gargoyle, this time—further down the path about thirty yards distant, leaping off through the trees. Naturally, Tryffin and Meligraunce gave chase at once.

The path twisted and turned. Every now and again, there was a root or a vine across the path that had to be stepped over or around. Afraid that he might stumble and set the forest on fire, Tryffin stopped for a moment where he found a bare piece of earth to extinguish his torch, and then continued on.

The trees on either side of the path grew so close together, the woven branches formed such a thick leafy canopy overhead, that without the torch it was very dim . . . and also very silent. The thick carpet of damp and decaying leaves on the forest floor muffled their footsteps, so it was like running in a dream, soundless and a bit unreal.

Eventually, however, reality intruded, reminding Tryffin that he was not entirely recovered from his wound or the sickness that followed. He came to a sudden halt and leaned up against the mossy trunk of an oak, clutching at the pain in his side, struggling to catch his breath. Meligraunce skidded to a stop beside him.

"Your Grace, there is no need for us to go so quickly. She is leaving an easy trail for us to follow."

And that was true: Heavier than they, for all she was so much swifter, the stone gargoyle left signs of disturbance among the leaves, and broken branches wherever an ivy bush flung a snaky arm across the path.

"Aye," said Tryffin, still gasping for air. "But I don't know if night ever comes here or not . . . or how long it lasts . . . and without her to guide us, we may never find our way out of the forest and back to Anoeth. The wood is a vast maze of branching paths, and to follow any of those pathways without knowing the turns, there is no telling where or precisely when we may come out."

There was a pounding of footsteps, the voices of men drawing steadily nearer. Back down the trail they had just been following appeared four armored figures, running fleetly: Garreg, Conn, Ciag, and Mahaffy. The surefooted Ciag was carrying a lighted torch.

"Prince Tryffin," cried Mahaffy, as they approached. "We thought we had lost you."

"A wonder you did not," replied the Governor, as the four arrived—not nearly so breathless as he was—and crowded around him and the Captain.

"Yes . . . well, it took us a while to recollect your movements, and a few failed attempts before we were able to follow you through the pattern," said Mahaffy. "We left the Sergeant and Rhiwallon behind. It didn't seem wise for all to go through."

Tryffin nodded. Considering how things had turned out, it might be just as well that someone had stayed in the crypt to tell Dame Brangwaine and the other witches what had occurred—just supposing there was anything even Dame Brangwaine might do to aid them now. Tryffin turned to his squire. "Do you recognize where we are?"

Conn swallowed hard, brushed a lock of brown hair off of his brow. "Yes. It is the place Dame Ceinwen brought us, when you and I and Garth were lost in the southern bogs two years back. There—there is an indescribable feel to this place, quite unmistakable. Only I think we must be in some part of the wood quite distant from the paths we followed back then, because the trees I remember were mostly oak and willow. I don't recall so many elms."

Mahaffy, of course, had not been with them at the time that Conn was describing, but Tryffin suddenly remembered that the young Lord of Ochren had been raised by Dame Ceinwen. "And you, Mahaffy, do you know this wood?"

"I believe that I remember such a place mentioned in my kinswoman's stories, but I have never been here," the youth replied, with a discouraging shake of his head.

Tryffin heaved a frustrated sigh. "Then we have little hope of finding our way back to Dame Ceinwen's cottage on the moors—or to any other familiar place. In truth, the shapechanger remains our only chance, and that is a small one."

. . . but of the Wandering Sod, and the Breathing Mist, and the Will-o-Wisp, and the Bearded Wood, this much only will I say: Any man who should chance to fall under their spell, he knows not where they will take him, nor when he will see his home again.

—*From* Moren Clydno's Book of Secrets

11.

The Hall of the Lord of Shadows

When Tryffin had caught his breath, when the pain in his side subsided, he and his men set off again, this time with Garreg leading, because he was the more experienced tracker. In spite of Ciag's torch, their path became increasingly dim, as the oaks and the elms began to give way to pine and yew—though phosphorescent trails of giant snails, crisscrossing the path or winding like silver ribbons up the gnarled trunks of the trees, added a little light along the way.

They went slowly and cautiously, Tryffin inwardly cursing his own weakness with every step, the weakness that kept them all to this dawdling, limping pace. At least the others had spared him the humiliation of a shoulder or arm offered as support— although once Mahaffy had extended a hand and started to speak, before apparently thinking better of what he was about to say and holding his peace—and for that Tryffin was grateful.

He gritted his teeth and plodded on. The situation facing him and his companions was grim, for now they had not merely to find and slay the shapechanger, but to force her to lead them back to Anoeth. Knowing they would kill her afterward, she was hardly likely to comply, nor would any threat move her. Indeed, her malice appeared to be so great it might actually please her to know, even as she lay dying, that her death would prevent them from *ever* returning to their own time and place. It was only a matter of time before the others realized this.

That being so, someone had to steady them all when they began to grow discouraged, someone had to maintain a calm air of authority, so that no one faltered, no one lost hope. And who should that someone be, if not the Governor himself? This was no time for him to be ill or exhausted; he had to muster every last bit of his strength and pray that it would be enough to see them all through.

They came out of the trees unexpectedly. One moment, they were trudging through the deep woodland, the next they were astonished at finding themselves on a narrow road winding down a rugged hillside. It was a moonlit night—just as it might be in Anoeth—but a light covering of snow lay on the ground, little flurries of flakes were still falling, and a sharp wind whistled through the crags.

"Remarkable," said Meligraunce. "I wonder if it is possible to grow accustomed to all this whisking about from place to place and season to season."

Shivering in the sudden cold, Tryffin shook his head. For all that, he was grateful for the thin white carpet of snow: The shapechanger's trail was clearly marked. Though if the snowfall continued long, those wide paw-prints might soon disappear . . .

Apparently, Garreg thought the same. After a moment of hesitation, while he adjusted his ideas to these new surroundings, the guardsman advanced down the trail, setting a brisker pace than he had before.

"Your Grace," said Meligraunce, striding along at the Governor's side. "Your cloak appears inadequate in this sudden change of weather. I think you ought to take mine as well."

By now, Tryffin's teeth were beginning to chatter and his limbs to tremble, whether with cold or exhaustion it was difficult to tell. His injured shoulder ached horribly. And the wind had such a biting edge to it, he thought he had never felt so keen a blast. Yet the other men seemed to keep warm merely by walking. No one else was shuddering as he was, no one else showed signs of such bitter fatigue.

There was a difference between *noblesse oblige* and rank stupidity. Much good he would do the others, lying frozen in a snowbank, Tryffin thought, as he accepted the cloak and gave the Captain his thanks in return. He wrapped the mantle around him and fastened the clasp; the dark wool was thick and warm, and he felt a little better almost at once.

He began to take note of his surroundings. The road was wide, and hard as stone beneath his feet; he guessed that it had been carved right out of the hill. Skeleton bushes grew thickly on either side, bushes dusted with a light sprinkling of snow which gave them the look of white heather. If he closed his eyes, if he allowed his imagination full rein, he might almost be able to *smell* the heather. Certainly, it was easy enough to picture how the hillside would look during the summer, when the heather and the gorse, the broom, the thistle, and the wild fennel would all be in bloom. Further up the slope, on a narrow shelf of earth and rock, was a stand of trees, oddly familiar. These, too, he could picture in full leaf.

In fact, Tryffin slowly realized, *everything* he saw was achingly familiar: every bush, every twig, every rock and ridge. And yet, at the same time, inexplicably alien. It was like spotting the face of your nearest kinsman in a crowded street, only to discover, as the man drew closer, the swarthy complexion of a foreigner, the inscrutable eyes of a stranger.

The road led through a narrow defile and started down. It was now little more than a steep slippery pathway, the footing uncertain, with sheer walls of rock on either side. *I have walked or ridden this way a thousand times. But that is impossible. I have never come this way before.*

A final turn in the path brought the Governor and his companions out on the floor of a long valley. On the far side of that valley stood a dark castle, perched on a rugged crag, silhouetted against the rising moon. The walls of the fortress were sheer, its slender towers, gracefully turned and fluted, soaring up to almost impossible heights. Tryffin felt his heart leap in his chest.

"Lord Prince," said Meligraunce. "It is no use going further, because the tracks have all disappeared. Also, there is no telling what sort of people live in yonder fortress. They may be friendly, they may be violently inhospitable. But if we go back to the wood, we can at least be certain that the trees will shelter us."

Tryffin shook his head emphatically. "I doubt we would find the wood still there if we tried to go back. It has a tendency to disappear as soon as you step away from it. And I *do* know what sort of people we will meet in that castle. This is Tir Gwyngelli, and that fortress is Castell Maelduin, where I was born.

"Only, it is all so changed," he added softly. "I do not see how it all could have happened in a few short years, since I was last there. Unless . . . unless we spent much, much longer in the Bearded Wood than we realized."

Those words were scarcely out of his mouth before something happened, something so weird and unexpected that a chill slid down his spine, and the fine hairs on his arms and the back of his neck stood erect. The wind blew a bank of clouds aside, revealing an immense yellow, pock-marked moon in close conjunction with a strange red planet.

There was a long, breathless silence, while everyone stood in astonished contemplation.

It was larger than the orange moon rising behind the castle, larger still, Tryffin slowly realized, than the silver moon which had been lighting their way, virtually unnoticed, all this while.

"It seems that I was wrong, after all," he said at last—perhaps unnecessarily. "This is not Gwyngelli, nor any part of the world we know."

Mahaffy cleared his throat, shifted his weight from one foot to the other. "I think we have ventured into the Shadow Lands, the Inner Celydonn."

The Governor turned to stare at him. Those names meant nothing, they stirred no memories. "And where might that be?"

"Not far beyond Dame Ceinwen's house on the Marches—that is to say, one may move from the Marches to the Shadow Lands very readily, but I am not absolutely certain of their actual proximity," said Mahaffy. "I can only tell you a little of all that might be told of that strange realm, but perhaps—perhaps we should sit down here on these boulders and rest a bit, Your Grace, while I relate all that I do know."

As Tryffin and the others complied, searching out seats among the tumbled rocks and making themselves as comfortable as possible, the young Lord of Ochren continued: "You must understand that I never had any magical leanings like my Uncle Cado and I was never Dame Ceinwen's pupil in that sense of the word. She only taught me the things that any nursemaid might teach her small charges. But she did tell me stories, wonderful stores, about the Breathing Mist and the maze in the Bearded Wood, and a great deal more besides. I often wondered if those stories were true, or just the sort of tales that old women will tell—because I must confess that it was a long time before I began to realize what an extraordinary woman Ceinwen was."

Ciag's brand was burning low, so he took out another, which he had been carrying in his belt all this while, set its head of flax and tallow aflame, and wedged it between two of the rocks. The Governor moved a little closer, so that he might warm his hands.

"I am trying to tell you that I am not sure how to properly explain what I scarcely understand myself," Mahaffy was saying. "The Shadow Lands, they are all *different*. The borders are constantly shifting, and there seem to be holes in the fabric of reality there. Some places are just like stepping into the past, because they are inhabited by the shadows—the ghosts, you would say, though they seem amazingly substantial—of ancient heroes and beautiful women, of the most wicked villains and the most splendid of kings . . . all the great folk of history and legend . . . who are doomed to repeat the same actions, over and over again, that they performed during life. Though a traveler from our world can only make the smallest changes there, *he* in his turn may be profoundly altered. Also, he can be killed by the inhabitants; they are quite substantial enough for that.

"But there are other lands inhabited by creatures that could never exist in our world, or by creatures that did exist in our world but no longer do so, or by the spirits of the unborn . . . or by the ghosts of people *and* places that might have been but never were. I have a feeling, Prince Tryffin," Mahaffy concluded, "that we have come to one of those latter places, a sort of shadow Gwyngelli."

Tryffin sat staring at his hands. This was all a bit much even for him to accept, for all that he had seen and experienced a great many curious things during his lifetime. "Ghosts of people, that I can easily believe. Ghosts of places, that is a little more difficult, though hills and valleys and deserts do have personalities, and often seem to be inhabited by some sort of pervading spirit that influences the people who happen to live there. But ghosts of moons and planets, of winters and summers that never were, that is simply incredible."

Yet the evidence was all around him: the rugged boulders on which he and his companions were sitting, the wind scouring the valley and the hilltops, the towers and spires of the castle . . . the huge second and third moons, and the baleful red planet hovering on the horizon.

Unless I am dreaming. Or have fallen ill and delirious again. Yet the events of the last several hours had proceeded in such an orderly—though perfectly astonishing—fashion, they hardly suggested either dream or delirium.

But while Mahaffy spoke, the snowfall had steadily increased, until it seemed to be reaching blizzard proportions, while the wind blew more fiercely than ever.

"Wherever we are, we must get in out of this weather," said Meligraunce.

"Either back to the wood or on toward the fortress, we must seek shelter somewhere."

"To the castle, then," said Tryffin, rising heavily to his feet. "No matter how weirdly altered we may find things here, my father's house could hardly be so changed that travelers would not find a warm and generous welcome there."

The night seemed to last for a windswept eternity as Tryffin and his companions crossed the stony valley and began to climb the winding road on the other side. The wind howled, and the snow continued to fall, in great crystalline flakes so large it was actually possible to see their shapes and beautiful, complex patterns. Tryffin was dimly aware that he had never seen, never imagined, anything like them before: brighter than diamonds, more delicate than flowers, colder and sharper than steel. Were it not for the pain, the weariness, weighting his limbs, he would have been completely enthralled.

At the same time, he had a vague sense that Mahaffy and the two men-at-arms were uneasy. Understandable, perhaps, at finding themselves in the land of their hereditary enemies. Even Conn and Meligraunce seemed to be struck with superstitious dread. But as there were so many wild tales linking the Gwyngellach with the Sidhe, the Fairy Folk, that was also understandable. Indeed, the Gwyngellach even encouraged those stories, and others which painted the land itself as incredibly rugged and savage. When travelers arrived, they were treated with every possible consideration . . . but the people of the Hidden Country (as they liked to call it) were not above *discouraging* those travelers before they even left home.

As the first lilac-tinted light of morning appeared in the eastern sky, there came signs of activity in the castle above. Fires were kindled, voices could be heard relaying a message along the walls, as one of the sentries spotted the weary little party trudging slowly up the long road.

A wild, ululating cry rose up from the gatehouse, an eerie wailing so cold and unearthly that it froze everyone but Tryffin in his tracks. While he, with no visible sign of emotion, calmly cupped his hands around his mouth, and responded with a blood-chilling howl of his own, a banshee caterwauling that echoed and re-echoed from one end of the valley to the other.

"Holy Mary, Mother of God," said Conn, under his breath, as he made the sign of the cross. He had never, in his wildest imaginings, supposed that anything half so ghastly could emerge from a human throat. "Is that a password . . . or a challenge?"

The Governor said nothing, but Conn had his answer when they reached the foot of the walls, and the gate swung wide open to admit them. Tryffin went through first, his step quickening with anticipation, the others trailing a step or two behind.

Yet it was the Governor, rather than any of the others, who came to a sudden halt in the middle of the torchlit courtyard and glanced around him with a dazed expression. Because his squires, the guards, even the sensible Meligraunce had—after all—been expecting something like this from the very beginning.

Tiny blue-skinned men and women, hunched and misshapen like goblins. Tall, almost impossibly beautiful lords and ladies, dressed in splendid garments of shimmering silk. Spirited black horses and great rangy wolfhounds. And other, stranger creatures besides, all gathered around, staring at Tryffin with glowing yellow eyes.

He knew then that he had not wandered into some misty might-have-been of the past, nor into a land where the ghosts of kings and wizards endlessly repeated the triumphs and the tragedies of their earthly lives. No, he had come to a place stranger by far, and yet completely familiar: Tir Gwyngelli as it existed in his own day . . . in the tall tales of travelers, in the imaginations of foreigners.

For this was elfland, and he and his companions had just arrived, entirely unexpected, at the court of the King of the Fairies.

They were immediately surrounded by a contingent of the goblin folk, armored after their own strange fashion: grotesque pot helms, ring mail, leather coats with all manner of odd bits of metal attached to them. They carried round shields the size of bucklers, banded with bronze. One little fellow, no more than three feet tall, carrying a pole arm perhaps six feet longer than he was himself, strode up to Tryffin with a great air of importance.

"Though you know the signs and signals to gain admittance, you are clearly strangers, and have no business to be here," he said, in a voice surprisingly deep and gruff in one so small. "We will take you to the King for judgment."

Meligraunce and the men-at-arms were reaching for their weapons, when Tryffin stopped them with an upraised hand. "We are content to yield ourselves to your King's justice. We are law-abiding men, and if we have violated any custom here, we acted in ignorance."

The men reluctantly sheathed their swords. "Your Grace," said Meligraunce, in the Governor's ear. "We cannot be certain that *these* are law-abiding people. They may be no better than outlaws and brigands, their 'King' a notorious robber baron. And even if all is done here according to law, that law may be unconscionably harsh, particularly where foreigners are concerned.

"No," said Tryffin, also very low. "This is my father's realm, no matter how artfully disguised. The laws will be fair and tempered by mercy."

Their goblin escort herded them in the direction of the keep. As Tryffin approached the vast stone pile, he slowly realized that it was exactly that: not blocks of limestone and granite mortared together, but the very substance of the hill itself, cut and chiseled and hollowed to form towers and courtyards, chambers and passageways, halls and galleries, out of the living rock.

Stepping through a graceful stone arch, they climbed a winding interior staircase. Opening off of the stairs on either side were low passageways and tiny, cell-like rooms, all connected by doors, and traps, and ladders too small for men to ascend, level on level of mazelike goblin accommodations—rather (so Tryffin imagined) like the chambers and corridors of a rabbit warren—where a vast number of the tiny blue-skinned inhabitants seemed to be carrying on with their lives: eating, sleeping, swilling, quarreling, backstabbing, and making love, all in promiscuous publicity.

Just as the Governor was beginning to wonder if the entire castle would be the same, they reached a landing near the top of the tower, passed under another arch, and moved through a series of larger and fairer chambers, then through an immense door that shone like silver, into a place full of light and color.

Tryffin and his companions looked around them in silent awe, for this was surely a place out of legend: a vast hall with pillars and alcoves and benches all beautifully carved out of stone, a firepit at one end of the chamber, in which an entire cherry tree was set on fire, and a ceiling glittering with gems and veins of precious ore. A feast was in progress, at long trestle tables set up down the center of the hall, and the array of silver and gold and crystal serving pieces fairly dazzled the eye.

No less splendid were the beautiful people seated at those tables, the jewel-like colors of their gowns and tunics glowing in the firelight. But outshining them all was the King himself: a tall elf lord with raven-dark hair, a golden crown blazing with sidhe-stones, and a cape made out of eagle feathers. On either side of him sat two muscular youths, in armor of silver mail.

"Prince T-Tryffin . . . it is your Uncle Manogan, your brother Fflergant . . . and you!" gasped Conn.

Mahaffy shot him a warning glance and whispered in the Governor's ear. "Your Grace, I forgot to mention: We must not tell anyone here the names of the lands that we come from. It is strictly forbidden."

Tryffin nodded as his escort of goblins prodded him toward the High Table. Conn had been wrong about one thing: The King did not resemble the Marshall of Celydonn so much as his brother Lord Maelgwyn, and the likeness there was striking— though the features were more finely drawn, and the eyes were a startling shade of amber rather than brown. Most disconcerting of all was the youth on the left, presumably the younger son; gazing into that face, so like and unlike his own, was a little disorienting.

The chief goblin held a whispered conversation with the monarch. "Nevertheless," the King said out loud, "we are not wont to use visitors quite so harshly. I commend your caution, but it is easy to see these men mean us no harm, if only by the readiness with which they surrendered."

As the guard of goblins melted away, the King gestured to Tryffin. "Welcome to Annwn and to the court of Avallach. If you are weary, rooms will be provided you. If you are hungry, then sit at my table and join in the feast."

Tryffin went down on one knee. Tears blurred his vision and a great lump rose in his throat. Viewed more closely, the King's likeness to Maelgwyn fab Menai was even more marked— heartbreakingly close, viewed through the eyes of a wandering son who had not seen home in too many years. Tryffin took the hand that was offered him and raised it to his lips.

"I think I should know you," said the King softly. "And yet I do not."

Tryffin shook his head. "Lord King, we are strangers here. We have come here pursuing a criminal . . . a woman who has slain numerous children that were under my protection."

There was a sympathetic murmur from the assembled courtiers—at least from those who sat near enough to hear him speak—and the King's oldest son sprang to his feet. "Father, if what he says is true, we should give him all the aid that we can. For you know that the murder of children is abomination, and that a woman should be guilty of such a crime is particularly indecent!"

It was then that Tryffin realized another thing that was very different about this place: Unlike his father's dining hall, where children were always present, waiting on their elders as hand-maids and pages, or seated on the laps of mothers or nursemaids and enjoying the feast if they were very small, there was not a single face in sight that appeared to be less than seventeen—unless it might be one of the goblin servitors, whose age it was difficult to determine. And he remembered that children were said to be rare among the Sidhe; which might explain why their lives were held as particularly sacred.

The King smiled indulgently. "Your indignation is admirable, Ffergus, but you are too impulsive. These men have not even asked for our aid . . . nor told us, yet, who they are and where they have come from.

"I see you have hurt yourself," he added, indicating Tryffin's left arm. "I hope this misfortune didn't befall you on my lands."

"No, that happened to me . . . a long way from this place. Lord King, I am Tryffin fab Maelgwyn. I do not think you would recognize the name of my father's kingdom; I was last there myself four years past, and I have been traveling much of the time since. In fact," he continued on truthfully, "it is so far removed from your kingdom, I wonder if I will ever find my way back again."

"I see," said King Avallach, nodding sagely. "It is most unwise to leave a place for such a long stretch of time, for you are almost certain to lose it—or return to find it almost unrecognizable. But what sort of land was it, at the time you left it? Was it mountainous? Was it in the desert?"

The King motioned him to rise, and Tryffin did so. "It was located by the sea. Though, strange to say, my people are not seafarers. The land is so beautiful, and the people who live there love it so dearly, that few men desire to leave it."

"Ah," said the King. "Then it must closely resemble Annwn, for we are also deeply attached to our native soil, and there is no place more beautiful . . . though some might regard it as rather wild. But tell me, Prince Tryffin, the names of your companions."

This Tryffin did, being particularly careful to omit Mahaffy's title as Lord of Ochren, introducing the boy only as a knight in his household.

"You have a very young household, and do not appear so very old yourself," commented the King, glancing from one face to the other. "Yet you say you have been traveling for four years. It seems very odd of your father, if I may say so, to send mere boys out into foreign lands, particularly as it is your object to apprehend a criminal who has slain many children already."

Tryffin released a long sigh. It had been a long time since anyone made mention of his age—except for his squires, who generally contrived to make him feel positively ancient, for all he was not much older than they were—and he found that it was a great relief to put aside the pretense of age and experience. Especially before this man with compassionate eyes, who so poignantly resembled his father.

"We were chosen by circumstances, not by design. Or if there was a design, it was that of the woman herself."

The King appeared to consider this. "Perhaps you are under a geas and don't even know it," he said at last. "And if that is so, it would be wrong—not to say extremely dangerous—for us to refuse to aid you in any way possible."

He summoned two of his goblin servants and instructed them to provide his guests with a comfortable chamber to sleep in and a private meal, "for they look too weary to join in our merriment here."

Then he smiled warmly on Tryffin and his companions. "When you have eaten and rested, I will send for you to attend me once more. Then we may discuss your quest more fully, and determine how I and my sons might aid you."

There was a man who lived in the parish of St. Sianne, who went into the village one day and met there his own Shadow, walking about as boldly as you please, and conducting business just as though it were a Christian. At this, the man became exceedingly angry and began to scold the inanimate thing.

"What a mischievous creature you are, and up to no good, that I will warrant you!" said he. "Begone from this place before I send for the priest and have him speak the Words over you."

Hearing the fellow speak, the Shadow made him a flourishing bow and walked out of the town with its head held high, leaving the man behind in the street, trembling with indignation.

> —*From* A Journey into Rhianedd and Gorwynnion, *by the monk Elidyr fab Gruffudd*

12.

Under Stars, Under Stone

It was never mid-day in the land of Annwn, it was always twilight or early morning. The sun was a tarnished golden disk, which rose now and again a short distance above the horizon, described a shallow arc, then disappeared, leaving the sky to the blazing stars, the triple moons, and a procession of wandering planets and silver-tailed comets.

"I have seen the sun a great ball of fire at the top of the sky, and the heat rising up from the land . . . but that was in other countries, when I was younger and able to travel from place to place," the King told Tryffin. "Night and day, they are a great mystery, and so are the shifting borders—once, I sought to unravel these riddles, but now no more, because the King of Annwn is bound to his native soil." He and Tryffin stood on a balcony near the top of one of the fluted towers, staring up at the star-scattered heavens. "In Charon, which lies to the north, there is a single moon; in the Summer Country, which bordered

Annwn on the west before it drifted away, there are twelve moons, all ghostly pale, strung out across the sky like a necklace of pearls. I suppose you must have seen things equally strange during your travels. But tell me . . . what is the sky like in your father's kingdom?"

Tryffin hesitated before he spoke. He must always remember that the man at his side, the stately figure in golden crown and eagle-feather cape, was not his own father, Maelgwyn fab Menai, whom he resembled so closely, but another sort of creature not even human—and therefore not to be entirely trusted. Tryffin must always remember to weigh his words, to stifle any confidence which sprang to his lips, and not reveal too much about himself or his companions. "There is a solitary moon, as in the place you just mentioned . . . Charon, I believe you called it? The stars are smaller and colder than they are in Annwn, and the nights can be fearfully dark. The day, however, is longer and brighter."

He ran a hand over the marble railing of the balcony. It was as cold as ice and as solid to the touch. Yet all this was shadow, all this illusion: the hill, the castle, the people inside, the food that he ate (for all that it satisfied him), the wine that he drank (for all that it warmed him), no more real than the lights in the sky, the unknown moons and comets and planets, which if they truly existed would disorder the cosmos, make a lie of everything he had ever been taught about the earth and the seven spheres.

"How long have I been here?" he asked, after a while. It was difficult to keep track, since the Fairy Folk ate, and slept, and woke, and conducted their lives, not by the rising or the setting of the sun, but according to various devices that recorded the hours: sand-glasses, and candles that burned at a measured rate, and mechanical things called clocks. Before coming to Annwn, Tryffin had only seen one mechanical clock in his entire life; it belonged to his cousin the High King, and was far less elaborate than the clocks of fairyland, which were operated by weights and pendulums and coiled springs.

"You have been here a week. The dawn has come seven times since you first arrived at our gate," said a voice—his own voice—coming from the shadows over by the wall. It was, of course, Prince Gruffydd, the King's younger son and Tryffin's elfin counterpart.

"So little as that?" said the Governor, under his breath. He was no longer wearing his arm in a sling, for the wound in his shoulder had healed, the broken collarbone mended, and he was nearly as strong and as healthy as he had been before the shapechanger's attack. Was it some magic peculiar to the realm of Annwn which brought so swift a cure—or some benevolent spell secretly worked by King Avallach, who declined to take the credit?

"Is it always winter here . . . always so cold?" Tryffin asked out loud. New clothes had been provided for him and his household of five, garments made of the remarkable cloth of fairyland, which flowed like water and blazed with jewel-like colors. The glittering cloak and long silky tunic he was wearing now were warmer than they looked, but barely sufficient to keep out the icy blast of the wind which seemed always to be blowing.

"There is spring," said the King of the Fairies. "When the sun rises a little higher and remains in the sky a little longer. It is warmer then, for the snow never falls and the air is still, and the trees grow leaves, the heather and the gorse are covered with tiny flowers, and the grass grows long and green. Then the leaves turn yellow almost overnight and fall to the ground, the blossoms wither and die. It is all so brief, you could hardly call it autumn, and as for summer . . . my two sons, who have never even crossed the borders of Annwn, have never seen it." The King smiled suddenly. "Ffergus, of course, believes anything I tell him, but I sometimes wonder if Gruffydd truly accepts that autumn and summer exist."

"I would not accept either one on any authority less than your own," replied Gruffydd. "But still, I would like to see them for myself, and discover if you have remembered these things accurately."

It was beginning to snow, a scattering of sharp, icy crystals, which the wind whipped around and threw in Tryffin's face. "Let us go inside," said the King. "I believe a blizzard is coming." As Tryffin had never seen the King mistaken about the weather—indeed, Avallach had an uncanny ability to predict what was going to happen hours or days ahead of time—he readily consented to go inside.

Passing through the door, Tryffin brushed against Prince Gruffydd and drew back with an involuntary shudder. The young elf stared at him for a moment, then shrugged and went on ahead, taking the stairs leading down to his father's apartments two at a time. The King stopped Tryffin by putting a gentle hand on his arm and drawing him out on the balcony again. "You dislike my son. I wonder why. To me, you seem very much alike."

Tryffin was not even sure how to explain it. When he first arrived in Annwn, he had actually felt drawn to his elfin counterpart, but as the days passed he conceived a horror of Prince Gruffydd's company. Now he had only to meet the brawny youth walking down a corridor to feel his skin crawl, and the very sight of that face—his own face, though with more pronounced cheekbones and finer features, and an eerie glow in the eyes—made his stomach clench like a fist.

Prince Ffergus was so like to Tryffin's brother Fflergant, with that same guileless, gullible charm, it was impossible not to feel some affection, but there was something in Prince Gruffydd that continually offended.

"Your son is younger than I am," said Tryffin. "And the resemblance is only superficial."

"Would you say so?" asked the King. Though the night wind was howling about him, not a hair on his head, not a feather on his cloak, was disturbed. When he touched Tryffin, there was a warm, tingling sensation—not Witchcraft, but Fairy magic, and some species of ward or magic circle. "But I would say that you are exactly the same age. Yet it is true that he lacks your experience of the world . . . perhaps his life has been a bit too sheltered. No wonder he strikes you as immature."

The Governor considered that possibility. His own nature was expansive, his temper forgiving; he was the sort of person who was always finding excuses for other people—not always wisely. He knew that his assessment of Prince Gruffydd was uncharacteristically harsh. He thought the young elf sly and deceptive, a man who spoke little, appeared to notice much, and acted indirectly, often through his older brother. At the same time, Gruffydd showed so little emotion, it was hard not to condemn him as cold and manipulative. And yet, might not all this arise from a lack of self-confidence, a sense that his talents were all untested . . . from immaturity as the King suggested?

And how much was due to the unsettling experience of viewing himself from the outside in?

"In truth, Prince Tryffin, I find the likeness between you and my son remarkable," said the King, as if reading his mind. "Are you quite, quite certain there is no kinship between us?"

Mindful that he was treading on dangerous ground, Tryffin shook his head. Why, he wondered, did Avallach surround himself with such powerful wards in his own fortress? What did he fear from his own household, his own sons? It was difficult to trust a man . . . no, not even a man, but a shadow . . . who was so mistrustful. "Surely any relationship would be for the King's Grace to determine, and not for me to claim."

The King smiled faintly. "You evade the truth like a Fairy. I believe you must be one of us, after all."

Now that he was completely recovered from his wounds, Tryffin rode out at dawn each morning to hunt for the child-killer. No sign of the creature ever appeared, though he and his companions rode further each time, down the valley and over the snow-covered hills, on the shaggy black Fairy horses, accompanied by the demon-eyed Fairy hounds, stretching the brief hours of daylight as far as he could and often riding back to the fortress after the stars had appeared in the sky. Yet with each sunrise came strange reports which seemed to indicate the shapechanger's presence somewhere in the countryside surrounding the castle, preying on the livestock owned by the goblin herdsmen. Sheep and goats and chickens kept disappearing, and ferocious nightmares attacked any goblin who closed his or her eyes for an hour's rest.

"Though no one has yet produced a single blood-drained carcass," said Meligraunce one morning. "Not a kid or a lamb. And the dreams are always exactly the same, with never a new or an altered detail."

"Yes," Tryffin agreed, with a sigh. "I sometimes wonder whether everyone is only repeating what they think I would like to hear. The Gwyngellach are prone to that sort of thing, and so perhaps are the Sidhe."

In the meantime, life in Annwn was seductively pleasant and easy. Tryffin and his men lived in bright, airy chambers, with vaulted ceilings and smooth marble floors, and it seemed that everything King Avallach owned was at their disposal, whether it was food and drink, horses, armor, or his goblin guardsmen, who served as an escort whenever they went out riding.

It took another week and three rides up the same road that he and his companions had followed on the night they first entered Annwn, before Tryffin found the Bearded Wood waiting for him at the top of the icy ridge. From a little distance, the thicket of trees and vines appeared dense and impenetrable.

Tryffin turned to the chief goblin, Dris. Darker than some of the other goblins, Dris was the deep, rich blue of the evening sky. He had sharp, intelligent eyes, and a beaked nose and chin so remarkably hooked that they almost actually met. Yet the Governor thought that he knew him, or someone very like him—Bron or Brandegorias Corynaid was the name he had gone by when he lived in Mochdreff—the dwarf that Lord Maelgwyn had used as a spy.

"It comes and it goes, that forest," said Dris, in response to Tryffin's question. "They say that the wood is very dangerous, and that those who but enter its shade never return again."

Tryffin spoke to his steed and turned back down the path. When Mahaffy came abreast of him, he said very low, so that the young knight should hear him but not any of the goblins: "I would be happy enough to enter the wood and see where it takes me—for I've given up all real hope of meeting my enemy here—had we not left Caig and Garreg inside the castle. They followed me through the pattern spell out of loyalty, and I will be damned if I abandon either one of them here in Annwn."

Mahaffy frowned. "Do you not think it odd, Prince Tryffin, that we never seem to ride out without the goblins . . . nor all of us leave the castle at the same time?" he asked softly.

"I do," said Tryffin. There was always some reason suddenly materializing that required one or two of them to stay behind: a summons by the King, a horse gone lame, a message sent astray. Always very plausible, but the coincidences mounted.

"The King is not so open and trusting as he would have us believe. Nor so much like my father as I first thought, for all that it hurts my heart just to look at him. I have seen him strike one of his squires in a fit of rage—and that is something that Maelgwyn fab Menai would never do."

The young Knight shook his curly dark head as though he were puzzled. "If I may say so, that's no great thing. It happens all the time elsewhere. If I had a gold coin for every time I was slapped or cuffed as a page or a squire, I would be a rich man today."

Tryffin's hands tightened on the reins. "Have you ever seen *me* do anything of the sort?" Mahaffy shook his head again. "And you never will. We believe it is demeaning to both parties involved. My brother Fflergant struck his squire once, when he was very angry and didn't stop to think what he was doing—he was but newly knighted and still accustomed to a certain amount of scuffling and knocking about with the other lads—but when he realized what he had done, he never forgave himself. King Avallach did it and never apologized, nor seemed to think that he had done wrong."

And yet . . . was it being quite fair, blaming Avallach for anything that he thought or he did? Tryffin asked himself. The King of the Fairies was only a shadow, a fantasy; he could never be anything else but what other men thought him to be.

The King gave Tryffin and his men free run of the castle—which was rather puzzling, since he seemed to distrust them whenever they ventured outside his gates—of which the Governor took full advantage by exploring the fortress thoroughly. It was and it was not Castell Maelduin. There were rooms in the place that did not exist in Tir Gwyngelli. At the same time, there seemed to be a great many *people* missing, as though life in Annwn might be much more perilous than anyone was admitting. Tryffin often wondered what had become of the women who ought to represent his mother and his sisters in this shadow kingdom.

"I am not going out riding today," he told Meligraunce one morning. "I wish to explore the rooms and the passages under the castle, the caverns deep inside the hill."

"Then I will come with you," said the Captain. "And with your permission, we will bring Garreg and Ciag with us."

Tryffin nodded his assent. The four men descended the long staircase, past the goblins' warren, with Tryffin in the lead, Meligraunce only a step behind. At the foot of the steps was a door of heavy oak, which the Governor opened; on the other side was a deep shaft and a spiral staircase leading down to the lower regions of the castle.

As the stone steps were narrow, the men went down in single file, down and down, passing many landings and doors. "Are we heading for some particular place?" asked Meligraunce.

"Aye," said Tryffin. "For I have taken it into my head—I am not certain why—that there may be pattern spells down here. One pattern spell in particular, that may lead us back to Mochdreff. And that the tombs under the castle may be the place to find them."

Reaching the landing he wanted, he passed through an archway and led his men down a long corridor. The walls were rough and the floor irregular, for this was a natural passage in the rock.

"Because the spell that brought us here was located in the catacombs under the church?" asked Meligraunce.

Tryffin shook his head. He had no reason so coherent as that, but was acting on intuition instead of logic, relying on instinct far more than he would have done back in Mochdreff, because he was here in this shadow of his father's kingdom.

He changed the subject. "Captain, I believe this castle is a regular nest of intrigues. I have never in my life been in a place where there were so many whispered conversations, so many surreptitious glances passing back and forth, such a great coming and going of messengers in the night."

Instead of a torch, Tryffin had brought a crystal lantern with him, knowing from his own experience at Castell Maelduin that air shafts leading down from the upper levels, some of them natural, some of them cut into the living rock, made the passages on this level drafty.

"And you do not recognize these same . . . intrigues . . . from your own home?" said Meligraunce. The Captain had not entirely conquered his dread of underground places. Now, as he moved down the long windy corridor leading to the catacombs, there was tension in every muscle of his body, but that tension was under control.

Tryffin smiled faintly. He knew what people outside Gwyngelli thought of his father: a brilliant but sinister genius, holed up in his outland fortress, spinning plot after plot. The Gwyngellach knew better, knew him for the wise and compassionate ruler that he was—albeit a man who never let anything significant which passed in his realm escape his notice. Yet the people of Annwn actually seemed to fear their King, and that was the source of most of the whispering, so many of the clandestine meetings.

Ciag cleared his throat. "Your Grace . . . that boy Dylan, one of the King's squires . . . do you know who I mean?"

The Governor nodded his head. Dylan stood out among the King's personal attendants because he showed traces of goblin blood. Though otherwise one of the tall, fair Sidhe, he had a faint blue cast to his skin and his features were a little coarser.

"One day when you were out riding, Garreg and I caught him working a spell in your rooms," said Ciag.

Tryffin raised a sandy eyebrow. "What sort of a spell, and how did you know? To say nothing of why neither one of you thought to mention the incident before."

The guardsman flushed and shook his head. "It was something

with salt . . . a circle he drew on the floor by the firepit. And I didn't tell you because I didn't remember; he gave me a look with those yellow eyes of his, and the—the whole thing passed right out of my mind. I believe he did the same to Garreg."

"Fairy Glamour," said Tryffin. "But why should you remember it now and not before?"

"What you said just now about whispered conversations." Garreg spoke up for himself. "Dylan was *talking* to the fire, Lord Prince, speaking very low. But I think that we walked into the room before he was quite finished casting his spell."

The Governor stopped by a sealed iron door set into the rock, and lifted his crystal lantern to examine the inscription and see who was interred on the other side. "The next time, I hope you will both know better than to look any of the Sidhe directly in the face."

Hours of searching the catacombs yielded nothing useful. From time to time, Tryffin's bones began to vibrate or his teeth to ache, but it always happened as he was passing under an arch or over a threshold, most likely the effect of a warding spell. There seemed to be plenty of wards in the castle up above, though they could hardly be intended to keep ordinary folk out, since he and his household passed through them freely. And that was another thing different from Tir Gwyngelli: There were no such spells of Witchcraft *or* Wizardry at Castell Maelduin.

Only one object of interest did Tryffin discover that morning under the castle.

"What do you make of this?" he asked the Captain, using one hand to clear the inscription on a marble coffin that was sitting deep in dust, all alone in its own separate chamber.

"Gwynhwyfara." Meligraunce read the single name out loud. "It is the Lady Guenhumara from Mochdreff, who married your grandfather and was killed in a landslide. Do you recognize this room and this coffin?"

"I do," said Tryffin, staring down at the marble box containing the bones of a woman whose fate had been of such interest to him twelve months past. *Guenhumara, Gwynhwyfara . . . Gwenhwyfar on the coffin below Castell Maelduin . . . it is the same name in different dialects.* In his attempts to learn the true and original cause of his family's feud with the Lords of Mochdreff, he had eventually uncovered Guenhumara's tragic history. It seemed somehow significant to find her waiting for him, in this ghost of Tir Gwyngelli. *Perhaps I did not learn so much as I imagined. Perhaps I should have followed the thread of events back even further.*

"It is strange to think that she was buried at Castell Maelduin all along, and that I visited her tomb so many times," Tryffin said to Meligraunce. "Yet I never wondered or asked who she was—all because someone did not wish to lay her to rest under her own Mochdreffi name."

Not all of the intrigues in Annwn were political. The Fairy Folk were exceedingly volatile, and made and unmade their friendships, loyalties, alliances, and romantic attachments on a daily basis. Moreover, the beautiful long-limbed women were very free with their favors, inclined to be passionately possessive so long as their interest lasted, ruthlessly fickle when they grew bored—and strangely intent on drawing the foreign Prince and his two young attendants into their toils.

Not for these elfin damsels the languishing look, the suggestive smile. Their attentions were so particular, their invitations so open and explicit, as to be positively brazen. The Governor steadily but politely refused them, not for fear that anything he did in Annwn would get back to Gwenlliant to cause her pain (which hardly seemed possible), but because he had heard of the dangers that awaited any mortal who bedded with the women of the Sidhe.

Also, there was a certain hunger that he sometimes detected in a pair of bright eyes that made him uneasy.

"Best not to allow them to gain any power over you," he admonished Mahaffy and Conn. "No matter how they may tempt you. And it would be folly to form any real attachment to these things that can't even be human."

"I would as soon bed with a viper as a Fairy woman," Mahaffy replied with surprising vehemence. "The way that some of the creatures watch me, I think they would like to suck the marrow right out of my bones."

Conn said nothing, but he looked so ill and uncomfortable that Tryffin stifled a smile and said, "I know very well that you can both be trusted to do what is right."

So it came as a deep shock, two days later, when Tryffin returned from the hunt at sunset and dismounted in the snowy courtyard, to be met by Meligraunce bearing the news that his squire had been arrested for "unnatural acts."

"Conn?" said Tryffin, feeling a little dazed. "Our Conn has

been arrested for acts of *perversion*? By all the Saints and the Hosts of Heaven! I doubt he has ever so much as found the courage to perform the act with his eyes *open*."

"Indeed, Your Grace, given the circumstances, I can't help thinking he may have been blinded by some Fairy Glamour," replied Meligraunce. "But perhaps you ought to hear the story from Conn himself. He is more likely to confide in you than he was in me."

"Yes," said Tryffin, stripping off his gloves. "Though I doubt he will wish to tell it even to me. Can you show me to the place where they have taken him?"

As it turned out, Conn had only been confined to the Governor's quarters. There were goblin guards outside the door, and everyone who entered was required to yield up his weapons, or else swear an oath not to aid the prisoner in escaping, but that seemed to be the extent of Conn's imprisonment. The absence of chains and dungeons was slightly reassuring.

"Tell me everything that happened, and by all you hold sacred don't hold anything back," said Tryffin, taking a seat in the antechamber. "I am not here to judge you, which is the King's prerogative, but to help you in any way that I reasonably can."

The boy from Gorwynnion was a miserable sight. His brown hair was rumpled and his clothes looked as though he had donned them hastily. As he stopped pacing the floor and took a seat on a stool at Tryffin's feet, he looked much younger than his seventeen years. "Prince Tryffin, I never intended to do anything wrong. And you know how the women are, running about in those gauzy gowns, so they hardly appear to be dressed at all, and the way that everyone . . . that everyone behaves. You would hardly think that the word *perversion* would ever enter their minds."

"The question is," Tryffin said dryly, "when and how it first entered yours."

He regretted saying that almost immediately, because Conn flinched and refused to meet his eyes. It was wrong to allow his own irritation at not finding himself completely in control during this dreadful situation to dictate his words and actions.

"It never came into my mind at all. They made me sit in a chair, Aoife and Morna, and they took turns sitting in my lap and kissing me. It seemed harmless enough, though I didn't quite like it so much as I thought I would, because their teeth were so sharp and kept getting in the way, and . . ." Conn shuddered at the unpleasant memory.

"But I did remember how you warned me; I didn't mean to lie down with either of them. But it was so . . . I didn't know how to discourage them without committing discourtesy to a lady. And they . . . they kept putting . . . that is, they both—"

"They touched you in ways that made you feel excited," Tryffin finished the sentence for him. "There is no reason for you to feel ashamed of a perfectly natural reaction. Tell me what happened after that."

"I don't even remember how we all ended up in a room with a bed, or where all the clothes went," said Conn, continuing to stare at the floor. "And one moment Morna was lying under me . . . and then I rolled over after I was finished, and suddenly Aoife was sprawled naked across me. And . . . and Mahaffy was right when he compared those women to vipers, because all that fair hair of hers was just like snakes, curling around my wrists and my neck. It was all so ghastly that I couldn't . . . even if I wanted to again so soon, I could never . . . Aoife kept telling me to try but it was just impossible! Then it no longer mattered because the room was suddenly full of goblins, and everyone was shouting and saying that I had committed an unnatural act, fornicating with two women at the same time."

Tryffin expelled a long, thoughtful breath, and he and Meligraunce exchanged a meaningful glance. Some of this sounded disturbingly familiar. "Describe to Conn what you saw at the inn in Anoeth, Captain."

This Meligraunce did, in careful and painstaking detail. But Conn shook his head. "It didn't seem like that . . . her hair was around my throat but I could breathe. And her face was well above mine, staring down at me—it was like looking into the eyes of a tyger."

"Well," said Tryffin, putting a comforting hand on the boy's shoulder. "I will plead your innocence before the King. I suspect they were out to draw you into one of their damnable intrigues, and that the guards knew in advance where and when they ought to arrive."

Meligraunce frowned. "I do not think, Lord, that you should say as much to the King. Somehow, I doubt he would wish to hear it."

"No," said Tryffin, rising to his feet. "But I will think of something to say to him, some way to move him, some way to convince him that Conn should not be punished."

The King was in his smaller audience chamber, surrounded by his courtiers, when Tryffin and Conn were finally summoned to appear before him several hours later. That was a room that showed more art in its making than any of the others, with fluted pillars of clouded crystal, and tall arched windows all along one wall, and a number of the ticking mechanical clocks. Outside, it was beginning to snow again, but the sky was clear to the east, and it was possible, through the diamond-shaped windowpanes, to see the white moon and the orange moon hanging in the blue-black sky.

Aoife and Morna attended the King, exquisitely gowned and bejeweled, and seemed to be enjoying their sudden notoriety. Poor Conn, surrounded by an escort of goblin guards, was unable to look at either one of them, so deep was his shame. But the two elf women stared at him boldly, even smiling a little to see him so flushed and apprehensive.

"Conn mac Mathowlch, you have committed a serious offense and in my realm," the King said sternly, from his seat on the dais. The throne was made of spun glass that had been specially treated until it was harder than steel, so despite its fragile appearance it was well able to bear his weight. "But before I pass sentence on you, you are permitted to say a few words on your own behalf."

Tryffin flipped back his glittering cloak and dropped to one knee on the lower step—and was surprised to discover how much he hated it. *Is it because I have lost all respect for King Avallach . . . or because ruling in the Emperor's name these last two years has spoiled me so badly that I dislike bowing my head to any man?* Yet he remained perfectly composed, rather than show anyone how much the gesture cost him.

"Lord King, I would like to speak in his place, as is my right, by reason of the vows of fealty and service we have exchanged. Conn did not know that he was committing any crime under your laws; he is a stranger here, as you know, and ignorant of your customs. Also, you may wish to take his youth into account. He is really no more than a boy, and I know that the Sidhe use children gently. I hope that his punishment, if indeed anything more than a reprimand is necessary, will not be harsh."

The King made a helpless movement with his hands. "I am

sorry, Prince Tryffin, for any grief or inconvenience this may have caused you. Yet there can be no doubt that Conn is guilty, since he was caught in the act, and not only did the guards witness his shame, but both women have sworn to his guilt."

Tryffin shot each of the women a sharp glance, and received in each case a complaisant smile in return. "I wonder, Lord, that you would take their word so readily, since if he is at fault, then so must they be. Perhaps even more guilty than Conn himself, since they knew what he did was forbidden and yet they encouraged him. But I see that Morna and Aoife are both in this room, and that neither of them is bound or guarded. If they are not to be punished, then why should Conn? I am sure that the King of Annwn will be able to explain to me all these things, though I find them so puzzling myself."

All this time, Avallach was smiling a sorrowful smile, as though these things pained him but he was powerless to change them. "Well, it was wicked to tempt young Conn the way that they did. On that we are in perfect agreement. For doing so, their reputations will be utterly ruined."

There was a kind of titter that went around the room, which, combined with the smug expressions on both women's faces, led Tryffin to doubt that Avallach spoke the truth.

"But the law is written in this manner," the King continued. "No man or woman may commit fornication with two partners at the same time, for that is a wicked and unnatural act. But since Morna and Aoife were not making love to each other, and each only with your boy Conn . . ." Avallach shrugged. "Obviously, neither of them has violated the law, and he alone is guilty."

To Tryffin, this logic seemed cruel and dishonest, but he could hardly say so. Certainly his opinion of the King and of his justice had now fallen so low, he hardly knew what might be the consequences if he spoke too frankly. He rose slowly to his feet, moved backward toward the place where Mahaffy and the Captain were waiting for him.

"Then I suppose there is nothing left for me to say, except to ask you the penalty." He still had hope, in this shadow Gwyngelli, that the law would be more merciful than it was in the north. And even in Gorwynnion or Rhianedd, the sentence would not be worse than a dozen stripes and a heavy fine.

"I wish it were less," said the King. "But the sentence is written in our Book of the Law. The boy is condemned to seven years' servitude."

Conn made a strangled sound, and Mahaffy and Meligraunce cried out in protest. Tryffin was stunned. He had been ready to offer himself in Conn's place, since he was responsible for his squire's behavior, but now it was several moments before he could speak. "Seven years . . . that is a long time, and surely a harsh punishment when he has injured no one."

The King shrugged again, lifting one shoulder under the eagle-feather cape—a gesture that was beginning to wear on Tryffin's nerves. "This law has been handed down for a dozen generations; I am powerless to change it. But as he is young, and because I wish to oblige you, Prince Tryffin, this much I may do for him. Conn's service will be light during that time. The loss of his freedom should be enough."

To Tryffin's way of thinking it was far more than enough. And a sidelong glance told him that Conn was pale and his face set, as though he were struggling for control. He did not dare to look at the boy directly, for fear that a single sympathetic glance would cause Conn to break down and lose his courage before all these people. Tryffin longed to ask for a look at this Book of the Law, but he did not dare risk offending the King.

"Is there no way that I can ransom him? No fine or compensation that I can pay on his behalf?" He tried to think of something he might offer, but aside from his sword and the silver dagger, he had so little—it was humiliating to think that even the clothes he wore, the shimmering garments of pearl-grey silk, had been provided by the King. Then he remembered his golden armguards, the thick bracelets he wore on his arms, and began to unfasten their clasps. "These are heirlooms of my house . . ."

The King waved his offer aside. "I have great vaults filled with things every bit as fine. Yet your willingness to ransom the boy with the little that you have moves me. And so I will tell you something which, being strangers here, you probably do not know.

"There was a geas placed on me by one of my father's wizards, when I was no older than you are now: that anyone who can best me three times at Chess may ask of me any boon that he wishes, and I must grant it if I am able," the King continued. "You may wish to rescue the lad in that manner. However, I must warn you, in all that time only one man has ever defeated me, and that is my youngest son, who has done so but twice. Also, there are certain conditions which bind any man but one of my own sons, once I accept his challenge to a match."

"And what are those conditions?" Tryffin asked quietly, suspecting they were going to involve something distinctly unpleasant, or the King would never have volunteered the information.

"The first condition," said the King, "is that as soon as *I* win three games the match ends. The second condition is that if any man should challenge me and fail in his intent, he must pay the penalty."

Through the corner of his eye, Tryffin could see that Meligraunce was shaking his head, yet he was determined to ask the question. "And what is that penalty?"

King Avallach smiled incredulously, as though he could not believe the question. "The sentence, of course, is seven years' servitude."

Tryffin clenched a big fist, gave the King a dark look under his brows. "It seems to be a popular sentence."

"In Annwn," said the King, "the penalty for everything is seven years' servitude . . . except when the sentence is death."

Conn spoke out for the first time. "Prince Tryffin, you must not do this. The fault was mine, and I alone should suffer," he pleaded earnestly.

And Meligraunce said the same. "Lord Prince, you cannot risk your freedom in this way. You are a man with many responsibilities elsewhere."

"Undoubtedly, your Captain speaks the truth," said the King, sitting back in his chair. "You are a man on a quest and must not turn aside. The last man who challenged me and lost is now a slave in my kitchen, though he was a powerful elf lord before that . . . I was harder on him than I will be on Conn, for I knew very well that he meant to ask for my crown. But I will make the boy my squire, and I promise that he will not find me a harsh master."

But Tryffin was determined not to leave poor Conn a prisoner in the otherworld all that time. Seven years in Annwn might be seventy back in the lands he knew, and the boy might return to find all of his friends and family dead. Certainly, there were legends enough about prisoners in fairyland who had suffered exactly that fate.

Tryffin turned to the Captain. "By God, Meligraunce, do you think I can't do this? The last man to defeat me was Maelgwyn fab Menai, and that was many years back." Though he dared not say so where the King of the Sidhe might hear him, Tryffin did not think he could lose to this shadow, this mockery, this creature that could only feign his father's wisdom and intelligence. "Do you really suppose that I would fail now, with so much at stake?"

"Unfortunately, Lord Prince, I had a notion that you may. The way that they play the game—"

"I am waiting," said the King, rising from his throne of glass, staring down at Tryffin from the dais, "to hear if you wish to challenge me."

Tryffin glanced at Conn, who was still protesting, and quickly made up his mind. "I will play you, Lord, and attempt to win the lad's freedom."

"That being so," said King Avallach, descending the steps, with his feathered cloak trailing behind him, "I see no reason to delay the contest. Shall we begin at once?"

Tryffin thought for a moment, then nodded his head. "I would sooner begin than put it off and keep young Conn in suspense."

The King made a gesture, and two of his squires left the hall, to return a short while later with a small table, a golden chessboard, and some ivory playing pieces. As Dylan and the other squire proceeded to lay out the men on the board, Tryffin felt a sinking sensation, a cold sweat break out on his skin. The pieces were set with emeralds and opals, and made to resemble magical beasts—harpies, manticores, griffons, gargoyles, dragons, and basilisks—and their arrangement across one corner of the board was completely unfamiliar.

He looked up from the board to meet the King's gaze. "I ask your pardon, Lord King. I seem to have promised more than I can perform. This is not the game of Chess that I know, not the game I have played in my father's kingdom."

He felt his face go hot; never before had he been caught boasting of a skill that he did not possess. "Perhaps you will allow me to withdraw the challenge, until I have had time to study this game . . . until I can provide you with . . . some better amusement."

A look of pure delight came into the King's amber eyes. "I fear that once the challenge has been made it cannot be withdrawn. Yet as you say, the contest would hold little interest, if you are really so ignorant. I will give you . . ." He paused and appeared to consider. "I will give you the time between now and sunrise to learn the rules and a little of the strategy." He pointed to one of the mechanical clocks, which stood on the floor at the back of the dais: a collection of silver gears and golden wheels encased in a tall crystal cabinet. "That is a period of twelve hours. More than that, a board and playing pieces will be provided for you, along with a teacher of suitable skill and experience who will come to your rooms this evening after supper."

With an effort, Tryffin concealed his dismay. "With the King's permission, then, I will retire to some quiet place to clear my mind, the better to receive those lessons at the proper time."

"Yes," said the King, his smile growing wide, and now it could be seen that he, just as much as the Fairy women, had a fine set of pointed teeth, "I think that would be best. For I ought to warn you that I would be very disappointed, should I find myself facing an unworthy opponent in the morning."

The trees have lost their shape under the snow,
their branches broken by the bitter weather.
Loch Gorm and Loch Shelligh are frozen; fish are
prisoners under the ice.

> —*from a poem found on the margin*
> *of a manuscript at the monastery*
> *of St. Mawban*

13.

A Cold Season in Achren

Winter came to the land of Achren, and still Gwenlliant and Grifflet lingered in the house of the twelve young priestesses. The short days and the bitter weather kept everyone indoors for most of the time, but there were many tasks to keep the women busy.

"There are visitors in the woods," said Maelinn one frosty afternoon, as she sat carding wool by the fire. "They arrived this morning, perhaps an hour after dawn." When the others turned to stare at her, she tossed her head and asked, "Did you imagine there could be men in the forest, *my* forest, and the trees not inform me?"

Gwenlliant sat quietly, forbearing to speak. Though it was true that Maelinn had not ventured beyond the clearing all day, and everyone knew it, she had also exchanged a few words in private with Ceri and Pethboc, who *had* been out in the early morning, and it was likely that one or the other had brought the news.

"And while the trees were telling you that," said Caithne, who had also witnessed the whispered conversation, "did any of the more talkative elms and hazels happen to also mention what manner of men they were?"

Caithne and Sceith were weaving charms out of feathers and scarlet thread, to be hung up over the beds in the loft and ward off "winter chills and inflammations"—so Sceith had informed Gwenlliant.

"Men from the High Prince's warband," Maelinn answered calmly, for once ignoring the redhead's sarcasm. There was much speculation among the other priestesses as to just how far her influence extended within the wood, whether Maelinn could actually speak to the trees, the birds, and all the animals as she claimed, or only (as Sceith and Caithne insisted) with the foxes and the owls, which were sacred to Maelinn's goddess, who had many different aspects and was invoked by various names—Goleuddydd, the Green Lady, and the White Cailleach were the most commonly used.

Gwenlliant, who listened in on these conversations but never spoke up, was inclined to the middle view. She had known the language of trees all of her life, and it was easy to see that Maelinn did not, but she thought that many of the birds, the owls in particular, acted as Maelinn's spies—the same as Pali, Ceri, and Pethboc did—and that whatever lived at the bottom of the well spoke with the High Priestess more often than to any of the others.

Yet it was difficult to tell how much Maelinn actually learned from the birds and the foxes, since Gwenlliant did not know their language herself. She had an impression, however, that the songbirds, at least, were far too scatterbrained to be of much use.

"I take them to come from Prince Caerthinn," Maelinn continued. "Because the linen they wore was very fine and they carried swords of real iron—or so I was informed." She glanced around the room. "Now, who would like to go with me to meet them?"

"I will go," said Pali, which was expected. She was Maelinn's most abject follower, as everyone knew.

"And so will I," said Regan, which was not, she being one of Caithne's closest friends. "You know that my father has been very ill for many months now, and they may have news of him," she added, a bit defensively. Her clan had holdings near Caerthinn's hall, so this was perfectly reasonable.

"Please," said Gwenlliant, "I would like to meet these visitors if I might. I know so little of the men of your land, for if you will remember, I have never even seen one."

Maelinn reached across and gave her hand a squeeze. "Then it is time that you did so; and of course you must come. Imagine, you have been here since summer and it is nearly the middle of winter, Gwenhwyach!"

From the others, Gwenlliant had gathered that the prevailing opinion was that the High Priestess treated her like a pet or a plaything, because she was younger and something of a novelty, with her strange coloring and her ignorance of their customs—of a similar sort had been her devotion to Caithne and Sceith when they first arrived, but that friendship had withered when the two sisters began to show too much independence. But Gwenlliant continued to believe that Maelinn's displays of affection were genuine. The High Priestess was proud and difficult, but she placed a high value on loyalty and friendship . . . so high, that anything which seemed like betrayal could apparently never be forgiven.

Maelinn put aside her wool and her combs, left her seat, and put on her squirrel-skin cloak. Gwenlliant, Pali, and Regan did likewise. It was too cold for her own plain cloak, so Gwenlliant wore one which had belonged to Maelinn; it was still very fine and lined with grey fur. Grifflet, she bundled up in all of his clothes, everything that still fit him, anyway. She never let him out of her sight, not for a single instant, took him everywhere with her, for fear she might lose him here in the past, should Dame Ceinwen ever work the magic to whisk her back home.

Outside, there was snow on the ground all around the house, and a dusting of snow up in the trees, but the path through the forest was bare, if a little bit icy and slick. Gwenlliant kept a tight hold on Grifflet's hand to keep him from slipping, and planted her own steps carefully.

The path was a familiar one lined with berry bushes, but Maelinn took an unexpected turning, and they suddenly came out of the trees in a small clearing which Gwenlliant had not even known was there. There was a round hut at the center of this clearing, a beehive of stone without any windows and only a single doorway built low to the ground. "What is this place?" said Gwenlliant. "And who, if anyone, lives here?"

"It is where visitors always stay . . . for if they are grown men, you know, they dare not approach our house and our well," said Maelinn. "While if they have business at the other temple, they may only come just within sight of the houses and not any closer—unless they should happen to be priests."

Gwenlliant had known all along there must be someplace like this, because the priestesses often went out into the wood and returned to the cloister, bearing sacks of wool or grain, or pottery urns, or other necessary things, which had obviously been left somewhere in the forest for them to take home as offerings.

Lowering her head, Maelinn used one hand to push aside the deerskin hanging in the doorway and went into the hut. Gwenlliant and Grifflet followed her in, and Pali and Regan arrived a moment later. It was dim inside, the only illumination a little cold winter sunlight coming in through a tiny smokehole at the top. The floor was made of packed earth, and the hut was bare of furnishings.

"There is no one here . . . they have gone on to the other temple, and may not even come back," said Regan, sounding disappointed. "They had a message for Gwythyr and nothing for us at all."

"No . . . see, they have left some of their things here," said Maelinn, gesturing toward a pile of blankets and furs against the wall, which no one had been able to see before their eyes adjusted to the dim light. "They obviously intend to spend the night, and we shall wait right here until they return." So saying, she pulled out one of the blankets and spread it across the ground, then seated herself cross-legged.

The other young women disposed themselves likewise, Gwenlliant taking a seat on the corner of Maelinn's blanket, and the other two spreading a fur out for themselves. Grifflet, however, made a thorough exploration of the hut, poking his little nose into all the darkest places, finding nothing there to interest him but a handful of pebbles, which he would have swallowed had not Gwenlliant prevented him.

They did not have long to wait before voices were heard in the clearing outside. Maelinn put a finger to her lips to silence her companions, and Gwenlliant pulled the little boy into her lap and whispered in his ear to keep him quiet.

The deerskin was moved aside, and three men came into the hut, all very dark and bearded. The smaller of the three wore a long white tunic and a crimson cloak, and something about his eyes, which were very large and expressive, was so like Maelinn that Gwenlliant had no trouble placing him as Gwythyr, the Priest of Cerridwen.

The other two wore stiff leather tunics, and what looked like light antique armor: armguards and gorgets and wide metal belts, which reminded her of some pieces that Tryffin wore on ceremonial occasions—except that *theirs* were made of bronze and other base metals and everything that Tryffin had was made of Gwyngelli gold.

At the sight of Maelinn and the other young women, Gwythyr drew back in surprise. Then he shook his head and said with a bitter-sounding laugh, "I should have known I would find you here, even without an invitation."

Maelinn responded with a challenging glance. "And since when does the Lady of the Wood and the Well wait to be summoned at anyone's convenience? Indeed, this is my own place . . . as are all places in the wood, except for that small bit of land my predecessor gave to yours . . . and so I shall come here anytime that I choose."

The other men appeared painfully embarrassed by Gwythyr's rudeness, and went down kneeling submissively before the High Priestess.

"Lady, your visit honors us," said one. He looked about nineteen or twenty and was excessively handsome, and except for the beard, which was short and precise, reminded Gwenlliant of Mahaffy Guillyn. "Indeed, we would have sent a message to pay our respects, but your brother . . . that is, Lord Gwythyr said—"

"I said I would not send one of my acolytes such a long way on a cold day," Gwythyr finished for him. He folded his arms over his chest. "These men have business with me and not with you."

Maelinn cocked her head to one side. "And what, I wonder, would that business be?" she asked, addressing her question to the Prince's men. Her dark eyes were flashing, and her red lips had parted in a predatory smile.

The man who had spoken before shifted his weight uncomfortably, so that his leather garments creaked. "If it should please the Lady of the Wood, the High Prince has summoned Lord Gwythyr to attend the Midwinter festivities at Caer Bannawg."

Maelinn went on talking to the messengers, completely ignoring her brother. "That is most interesting, Tadhg. And so you say Gwythyr is summoned but I am not? I believe that I have been slighted."

"No, no," said Tadhg. A sheen of sweat appeared on his brow, and his whole aspect was so contrite, his manner so abject, that Gwenlliant thought, *These men are truly afraid of Maelinn. She is an important person, a powerful person in the world beyond the wood, and it is only because her companions are also important and powerful, though to a lesser degree, that they do not tremble before her the way these men are trembling now.*

"That is . . ." the unfortunate Tadhg was stammering. "I am certain the Lady would be welcome if she chose to come. In truth, it was your brother Lord Gereint who suggested to Prince Caerthinn that Lord Gwythyr might wish to celebrate the rituals at the Midwinter Feast, as the Lady of the Wood was gracious enough to visit during the spring. So of course no slight could have been possibly intended."

At this, Gwythyr looked much amused, and something twitched at the corner of Maelinn's mouth; she might have been sharing his amusement, or it might have signaled intense irritation. "Of course," she said sweetly. "And that being so—and because you have explained the situation so clearly—I believe I will accompany you to Caer Bannawg, after all."

Her brother's smile instantly faded. "You cannot do that," said Gwythyr, unfolding his arms and putting his hands on his hips, under the scarlet cloak. "Prince Caerthinn sent horses for me and my attendants to ride, but as you were not expected there are none for you and your women. Unless . . . but no, it is a long walk to Caer Bannawg, and a cold one this time of year."

Maelinn sniffed. "And do you think that my only choice is walking or riding?" she said, very low. "I think you know better than that."

Tadhg and his companion put their heads close together, exchanged a few whispered words between them. "If it please you, Lady Maelinn," said the older and plainer man, clearing his throat, "we have come provided with sufficient gold to buy horses in Tremoc where we left the others . . . the village, as you know, is only two or three miles distant, and we can make the arrangements tonight if you wish. Only we will need to know how many companions you will be bringing with you."

Maelinn considered for a moment, then turned to Gwenlliant. "Can you ride, Gwenhwyach?"

Gwenlliant felt her heart leap with excitement, at the thought of meeting Prince Caerthinn and his friend Mabonograin, and of all she might learn at Caer Bannawg—perhaps the very thing she had come into the past to discover. "Yes," she said. "But . . . the horse will have to be very gentle, since it will have to carry Grifflet as well."

"I would like to go also," said Regan, lowering her voice to an urgent whisper. "Maelinn, I know you would prefer somebody else, but I have good reason—"

"I know your reasons, and of course you may come," Maelinn replied, also under her breath. "Do you think I would keep you from your dying father for petty spite? You listen too much to Caithne."

Regan flushed. Gwenlliant could see that it had cost her a great deal to ask Maelinn for this favor, and that she was both relieved and a little embarrassed that the answer had come so swiftly and generously. "You are very good, Maelinn," she said contritely. "I see my error and I will correct it."

But the High Priestess shook her head. "Do not take this as a sign of friendship or an attempt to regain your good will, Regan. I know where your loyalties lie, and it matters very little. Only remember, after this, that I always do what is right, whatever my own feelings may be." She glanced over at Pali. "You will ride with Pali, because she is afraid of horses and you are not."

The men appeared greatly relieved that her party would be so small. "Three horses, then. That will be easy enough," said Tadhg, with a sigh.

Maelinn rose gracefully to her feet. "Then it is time that my companions and I began to prepare for this journey. Where shall we meet you and at what hour?"

"That shall be for you to decide," said the older man. "So long as we arrive before the festivities begin, four days from now—"

"It is best that we leave tomorrow morning, then, in case there should be delays along the road," Maelinn broke in. "We shall meet you at the stone circle below the wood, an hour after sunrise."

With a triumphant glance in the direction of her brother, who grimaced and then made a flourishing bow as she walked by, Maelinn walked out of the hut, followed by Gwenlliant and the other women.

"What do you think of Gwythyr? Is he not handsome?" Maelinn said in Gwenlliant's ear, as they walked down the icy forest pathway.

That was rather a surprising question, considering the apparent animosity between them. "I think your brother has a great air of elegance . . . but also of arrogance," Gwenlliant answered truthfully. "And I thought he was very unpleasant to you. Why did he not wish you to visit the High Prince?"

Maelinn laughed. "He was only jesting. Of course he wishes

me to go along. Or rather, it was only a test to see if I should be strong enough and determined enough to resist him. It is always so with the Sons and the Daughters of the Boar. We appear to be a quarrelsome clan, but we contend among ourselves only to increase our strength and refine our cunning; we are really quite affectionate among ourselves."

She smiled at Gwenlliant's expression of disbelief. "You will see in the morning how it is. Now it has already been decided that I am to make the journey, my brother will make every effort to be a good companion along the way."

The morning dawned clear and cold. As they had already bundled together everything they meant to take with them the night before, Maelinn and her traveling companions had only to dress and break their fast before leaving the cruck-built house and beginning the short walk to the stone circle at the edge of the wood.

The men and the horses were already waiting for them, just outside the shadow of the trees. Gwythyr was accompanied by two young boys in grey, apparently acolytes. Just as Maelinn had predicted, the priest's face lit at the sight of his sister, and he came striding to meet her. "So," he laughed, as he took one of her hands between both of his, "you did not insist on coming out of perversity only, but really intend to grace us with your presence. It is more than we deserve, but we shall strive to be worthy."

Maelinn laughed also, standing on her toes to give him a kiss on the cheek. "That will teach you to take me more seriously after this." Her eyes were sparkling with excitement and pleasure—not for the journey only, Gwenlliant guessed. She really did seem to enjoy her brother's company, and he to delight in hers this morning.

In fact, Gwythyr seemed so determined to make himself agreeable, he helped Maelinn to mount her pretty cream-colored mare and then turned to offer the same service to Gwenlliant.

"Gwenhwyach, is it not?" he said, as she settled herself in the saddle, atop a sedate-looking dapple-grey. "You are not one of the twelve priestesses, though you are dressed like one of them." The blue wool gown was in her bundle, waiting to be worn at the Prince's court, and she was wearing a gown of saffron linen which had belonged to Caithne, along with Maelinn's fur-lined cloak.

Gwenlliant shook her head and tried to take back her hand,

which the priest was still holding. His grip tightened for a moment—just long enough to demonstrate that he would not brook resistance—and then he released her, turning to sweep up Grifflet and hand him up to her. "Of course you could not be, or else you would not have brought your little brother into the temple with you."

She took Grifflet and helped him to straddle the saddle in front of her, showed him how to hold on for himself, at the same time assuring him that she would not let him fall. When he seemed comfortable and secure, she looked up again, to see that Gwythyr was still standing there, still watching her. She felt a burning blush rise in her cheeks. Only one man had ever dared to look at her that way, as though wondering what she looked like under her clothes, and that had been Calchas fab Corfil. More than that, her hand was still throbbing from the crushing grip he had given it, and she was certain he had hurt her on purpose.

"Not her brother, but her son," said Maelinn, sounding considerably less good-humored than before. "She is the widow of a very powerful man . . . see the ring and the bracelet he gave her? She is not for you, Gwythyr. You will have to do your wooing elsewhere."

Gwenlliant, watching the interest fade from his eyes, felt a mixture of relief and disgust.

He is even worse in his own way than Calchas, who at least wanted me, who at least felt a kind of twisted affection, she thought, as the priest shrugged his shoulders and backed away. *But this Gwythyr is more like Rhun of Yrgoll, one of those men who see women only as playthings or prizes, and think that they have done something remarkably clever whenever they deflower a virgin.*

"Do not worry," said Regan, bringing the gelding that she shared with Pali around on the other side, as Gwythyr moved away. "He does not bring any of his wives with him, which almost certainly means that he is seeking to acquire a new one, but it is the Princess Tinne he is after, not you. It is just that he likes to show his power over women whenever he can—that is why he became the Priest of Cerridwen to begin with . . . three wives, and all of them sworn to silence and to the temple for life, and therefore unable to resist his will in any way."

"That is not fair; you know he had a vision which told him the goddess Cerridwen wanted him," said Pali. She was holding on to Regan's waist as if for dear life, and the face inside the hood of her red squirrel cloak was white and terrified. She really was deathly afraid of horses, but her loyalty to Maelinn impelled her to make the journey.

That loyalty, however, only extended so far, because she added in a whisper, "Yet I do not like him much, either, Gwenhwyach. Maelinn was only teasing about him wanting to marry you, but you would do very well to stay out of his way."

Gwenlliant nodded grimly. And she thought, *If he tries to put his hands on me ever again, I won't even care if he learns I am a witch. I will crush his bones into dust, if I must, to keep him away from me.* He might be no more than the shadow of a man long dead, but for all that, she was not about to allow him to take any liberties.

In Annwn, the hour for supper had already passed. In his tower bedchamber, Tryffin was pacing the floor, still waiting for the chessboard and the teacher "of suitable skill and experience" which King Avallach had promised to send him.

"I suppose," said the Governor to Meligraunce, who was striding along at his side, "that you were trying to tell me they play Chess differently among the Sidhe, and fool that I was, I would not listen."

Meligraunce shook his head. "The fault is mine, for being so hesitant . . . I was not entirely certain that it *was* a different game, for as the Governor knows, I do not play Chess myself. And I have only seen it played once, here in Annwn. Had I known it would later prove important, I would have paid closer attention."

Tryffin dropped a hand on the Captain's shoulder. "I imagine they do not play the game often, at least not where they might catch the King's eyes, lest he take a desire to grow proficient at the game as a veiled threat to his position and power."

He paused by the raised hearth in the middle of the room, stood gazing into the flames. There was half a tree lying on the immense stone slab, the crown of an appletree with the leaves still on, which had been burning for days and days without being consumed, and the flames were silver and purple. Whose sorcery made that fire, Tryffin did not know, but he suspected it was the work of King Avallach himself; he did not seem to be the sort of man who would keep elfin wizards or warlocks more powerful than he was under his roof.

"Tonight in the hall down below was the very first time I had even spotted a chessboard since we arrived . . . though I have seen the Sidhe playing at cards, or dice, or Fox and Geese . . . and any number of similar pastimes."

Meligraunce cleared his throat. "If it should please you, I would like to share your lessons."

Tryffin turned to stare at him. "By all means, do as you like. But why this sudden desire to learn to play Chess? I have offered to teach you often enough—I think you would make an interesting opponent—but you have always regarded the game as . . . what? Too frivolous, or simply above your station?"

The Captain shrugged. "How I have regarded the game in the past seems unimportant now. If you should fail to rescue Conn, I have an idea that I might wish to challenge King Avallach myself . . . once I have gained a little proficiency."

"No, Meligraunce, it would be my turn first," said Mahaffy fiercely. He and Conn had come into the room from the antechamber so quietly, Tryffin had not even heard them enter. "I don't pretend to your sagacity, but I have been playing the game since I was a little lad, and the rules here can't be so *very* different. No, Prince Tryffin, I am determined to do it," he added quietly, when the Governor opened his mouth to protest. "And with far better reason to do so than Meligraunce—who might just as well be serving you here as elsewhere. You are needed back in Mochdreff, and the fate of the people, my own people, depends on your safe return."

Tryffin crossed the room, flung himself down into a chair by the window. "I wish I had kept that more clearly in mind, before I tried to play the hero and rescue Conn. Sweet Jesus! I have a wife and a son that I may never see again, if I don't find my way back to Mochdreff."

"It is my fault," Conn said miserably. "No one is saying so, but we all know the truth. I wish I had died before I brought you to this."

Tryffin shook his head. "You may be partly to blame for your own unfortunate plight—and I hope to God you have learned a valuable lesson—but *my* peril comes entirely through my own self-conceit, for which it appears I will soon be justly punished."

He signaled to Conn, who crossed the room and knelt down at his feet. "This may be the very last time I am ever to command your service, Cousin, so listen carefully." As the relationship between them was so distant that neither the Governor nor Conn ever alluded to it, this form of address immediately fixed the boy's attention. He knew that what Tryffin said next would be very important. "No matter what may happen to me, you must serve the King to the best of your ability and with all the loyalty and good will that you can muster. With his favor, you may have an easy and pleasant life here in Annwn; without it, things could be painfully difficult, nor would you be doing me a shred of good by earning my displeasure."

"If you are to be a scullion down in the kitchen, then so will I be," said Conn, fighting back tears. "If you are a groom in his stables, I want to be the same."

Tryffin shook his head. "I doubt that Avallach has gone to such lengths merely to gain another potscrubber or stableboy. I believe he was sincere when he offered to make you his squire, but I think he has something considerably more difficult and dangerous in mind for me."

"Then you think that it was all a trap," said Meligraunce, frowning thoughtfully. In the firelight, the planes and the angles of his lean, intelligent face were more pronounced than ever. "With Conn as the bait to draw you in. I recall that you thought the guards arrived far too conveniently. But if that is so . . . why did the King hold his hand so long? We have been here, by my count, almost three weeks."

"He *didn't* hold his hand," said Mahaffy, folding his arms and glaring into the fire. "Most likely, he has been setting his traps from the very beginning. It is just that we have managed to avoid them. When we first arrived here, one of his squires tried to challenge me to a duel over some trifling matter, but I refused. A few days later, I learned that challenges of that sort are strictly forbidden inside the fortress. I assumed at the time that the penalty would be light, or Dylan would never have challenged me . . . and so it would have been light for the King's squire, who probably owes him seven years' service, anyway."

Tryffin and Meligraunce exchanged a glance, remembering that this same Dylan was the young elf that Garreg and Ciag had caught apparently working spells in this very room.

"But I would be the one in trouble now, instead of Conn," Mahaffy continued, "had I agreed to fight him."

"You were much wiser than I was," said the boy, rising to his feet. "If only I had shown the same good sense."

Mahaffy made an impatient gesture. "Don't be tiresome, Conn—it was not the same sort of temptation at all. Do you think I *wanted* to fight Dylan? What honor could I gain as a belted knight dueling with a squire, and a half-blood goblin at that? It was pride, not good sense, that kept me out of trouble . . . the same pride that usually trips me up. And you have probably sidestepped trouble a time or two, without even realizing that you were doing so. We none of us know their laws or their customs, and it was only a matter of time before one of us made a serious—"

He was interrupted by a knock on the door. When Conn went to answer it, one of Prince Gruffydd's attendants, an elf named Brion, came into the room followed by two goblins carrying a carved wooden chest between them.

"I take it," said Tryffin, with a wry smile, "that you have been chosen to teach me the game of Chess as the Sidhe play it?" This Brion had one of the youngest faces in the castle, younger even than the half-goblin Dylan, and though it was difficult to guess at a Fairy's age, Tryffin thought Brion was still a child. He was also different from the others in that his hair was white, his eyes silver, and his ears ever so slightly pointed.

"I play the game with Prince Gruffydd often, and I am accounted a very good player," Brion responded, rather stiffly. "It was Prince Ffergus who sent me, out of sympathy for your plight. But if you would prefer someone else . . ."

"No, no," said Tryffin, rising from his seat. "I am grateful to Prince Ffergus for sending you . . . and also Prince Gruffydd for sparing you."

If there was any Fairy the Governor was inclined to trust, it was the King's warm-hearted and impulsive older son. Also, Brion had always struck him as comparatively intelligent and honest—Tryffin might have wanted an older and more experienced teacher, but as it hardly seemed likely that one would be offered, he was happy enough to settle for this one.

"Pour me a cup of wine, Conn, and also one for Brion," said the Governor. "This promises to be a long and thirsty night."

And Cerddin's fortress was called Castell Carbonec, *which for many years after his death was avoided as a haunted and uncanny spot.*

—*From* The Nine Sorrowful Tales of
the Misfortunes of Mochdreff

14.

Juniper Wine

Caer Bannawg was built on an island in a lake, with a causeway going out from the shore to the wooden stockade which surrounded the fort. Whether the island itself was natural or had been created by men, with earth and timber pilings, was not precisely clear, but it was so nearly symmetrical with its four equal sides and nearly square corners that the latter seemed likely. Gwenlliant had not really been expecting a castle made of stone like the ones that she knew, but this crowded little village with its low buildings of various sizes and shapes, and the great wooden hall of the High Prince rising up above the rest, came as something of a shock.

The ground for one thing was undeniably muddy, and the straw which had been put down to absorb the moisture did *not*. There was not even a flagstone pathway to offer a dry place to walk, and with the sheep and the cattle and the horses milling around, to say nothing of the people, there was very little room for walking, anyway.

Gwenlliant dismounted gingerly and refused to put Grifflet down, for all that he struggled in her arms and demanded to be allowed to walk. She knew she would be a long time cleaning him up, if she once let him down into the mud. Meanwhile, Maelinn and the others were holding up their skirts and making faces, as though they had forgotten what a dirty place it was. As for Gwythyr, he only smiled unpleasantly and said to his sister,

"You insisted on coming here in the wintertime . . . what did you expect?"

"I expect," said Maelinn, with her head very high, "that when I next venture out into the air, there will be a path of clean straw between the house where I am staying and Prince Caerthinn's hall."

"That will be seen to immediately," said Tadhg, lending her a hand up the low embankment leading up to the house of the Princess Tinne, which had unoccupied rooms specifically set aside for Maelinn's infrequent visits.

Inside, it was dry and clean if a little dark, with a narrow set of steps leading up to those rooms. The entire ground floor was given to the Princess and her handmaidens; the story above was reserved for guests.

At the top of the stairs was a large room, a sort of solar with a line of shuttered windows along one wall. When these were opened, the room was quite sunny and pleasant, and proved to be well furnished with tables and benches and stools, and a single chair with a low back and a red velvet cushion. "We shall need rushlights, linens, rugs, sleeping furs, dishes, wine, and food," said Maelinn, glancing around her.

"I will see to it personally," said Tadhg. "Had you been expected—"

The High Priestess cut him off with a motion of her hand. "Where is my brother Gwythyr to stay?"

"In the house of Lord Gereint, where he shall want for nothing. As soon as I have reported to Prince Caerthinn and informed him of your presence, I will send in servants with all that you need," said Tadhg.

Maelinn nodded and allowed him to go. "Well, Gwenhwyach, what do you think of this place?" she asked, with a sweeping gesture.

Gwenlliant put Grifflet down on his feet. "I think it is not so nice as the place where we live, but I am very eager to meet your High Prince . . . that is, if I am permitted to do so."

"That can be easily arranged," said Maelinn. "He will undoubtedly arrange a feast in my honor tomorrow, and you shall attend me."

In the morning, the Princess Tinne came to pay her respects, along with her five handmaidens. She was very young and exceedingly pretty, with a pale face and a remarkable amount of

dark hair, which she wore in numerous thick braids, looped up
and pinned in place with jeweled hairpins. *She* curtsied low to
Maelinn, who responded by taking her hands, lifting her up, and
kissing her warmly. Though they were very easy and pleasant
together after that, yet it was clear to Gwenlliant that the Lady of
the Wood and the Well far outranked the High Prince's sister.

Tinne wore a gown of creamy wool marvelously embroidered
about the hem, and a number of bracelets, made of almost every
material imaginable: gold and silver, bronze and copper, wood
and bone, jade, amber, ivory, and seashell. For all her sophisti-
cated dress, she looked frail and childlike under her crown of
heavy braids . . . and rather as though she might prefer to sit
down on the wooden floor and play with Grifflet, instead of
sedately on a stool, speaking of alliances, treaties, marriages, and
politics with Maelinn.

"You have a very sweet little boy," she whispered to Gwenlliant. "Until last winter, I lived with my own young brother and
sisters . . . and now I have a house of my own as you see and
live in great state, but I *do* miss the children."

And this, thought Gwenlliant, *is the girl that beast of a
Gwythyr seemingly intends to take into the temple and make her
his wife.* It was something Gwenlliant would have given much to
prevent, but aside from the fact that she had no idea how, she had
come into the past to observe and to learn, not to interfere. *It all
of it happened a long time ago, if it happened at all . . . and is
long past hurting or helping, anyway.*

But that was small consolation. For the first time, Gwenlliant
began to understand Dame Ceinwen's teachings, how painful,
how truly heartbreaking it was if you allowed yourself to care, to
see these shadows repeat their old sorrows, follies, and disasters
and be powerless to act, unable to halt the inexorable march of
events.

Gwenlliant sighed. After all, she had no idea how it would
really turn out, and the Princess appeared to be a pliable,
biddable girl—perhaps she and Gwythyr would get on very well.

The expected invitation to a feast in the hall arrived in the
morning, so by late afternoon Maelinn and her companions
began to prepare for the festivities.

Gwenlliant, of course, put on the blue-violet wool, while
Maelinn arrayed herself in the green silk gown she had once
described as a gift from Mabonograin. Regan and Pali had
nothing so fine, but they did put on all of their jewels and

ornaments, as did Maelinn, and the four young women took turns dressing each other's hair. In their cloaks of silky soft furs, they looked regal and imposing.

Down in the yard, the way to the hall was covered with clean dry straw as promised, and people drew back respectfully, making way for Maelinn and her attendants, bowing their heads—some of them even going so far as to kneel down in the mud—as the three young priestesses walked by. This, thought Gwenlliant, as she and Grifflet brought up the rear, was what Maelinn lived for, this awe, this majesty, this power. But in order to achieve it, in order to experience and wield that influence a very few weeks out of the year, Maelinn had to live apart the rest of the time, remove herself from the temporal power of the court, and accept the isolation of the cloister in the wood. It was little wonder that her powerful frustration, her longing for the life she had left behind, made her occasionally difficult to live with. Gwenlliant thought that Caithne, Sceith, and the others might understand that, and not spend so much of their time and energy plaguing the life out of Maelinn.

The banquet hall was lighted by torches, and it was a magnificent structure inside, the roof supported by a double row of wooden columns, as beautifully carved as the beams and the pillars in the house in the wood. There was no dais or High Table as Gwenlliant might recognize it, but half of the room had a raised floor which was covered with bearskins and wolf pelts and smaller furs sewn together for rugs and pillows, where the High Prince might recline at his ease with the men of his warband, their wives, and such noble and powerful lords and ladies who joined him at the feast.

Gwenlliant knew Prince Caerthinn at once, for not only did he wear a thin band of gold encircling his brow, but he was just as Maelinn and the others had described him: plain, dark, dull, and dissatisfied-looking. That changed when he turned to address the lively young man sitting beside him, drinking mead from a wooden beaker; then his face lit up and he appeared quite pleasant, talking and laughing with his odd companion.

"Who is that?" whispered Gwenlliant, as she took a seat on the platform with Maelinn, Pali, and Regan. "The man with the golden rings in his ears?"

"That is Mabonograin, the Prince of the Hill Country. You have probably never seen anyone like him before," said Pali, sitting down on a sheepskin rug.

Gwenlliant shook her head. If this animated little man was related to Tryffin, it was hard to see it. But then, the pure Gwyngellach, like the true Mochdreffi, were a slender, dark-eyed race. Mabonograin wore his brown hair down to his shoulders, all except a great knot which he wore at the back, and his face, strange to relate, was covered with delicate whorls and spirals which someone had painted in blue. The result, while not unattractive, was highly barbaric.

"Is that woad?" asked Gwenlliant, under her breath. "Does it ever come off?"

"It wears off slowly, and then he has it painted all over again," said Regan. "I do not care for the effect myself, but some women think that it makes him look virile. Or . . . perhaps it is just Mabonograin they like, and they would say the same if he dipped himself in mud and stuck straws in his hair instead."

Prince Caerthinn had spotted Maelinn by now, and he poured her a goblet of mead with his own hands, and sent it by one of his servants, who presented the cup on bended knee. Maelinn accepted it graciously, drank, and then passed the goblet on to Pali and Regan.

Maelinn was in her element, smiling and talking to the people on every side of her, merry and affectionate even with Regan. *This is where she is at her best, this is where she ought to be,* thought Gwenlliant. Yet she knew very well that without the status she gained as High Priestess, her friend would be no happier here than she was at the house in the wildwood.

The evening wore on, the torches burned low. Someone gave Gwenlliant a wooden cup, somebody else filled it, not with mead, but with something that tasted of juniper and spices. Regan told her it was a sacred beverage, which the folk of Achren drank only at this time of year; it was supposed to bring on dreams and visions, though only in those who already possessed a touch of the second sight. The food went around on wooden platters, roasted fowl, honey cakes, baked apples, and a great deal more, which everyone was apparently expected to reach for as the servants passed by, and eat with bare hands.

Regan left early, because a man had come to escort the young priestess to her father's house, five miles distant, and she wanted to arrive before nightfall. Maelinn and Pali had their heads together whispering. Gwenlliant was aware of curious glances directed her way. Some people seemed friendly and inclined to speak, but she had no time for conversation; she was too busy feeding Grifflet and watching and listening to all of the things that were happening around her. Also, she was beginning to feel dizzy, for the juniper-berry wine was highly intoxicating.

It was very clear that Tinne and Mabonograin were deeply in love. They did not speak to each other, they never touched, but there was a kind of burning consciousness between them, and the cheeks of the Princess turned red, the face of the Prince under his blue paint went white and strained, whenever their eyes met.

At last, he could no longer keep silent. "Will you go riding tomorrow?" he asked, very low. There was a tenderness in his voice, a protective quality to his posture as he leaned over to speak in her ear, that might just as well have shouted their passion to the entire hall.

Tinne shook her head, refused to meet his gaze. "I have too many guests to attend to. Also . . . the Priest of Cerridwen asked me already, and I said no," she said, in a soft, breathless voice. She made a tiny gesture in the direction of Gwythyr, who was sitting on a bearskin with a man very much like him but considerably older, watching the young couple with covetous eyes.

Gwenlliant looked back at Tinne and Mabonograin, and she was suddenly assailed by a strong presentiment, a premonition more powerful than any she had ever experienced before. The air was filled with the stench of burning, a strong wind was blowing ashes in her eyes, and all around was the clatter of steel and voices crying out as if in great anguish. The vision did not last very long, but after it had passed she felt weak and drained.

And she thought to herself, with a rising sense of pity and horror, *This is where it all begins, perhaps a thousand years of hatred and bloodshed . . . not with stolen lands, or with evil magic, not with mighty princes contending for power . . . but here in this hall with these two gentle people who have fallen in love.*

After that vision, it seemed too much to bear, seeing the two young lovers together, so Gwenlliant spent the next few days avoiding them both as much as she could. Unfortunately, that also meant that she missed many chances to be presented to Caerthinn the High Prince, for he and Mabonograin were nearly inseparable.

Yet the day came when Maelinn was out walking with

Gwenlliant and Grifflet, along the rocky causeway toward the shore—because the afternoon was mild and there was no better spot to take a little air—and met Caerthinn and his warband along with Mabonograin, returning from a morning ride.

"I think it is time that you told me the name of this mysterious maiden, who has everyone talking about her eyes and her hair," said Caerthinn, smiling down from his horse. He was in good spirits after the air and exercise and inclined to be expansive.

"Show him your ring, Gwenhwyach, and then we shall see if the Prince is satisfied or the mystery deepens," said Maelinn, and Gwenlliant did as she was told.

The Prince stared for a long moment at the ring, then spread out his own fingers, that she might see the gold encircling the smallest finger of his right hand. The rings were identical: the same great unpolished stone, the golden band enscribed with signs and symbols . . . they were not just identical, Gwenlliant realized, they were the same ring.

"They are plainly the work of the same craftsman, yet my friend told me the ring was unique," said Caerthinn.

Mabonograin dismounted to take a better look. "I was told there was not another one like it . . . it appears that I was misled." He took Gwenlliant's hand in his square brown one and examined the ring carefully. "This is certainly the gold of my native land, and the gem is made of the bones of the dragons under the earth."

When he touched the band, Gwenlliant *felt* the metal grow warm and pliable, as though it were eager to leave her finger and slide onto one of his, that ring which had clung so tenaciously for many long months. *The gold knows its master,* thought Gwenlliant.

Then she caught her breath, realizing she had finally found her way back home. As soon as she learned what she had come here to learn, as soon as she was ready to summon up the Breathing Mist, she had only to find this Mabonograin again and ask him to remove the ring.

But Mabonograin had lost interest in the ring and was staring down at Grifflet, with a smile in his warm dark eyes. "Is this your son? He is a fine boy, you are a very fortunate woman."

Gwenlliant felt a lump rising in her throat, a sudden stinging in her eyes. The language was different, but the lilting accent was unmistakable. "I wish," she said, "that his father was here to hear you say so."

❧❧❧

In Annwn, Tryffin stood watching the goblins laying out the Chess pieces on the wooden board, the little carven figures of fabulous beasts. Along with the board and the men, two wax candles came out of the chest, tall white candles with thin metal rings set into the wax at regular intervals, which the goblin servants set out on the table to either side of the board.

"And what is their purpose?" the Governor asked, turning to Brion, though he thought he knew.

"The candles are lit to determine the time we may each consider our moves," said the boy with the silver eyes. "No more and no less than the time that it takes for the flame to burn from one circle to the next. Were the game not played in this fashion, a match between masters could be interminable."

Tryffin nodded. It seemed like a reasonable precaution, though it was bound to favor the more experienced player. "And if the game is not over when the candles burn down?"

Brion shrugged. "Then new ones are immediately provided. I used to play with my brothers many such games, in which we burned through a half dozen candles . . . but I have never seen King Avallach or Prince Gruffydd take more than a candle's worth of moves to crush his opponent."

They sat down to play, and Meligraunce, Mahaffy, and Conn gathered around to observe. Brion, as it turned out, was a very good player and an excellent teacher, explaining the rules and the moves clearly and patiently. Except for the candles and the initial placement of all the pieces, it was not so very different from the Chess that Tryffin was accustomed to play. Unfortunately, it was easy to see that even such changes as there were altered the strategy in some important ways.

The night went by slowly, and the Governor played several short games with the young elf, before he could even accomplish a draw. By then, Brion was rubbing his eyes as though he were sleepy, and his play became sloppy, allowing Tryffin to win the next game far too easily. When the Governor sent him off to bed, Mahaffy and Meligraunce took turns filling his place. Neither provided much of a challenge; Tryffin won game after game.

Two hours before dawn, Brion returned, bright-eyed and alert, ready to continue with the lessons. As he took his seat on the other side of the table, Tryffin noticed that a section of his tunic was damp and sandy—and now that he came to think of it, there was always a patch of wet somewhere about the boy. This morning, there was a strong odor of seaweed as well.

"You are not like the others . . . the King and his sons," said the Governor. "Neither are you one of the goblins."

Brion nodded. "I am a glastyn. There are not very many of us, but in truth, Prince Tryffin, we are an old proud race. Unfortunately, few have found favor with the King of the Fairies and I am the only one of my kind at court."

Tryffin continued to regard him with a speculative gaze. "When I first came here, it seemed to me that there were many different people, many kinds of people. Some of them . . . rather eccentric in their appearance. Since then, I have wondered if I might have been mistaken that very first night."

"No," said Brion, "you were not mistaken. And they are all still here, but cloaked in illusion to make them fairer to your sight. It was the King's idea—to keep you and your companions from becoming frightened. They are most of them fuathan, you see, and people of your sort usually find them rather intimidating."

"Fuath," said Tryffin, his fingers curling around the arms of his chair. He knew something of that species of Fairy from his nursemaid's stories, and none of those stories ended very pleasantly for the mortal men involved. "Morna and Aoife are fuathan . . . why did I never guess that before?"

"Ah well," said Brion, with a wide grin, "most likely because the guards arrived before they were finished with Conn. Had he returned to you spouting poetry with his wits all gone, you might have suspected something then.

"Of course," he added, with an offhand gesture, "they are only women, Aoife and Morna. The men of that race are much worse."

They played another game, much longer than any had lasted the night before, and this time the Governor won. "You seem to have mastered this form of Chess with amazing speed," said Meligraunce.

But Tryffin shook his head. "With all due respect to the skill of young Brion, I would have to play a number of games with someone whose skills match those of the King, before I could learn the subtler points of the strategy."

Meligraunce shrugged. "And you have two games to do so, Your Grace, playing the King himself."

Tryffin smiled at the Captain's confidence. "That hardly seems sufficient. Yet I will try to draw out the contest as long as I can, in the hope of picking up something."

"I hope that you do win," said Brion, surprisingly. "That is, I don't see any chance that you will, but I wish there was. You learn so quickly, you deserve a much better chance than the King has given you."

When Avallach sent up one of the goblins to fetch him, Tryffin and his attendants went down to the audience chamber, where they found the golden board and the jeweled playing pieces still left out from the night before. The King took a chair on one side of the table, and Tryffin sat down facing him. The court gathered around them to view the contest.

The first game, the King won with demoralizing ease, capturing several of the opal and ivory men early in the game, then checkmating his opponent in less than an hour.

The Governor ground his teeth in intense frustration; even accounting for the speed with which the game progressed, because of the candles, he should have been able to do better than that. He did not see how he could possibly prevail in the games to come. Yet he had learned a little, a very little, by observing the King, and he would try to remember and to adapt what he had learned to his own style of play.

Resolving to put all emotions aside and turn his entire attention to the contest, he began the second game. He lost fewer men but still was defeated with what he considered humiliating ease.

"We have been here all of the morning," said King Avallach, pushing back his chair, "and the long night is coming. And though it has been reasonably diverting, I believe I would like to resume the match a little later. After I have taken a walk in the gardens while the daylight lasts, and then, perhaps, a bite to eat."

Tryffin readily agreed, glad of the chance to get out of his chair and stretch his legs.

"Your Grace," said Meligraunce, as they walked out on the battlements. "Perhaps you should take this opportunity to get some sleep. You look rather tired."

"No," said the Governor. "Fresh air is what I need, to clear my head."

"By God, I was impressed," said Mahaffy, bringing up the rear. Conn, they had been forced to leave indoors; he would not be allowed outside until his fate was decided. "The King is a brilliant player but you did very well."

Tryffin clenched his fists, controlling an urge to pound them on the parapet. "It isn't enough to do very well," he answered grimly. "I have to start winning."

An hour after sunset, they were back in the audience chamber, and the third game was well under way. This time, Tryffin played cautiously, but with better success. He captured two pieces, evaded several traps, yet it was clear that the King retained the advantage.

"It should be obvious that you cannot win this one," gloated Avallach, several hours into the game. He made his move, blew out his candles, and delicately removed the golden ring, as one of his squires lit Tryffin's candle with a bit of burning straw. "Why will you not admit that I have beaten you?"

"How can I, considering what is at stake here?" Tryffin replied wearily. Staring down at the chessboard, he suddenly realized the pieces were not made of ivory as he had originally supposed, but of polished bone.

Possibly the remains of some previous opponent who lost and paid the other penalty, he thought grimly. Then scolded himself for allowing such morbid speculations to enter his brain.

Yet he was finally beginning to see the possibility of a stalemate. He thought Avallach must also, and that was why he had suggested that Tryffin concede the game.

After another hour, even the King had to admit that the game was a draw. His squires gathered up the playing pieces and began to arrange them for another game.

"It is late, and I begin to long for my bed," said Avallach, with a note of impatience in his voice. "We shall play again in the morning."

Tryffin released a long sigh of relief, as the King and his attendants left the room. According to the crystal clock on the dais, he had bought himself another eight hours in which to learn the game, and he meant to make the most of them.

. . . at Penngaren, Mabon and his warriors fought with the boar for three days and three nights, and all that time there was a great slaughter of men and horses. In Cormelyn, the boar stood his ground, and Eri, Caradawg, Cynan, and Erwm were all slain.

Prince Mabon followed the boar Ysgithrwyn the length of Mochdreff and back again, all in seven days. But except for a single silver bristle, Mabon and his men got nothing for their efforts.

—From the Oral Tradition of Tir Gwyngelli

15.

The Schemes of Great Men

It was snowing at Caer Bannawg, a fair omen on the day of the Midwinter Feast—or so Maelinn said. Gwenlliant was not so certain; she carried a great weight over her heart, and she felt sad and angry and homesick and rebellious all at the same time. She wondered if it was something she sensed, something terrible that was about to happen, the inevitability of which was hanging in the air like thunder, or was it just because she was thinking of Christmas and Tryffin, and wanting them both?

Tryffin, of course, was centuries distant in another Mochdreff, and as for Christmas: Someone was celebrating it somewhere if this was the year that she thought—but not in Achren. Yet there were aspects of the Midwinter Feast that were not very different. The Prince's hall had been decorated with evergreens—pine and holly and ivy—and a great round sun cut from a sheet of bronze had been hung from the rafters. The sun had thirteen rays, symbolizing the lunar months of the year. Yule logs blazed on every hearth, boughs coated with oil in which bayberries had been soaked, to make the wood burn hotter and produce a fragrant smoke. The children made wreaths of whatever greenery they had on hand, which they would burn for luck shortly before the festival, and all of the women and many of the men wore necklaces made of acorns painted scarlet.

Maelinn wore several of these necklaces, including one in which the acorns had been painted gold. She had put by all of her ordinary jewelry, because she was to perform the ceremony of Returning Light in Gwythyr's place, and everything she would wear to the Feast that night was prescribed by ritual.

She began dressing early in the day, with Regan and Pali to assist her. She had to bathe first, in water and then in milk, after which her face and her hands were painted a chalky white and her eyes lined with kohl. The effect was nearly as barbaric as Mabonograin's woad, but at least it would be gone tomorrow. She wore three different gowns, piled one over the other, black, saffron, and scarlet on the outside. Then she donned the necklaces, and a girdle of mistletoe with the berries still on.

After that, there was "only" the lengthy process of arranging her hair, in dozens of tiny braids, which in turn were woven together in an elaborate net—the procedure took hours, with Maelinn sitting restless on a stool and the other young priestesses chattering over her head as they plaited her hair.

"Maelinn," said Pali, after a time, "where did you put the crown of leaves you were wearing last night?"

Maelinn tried to think. "I don't remember taking it off when I . . . no, I did that earlier, because the leaves were scratching. Oh, Pali, I believe I left it behind last night."

Regan looked across the room to Gwenlliant, who was just beginning to ready herself for the Feast, combing out her long pale hair. "You will have to run to the hall and see if you can find it, before one of the children takes it for a wreath and throws it into the fire at noon."

Gwenlliant nodded, bundled up her hair in a rough knot, until she would have time to do it right, and threw on the grey cloak. She was bending down to pick Grifflet up off the floor, where he was playing, when Maelinn stopped her.

"Leave him with us . . . why should you not? You'll go more quickly without him."

Gwenlliant flushed, stood hesitating, not certain what to do.

"You never leave him with any of us, though he knows us very well and would not be frightened. Why won't you trust your friends, Gwenhwyach?" Maelinn asked softly, sadly. "Why won't you trust *me*?"

Now, it happened that Gwenlliant had been waiting so long for someone to notice the obvious and ask that question, that she had already forgotten how she meant to answer it. So it was a moment before she remembered that the truth could not hurt her. "It is because I came by the Breathing Mist . . . and I always wonder what would have happened to Grifflet if I hadn't been holding him at the time, or if I put him down for even an instant."

Maelinn's look of disappointment faded instantly. "Is that all it is?" she said, with a smile. "But I never met anyone stolen by the Mist more than once—it is like lightning striking you, a rare occurrence—besides, the fog cannot come when it is already *snowing.*" Regan and Pali nodded their agreement. "You can safely leave him with us this one time."

Put that way, Gwenlliant did not know what else she could do. She did not wish to risk offending Maelinn, who was so particular about matters of trust and loyalty—without whose friendship she certainly would not have been admitted to Caer Bannawg, or be living with priestesses in the wood, and on whose continued favor anything Gwenlliant might wish to accomplish in the past so clearly depended. So she dropped a kiss on the top of Grifflet's head and left without him.

Outside, the air was filled with whirling snowflakes, icy crystals that stung when they landed, but at least the way to the hall was clear: The cattle and horses were all huddled together in tight little groups over by the great wooden wall. Gwenlliant pulled up the hood of the fur-lined cloak and went as fast as she dared over the slippery ground.

When she reached the hall, she slipped past the big double doors and moved through the shadows among the pillars. The vast chamber was dark, except for some glowing embers in the firepit; the servants were elsewhere, either in the cooking houses preparing the feast, or running errands for those who were. But as she approached the platform at the end of the hall she realized that the place was not empty, after all. A single torch burned on the far side of one of the columns, and three men were sitting among the furs and pillows, near the place where Maelinn had been the night before, drinking and apparently quarreling, because their voices were low but angry.

Gwenlliant paused, uncertain, for she recognized the voices of the High Prince and the Priest of Cerridwen, and she thought it might not be wise or safe to interrupt them. Standing still in the shadows in the grey cloak, she was practically invisible, and the men were intent on their argument, anyway.

"It is the duty of a prince to keep his promises," Gwythyr was saying.

"It is the duty of a prince to do all in his power, but since Maelinn is here, what would you have me do? It is her right to lead the celebration," said Caerthinn, "and it is certainly not for me to ordain your rituals, anyway."

Gwythyr laughed nastily. "Is that what you thought we were discussing, Lord Prince? But that is a small matter beside my real grievance. Have you forgotten the promise you made two years ago, to give your sister to the temple?"

"I promised my sister to the cloister in the wood, not to the goddess Cerridwen, and not for a life of service. She was to be Maelinn's successor, as you very well know, when the three years had passed . . . now Maelinn says she will continue for nine, which is certainly her right but completely unexpected," said Caerthinn.

Gwenlliant shifted in the shadows, moving closer so she could see their faces. The third man, the one who was taller and bulkier than either of the others, who had so far remained silent, was Gereint, the priest's elder brother.

He spoke now, in tones of heavy sarcasm. "Unexpected? Can you really say so? I should have thought that the one thing certain in all of Achren was that Maelinn would hold on to her power as long as she might."

Prince Caerthinn made an impatient movement with his hand. "I thought she would wish to marry, they usually do, and the gods know she is a beautiful woman, who would have no difficulty finding a husband."

Gwythyr and his brother exchanged a knowing glance. "A husband, yes, but not one to suit her ambitions or her rather particular tastes, and can you see her living on in Gereint's house as an unwed woman without any power? But that is quite beside the point," said Gwythyr, those slender, hurtful fingers of his wrapping themselves around a beaker of mead. "Maelinn will stay where she is, there is no other way for you to keep your promise, and the goddess Cerridwen wants your sister Tinne."

Caerthinn shook his head. "Say rather that *you* do. As does Mabonograin—who agreed to wait the three years, as she is still so young, and even provided gifts for her to take to the temple . . . but he will not wait forever."

Lord Gereint snorted contemptuously. "Mabonograin. You would give him Tinne, the sister you love, to be taken away where you would never see her from one year to the next . . . to live among the barbarian Hillfolk and their filthy customs . . . and yet you deny her to the temple, where she would be safe and sheltered, honored and powerful, and only a two days' ride from this very spot."

Caerthinn lifted his cup to his lips. "The difference is that she loves Mabonograin, and would be happy with him, no matter where he takes her . . . and the customs of the Hillfolk are no more barbaric than our own. Also, she would come back to visit often; she and Mabonograin both, for both of them love me." He put a conciliatory hand on Gwythyr's shoulder. "Wait another two years, and you can have Fearn . . . she is very devout for a child her age, and you know she admires you. I believe she already aspires to the temple of Cerridwen."

Gwythyr frowned, not in the least pacified. Watching him, Gwenlliant thought, *He does not wish to wait for the younger sister, because he wants them both. Tinne now and Fearn later.* And she did not know so very much about the religion of these people, but she thought it must be very wicked, even among pagans, for Gwythyr to use his position to satisfy his lusts, or to force a young woman into the service of his goddess without a true vocation.

"I tell you the goddess Cerridwen will not be denied. In truth, she is already angry that she receives so little respect . . . from Prince Caerthinn, and from his people."

Now it was Caerthinn's turn to sneer as he spoke. "Twelve years ago, nobody knew of your goddess Cerridwen. It was only one of the lesser names of the White Cailleach, and not one of her aspects that inspired much popular worship, either. Now there is an entire cult devoted to her, a temple, a priest, three priestesses—who live together in a fashion which many regard as scandalous. And do not bother to tell me that it was ordained by the goddess herself, for I have heard that story before—a half dozen acolytes, and if I have not lost count, seventeen sacred swine. If there is any god or goddess who ought to feel satisfied, it is the goddess Cerridwen."

"You cannot know what the goddess feels or wants," said Gwythyr. "That is reserved for those who serve her, as I do. She came to me in a dream, not two nights past, saying that if Tinne is not consecrated to the temple by the first day of spring, there will be plagues and disasters."

Caerthinn rose to his feet; apparently, he was growing weary of this discussion. "You forget to whom you speak, Gwythyr," he said haughtily. "Who serves the gods and goddesses if not the

High Prince? And if Cerridwen requires Tinne, no doubt she will send me a sign that I can see for myself . . . and not one of these dreams of yours, that always seem to promise whatever you desire at the moment."

When the men were gone, Gwenlliant moved through the shadows and retrieved the crown of oak leaves and gilded acorns, which she carried back to Maelinn in the Princess's house.

As no one needed her after that, she finished dressing her hair, cleaned up Grifflet and changed his little tunic—a task she had left until it was nearly time to go down to the Feast, for fear that he would get himself dirty again almost at once—then opened one of the shuttered windows and stood looking out. By now, there was a great deal of activity down below, people milling around between the various little houses of daub and thatch and Prince Caerthinn's great wooden hall. She began to share a little of their excitement.

Turning around, she caught Maelinn watching her. "And so you are beginning to feel it . . . it is going to be a great occasion, a portentous night," said the High Priestess. "Everyone will be watching me celebrate the ritual, and then there will be wonders and marvels for everyone to see."

Gwenlliant frowned, thinking of what Caerthinn had said about a sign from the goddess. "Are you certain of that, Maelinn?"

Her friend laughed. "Gwenhwyach, you have lived among us long enough to know . . . it is not beyond my power to produce visions, even wonders. Indeed, it is necessary for me to do so, because ordinary people are impressed by these things and would begin to doubt that I was a true representative of the goddess Goleuddydd, if I did not display my powers every now and again."

"But it is just your own magic," said Gwenlliant. She thought of the twelve young women performing their rituals in the forest, where there was no one to see them. "You do believe in your goddess, that I know . . . so why don't you leave it to her to make a sign?"

Maelinn exchanged an amused glance with the other priestesses. "Because she never does so at our convenience, only at her own. And the people expect something from her much more often than that. Besides, it *is* her power . . . indirectly. From where else could my gift come?"

To that, Gwenlliant had no answer. Magic was something you learned, that anyone could study, but it took an inborn gift for the spells to *work*. If she believed, as she more or less did (despite what certain narrow-minded people said), that her own gift came from God, then it was not surprising that Maelinn credited her gods and goddesses—who at least had no priests running about attempting to suppress the practice of any magic that did not belong to the Church.

Somewhere down below, a gong sounded, summoning them to the ceremony and the feast afterward.

"It is time," said Maelinn, taking a deep breath to steady herself, clasping her chalky white hands together. "You must take Grifflet and go on ahead of us, or you will never find a good vantage point from which to observe the ritual."

By the time that Gwenlliant arrived in the hall it was already crowded, and a great wall of bodies stood between her and the area around the firepit where Maelinn would perform the ceremony. But she met Tadhg just as she stepped inside, and he took matters immediately in hand.

"As it is your first time, you must see it all," said the young warrior, snatching up Grifflet and elbowing a way for her through the crowd. He showed her a place near the edge of the platform, where someone could stand with her back to a pillar and watch everything that happened on the level below, and then he was gone before she could thank him. Gwenlliant doubted he would have heard her, anyway, because the noise by now was tremendous.

But everyone fell silent when Maelinn swept in, escorted by Pali and Regan, with the Priest of Cerridwen and his acolytes trailing behind. Gwythyr, though by no means as spectacular as his sister, had also painted his face and arrayed himself in numerous layers of clothing, black, white, and scarlet. He wore a cloak so long and heavy that the two young boys in grey had to carry the hem of it.

The High Priestess stopped about ten feet from the fire, to receive Prince Caerthinn and his sister, as they knelt for her blessing. Tinne was delicate and beautiful in a gown of saffron sewn with brass medallions to match the great bronze sun hanging from the rafters, and she wore a wreath on her head, made of the holly for which she was named. Caerthinn wore light armor, over a garment of silk, and a circlet of gold banded with pale yellow stones.

As the Prince and his sister retreated, Maelinn moved toward the firepit. Gwenlliant saw now that the sun was suspended by ropes in such a way that it could be raised and lowered. Men were working the hempen ropes now so that the solar wheel descended, dipping down until the flames just licked the rim, as someone played softly on a flute, and Maelinn spoke the invocation.

Gwenlliant felt a chill slide down her spine. There was real magic, real power, at work here; she could feel it and taste it, though beyond the fact that it was something too great to manifest as mere illusion, she could not say what it was. But when Maelinn began moving her hands, Gwenlliant could *see*: strands of fire on the air, threads of glowing force that Maelinn was weaving into a net as complex as the woven braids in her hair.

Then there was a roar like thunder, and the whole hall shook. The ropes holding the bronze sun just above the fire seemed to dissolve, and the solar wheel plunged into the heart of the flames, landing at the bottom of the pit with a loud clang and causing sparks to fly in every direction. Maelinn fell back in a dead faint, into the arms of Pali and Regan, who despite their own startlement were able to lower her gently to the floor.

Before anyone had a chance to recover from this unexpected turn of events, the large doors at the end of the hall flew open and there was a harsh squealing and a grunting, the scrabble of sharp hooves on the wooden floor . . . soon drowned out by shouts and screams of terror as everyone realized there was a wild boar running loose in the hall.

Gwenlliant picked up Grifflet and held him close, while chaos roared around her. People were pushing and shoving and trampling each other in their efforts to get out of the hall by any means possible, but she was comparatively safe in her place by the pillar and she had no intention of moving.

Gradually, the screaming subsided, the crowd grew still. Down on the floor by the firepit, among the scattered glowing embers, the boar lay bleeding out its life with a spear through its neck. It was a moment before Gwenlliant realized who was the man in golden armor holding on to the shaft of the spear, driving the point even deeper into the boar's throat: Mabonograin, gone pale under his blue paint.

Maelinn had revived, and insisted on standing. She glared at her brother Gwythyr, as though she suspected him of interfering with her ritual. Yet Gwenlliant knew that the High Priestess would say nothing, make no open accusation—not so much out of loyalty to Gwythyr, but because acknowledging that he, or anyone, had the *ability* to tamper with the signs and the portents would call her own power into question.

That Gwythyr had arranged the whole thing, Gwenlliant had not a single doubt. He had probably arranged it long before his conversation with the Prince. And while Gwenlliant had not seen Lord Gereint, the other brother, initially leave the hall, she had certainly noticed him slipping in through the open doors at the height of the commotion. While Gwythyr had provided the magic to disrupt the ceremony, causing the thunder to clap and the ropes to dissolve, it was probably Gereint who had provided the wild boar.

Meanwhile, there were two men dead and a great many people injured, including women and children, some slashed by the tusks of the boar, others who had fallen during the panic and been trampled by the crowd. Maelinn turned away from her brother with a contemptuous gesture, then bent down to minister to one of the wounded children. Pali and Regan did likewise, moving among the dead and wounded to see what help they might give.

As Gwenlliant continued to watch from her vantage point by the pillar, Prince Caerthinn stepped out of the crowd, leading his sister by the hand. Tinne was pale, and visibly shaking with the shock of recent events, but she held her head high—even though she must know what was going to happen next.

"Cerridwen has given the sign that I asked for . . . and may the gods and my own people forgive me my arrogance in requesting it," said Caerthinn, bowing his head. "The blood of the fallen is on my hands, and there is little I can do to make atonement, beyond giving my cherished sister to the goddess . . . and to you, Gwythyr."

No one said anything, no one protested—not even Mabonograin, who stood, apparently stunned, still holding the bloody spear which had slain the boar—not even when the Priest of Cerridwen took Tinne's shaking hand in his strong grip, and flashed his dangerous smile.

In Annwn, another night was far advanced, when Tryffin (after another stalemate earlier in the day) captured the King's dragon and achieved his first victory. Avallach, who seemed impatient the night before, accepted this first defeat amazingly well.

"And so you have not only won this game, but another night of freedom," said the King, with a winsome smile. "You are truly remarkable, my young friend. I look forward to continuing the contest tomorrow."

Tryffin rose, and watched the King and his attendants leave the room, before dropping back into his chair with a sigh. "I believe he may be toying with me," he said, under his breath. "I think that he meant me to win that one, else why should he seem so pleased?"

"Because he knows you are tiring," said Meligraunce, coming from behind the chair. "For all you are so good at concealing it, he can read the exhaustion written on your face, and he believes it will soon begin to affect your judgment. As it cannot fail to do—since you have not slept at all these last two nights. Your Grace, you need a good night's rest far more than another night of practice."

"Perhaps," said Tryffin. "In truth, I don't know." He saw that Brion was moving toward the door and called the young elf back. "Will you not be joining us again this evening?"

Brion hesitated, then came back into the room. "I am sorry, Prince Tryffin, but I was told it was all a mistake. That is, the King told Prince Ffergus to send up one of his squires, and he was not pleased to learn that Ffergus had borrowed me from his brother and appointed me as your teacher instead." He smiled regretfully. "Also, I should not have attended you that second night, because that was not part of the King's original promise."

"By my faith," said Tryffin, "I hope you are not in any trouble on my account."

The young elf shook his head. "It seems that I am not, as it was all Prince Ffergus's doing. He is a favorite of the King, as well as the only man in Annwn that he trusts without reservation."

It was a moment before the Governor absorbed all the implications. "The only . . . then he does not trust Prince Gruffydd in the same way? I wonder why not."

Brion shrugged, made a humorous grimace. "It is not so much that he mistrusts Prince Gruffydd. Let us just say that the King occasionally finds his younger son's remarkable intelligence . . . disconcerting. In truth, it was only today that—"

"Yes?" said Tryffin, when he did not continue.

Brion cast a silver-eyed glance over his shoulder, making certain there were no unfriendly ears nearby to hear him. There were goblins at the far end of the hall extinguishing the torches, climbing up on each other's shoulders to reach the brackets, but none of them was close enough to worry about.

"I should not speak of this . . . indeed, I should not even linger here . . . but this much I will tell you. When the King went out for a walk between games, I followed after him, and chanced to hear part of the conversation. He was scolding Prince Gruffydd for being so abominably clever . . . it was all said in jest, yet there was something in the way that he said it that made me suppose he was really in earnest."

"I wonder,"said Tryffin, when Brion had left the room, "if it was really Prince Gruffydd he was complaining of . . . "

He ran his fingers over the carvings on his chair, thinking that over. It was hard to know how much the King knew or guessed, whether he had divined the true relationship between Tryffin and Gruffydd, that it went much deeper than a close resemblance and a similar turn of the mind.

But there was no use worrying about that, with more immediate matters to consider. Tryffin rose from his seat and headed slowly back toward his bedchamber.

"Your Grace," said Mahaffy, walking along at his side, bright-eyed despite the lack of sleep. The Governor knew that he and Meligraunce were getting by on grim determination, but Mahaffy seemed to exist on nervous energy alone. "I have been watching the King's moves closely . . . paying more attention to his game today than I have to yours. And I wonder if you noticed that the piece known as the griffon may be the key to his strategy. He seems to protect the griffon, which is admittedly of little use while the board is full of men, with surprising zeal . . . and has often employed the piece to devastating effect in the endgame."

Tryffin thought that over as he climbed the stairs. "I think that you may be right, Mahaffy—and you, too, Meligraunce. I must be growing tired if I failed to notice that myself."

He considered a while longer, trying to remember what had occurred during each of the games. "It may just be that you have saved me, Mahaffy. Thinking back, I see that when Avallach can't gain a swift and easy victory, he depends on the griffon to gain an advantage. What I must practice tonight—after a few hours of sleep, Meligraunce, a brief nap only—are ways to capture that piece early in the game, or else render it helpless."

Put not your trust in the Folk of the Hills, for the Sidhe are given to half-truths, evasions, and double-edged meanings . . . and while they will not be forsworn, it is highly advisable that you make very certain just what it is they are actually promising you.
—Advice given by old women and nursemaids in Camboglanna and parts of the south

16.

The Grail of Shadows

Tryffin sat facing the King of Annwn across the golden chessboard. The room was crowded with Fairies and goblins, who had gathered around, eager and expectant, no doubt anticipating victory for their King, a final, crushing defeat for himself.

In truth, he had spent so many long hours over the game, had gone without rest, exercise, and food, these last three days and nights, that he was almost willing to put an end to it, to give up now, if by doing so he might be reasonably assured that he would never be required to play the game again in his life.

He was almost willing to admit defeat, but not quite.

The candle at his side was burning low. Tryffin reached out slowly and moved his bone and opal basilisk forward three squares. "Check," he said wearily. "And mate."

There was a stir throughout the room. The King gave him an enigmatic glance across the table. "And so, we are even now, at two games each. It has been a most interesting experience, Prince Tryffin, but perhaps you grow as weary of the game as I do." Avallach paused, as though considering his words. "If you are willing, we can end the match now and call it a draw. I would not require your service, you would not ask a boon."

Tryffin sat back in his chair, passed a hand over his eyes. "You said that once the challenge was made, it was impossible to withdraw."

Avallach shrugged, his golden eyes reflecting the candlelight. "Did I say so? But of course I meant you could not withdraw before we had played at least three games. We have played twice as many, and the rules of the challenge are satisfied . . . *if* we can agree that neither of us has defeated the other."

"Prince Tryffin," said Conn, in an urgent whisper. "You should do as he says. You have done far more than anyone could expect—"

The Governor silenced him by raising a hand. "After all I have risked for this boy already, you think that I would abandon him now?"

"Truth to tell," said the King, lounging elegantly in his chair, still with a thin smile on his lips, "I think you would be wise to do so. But if you want time to think over your answer, you may take all the time that you need."

Tryffin shook his head in abrupt denial. "No . . . I have already decided, and the answer is no."

Again there was a murmur and a rustle, passing throughout the room. Tryffin was not certain whether he had just done a very wise or a very foolish thing. "Very well then," said Avallach. "We shall play again after supper, when undoubtedly one of us shall have the victory."

As he had the night before, Tryffin remained in his seat while the King and his court filed out of the audience chamber. "Am I mistaken," the Governor asked Meligraunce, "or does my candle burn faster today?"

"Your Grace, I believe that it does, and that your turns have been considerably shorter than those of the King. Whether he has managed this through some spell or merely by putting something in the wax, I cannot begin to guess."

"It is a good sign that he is trying to cheat you," said Mahaffy hopefully. "At least . . . it is a good sign so long as he doesn't succeed. He must know by now that you are the better man, that you have the better mind and the greater skill. Also, he was ready to end it. I believe that he is frightened of you."

"If that is so," said Tryffin, with a sigh, "he may find some other and better way to cheat me. And if he does, I shall hardly be in a position to protest or accuse him."

"You are wishing that you had accepted his offer," said Conn morosely. "Perhaps if you tell him, when he comes back, that you have changed your mind . . ."

"No," replied the Governor. "As great a fool as I was to

challenge him in the first place, I think I should be an ever greater fool to withdraw now. Because considering what the King has done to bring me to this pass, I don't really believe that it would be possible to win my freedom by an act of cowardice, a display of weakness."

"Say rather, a display of good common sense, and an eye toward your responsibilities elsewhere," said Meligraunce. "Lord Prince, if it please you, take what the King offers and accept your own freedom, and I will play him for Conn's."

A faint smile played across the Governor's face. "You think that you can succeed where I would fail, Captain?"

"I think," said Meligraunce, "that you are too great a man to risk yourself in this way. But if Conn's freedom means so much to you, then I am willing to hazard myself in that cause."

"Before God." Tryffin laughed softly. "And so I should lose my good right hand, attempting to recover what may already be mine . . . if the King is so certain that I will win he is willing to offer me terms. That hardly sounds like good common sense to me."

He went out for a walk, then joined the King and the rest of his court in the feast hall for supper. He drank sparingly of the wine and ate only those dishes he had seen go to the King and his sons first. It did not seem likely there would be anything to affect him in anything that he was served, with Conn and Mahaffy both acting as his tasters, but there was no sense taking any chances.

When it was time to go back and play Chess, he walked slowly back to the audience chamber and took his seat on one side of the golden chessboard. He gazed down at the playing pieces with immense loathing. "Have you changed your mind?" said the King.

Tryffin shook his head. "I begin to suppose this game was invented by inquisitors and torturers," he said, quite truthfully, "but no . . . I mean to continue."

It was the King's move first, so Dylan touched a flame to his candle. A mere formality, since the first move was always the same, and took no time at all to decide. Except that this time, instead of moving one of the lowly harpies, Avallach brought out a manticore, leaping it over the other pieces, two squares forward and one to the side.

He is bluffing, thought Tryffin. *He wishes me to believe that he holds entire complex strategies as yet unrevealed, and that he will use them to crush me now. But if that were so, why would he fall back on trying to cheat me, or forbid young Brion to visit me last night?*

He studied the board and when it was time to move, pushed one of his harpies forward. "By the Sun and the Stars, you are not a very imaginative player," said the King.

Tryffin only smiled. And two moves later, when he captured one of the King's griffons, he watched Avallach grow suddenly intent, planning his next move.

It proved to be a long game. The candles burned down and had to be replaced. Outside the window, all three moons crossed the sky in procession, then dipped below the horizon. There would be no sleep tonight, no abandoning the game until morning, because morning was practically there.

The crystal clock chimed the hour of six, which at Castell Maelduin, or Caer Ysgithr, or any civilized place would be the call to early prayers. Tryffin moved his remaining gargoyle. "Check and mate."

There was a lengthy silence, while the King studied the board to make certain that this was so. "The victory is yours," he said at last, "and so is the boy, Conn."

Conn put his hands on the table to steady himself, so great was his relief. Everyone in the room began to talk at once.

Tryffin leaned across the board so that Avallach might hear him. "And are you so certain it is the boy that I want now . . . and not all of Annwn?" he asked softly.

The King did not even blink. "And *shall* you ask for my crown and my lands, Prince Tryffin?" he asked, with a disbelieving smile.

Tryffin felt a strong temptation come over him, a desire to say yes, just to see that smile fade from the King's face. "I remember you told me the King of Annwn is bound to the soil. I did not risk my freedom, just to accept a different and more lasting form of servitude. You may keep your kingdom and give me young Conn instead."

Avallach laughed. "And besides that, you would not remove a crowned and anointed King without just cause. As I knew from the very beginning. I am a very good judge of character."

Tryffin spent a moment mastering his more violent urges before he replied. "So you risked nothing and I risked all," he said, a bitter taste flooding his mouth.

"Very true," said the King, rising from his chair. "And so it may be plainly seen, you are my superior at Chess but I am the wiser man."

Tryffin was at least wise enough to ignore the provocation, and stifle the retort that came into his mind. He stood up, and watched the King leave. Then he motioned his own people over to the window, where nobody else could hear what he said. "I don't like this. He has done everything possible to see that I lost and still give the impression that I had a reasonable chance of winning. And then when I did win, he accepted the situation with remarkable grace. I believe it was all a sham from the very beginning: the law, the geas, the challenge, and the conditions."

"To what end?" said Meligraunce, his brows pinched together in thought. "I admit that it all looks very strange, but I cannot fathom what the King meant to gain by any of it, unless he truly wished to make you his servant for seven years."

Tryffin let out a long breath. "It seems to me that it was meant as some sort of a test. Though what Avallach thought he would learn and how he meant to use that knowledge afterward, I have no idea. Nor do I intend to stay and find out."

He lowered his voice, though he had not been speaking very loudly to begin with. "We are leaving this place as soon as it is dark again—if we have to climb over the walls to do so."

They went upstairs, drank wine, discussed plans for escaping the fortress, and nibbled on the light repast the King sent up to them. Then Conn and the men-at-arms closed all the shutters, blew out the candles, and left Tryffin alone for a few hours of rest.

He stretched out on the big feathery mattress and instantly fell into a deep dreamless sleep. But he woke suddenly, he did not know how many hours later, when the door burst open, and the darkened bedchamber was immediately full of goblins in armor and pot helms, brandishing their axes and pikes.

He sprang up from the bed and caught up his sword, just as Conn and Meligraunce came hurtling through the door, similarly armed. But the King's guards had the advantage of surprise and superior numbers; the struggle was brief but decisive.

Tryffin found himself in a corner, facing a semi-circle of pole arms, all pointed in his direction. Conn and Meligraunce had lost their weapons and were under restraint, and more goblins came into the room, escorting Mahaffy, Garreg, and Ciag, who were similarly disarmed and helpless.

"I would say, Prince Tryffin, that it would be to your advantage to surrender," said Dris, waving his outsize poleax.

"If we are to be arrested, then what is the charge?" Tryffin demanded, keeping up his guard.

"You are not under arrest and there is no charge," said his elfin counterpart, Prince Gruffydd, coming into the room with a crystal lantern in his hand. "It is just that my father desires to enjoy your company a while longer, and he entertains some suspicion that you are planning to deny him that pleasure."

"My apologies if I wrong you in any way," said Tryffin, staring into that high-boned face that was so like and unlike his own. "But I am afraid that I simply do not trust you."

Prince Gruffydd shrugged, staring back at him with expressionless green eyes. "Who would know better than you if I were lying? You know the twistings and the turnings of my mind just as well as I know them myself. Better perhaps, because you know not only what I am but all that I could be under other circumstances. You are more of a puzzle to me than I am to you, yet I knew very well that you were planning to leave tonight."

Tryffin considered that. The King's son spoke the truth: If he could not exactly trust this shadow of his, at least he should be able to anticipate all of his tricks. "Very well then, I should like a straight answer. If I put down my sword and make my surrender, will my people be harmed?"

And he wondered, but he did not ask, how long the King and his sons had known who he was and where he had come from.

At Gruffydd's signal, the goblin guards retreated an inch or two. "If they do not persist in attempting to escape . . . in which case they might suffer some unintentional damage . . . no one will be harmed in the least," he said. "Neither directly nor indirectly. They will only be moved to another chamber, where it will be more difficult for them to escape."

Tryffin lowered his blade. "Then on those conditions and no others, I surrender."

They were removed to one of the rooms under the hill, not really a dungeon, for it was very large, well lit by candles and torches, and comfortably furnished with beds, chairs, tables, rugs, and everything else that was needed—and all of the best, from the linens on the beds to the silver cups and plates laid out upon one of the tables. Yet it was a prison for all that, and a very secure one, with no windows and only one door, made of stout planks of oak.

Tryffin made a thorough search of the chamber. There were air shafts cut into the rock, but too small to suggest any ideas. Since no other possible means of escape immediately presented itself, Tryffin decided to continue his nap, at least until the King sent for him.

That summons was a long time coming, giving him time to sleep, wash, and dress, using a basin of water brought in by the goblin guards at his request, and the garments he had worn when he first entered Annwn, which he found waiting for him in the clothes chest at the foot of his bed. He was beginning to understand that the King did not mean either to harm or to intimidate him, only to make certain of his continued presence for as long as it should please Avallach's fancy.

His appetite returning, Tryffin asked the next goblin who came into the room whether dinner would soon be served. "For these others, yes, but if you are ready, it is time for you to appear before the King," said the guard.

Tryffin nodded and went out, with a goblin escort. They walked along with their axes in their belts, and their pole arms elevated. Apparently, they knew him well enough not to expect an attempt at escape, with his companions securely imprisoned below.

They took him to the King's private apartments, where as soon as Tryffin arrived, Avallach dismissed his squires and his other attendants. "I trust that you have rested and that your mind is clear," said the King, when they were alone together in the glittering glass chamber.

"I have, and I believe that it is," answered Tryffin, taking up a position by the fire. For every effort that had been made to make his prison comfortable, it had been drafty and damp.

"That is good," said the King. "For I have much to say to you and it is important that we should reach a perfect understanding. Indeed, your entire future depends on it."

The Governor nodded grimly and waited to hear more.

"I wonder," King Avallach continued, "how long you thought you would be able to fool me? Beyond your obvious resemblance to my younger son, there was your air of belonging and not belonging, the way that you seemed to know your way in places you could not possibly have been before, and so much else . . . you are a man of the Otherworld, that much is plain.

"Oh yes," he said, in answer to Tryffin's sharp look of inquiry. "I know something of the world you come from. It is a strange realm, they say . . . where the fabric of reality has not that natural fluidity we know here but possesses a curious rigidity . . . where everything is frozen into a terrible sameness, and the borders of kingdoms and principalities change only according to the whims of powerful men, and never of themselves. Yet there are places in your world which are outwardly similar to places here, where a man might meet with his own living image. They say that a man who passes from that outer world into this one—or from this world into that one—gains great and terrible powers. Would that I might go there and attain such powers for myself, but I would wither and die if I left Annwn."

Tryffin lifted his brows in amazement. "I can assure you, Lord King, that I have no such powers. Not any that I am aware of, anyway."

"And yet, those very same powers were in part what betrayed you. From the very first night you arrived here, you and your men have been passing through wards that ought to be impenetrable. Also, there was the incredible rapidity with which your wounds healed," said the King. "Other powers may reveal themselves as time goes on."

Tryffin walked over to the nearest window and stood looking out at the golden disk of the sun coming up over the hills, in a wreath of violet flames. "Even if these things are true . . . by what right do you hold us here against our will? And having decided to do so, why wait to reveal your intentions until now? Why did you not have us confined the first night we arrived here; why pretend to be so friendly and so helpful in the meantime?"

The King made a steeple of his long white fingers. "I hold you by my right as the King of Annwn, which land you entered without my permission, and also because I expect some return for my generous hospitality over these last weeks. Did you really think that would be offered to you without any conditions attacked? There are always conditions for everything."

"Not for hospitality, not in my father's house," said Tryffin, and he could not keep a certain bitterness out of his tone. "Yet I see now that I was mistaken, thinking the resemblance between you and him went any deeper than your skin."

"There is something I want you to do for me," said the King.

"It is true that the method I have chosen to gain power over you is a crude one, but what am I to do? You have avoided or resisted all of my spells, all of my attempts to entrap you. It is said that one can gain power over a man of your world by merely speaking his name. But you are not a fool, and neither am I—I know very well that the name you have given me must be a false one."

Neither by a word nor a look did Tryffin show his true reaction—though he immediately resolved to ask Mahaffy how he could possibly have forgotten this very important piece of information. He just smiled his blandest and blankest smile, as if to agree that he could not possibly have made so simple and foolish a mistake as to reveal his true name.

"You have already guessed, of course, that the Chess match—whatever else I may have hoped to gain by it—was in the nature of a test," the King went on, shrugging a broad shoulder under his feathered cloak. "I wanted to learn two things: The lengths you would go to in order to protect your young attendants. And if you had the intelligence to succeed at the task that I had planned for you. For that purpose, it proved to be a better test than I had imagined, for it never occurred to me that you would not know the game . . . or that you would be able to master it over the course of three days."

Tryffin turned away from the window. "There are certain similarities between Chess as you play it and the way I was taught, or I could never have done it."

"Still," said the King, "it was a remarkable feat, and as I have said before, you have a remarkable mind. I am very glad that Prince Gruffydd is not so like you as he might be; that would make life very much more difficult for both of us. However, you are rather too trusting, or at least inclined to give others the benefit of any possible doubt. I believe this is a common failing with men who themselves are honest and reasonable; they cannot overcome a certain expectation that others will wish to be the same. Perhaps your experiences here have taught you better, have awakened you to possibilities of deceit and duplicity you never imagined, and you may yet live to thank me for opening your eyes."

"It has never seemed to make any difference in the past," Tryffin remarked, with a wry smile. "I believe it must be some sort of flaw in the way I am made, that renders me incapable of learning that particular lesson."

"Ah well," said the King. "As you are now suits my purposes very well. Pray take a seat, for what I am going to explain to you may take some considerable time."

Tryffin did as the King advised, pulling up a chair beside the great marble fireplace, and settling down in it.

"There is a land on the northern border of Annwn, a place that I may have mentioned before. Its name is Charon, and it has remained there for as long as anyone can remember, which is an unusual occurrence, but not unknown. Generally when this happens, it is because the two lands so linked share some mysterious common destiny, or when they are held in place by the strength of some powerful desire—such as my own desire, which I shall explain to you presently."

On a table beside the King's chair were a number of scrolls and parchments. Avallach picked up one and passed it over to Tryffin. "This is a map of Charon, which you may wish to study."

Tryffin accepted the parchment but did not unroll it, intent on the rest of the King's explanation. "Charon is ruled by a great warlock . . . not a man of the Sidhe, but one of your own sort, yet possessing powers that rival my own. This warlock—his name is Garlon—happens to own an object of surpassing beauty, a chalice set with an immense and unusual gem, which is said to possess miraculous powers. When I was much younger, before my father died and I was bound to the land of Annwn, I saw that chalice and was instantly consumed by a desire to obtain it and make it my own. Since that time, I should tell you, I have tried one scheme after another to obtain this prize, yet for all my attempts to buy, barter, or steal the miraculous vessel, I have never succeeded in doing so. At last, weary of countering my attempts, the Lord of Charon worked a mighty spell to ward his borders, so that no creature born of Annwn can pass over. You, Prince Tryffin, will naturally be immune to that spell."

Tryffin frowned. "And so you expect me to play the thief and steal this cup for you, in order to win my freedom and that of my companions?" he asked incredulously.

"I expect you to bring me the chalice, but I am indifferent as to the means you employ in order to obtain it," said Avallach. "You may do so honestly for all of me. But you need not scruple to steal from this warlock, for though he began his reign very well, he has become a harsh and cruel tyrant over the last twenty years.

"You need not take my word for this," he added, in response

to Tryffin's doubtful look, "since you will see for yourself when you go to Charon, but really the cup and its remarkable powers will be much better off here in Annwn. However, if you think otherwise, you and your friends may go on living, in perfect comfort but regrettable confinement, here in my fortress for the rest of your lives."

Naturally, this was not a circumstance which Tryffin was eager to prolong. "But how do I know that you will set us free if I do as you ask?" he said, eyeing Avallach narrowly.

"You cannot know," replied the King. "But what other choice do you have? Also, you might consider that I am not such a bad fellow. There are any number of ways that I might force you to do my will—I could torture your young attendants, I could kill one of your men as an example, I could throw you into my darkest dungeon—yet I don't threaten to do any of these terrible things, because I am a man with a conscience.

"In truth," he added, showing his pointed teeth, "it all depends on the strength of your desire to go home again."

Tryffin put by the map, stood up, and began to pace the floor. "May I ask you one question? Was the shapechanger ever really here in Annwn?"

"No," said the King, with astonishing candor. "Or yes, according to your own story, for she led you here, did she not? But not very long, I should think. Certainly the stories that you heard, which convinced you to keep looking here, were all of them lies. At this moment she might be anywhere, I suppose."

Tryffin ground his teeth. "Even back in . . . the place that I came from . . . slaying children. While I remain here unable to stop her. Does this idea not trouble you at *all*?"

The King gave a careless shrug. "It certainly might do so if I were not aware that it is possible to twist time moving from one world to another. Come, Prince Tryffin, you must know as well as I do, that you can return to your own place at the very same instant you left it, or at least very shortly thereafter."

Tryffin could see that there was no use trying to convince the King that he did *not* know anything of the sort. Besides which, it was at least as reasonable a possibility as the reverse: that days spent here would be years in the real Celydonn.

He continued to prowl through the chamber, thinking the whole thing over. "And what will you do with this wondrous vessel, if I bring it to you?"

"I will keep it only to treasure it," said Avallach. "My power in Annwn is already absolute, and dreams of conquest hold little appeal for a man who can scarcely venture beyond the walls of his own castle."

That much Tryffin was ready to believe. "Well, I am willing to go into Charon, to look around me, and see if it's even possible for me to do what you ask," he said at last. "But more than that I cannot promise."

"That is fair enough," said the King, extending a hand which Tryffin could not bring himself to clasp. "Indeed, I would have been disappointed if you made any rash promises. Mahaffy and Conn, of course, must remain behind as hostages, but you may take one of the others along to assist you. No doubt you will choose Captain Meligraunce, as he is most likely to prove useful."

"Yes," said Tryffin, "if I can only take one of them, it must certainly be Meligraunce." As that was decided, he sat down and opened the map.

"You must enter Charon by the usual way, over the mountains," said the King, as Tryffin studied the parchment. "But once you have obtained the chalice, you can return much more quickly. Under Garlon's fortress there are many prisons, storerooms, and other chambers. There is also a sort of archway in the natural rock. That is one of the places where the fabric of reality is particularly thin and fluid, and it is possible to pass from Charon into this realm simply by walking under the arch."

"Like the last part of a pattern spell," said Tryffin, glancing up. It was a moment before he remembered that he had never encountered one of these spells—or even a knowledge of them—outside Mochdreff.

But the King seemed to know what he was talking about, so perhaps such spells were commonplace in the Shadow Lands, after all. "Yes, very like. Only different, because it is not necessary to walk any sort of pattern first."

Something about this, the idea of the arch in the rock, the ways of pattern spells, nudged an idea at the back of Tryffin's mind. But the King was still talking, so he put the thought aside to be considered later, at some more suitable time.

"My sons and an escort of goblins will take you as far as the border. Also, horses will be provided for you . . . though not of the breed of Annwn . . . and supplies for a journey.

"Of course," he added, "once you have crossed into Charon, there is nothing that anyone here can do to offer you assistance, no matter what happens to you."

*And he saw before him a hot, dry, withering land. Where there
should be water there was only dust. Where there should be
prosperous towns and populous villages there was only rock.
And where there should be vineyards and orchards there was
only sand.*

Dust, rock, and sand: a land of dry bones and no water.

—From The Vision of St. Pellam

17.

Water Among the Rocks

In order to prepare for the journey into Charon, the King took
Tryffin down to the cavernous treasure rooms under the hill.
There, among piles of gold and silver coins, wonderfully painted
shields, fabulous crested helmets, and entire suits of jeweled
plate armor (for ceremonial purposes only), Tryffin eventually
located some pieces of plate and mail which closely resembled
the black and gold armor he had left behind him in Anoeth.

"I suppose," said Tryffin, "these belonged to Prince Gruffydd." If they did not, and if the person who had owned the
armor before had died, he could not accept them—for he was
forbidden by geas to take iron from the dead.

"Yes," said the King, standing by the door with a crystal
lantern in his hand. "Which he has only recently put aside in
favor of the silver mail that he affects now. As you and he are
exactly the same size, this armor should certainly fit you."

Tryffin glanced up from his inspection of the armor. There
appeared to be a spell on the mail, one that set the bones in his
hands vibrating and warmed the blood in his veins, but he
thought it was harmless. Probably no more than a charm to bind
the iron rings one to the other and make the armor more nearly
impenetrable. "I will need a shield as well."

A shield was provided for him, one blazoned with a great

192

golden comet on a sable field sprinkled with silver stars. There was no need to choose armor for Meligraunce, who had been wearing his own when he entered Annwn, but Tryffin did ask for and receive a shield for the Captain.

"If you don't mind my asking," said Meligraunce, as he and the Governor prepared to depart, "I would like to know whether you think we have any hope of accomplishing this quest at all."

"If this Garlon is so powerful as King Avallach says . . . if the King himself, with all his resources of men and magic, for all his plots and schemes over twenty years' time, has not been able to obtain the chalice for himself . . . I cannot really believe that we will be any more successful," said Tryffin. "And yet . . . I think we owe it to Conn and Mahaffy, and to Garreg and Ciag, to at least go into Charon and see for ourselves what the chances are. If it appears to be truly impossible . . ." He shrugged. "Then I suppose we will have to do all in our power to return to Anoeth, defeat the shapechanger, and then with men and weapons at our disposal, *try* to find our way back to Annwn in time to effect a rescue."

"You do not sound very hopeful about that," said Meligraunce.

"I don't see much hope wherever I look," replied the Governor, "for all that I try to put an optimistic face on everything. Though we should have no trouble getting inside Dinas Garlon, because the warlock is apparently known for his hospitality. And not—so the King informed me, with a vile smirk—the sort of hospitality we have enjoyed in Annwn."

"And what of those fabulous powers we are supposed to possess, being men of the Otherworld?" said Meligraunce, as they walked down to the stable where the King's two sons and an escort of goblins were waiting with the horses.

"Those may appear in their own good time, but I very much doubt it," said Tryffin, shaking his head. "For myself, I think they may only augment such power as a man has to begin with. I do not imagine that many travel between the worlds unless they are already great wizards or witches, pagan priests or Adepts. Any power that you and I may discover within ourselves may not be enough to do us much good."

Charon was a hot, bright land. After the almost continual twilight in Annwn, it was like journeying into Hell to cross over the border and discover that glaring sun in the sky. To make matters worse, it appeared that Tryffin and Meligraunce had arrived near the end of a long, dry summer.

They rode for many hours across a rocky wasteland where the very air tasted like iron, an eternity, it seemed, of sun-baked earth and riverbeds filled with dust. But on toward evening, they came into inhabited country. It was not much better there, because the castles and the villages were mostly in ruins, and there seemed to be endless fields of withering vines . . . yet now and again, amidst that desolation, could be seen a small village clustered around a well or a fountain, a group of tiny cottages each with its own flourishing garden, and sometimes on a hillside in the distance, what appeared to be a castle surrounded by a thicket of trees and bushes.

At sunset, the Governor and Meligraunce stopped in one of the villages, to ask shelter for the night. There was no inn or public house for travelers to rest, but the mayor of the village was willing to give them a place in his stable with the asses for the price of a silver coin. This, Tryffin paid him readily, over the Captain's protest.

"By God, I know it is exorbitant," Tryffin whispered, in his henchman's ear, "but it is Avallach's silver."

"And I suppose you would be willing to haggle if it were your own?" said Meligraunce, with a sigh.

Tryffin shook his head. "No, I would not." But then he handed over the bag full of coins. "You may handle the money after this, Captain. There is no telling how long we will need to make this last, and I've no doubt at all you will manage it far more wisely than I would."

They slept that night in a thin pile of straw, rose reasonably refreshed in the morning, ate breakfast out of their saddlebags, and resumed their journey.

As the morning progressed, the land became a little more hospitable; there were even patches of green growing wild among the rocks. At noon, their road led them through a forest of thorns and branchless tree trunks, bleached and rotting. The trail twisted and turned, took them through a clearing where the ruins of a cruck-built house with a well could be seen, then into the forest of thorns again. At last they emerged, quite unexpectedly, on the banks of a flowing river, spanned by a vast stone bridge.

Tryffin drew in on the reins, sat staring out across the broad face of the water, which was dark and muddy but swiftly moving. "This will be the river Acheron, for there is no other river of any considerable size according to King Avallach's map," he said. "Yet I never expected so great a flood in this Purgatorial wilderness."

They crossed over the bridge, the horses' hooves clattering on the wooden timbers. As they approached the rocky banks on the other side, Meligraunce pointed, indicating a hill surmounted by a formidable-looking fortress, rising up in the middle distance. "That would be Dinas Garlon, I suppose. But what is that I see on the road?"

Down the long white track from the castle came a straggling line of dusty pilgrims, all in dull black. At the head of the procession rode a stern man on a white horse, a man clad in the rough sackcloth garments of a holy man, though a glint of armor could be seen beneath his open robe. There were other clerics as well, barefoot, tonsured, trudging behind him with their heads bowed, and beyond them the ranks of the faithful, wailing and beating their breasts as if in penitence.

"It looks like some sort of pilgrimage for the remission of sin," said Tryffin, as he and the Captain stopped to watch.

But when the procession reached the banks of the river, two of the monks of the humbler sort waded out into the shallows, and began to conduct a mass baptism of the noisy penitents, who went wallowing and thrashing into the muddy water on their knees, and then went eerily silent as soon as they received the sacrament.

"Have we wandered into a land of pagans?" said Meligraunce, under his breath. "A land where the Church is only just beginning to gain a foothold?"

There had been no signs of any religion in the Fairy realm, but that was to be expected.

Tryffin shook his head. "I seem to remember that every village we passed through had its own little shrine or chapel, and though I don't recall looking at any of them closely, they had . . . a sort of Christian look about them. It may be that there are schisms here in the Shadow Lands, just as there are in Mochdreff, and that this is a sect that does not believe in infant baptism."

"Heretics," said Meligraunce, frowning darkly, and he made a pious gesture, unthought and reflexive. "Like the Black Canons, or whoever built that damnable church where we ran the shapechanger to earth."

Tryffin repeated the gesture. "We have no way of knowing if the church and the shapechanger were truly connected, except by the accident of a powerful pattern spell being located down in the crypt. Last summer, when Gwenlliant was missing and we believed she was under the influence of the Black Canons, I learned all that I could of the various schismatic orders. Truth to tell, there was not much to learn, because most of their sects are extremely secretive. I do recall that the Black Canons reject infant baptism, but so have other, more harmless groups. Some even went so far as to reject the cross as an object of veneration, but we know that was not true of the church that Gwenlliant visited with Dahaut."

He remembered, with a shudder, what the pages Cei and Elffin had said afterward, of the ugly, threatening figure on the cross, the wine tainted with goat's blood, and the bread made with ground-up bones. And Mahaffy's description of the Black Canons: *"They are evil incarnate. But while those who make up the congregation radiate evil during the Mass, the Canons themselves give precisely the opposite impression. It is as though they have so thoroughly absorbed their own wicked principles, made a virtue out of vice and vice out of virtue, that even to those who are sensitive to such things, they appear perfectly harmless."*

As did the monks doing baptisms down in the muddy water. But the stern armored man on the white horse, watching the entire ceremony from the banks of the river, had the face of a fanatic, cold and merciless.

Tryffin was just turning toward Meligraunce, about to speak, when something caught his attention: an unpleasant odor riding on the breeze, a hint of graveyards and of rotting carrion. He glanced quickly around him in every direction, half expecting to see the vampyre Madonna in her brown cloak poised on the riverbank, or a stone gargoyle come galloping across the bridge. But of course there was nothing of the sort, no indication that the shapechanger was anywhere near. Most likely he had only caught the stench of some charnel house in the vicinity of the fortress, carried all this distance by the rising wind.

Then all thoughts of his enemy flowed from Tryffin's mind, as he spotted a lone woman in a rough dark robe approaching the river, kneeling down on the bank, beating the heels of her hands together . . . a slender young female who, even with her hair covered by a veil and her face shadowed, he recognized instantly.

He rose up in the stirrups, was about to call her name, when the lady gave a slight shake of her head, and a sign indicating that he should remain silent. Feeling a little dazed, he sat down in the saddle again.

But Meligraunce had already noticed the Governor's suddenly rigid posture. "Your Grace, what do you see?"

Tryffin shook his head, never taking his eyes off the woman, who had finally ceased bruising her wrists, and was scooping up a handful of dust, and marking herself under the veil.

"I hardly understand myself, how such a thing has come to pass," he said quietly. "But that lady there—the woman just prostrating herself on the rocks—that is my cousin Gwenlliant."

The road leading uphill to the limestone fortress was lined with appletrees. In fact, an orchard covered the lower slopes of the hill, and most of the trees were heavy with fruit. As he and Meligraunce rode up the lane, the Governor kept looking around him. There was something almost familiar about the lay of the land—*not* in the way that Annwn was familiar, but as though the shape of the hill and the general contours of the castle above reminded him vaguely of some other place.

When they reached the walls, which were high and sheer with rows of spikes around the top, the gate stood open and the portcullis lifted—but armed men barred the way, asking what business brought them to Dinas Garlon.

"We have come a great distance," said Tryffin. "But the fame of your lord is so great, we have heard that he never turns travelers away and that we have only to ask for shelter at Dinas Garlon to be taken in."

"That is true," said one of the guards, with a nod of his head. He had straw-colored hair and a tanned face, and his manner was friendly. "Though the guest house is maintained by order of the Lady Guenwyn."

He lowered his pike and stepped aside, so they might enter the shade of the gatehouse. "You may keep your armor, but your weapons must remain with us here."

While this had not been exactly expected, it was perfectly reasonable since they were strangers. For all that, it was difficult for Tryffin to relinquish the silver dagger.

Still, he told himself, *in all the lands of all the worlds there are, what makes me think I will meet the shapechanger here?* He could not expect to find her standing at his side every time that he caught even a whiff of bad odor.

"This dagger," he said, as he turned it over to the guard with the pike, "was a gift from a great lady. I hope you will guard it well and keep it safe, for I would hate to lose it."

"It will be returned to you whenever you decide to depart," said another of the guards, an older man with an air of quiet authority. "Or if you should stay for a time . . . once you have established a good name and a good character, you may carry your weapons again."

Tryffin and Meligraunce exchanged a puzzled glance. The guards seemed so friendly and helpful, the rules so just and so reasonable, it was difficult to believe that the man who ruled here was the same cruel tyrant that King Avallach had described to them.

"There is one other condition," said the first guard. "Before you can enter, you must give us your names."

Mindful of what Avallach had told him, that to give his name would place him in danger—and yet being forbidden by geas to tell an untruth—Tryffin had already arranged for Meligraunce to do the speaking, should a situation of this sort arise.

"My name is Brandegorias," said the Captain. "And this is my master, Maelwas fab Garan." It would be possible for Tryffin to respond to this without deceit, since it was all part of his name: Tryffin fab Maelgwyn fab Menai fab Maelwas fab Garan fab Maelgwyn fab Maelduin fab Pwyll.

Under those names, they were passed through into the outer courtyard, and one of the guards, a young fellow in patched leather and miscellaneous bits of plate armor, came along to show them the way to the house set aside for the entertainment of wayfarers.

"Food and drink will be provided you both for three days. After that, you may stay as long as you please, but you must pay for what you get . . . either with coins or with service," he explained, as they crossed the yard, passing a well, a forge, and a number of brightly colored awnings and open stalls where the castle craftsmen plied their trades. "The Lady Guenwyn is generous, but her wealth is not inexhaustible, and she wishes to benefit as many travelers as she possibly can."

Again the name of this woman that King Avallach had

neglected to mention, prompting Tryffin to ask, "And the Lady Guenwyn is Lord Garlon's . . . ?"

"She is the Chatelaine here, and Lord Garlon's younger sister. A most amazing woman, and you will be fortunate if you are allowed to meet her," replied the guard, as he opened a wrought-iron gate and ushered them into a garden where grapevines and lemon trees grew. "She is one of the great marvels of the world, that I can tell you."

Tryffin smiled faintly, thinking he understood the cause of the young man's enthusiasm. "She is very beautiful, then . . . and perhaps also very charming?"

But the guardsman only laughed. "I believe you might call her a fine-looking woman but she is certainly no beauty. And she can be a little too brusque to be accounted charming. I am surprised that her fame does not extend so far as that of her brother," he added earnestly, "for she is a great sorceress in her own right—some call her a witch, others a healer and prophetess, but I say that she is a very good woman and the most compassionate heart in all of Charon."

"Before God," said Tryffin, to whom it was now becoming clear why Avallach had failed to mention Lord Garlon's sister. "I think I should count myself fortunate to meet her, if she is all that you say."

There was no feasting in the house set aside for travelers by the Lady Guenwyn, just good plain food: barley bread and fruit, lettuces, and a broth made with millet, served three times a day in the common dining hall. The house was built of stone, white-washed within and without, and was kept as clean as a building with a dirt floor could possibly be. Besides the common room, which took up most of the place, there was also a loft above, where women and children slept when there were any in the house. But now there were only men, who slept in rows on the floor, on rough sheepskin robes provided each evening by the two old men who maintained the place in the Lady's absence. It seemed to Tryffin that this Guenwyn was extremely practical in her charity, and that it was a solid and ongoing concern, not something brief and flashy, calculated to win admiration, then to be cast aside as soon as it had served that purpose.

The guest house was also a good place to gather information, because there were men there—peddlers, mendicants, and wandering friars—from all parts of Charon. And after a good meal and the single tankard of ale that was provided, some of them were inclined to become expansive. For Tryffin, who had the ability to draw out others, simply by looking sympathetic and listening patiently, it was the perfect opportunity to learn everything that he wanted to know.

After the first day, he was able to piece together a brief history of Charon, over the past twenty years: Not long since, Charon had been even more barren and desolate than it was now, but it was said that Lord Garlon himself had saved the land and the people by "the sacrificial act of contrition." No one seemed to know exactly what this act of contrition was, only that it involved some form of holy White Magic, and had apparently left deep physical scars that would remain with Garlon for the rest of his life. Nevertheless, everyone was firmly convinced that it was Garlon's act which had "released the waters and caused the river Acheron to flow again." Though the land still remained largely infertile, wherever there was a well, a spring-fed pool, or a river, it was now possible to grow things in abundance.

Of the chalice with the gemstone, Tryffin learned rather less. It was apparently *not* part of the magic which had brought a partial healing to the land, because it had arrived in Charon some time afterward, but it seemed to be the source of much of the power that Garlon had acquired later, which gave him his reputation as a sorcerer.

"Yet before I came into Charon, I heard it said that Lord Garlon was a hard man and a cruel master. How could such a story have started?" Tryffin asked the wandering tinsmith who had provided most of this information.

Then seeing how the man's face suddenly closed up, he added hastily, "I beg your pardon. If the story were true, it would not be wise for you to answer my question, and if it is not, then you are rightly insulted by my impertinence in asking."

The smith shook his head. He was a weather-beaten man with shaggy brown hair and a thin beard. "There are some things safer for *me* to say than for *you* to hear, Lord Maelwas. For it is plain to me by the way that you speak and the way that you hold yourself that you are no ordinary wayfarer, but a great man in your own country."

Tryffin frowned thoughtfully, finding this decidedly ambiguous. "I don't understand, and I wish you would tell me everything you know. I will not repeat anything that you tell me abroad, for I know when to speak and when to be silent."

The man sighed. "Perhaps it is better for me to speak now than for you to go about asking questions that might make trouble for you." He sat chewing on a piece of barley bread, as if he needed time to choose his words, and then he began: "For many years, you could not find a wiser or more temperate or more compassionate ruler than our Lord Garlon. But in recent years . . . the taxes have been cruelly heavy, and he makes new laws all of the time, each one harsher than the last. You must understand, the people are not ungrateful for what he has done for them, and they attempt to obey his laws, but news travels slowly and sometimes these new laws are broken out of sheer ignorance."

"And how are the lawbreakers punished?" asked Tryffin, picking up an apple, taking out his dirk, and beginning to cut the fruit into sections.

"Now, that is the strange thing . . . for a true tyrant uses terror as his weapon, does he not? You are maybe imagining hangings and burnings, scourgings and mutilation, but that is rarely the case. For the most part, he levies heavy fines, which if they cannot be paid in coin are paid with the lawbreakers' lands and possessions. And you know, Lord Maelwas, that men may die by other means than the rope or the axe: Starvation will do it, and so will disgrace, poverty, grief, and the maladies that all of these other things breed."

"Yes," said Tryffin quietly. He slipped the dirk back into its scabbard and offered his companion a section of the apple. "I know that they can. But you said . . . it was safer for you to speak of these things than for me to hear them. What did you mean by that?"

"I mean that Lord Garlon for all I have told you remains a reasonable man. That is . . . he knows that people will grumble, and that this grumbling is mostly harmless. So if the common folk complain of their lot, he does nothing at all. But . . ." The tinsmith lowered his voice. "Certain powerful men who have spoken out against him, men who were in a position to oppose his will, have all died, or suffered great misfortune . . . always by accident, it seems, yet always at the moment when Lord Garlon is threatened. If he were an ordinary man, one might call these coincidence, but as he is a warlock . . . everyone believes that he causes these 'accidents' to happen."

Tryffin sat staring down at the toes of his boots. "He seems to be a very complex man, Lord Garlon. Not so good as he might be—or so bad." And he thought of that other complex man, King Avallach of Annwn, and wondered: In whose hands would a chalice with miraculous powers be likely to cause the least grief, the least mischief to others?

"In truth," said the tinker, "there are some who say if he would only allow the Lady Guenwyn to influence him more, he would be the kindest and wisest ruler that was ever born—though others say if he would only listen less often to the dark witch and more often to Lot of Caer Sant, he would see his way clear, and follow the path of a righteous man."

But when Tryffin asked him to explain further, the tinsmith would say no more. Lot of Caer Sant was the warrior monk that Tryffin had seen down by the river—he had learned that much talking to other people—but he had to wait another day, until Meligraunce could provide him with more information.

"According to the guards at the gate," said the Captain, who had rapidly ingratiated himself among his counterparts at Dinas Garlon, "this Lot is the most powerful man in the very powerful militant order, the Knights of Jerusalem, and some folk call him a wicked sorcerer, others a saint, all for the miracles that he performs. Beyond that, he is Lord Garlon's friend and his most trusted advisor."

They were walking in the outer courtyard, among the craftsmen's stalls and tents, so Tryffin lowered his voice, to keep others from overhearing. "It seems to me that Charon has more than its fill of miracle workers, and no one seems able to agree which ones are given their powers by divine will, and which are in league with infernal powers."

"That is my impression also," said Meligraunce, as they passed a stall where a man was making leather saddles. "Though from all I have heard, if I were asked to form an opinion of my own, I would say that the power of good in this land is mostly vested with the Lady Guenwyn."

Tryffin nodded. "I believe you are right. But what . . . what of my cousin, the Lady Gwenlliant? Have you seen her here, does anyone know anything about her?"

Meligraunce made a helpless gesture. "I thought, once, that I spotted her from a distance, but she was gone again before I could approach her. And you asked me to be discreet, so I could not inquire too widely. The guards at the gate know of no one by that name, but that is hardly surprising. She is likely to be using a false name just as we are."

The Governor paused to stare up at the central pile of the fortress, the many-towered keep where they had not yet been permitted to enter. The place had a closed, forbidding aspect, for many of the windows were barred, and the rest were too high or too narrow to be accessible. "Dear God, how I want to find her . . . how I want to speak to her. But she made it quite clear that I was not to approach her in the sight of others, and I ought to respect her wishes . . . at least until I have a better idea what she is doing here."

"In the meantime," said Meligraunce, bringing him back to earth, "we will soon have the chance to see and perhaps to meet some of these other important people we have heard so much about."

Tryffin felt a slight quickening of interest. "And how is that?" he asked, as they wandered across the yard, toward the garden with the lemon trees.

"There will be a service in the chapel tomorrow, at which Lot of Caer Sant will celebrate Mass and the chalice will be displayed to the populace, as it is three times a year," said Meligraunce. "In the afternoon, there is going to be some sort of ceremony involving the Lady Guenwyn—a public healing, I believe. That is supposed to be rather more common, but still worth seeing."

Tryffin stopped with one hand on the iron gate, thinking that over. Both occasions seemed likely to attract great crowds of curious people, and perhaps . . . perhaps Gwenlliant would be there among the rest.

"Then I think we should make every effort to be there," he said.

In Glangogledd, a priest there told me of a scandal which had occurred in that very village during his grandfather's time.

It seems that there was a young woman who, being of a wayward nature and extremely wild and uncontrolled in her ways (though she came of a good family, and her parents had both been respectable people), would go out by stealth from her mother's cottage, when the nights were long, and dance in the moonlight with the wolves and the foxes.

—*From* A Journey into Rhianedd and Gorwynnion

18.

The Moon of the Wolves and the Foxes

They left Caer Bannawg in the cold, sad hour just after dawn. Already mounted, with Grifflet cuddled under her cloak, Gwenlliant watched sympathetically as Tinne and Mabonograin made their farewell.

Pale but dry-eyed, the Princess was doing her best to be brave and dignified. Mabonograin showed more visible signs of inner turmoil; his lips were compressed in a hard line, and there was tension in every line of his wiry body. Yet he, too, had apparently accepted the situation, was going to let her go from him without protest or interference; had resigned himself to the fact that Tinne must do her duty, whatever the personal cost to her or to him.

It was a great deal harder for Gwenlliant to hold her tongue. She knew that it was all a lie, that Gwythyr had cheated them both out of the life they were meant to lead. And she had an idea, knowing what she knew of future events, that as a result of that cheat everyone was going to suffer in ways that would have shocked even Gwythyr out of the course he had chosen, if he had been able to predict any of the consequences.

It was all very easy up until now, there was nothing I saw that I wanted to change, nothing important enough that it would have mattered, anyway. Gwenlliant shivered and retreated inside her borrowed cloak. *But these are events that are meant to happen, and interfering will do no good. In truth, I could only make it crueler and harder, by delaying the inevitable.*

She wanted very much to go home, back to her own time and place, or at least to Dame Ceinwen on the Marches. She did not want to stay and see events play themselves out to their tragic conclusion. *But I have to stay a little longer; I still don't know exactly what happened to disgrace Caerthinn, or how the feud really began.*

Or if only she could gain mastery of the shapechanging magic, her time in Achren would not have been wasted.

Prince Caethinn had not come down from his bedchamber to say good-bye to his sister, which made Gwenlliant think less of him. Perhaps he thought it would be easier for Tinne, sparing her the sight of his unquestionably genuine grief. But Gwenlliant thought that a good brother would have been strong enough to put that grief aside, and to lend his sister a little of that strength in a situation that had to be far more painful for her than it was for him.

Mabonograin assisted Tinne into the saddle, gave her one last tender glance, then turned on his heel and strode away, before his feelings could overmaster him. Maelinn, who had been standing apart talking to her brother all this while, came over and took one of the Princess's hands, held it to her cheek.

"It has been decided. You will *not* go directly to the temple of Cerridwen, but will spend some time in my house first. While you are there, you shall make peace within yourself, learn something of your duties as a priestess, and dedicate yourself to the new life to come. Don't you think it will be easier and pleasanter so?"

Tinne nodded wordlessly. Gwenlliant did not know what Maelinn had done or promised to gain this concession from Gwythyr, but she thought it was a kindly gesture. Probably Maelinn was feeling a little bit guilty—not only because she knew what Gwythyr had done and would not speak out, but because it was her own decision to continue on as the Priestess of Goleuddydd that had caused these things to happen—yet it would not be unlike her to do the thing out of kindness alone.

Besides which, Gwenlliant reminded herself ruefully, Maelinn had probably justified everything in her own mind already. She was very good at finding excuses for whatever she wanted to do.

Gwythyr cleared his throat. "However, I will not wait forever to claim my bride. She must be ready to come to me by the next new moon."

Maelinn, who had been all sweetness and sympathy a moment before, turned swiftly and gave him a spiteful glance.

"You make a mockery of sacred mysteries, by regarding Tinne as your bride first, the chosen of your goddess second," she said coldly. "I should advise *you* to make good use of this time of preparation, by asking Cerridwen to grant you a better understanding of your duties and your obligations . . . and how to put the will of the gods above our own."

Gwythyr said nothing, only gave the High Priestess a smoldering glance. The rebuke was an apt one, as he must certainly realize, but that did not mean he liked it any better. Or that he was going to make any effort to amend his thinking.

Tinne was a dismal presence in the house in the wood. She trailed about, sad and silent, with her hair unbraided and her feet bare, and when anyone asked her to assist with the cooking, the milking, or the spinning, she performed those tasks in a half-hearted way that was really not very helpful.

Eventually, Maelinn grew impatient. "I have already done all that I can to make her way easier, and you would think she might show a little gratitude, as well as a little more spirit. If she raged against her fate, if she wept and stormed and stamped her feet, it would soon be over, but this moping about is useless and depressing."

It seemed to Gwenlliant that it was everyone else who made Tinne so determined to remain miserable. If people would just stop telling her that she ought to cheer up, she would no longer feel any need to assert her right to be just as dreary and doleful as she liked, and would soon grow resigned all on her own.

"Besides," Maelinn added, with a sniff, "I do not see why it was necessary for her to bring *all* of her possessions with her, so many chests and bundles and bags—as though we need her things cluttering about, or Gwythyr will allow her to live in such state, once she goes to him at the temple of Cerridwen."

"Let that be decided at the proper time," said Caithne, rising to Tinne's defense, simply because it had become a matter of habit to oppose Maelinn, not because she felt any sympathy for Tinne. "Besides, quite a number of the things that she brought with her were intended for temple offerings."

But this did nothing to placate Maelinn—in fact, the mention of offerings only served to increase her irritation.

In all that house, Gwenlliant was the most sincerely sympathetic, having once so narrowly escaped the same fate: marriage to a man that she feared and loathed. *At least,* she thought, *had I grown sufficiently desperate, I might have escaped to live in a convent. I don't think that I would have* liked *being a holy sister, lacking a true vocation, but at least the Church would have offered me that one safe refuge. But Tinne has to take the convent and Gwythyr, too, and that really seems an unbearable fate!*

Sensing this sympathy—and perhaps because Gwenlliant was the closest in age—the Princess sought her out, and soon they became good friends. Though she never spoke of the future, Tinne would become cheerful speaking of the past, when they were alone together.

Tinne's brother, Gwenlliant soon realized, was weak, though his sister never said anything against him. It was easy for Gwenlliant to see these things, because she had lived in the halls of power most of her life. Caerthinn had been chosen to succeed his maternal uncle as the High Prince simply because he was the only nephew. He was not a brave man, in battle or elsewhere, and spent most of his time avoiding difficult decisions and confrontations. And he was always making promises he was too lazy to keep, then depending on somebody else to carry them out. When Gwenlliant thought of Tryffin, who was always so strong and tireless in carrying out his duties, who faced every challenge with courage and honesty, it was hard to feel much compassion for Caerthinn. Still, he had clearly been thrust into a role of power and influence he was simply too small a person to fill, and for that reason he ought to be pitied.

Mabonograin appeared in a more favorable light: generous, demonstrative, energetic, and loyal. Unfortunately, he was also impulsive and tended to act according to the promptings of his heart rather than his head.

What was really needed in Achren, at the court of the High Prince, was some good common sense, thought Gwenlliant, feeling suddenly very much older than all of them.

"Gwenhwyach, I have something to show you," said Tinne one day, speaking very low, and glancing around in a cautious, conspiratorial sort of way. "The others don't know and I do not mean to tell them, but it is something I would like you to see, for I am sure you will admire it and will understand exactly what it means to me."

Naturally, Gwenlliant was curious, and more than willing to accompany the other girl up to the loft, where it was cool and shadowy under the roof, and everything smelled of earth and feathers. Tinne opened one of the wooden chests she had brought with her and took out a bowl-shaped object wrapped in silk.

"You must promise not to tell Maelinn, for she saw this once and wanted it . . . she might find a way to claim it, if she knew it was here," said Tinne, very low.

"I promise," said Gwenlliant, kneeling down on the floor beside her, the better to see the object she held.

The wrappings fell away to reveal a sort of crystal loving cup, with golden handles and a golden rim set with lesser gemstones around the top. In the dim light of the loft, the cup shimmered and glowed, as though it possessed some luminous quality of its own.

"The bowl was made from a single sidhe-stone," said Tinne. "Mabonograin gave it to me, when . . . when we first knew that we were in love, in the days when we thought I would come here and take Maelinn's place. It was to be an offering to the Green Lady—now it will go with me to the temple of Cerridwen."

Gwenlliant reached out tentatively to touch the cup. It was true that sidhe-stones were often quite large, which was why—unless they happened to be those with magical powers—in spite of their beauty, only the really enormous ones had great value.

But she had never seen or heard of a stone to match the one she was looking at now, either in size, beauty, or luster. "Does it have any powers . . . is it one of the magical stones?" she asked in a hushed voice.

Tinne shook her head. "Not that anyone knows. But everyone thinks that when it is consecrated to—to one of the gods or goddesses, any powers it has will be finally revealed. That is why Gwythyr wants it, and why Maelinn would rather it stayed here with her than went to him. And I . . . even though it is so beautiful a thing and it came from Mabonograin . . . sometimes I wish I had never seen it, because I think it was the beginning of all my troubles."

As the stone was so large and perfect, it was not surprising that so many people wanted it. If it was magical, its powers would be formidable.

"Truly," said Gwenlliant, "it is a marvelous thing. But if Gwythyr and his goddess only wanted the cup, I think they might have found a way to get it, and leave you alone. You should cherish this gift that Mabonograin gave you, and not let anything spoil your pleasure in its beauty."

Tinne nodded, with tears in her eyes, as she wrapped the cup in its silk covering and hid it away again.

After that, Gwenlliant thought of the sidhe-stone cup often, wondering why she had never seen or heard of it before. It was hard to believe that anything so beautiful and valuable could be allowed to be lost or destroyed, even in a thousand years.

There was a sudden air of excitement in the house. Gwenlliant knew that it had something to do with the waxing moon. It was always at the full moon that the twelve young priestesses went out into the forest to dance all night, bare-skinned during the summer months, scantily clad when the ground was covered with ice and snow. But it seemed that the first full moon after the Midwinter Feast was somehow special—the Moon of the Wolves and the Foxes, said Maelinn; Owl Moon, Hawk Moon, the Moon of Ravens and Magpies, said Caithne and Sceith; and for once Maelinn had laughed at the contradiction—and so this dance would be special as well.

The Princess had been invited to join them, but she declined, so when the night came, when darkness crept in, Tinne went up to bed long before moonrise. Gwenlliant, who had *not* been invited, did likewise, slipping in under the blankets and furs beside Grifflet, who was already sleeping, taking his warm little body in her arms for comfort. At times like this she was painfully aware that she was not, after all, really a member of this unusual household, but only a stranger offered temporary shelter.

She must have been asleep when the others went out, because she heard nothing of their departure, but she woke, a short or a long time later, with the moon in her face. Someone had neglected to fasten the latch on the one window, and the shutter had blown open.

Gwenlliant slid out of the bed to close the window, walked

barefoot across the loft . . . but paused with her hand on a shutter, because something extraordinary was happening down below.

The forest had come to life: The moon-silvered trees were all swaying and crooning as if in a high wind, but the air was completely still—not a hint of a breeze, not the slightest movement of the chilly air on her face, to account for the open window or the motion of the trees. But sitting in a circle around the edge of the clearing were the wolves and the foxes who lived in the wood—silvery grey and autumn red against the white drifts of snow—staring up at Gwenlliant, with their wild, dark, expectant, questioning eyes, inviting her to come down and join them under the moon.

She turned from the window and started toward the ladder, then hesitated, standing in the middle of the loft in her thin nightdress. Because what of Grifflet? She could not take him with her into the forest, among all those wild creatures, yet she hated to leave him behind.

Then she remembered what Maelinn had said at Caer Bannawg, that the fog could not come when the snow was falling. It was not falling now, but she thought it was far too cold for the Mist to rise . . . and besides, she had lived in this place for half of a year and the Mist had not come to snatch her away. Also, if the little boy should wake in the night and call out, Tinne was there to see to his needs.

Any by now, she was entirely caught up in the enchantment of the night, her blood singing, her bones humming, a warm tingle spreading across her skin. She *had* to go down, she was meant to go down, or else why had the wolves and the foxes appeared to escort her?

On the day she first wandered into the wood, Gwenlliant had imagined a night of impenetrable blackness, but that was in summer with the leaves on the trees, blotting out the moon and the stars. Tonight, the trees were all bare except for the yews and the evergreens, and the forest was bathed in moonlight. That would hardly have mattered in any case, because she had no need to find her way, moving with the tide of the forest beasts, who pressed their furry bodies on all sides of her, carrying her along with them. And there were owls in the air, just as she had envisioned them, flitting about from tree to tree, some of them swooping so low that they grazed her hair. One even landed for a moment on her shoulder and rode there for a time, murmuring in her ear, then departed with a whoop and a rush of wings.

Then suddenly she was alone, standing on the edge of a clearing, in the shade of a whispering yew—her escort of wolves and foxes had simply disappeared, and the owls had done the same. They left her, shivering a little because the night was so cool, barefoot in the middle of the forest.

But not alone, after all, because all the twelve priestesses were gathered in the clearing—Maelinn, Pali, Ceri, Pethboc, Sceith, Caithne, Regan, Tiffaine, Ettare, Gleis, Mai, and Morfa—her twelve friends and three strangers, perhaps the silent priestesses from the temple of Cerridwen. None of them spotted Gwenlliant, standing under the sheltering yew, and she thought that was perhaps just as well, since the invitation had come from the beasts and the birds and not from any of the women.

They stood in a circle facing in, all dressed as Gwenlliant was in their white night-shifts with their hair unbound, their mantles and cloaks lying like pools of shadow on the ground at their feet, as though carelessly dropped there. They were humming a tune very low, under the breath, the same tune without words that the trees were crooning, the same tune that Gwenlliant's blood was singing, and their arms were upraised toward the moon.

Suddenly, there was a shimmering in the air around Maelinn, and a great cry was torn from her throat, whether of joy or of pain it was impossible to tell, for her face contorted and her body writhed . . . then Maelinn was not there at all. A great brown owl rose up in her place, batting its wings wildly, then those wings caught the air and the owl went soaring off into the night sky.

Now Gwenlliant knew why Maelinn and Sceith and Caithne had laughed together, so strangely companionable. The Moon of the Wolves and the Foxes, Owl Moon, Hawk Moon, the Moon of the Ravens and Magpies . . . it was all these and more, for its true name was the Shapechanger's Moon. And one by one, the other young women *were* changing: into a crow, a sparrowhawk, falcon, magpie, chough, rook . . . the transformations came so swiftly that it was impossible to keep count.

The last was a bewildered white raven, fluttering in the darkness under the yew, rising to the branches on uncertain wings, and balancing there for the briefest of moments while the reality of what had just happened flooded into her mind . . . then Gwenlliant launched herself into the night sky and flew away with the moonlight on her wings.

There was a great press of bodies in the Dinas Garlon chapel. Arriving late with Meligraunce, Tryffin had to settle for a position near the door, instead of a place on the benches near the front, which his fine clothes and that indefinable air of rank and distinction would have entitled him to, even here where he was not known. Fortunately, both he and the Captain were tall enough to see over the heads of the people standing in front of them, with a clear view all the way to the altar.

It was not like any church that Tryffin had ever seen, so bare and cold and somehow threatening: walls of naked unfinished stone, a lofty ceiling lost in the shadows, and no ornamentation except for some stained-glass windows depicting grisly martyrdoms in dark, disturbing colors: viper green, midnight black, storm purple. The place in the sanctuary where the crucifix ought to be was empty, and on the altar, which was covered with a blood-stained cloth, instead of the cup and plate, there rested a hammer and a long silver spike. The congregation seemed to feel some lack of sanctity, too; the way they were shoving and jostling to get the best places, they seemed more like the crowd at a bear-baiting or other spectacle than a community of the godly going to worship.

Glancing around him, Tryffin saw there was an oriel near the back, with a gallery for the Lord and his household to sit. They were filing in now, in their silks and furs, prayer books in hand, then sitting down on a bench near the rail. These noble lords and ladies, at least, were silent and seemed to have their minds on higher things.

The Governor nudged Meligraunce and indicated the party up in the gallery. "Do you know which one is Lord Garlon?"

"The gaunt man with the restless eyes, according to the description of the men at the gate. Yes . . . see, there are scars on his hands," said the Captain, very low. "By God, I think it would be a fine thing to be lord of a mighty fortress like this, but I do not think I would like to live in the mind behind that face."

Tryffin nodded. Everything about Lord Garlon denoted great mental suffering: the nervous, bloodless hands that were never at peace, the inward stoop of his shoulders, the wide, tormented eyes. "He looks like a man who has bad dreams. No, worse . . . like a man who is slowly going mad, and knows it."

There were three women up in the gallery, beautifully gowned and bejeweled, with veils over their hair but their faces uncovered, but as none of them bore any striking resemblance to Lord Garlon, it was impossible to guess which one was his sister.

"She is not likely to be here," whispered Meligraunce, in response to Tryffin's question. "I have heard she will not set foot inside a church where Lot celebrates the Mass. It would appear that they disagree most bitterly on matters of doctrine . . . though the Lady, in any case, has never been one for public worship, preferring to make her devotions alone in her private chapel.

"Which apparently makes it that much easier for Brother Lot and his followers to denounce her as a pagan sorceress, for all her good works," he added, under his breath. "Were it not that she stands so high in her brother's favor, as well as the love of the people, they would probably have burned her a long time ago."

Tryffin frowned thoughtfully. "This Lot has sufficient power to do that . . . to a woman of noble birth?"

"So I have been told," said Meligraunce. "It seems this Pellamian Heresy has spread like wildfire in less than five years . . . half the country converted and the rest considering it. And the Knights of Jerusalem, as Lot and his order are called, appear to be the sort of dangerous fanatics who would welcome an opportunity for a purge and a holy war."

He might have said more, but just then there was a rustle of movement, a ripple of excitement, as a door near the altar opened and a procession came through, all in rough black sackcloth except for Brother Lot, who wore robes of scarlet and gold. Two scrawny young acolytes carried the cup and the covered plate.

"We'll move forward with the rest when it comes time to receive Communion," Tryffin whispered, in the Captain's ear, "because I want a closer look at the chalice. But there is no need to take the bread or the wine. In truth, I would rather avoid it if at all possible."

"As would I," murmured Meligraunce.

The Mass proceeded in a familiar fashion. It appeared that the Pellamians, no matter how strange their doctrine, were highly orthodox when it came to ritual. It was a simple ceremony of the same sort practiced by conservative clerics in Mochdreff and Perfudd, with overtones of the northern rite.

As the Host was elevated, Tryffin felt a hand on his sleeve. "Your Grace, look," hissed Meligraunce.

He turned his eyes in the direction that the Captain indicated. A number of young men and women were silently entering the chapel by the door near the altar, among them a particular young woman in a long black gown and a misty grey veil. One by one, they prostrated themselves before the altar, then rose, moved toward the rail, and knelt down with their heads bowed.

Tryffin caught his breath. "Gwenlliant. I was beginning to think I had dreamed that encounter down by the river. But why did she come through the priest's quarters? Why does she kneel with those others by the altar, away from the rest of the congregation?"

Meligraunce cleared his throat. "Your Grace, do you think it possible, the Lady being still a virgin . . . that is, I do not know if there are Pellamian sisterhoods related to the Knights of Jerusalem, but if she has taken some sort of vow . . . ?"

Tryffin felt like the earth was slipping away beneath his feet. Gwenlliant forget her wedding vows, enter a convent, and become a nun—and not even in the real world, but here in this land of ghosts and shadows—rather than return to him? It was not what he would have expected of her certainly, yet it would explain much that was puzzling: about her presence here now, and the way she had turned away from him down by the river.

Then he shook his head emphatically. "No, I will not believe that until she tells me so herself."

Tryffin began moving toward the altar with the rest of the crowd, but also trying to make his way in Gwenlliant's direction. He was not successful, and found himself on the other side of the nave by the time he reached the front.

But by then, his eyes were on the chalice: a great silver cup, banded with gold and set with many precious gemstones, including an immense sidhe-stone. From a distance, he had not noticed the aureole of light which surrounded it, a pearly radiance that extended in every direction for about a yard, and limned everything that passed within it with a shimmering silvery fire.

That, however, was not what caught his attention. Because the silver cup was an illusion, a misty veil, covering the deeper and darker mystery which was the real chalice. That second cup, the true chalice, was like a shadow at the heart of the mist: a crystal vessel without any stem, as red as wine, as red as blood. Those who appeared to drink from the silver cup were left dazed and euphoric, but they were obviously inducing that state themselves; it was a kind of hysteria. The illusion had nothing to give them, and as for the real chalice . . . if it had, it was not distributing that manna today.

Afterward, in the flagstone-paved yard outside the chapel, Tryffin was angry. "It was all a sham . . . all done for show. Those people went there expecting a miracle, the revelation of some holy mystery, and there was nothing of the sort. There was a power at work there in the chapel—I could feel its influence— but that power has nothing to do with Mass or Holy Communion, and Garlon and Lot must know that as well as I do."

Meligraunce frowned thoughtfully, walking along at his side. "But how can you be certain? Would it not take someone with a religious vocation to determine whether the object was holy or not?"

Tryffin sighed. He was reluctant to tell Meligraunce exactly what he had seen and felt, so he contented himself by telling half of the truth. "If the chalice was holy, I might well have felt nothing, but not such a very strong presence of . . . of some *earthy* power."

They passed through a gate into another courtyard and continued on through the series of gates and archways, court- yards and gardens, which made up the outermost ring of the fortress, while the Captain mulled that over.

"It was not, then, something you perceived as evil?" he asked at last. "You are only disturbed because it was a lie?"

Tryffin nodded. "Because it was a lie, yes. And because I am wondering what evil—in Lot of Caer Sant or Garlon of Charon—that lie was meant to conceal."

By now, they had arrived at the place in the outermost courtyard where the ceremony of healing was supposed to take place. The Governor was hoping he would not be disappointed, and that the Lady Guenwyn would *not* prove to be as great a charlatan as her older brother. There were a number of people in the yard already, gathered around the stepped stone platform where she was supposed to appear, and Tryffin was startled to note that a fire had been built in the middle of the platform, and a large iron cauldron was hanging from a tripod over the blaze.

But he had already noticed his stocky friend the tinsmith among the other spectators, so he asked the man for an explanation.

"Ah, Lord Maelwas, I am glad you are here. It is a remarkable ceremony, the Washing of Souls . . . or so they call it in the village I come from," said the tinker, stroking his thin brown beard. "But you must see it for yourself; I could not possibly do it justice."

While the tinsmith spoke, a slight, straight figure in a grey velvet gown was approaching the platform and mounting the steps. If this was the Lady Guenwyn, the guard at the gate had described her perfectly: a handsome woman at best, not young or beautiful certainly . . . but dark and elegant, with a lively, intelligent face, and an air of self-possession that some might find a little daunting.

"By Our Lady of Mercy," breathed Meligraunce, on whom she seemed to be having a very different effect, "if it were not such a great impertinence, I believe I would fall in love."

Tryffin, who had never seen the Captain bedazzled before, was suitably intrigued. Yet there was no time to ask questions, because with the Lady's arrival a great many others had converged on the courtyard and the ceremony was already beginning.

A grey-haired woman with a lined face and bitter dark eyes was climbing the stairs to the platform, with a hesitating step. When she reached the top, she stood a moment, as if uncertain what was expected of her, then reached back and undid the lacing of her ragged brown dress, shrugged her way out of the gown . . . and stepped away, with a kind of a shudder, from the pile of dirty cloth. Quicker than thought, before the woman had time to change her mind, the Lady Guenwyn snatched up the garment and plunged it into the boiling water.

Tryffin and Meligraunce waited to see what would happen next. The sorceress stepped toward the grey-haired woman— who was shivering mightily in her short dingy shift, for all the heat of the day—placed a comforting hand on one scrawny bare arm, and whispered something into her ear. What she said, Tryffin could not make out, yet it seemed to communicate some peace of mind to the shuddering woman. Her trembling stopped, almost immediately, and when Guenwyn brushed a light kiss on the woman's forehead, a beatific smile appeared on her lined face.

Then the witch reached down through the steam rising from the iron pot, put her hand into what certainly must be scalding water, and drew out the dress. The crowd gasped, and even Tryffin caught his breath sharply. For the gown, which had been tattered and brown when it first went in, was now beautifully mended—and had apparently been dyed a fresh spring green.

As the woman left the platform, clutching the gown to her breast, still with the same dazed smile on her face, the Governor glanced around him. There appeared to be many waiting to take her place. If the Lady Guenwyn was playing some mountebank's trick with another gown already in the cauldron, she could only manage to deceive the crowd a few more times before she ran out of fresh garments—or else bring the ceremony to a close.

She did neither one. Men and women kept streaming up to the platform: a monk in a stained white habit, which came out of the cauldron a deep, ecclesiastical purple . . . a weary old man in dull robes of mourning, which turned many shades lighter to a startling blue . . . a painted harlot in harlequin silks, who approached with a swagger and departed, blushing like a maiden, with a gown the color of sunshine over one arm . . . and many others besides, so many that Tryffin soon lost count. Not one did the Lady Guenwyn turn away, not one left her without signs of mental and spiritual renewal plainly written on his or her face.

"And this is the woman that Lot and his followers call the dark witch, apostate, and a pagan sorceress," Tryffin said, with a wondering shake of his head. "The marvel is that the people do not band together and honor this Guenwyn as a living saint."

"Many would," said the tinsmith, beside him, "but the Lady herself will not have it. She insists that she has no holy vocation, and that the rite you have witnessed is no washing of souls—as it would certainly appear—but only the ancient craft of the white witch."

"Whatever it is," said Tryffin, looking down on his shorter companion, "it is more truly and wholesomely magical than anything I have seen since . . ."

"Since . . . when, Lord Maelwas?" asked Meligraunce, when he did not continue.

But the Governor was staring at the Lady as she descended from the platform, crossed the courtyard, and disappeared through one of the iron-bound doors leading into the inner fortress. "I don't remember. For a moment I was almost reminded of something, but it has since passed out of my mind."

And there came, at that time, an order of humble mendicant friars into the land, and they went from one village to the next, healing the sick, speaking words of comfort to the dying, and doing much good. It was said that their prior was a youth with remarkable powers, one who had worked many wonders and miraculous healings, remarkable, too, for his saintly nature and the fervor with which he served God. He had been born of a noble house, even of the line of the Lords of Mochdreff, but had put aside the privileges of his rank and all worldly pomp and splendor, because of his extreme holiness.

At last, men of the court came seeking this holy youth, to tell of the plight of their young lord, and how he was dying of the wounds that he had inflicted on himself. "But if you will see and speak to him," they said, "if you cannot save him, at least you may give him peace as he passes out of this life."

And the youth said, "I will come; let the Lord of this land look for me."

. . . but when he arrived at the fortress, it was not as a humble friar. He rode in through the gate on a white stallion, and he wore rich garments of purple cloth over a suit of glittering silver armor. He carried something with him, an object which he handled at all times with great reverence, but it was veiled like a mystery.

The guards at the gate escorted him to the place where their lord lay dying. The miracle worker did not wait to be greeted or acknowledged, but spoke up boldly at once. "What," he asked, "will you give in return for healing?"

And Garlon, believing that Lot was a holy man and that he served the Lord God Almighty, answered without hesitation, "I will give whatever is required, nor will I ever make complaint afterward that the price was too high."

—*From* The Madness of Garlon and
the Waning of Charon

19.

The Assembly of the Wicked

In the morning, the Lady Guenwyn came to the guest house, as she did every six or seven days. Tryffin, who had reached the point where he had either to work or to pay for his keep, had asked for an introduction from one of the men who ran the house for her.

"I am told," said Guenwyn, crossing the common room, threading her way between the long oak tables and benches, to speak to him, "that you are the younger son of a petty lord, turned knight errant, now seeking service in some noble house."

This bit of deception had been conveyed by Meligraunce, allowing Tryffin to answer truthfully now, "I would deem it a great honor, Lady Guenwyn, if I were allowed to serve you."

Her penetrating dark gaze passed from his face to the Captain's. "And I suppose that your friend would like to serve at your side?"

Tryffin nodded. "We have been inseparable for many years, and we would not wish to be parted now. Also, he is a very valiant man."

She was dressed very simply, as she had been the day before, this time in a gown of midnight-blue velvet, with a ring of keys suspended from her girdle. She looked the perfect Chatelaine—brisk, efficient, and sensible—but the heavy dark hair, which was a little wild, and something that quirked at the corner of her mouth made her seem a great deal younger than she obviously was.

Guenwyn was silent so long that Tryffin thought she meant to refuse them both. Then suddenly she smiled. "Well, you are certainly big enough. I would be well defended with two such giants guarding me . . . also, I can see by the way that you move that you are both fighting men. I consider myself a good judge of character and better than most at reading faces. You would serve me well, I think. Yet you ought to be warned that I have powerful enemies and that guarding me might be very dangerous."

"If there were no danger, then there were no honor," said

Meligraunce, standing stiffer and straighter than ever. "Nor any use for us, either."

"Very true," said the Lady, with a humorous glance. "I can see that you are a man of exquisite practicality, and that is something I am looking for also. Well then, you may come to me tomorrow; ask the guards at the gate to return your weapons and show you the way to the tower where I live."

She offered them each a hand, which they kissed respectfully (Tryffin was interested to see a burning blush come over the Captain's face as he did so). She would have left them then, was turning to do so, when Tryffin asked her a question.

"Lady, you have no one to guard you now . . . and I noticed yesterday that no one attended you at the ceremony in the courtyard."

Guenwyn paused and glanced over her shoulder. "When I go abroad by day, I am safe enough, for no one would be foolish enough to attack me openly, as I have many friends and defenders wherever I go. But when I am in my own rooms or walking the dark corridors, then I make certain I am always guarded."

Serving the Lady Guenwyn proved to be easy and pleasant. Tryffin and Meligraunce were given the day watch in her tower apartments, immediately after she had made her morning rounds of the castle performing her duties as Chatelaine, which meant they had nothing to do most of the time but sit in the octagonal antechamber which led to her bedroom, her stillroom, and her private chapel—which places they were never expected to enter, unless she should call them—and amuse themselves playing cards, dice, or Nine-Men's-Morris, while keeping alert for her summons, should it ever come.

At sunset, they were free to do as they liked, either return to their tiny, cell-like rooms in the guard's barracks, eat supper in the hall with the rest of the household, or seek what amusement pleased them elsewhere. As he now had the run of the entire fortress, Tryffin spent most of his time looking for Gwenlliant. He was growing impatient to speak with her, and besides, the presence of Garlon of the haunted eyes, and the pale-faced fanatical Lot, even at the other end of the vast banquet hall, generally robbed him of his usual appetite. As he was only a simple guardsman, neither of them spoke or noticed him at all, and that was exactly as Tryffin wanted it, having no desire to make the acquaintance of either gentleman. It would also, he told himself, make it easier, in terms of conscience, to rob Garlon when the time came.

The cup, he had learned, was kept in a grim black tower at the heart of the fortress, in a small secret room, which could only be reached by passing through seven locked doors, up seven flights of stairs, and down seven long corridors. No one had access to the tower at all, except Lord Garlon, Lot of Caer Sant, and the Lady Guenwyn, along with such guards or other attendants that might accompany them. Since Tryffin's day began when Guenwyn's rounds of the castle ended, he had never entered the tower himself, nor did it seem likely that he would be permitted to do so anytime soon. Until he did, it was impossible to form a plan for stealing the chalice.

"There is a lady here . . . perhaps you can tell me who she might be," he asked one of his new acquaintances, a burly guardsman who took the night watch outside Guenwyn's chambers. After many evenings of useless searching and no further sign of Gwenlliant, he was ready to toss discretion to the winds and make some inquiries. "She appears to come from a place in the north that I visited once, for her hair and her eyes are an unusual color, and moreover, she has the look of a lady I knew when she was only a little girl."

The guardsman answered immediately. "If you mean the woman with the white hair, that will be the Lady Gwenhwyach."

At this, Tryffin felt a curious mixture of apprehension and relief, any doubt he might have that it was really Gwenlliant completely dispelled. Gwenhwyach was a name in their family, one that would immediately suggest itself if she was looking for something to call herself.

"Gwenhwyach, yes," said Tryffin, feeling his pulse begin to race. "I believe it is the same lady, then. Where would I find her?"

"In the chapel or the garden," the man replied, with a shrug. "Or in the scriptorium with the other scholars. I do not know where she sleeps . . . unless it should be with Brother Lot."

For a moment, Tryffin thought he had misheard him. When he decided he had not, he was aware of a sudden savage desire to rip something apart—and the man he was speaking to seemed a good place to begin.

"Why should you say that?" he asked, as steadily as he could. "Is the lady . . . not virtuous?" He rested his hand on the hilt of his sword. "It would be a vile thing for you to blacken her name without good cause."

His companion grinned sheepishly. "Well, you are right. And if the lady means something to you, I ask your pardon. I know nothing against her, except for her association with Lot of Caer Sant, which is probably innocent enough. But they are a strange group, the Order of St. Pellam, and I sometimes think not so chaste or so holy as they would like the rest of us to believe. Besides, if you will pardon my saying so, she is much too pretty to become a nun."

Tryffin let out his breath. "The Order of St. Pellam . . . those are the lay brothers and sisters who are servants and students of the Knights of Jerusalem? They do not take binding vows, nor swear themselves to the order for life?"

The guard shrugged again, took a step sideways to put himself out of Tryffin's reach. "I don't know what vows they take. I have never known any of them to leave the order, but that may be a matter of choice. If you want to know, you had better ask one of them yourself."

Tryffin nodded. Now that he had someplace to begin looking, he thought that was a good piece of advice. "That I intend to do," he said. "As soon as I find the opportunity to speak to her alone."

Five days later—and no closer to conceiving a plan to obtain the chalice—Tryffin's nightly vigil outside the scriptorium was finally rewarded, when a familiar figure in a trailing black gown and misty veil moved toward the building. He stepped out of the shadows and called her name softly, just as she was crossing the threshold. She stopped just inside the arch of the doorway and motioned him to follow her.

Moving lightly and swiftly—and without glancing back to see if Tryffin was keeping up with her—she led him up a winding staircase, down a long gallery, and finally into a round chamber which had the look of an alchemical laboratory, with vats and ovens, glass vessels and brass tubing, and a number of books and parchments scattered across a long table.

"And so, Cousin, what do you want from me?" she asked harshly, as she lifted her veil.

He was as shocked by the tone of her question as by the face that she showed him. It was the same fine-boned face, the same dark violet eyes, that he had known and loved for years, but considerably older, and Tryffin (who had spent a good portion of his life wishing Gwenlliant would grow up a little faster) felt it like a blow. She had not overtaken him yet, appeared to be about nineteen or twenty, but the enchanting child that he remembered so well was gone.

Something . . . it might have been pain, it might have been some more complex emotion . . . crossed her face. "You do not seem to like what you see," she said softly.

He took her hand and kissed the tips of the fingers, then held it to his heart. "I am seeing what I hold most dear in the world, but I must admit that I did not expect to find you so changed."

After a moment, she drew her hand away. "I have been wandering in and out of these shadows for a long time," she said wearily. "I believe it has been longer for me than it has been for you."

He tried not to show how badly she had hurt him with that single gesture. "We were to meet at Dame Ceinwen's house on the Marches on Midsummer's Day, or had you forgotten?" he asked, around the sudden obstruction in his throat.

Gwenlliant gave a careless shrug. "And so we shall . . . when I am ready to return to our own time and place. I shall keep my promise, but you must keep yours as well: not to claim me until I have gained sufficient mastery of my craft." She turned away from him and began sorting through the scrolls on the table.

She was so cold and so distant that Tryffin was tempted to shake her, though he had never laid hands on a woman in his life. Yet he reminded himself that it was natural, under the circumstances, for her to view him as a stranger, and he tried very hard to be patient. "But why are you here in Charon, and not with Dame Ceinwen?"

"As to that," she said, her fingers closing on one of the scrolls, "we had reached a place where there was no going forward. It is the way that young witches and wizards are taught . . . I was too old for the one, not suited to become the other . . . so Dame Ceinwen wished me to study with an Adept. She had intended to apprentice me to a certain wizard, but that plan went awry, and by the time we were able to take it up once again the old man had already died."

She continued to speak with her face averted, partly obscured by the shadow of her hair, so it was hard for him to interpret her expression, but he thought he saw a brightening of her eyes as she went on. "So I was forced to leave the child with Ceinwen and search through the past for other teachers. I have been with Cynfarch in Rhianedd and Gandwy in Perfudd, before his fall, and now I am here."

"And who is your teacher now?" he asked, though he was certain that he knew the answer. "Are you Garlon's pupil . . . or the Lady Guenwyn's?"

"Neither," she said, fingering the long silver spike that she wore like a cross on a chain around her neck. It was, he had learned, the emblem of the Knights of Jerusalem and the Order of St. Pellam, supposed to represent one of the nails of the crucifixion. "I am apprenticed to Lot of Caer Sant. He is the only Adept in Charon: warlock, priest, and wizard in one. Those others, Garlon and Guenwyn, they dabble in Wizardry and the holy mysteries as well as their own low Witchcraft, but they cannot hope to rival Brother Lot."

He continued to study her, looking for something, something in the way that she spoke, some expression crossing her face, that he might recognize. "I can remember a time when his heresy would have shocked you. God knows, I never would have thought to see *any* of my Rhianeddi cousins, least of all you, reject the cross."

The look that she gave him was not a pleasant one, but she only replied in the mildest of tones, "Well, I have seen much more of the world. Like you, I have become tolerant. What do the trappings of religion really matter, so long as we serve God in our hearts?"

As there was nothing in this with which he could honestly take issue, he abandoned the subject. "You saw me the day of the procession down by the river . . . yet it seems you have been avoiding me ever since. May I ask why?"

She moved around to the other side of the table, as if she wished to put some barrier between them. "It is because of Lot . . . he is a stern man, and would never have accepted me as his apprentice if I were not a virgin. That is why I do not wish anyone to know who you are, or what we have been to each other. If it were known that I had a husband, who would believe in my chastity?

"I sometimes wish," she added, with a hardening glance, "that you had made up your mind to do something about this ambiguous state of mine, neither maiden nor wife. It is very uncomfortable."

There was something so cruel and contemptuous in the way

that she said it—as though he might have been more of a man had he steeled himself to force his attentions on her—that Tryffin was stung into an uncharacteristically harsh retort. "Before God . . . your chastity, if not your innocence, was in a very questionable state before I ever married you."

As soon as he said those words, he wished them back again. But she only answered more coldly than before. "That is true, Cousin, but Calchas is dead. Whatever there was between us once, it cannot concern me now."

"Calchas is dead," he agreed, under his breath. "And it begins to look as though you would like it equally well if I were dead, too."

He was turning to leave when she spoke his name. When Tryffin looked back, she was holding a piece of dark metal in her hand. "I saw you in the hall two nights since—I do not believe that you saw me—but you dropped this."

It was an iron cross, crudely made, lying in the palm of her hand. He was astonished that she should imagine that it belonged to him. "Not mine . . . no," he replied, with a shake of his head.

"Then it belongs to Meligraunce. He was with you then, as I remember. One of you must have dropped it," she insisted, the violet eyes growing wide.

As she continued to hold it out, he finally took the cross to examine more closely. "I have never seen the Captain wear something like this. If he wore any ornament at all, it would not be anything so ugly and common."

"Well then, it is likely to belong to one of the other guards," she said, turning away with a dismissive gesture. "You must take it with you and ask them, for it is plain enough that I cannot keep any such thing here with me."

After that night, he was as careful to avoid Gwenlliant as she was to avoid him.

"You have seen her and spoken to her," said Meligraunce the next morning. "I have not seen such a look on your face since that time she left Caer Ysgithr and nobody knew where she was. Yet it is hard to believe that the Lady Gwenlliant could be so cruel. Do you think that Lot and his ungodly brethren have the lady under some spell?"

"I wish that I knew," said the Governor. "By God, I wish that

I knew. Until I do, I will not go near her, for she has made it quite clear that she does not wish to see me."

As the days passed, he began to find Dinas Garlon more and more hateful. If it were not for Mahaffy and Conn, Garreg and Ciag, imprisoned in Annwn . . . had he been sure that Gwenlliant had her own free will and was not under any sinister spell . . . he would have shaken the dust of Charon from his heels in a moment, and been searching for a way back to Anoeth.

As to the right or wrong of stealing the silver goblet at all, even supposing that it could be done, he was still undecided. It was difficult to make up his mind about Garlon: whether he was essentially a good man forced to take harsh measures to hold his disintegrating realm together, or whether he was the tyrant that King Avallach would like Tryffin to believe.

And what did any of it really matter? None of this was real, it was all illusion, though illusion that might keep him and his men ensnared for a very long time. Yet it was very difficult to determine where true morality might lie in dealing with people who were really no more than ghosts and shadows.

About Lot of Caer Sant, Tryffin had very few doubts. If the man was not a dangerous fanatic and perhaps something even worse, it was more than he was willing to believe. Seeking to learn more, he began to ask more particular questions of the other guards—at least of those who seemed to have no connection with Lot and his sect—until someone suggested that he speak to the Lady Guenwyn's confessor, an elderly friar who was something of a scholar, and was said to cherish conservative views on all matters of doctrine.

As the Lady Guenwyn had left the castle, and had not taken him with her, Tryffin went looking for Brother Airem the next afternoon, and found him in the garden behind the chapel, pouring water from a wooden bucket on a patch of wilted herbs.

"The Pellamian Heresy . . . yes, I know more of their wickedness than I would like. And yet perhaps far less than I should," said the friar, in his creaking old voice. "They are dangerous, dangerous. Not only do they have the effrontery to reject the cross in favor of the passion nail, but they claim to practice a more ancient and pure form of the faith than the established Church."

"And on what do they base this claim?" asked Tryffin, sitting down on a wooden bench in the shade of a walnut tree. As he already knew, this was the standard practice with most heresies.

"What their arguments are, I do not recall," said Airem, sitting heavily down beside him. "But this I have heard: that the sect was known in pagan times, when it cloaked itself in the guise of the Old Religion. Indeed, they say this cult has existed in many times and places under many different names, and whenever there is any attempt to stamp it out, it continues in secrecy for a time, then takes a new form and another name."

Tryffin felt a sick feeling growing in the pit of his stomach. "It is not then, really, a Christian heresy, or an aspect of the Old Religion, though it has presented itself as both, to win favor with the people?"

"So it is said," Brother Airem replied. "But of this I am certain: It is the cult of all evil. Whatever evil powers there are in the world, be they infernal or pagan, they are at the root of the Pellamian Heresy."

Tryffin sat staring sightlessly before him. He was thinking of that other cult of all evil, the Black Canons. Could they and the Knights of Jerusalem, the Order of St. Pellam, be somehow related? Brother Airem said that the sect took on many different names in many different places—and if the cross and the passion nail were not genuine objects of worship among them, but merely adopted for the sake of appearances, then the difference between the orders was negligible.

It was even more chilling to think that the fact Gwenlliant had once fallen under the spell of Father Idris and his infernal relics might make her that much more susceptible to a similar evil influence on the part of Lot of Caer Sant.

"I thank you," said Tryffin, as he rose to go. "You have given me a great deal to ponder. If I have further questions to ask, may I see you again?"

The old man nodded his head. "You appear to have a good understanding for a man of the sword. You may come and visit me as often as you choose."

It was later than usual, that night, when Tryffin returned to his cell-like bedchamber, after pacing the corridors for many hours, deep in thought. Moonlight was pouring into the room through an arrow slot in the wall, so he needed no candle in order to undress; he left the short stub of tallow lying on the table beside his bed unlit.

As here at Dinas Garlon he was only another of the guards in the castle, Tryffin had (with difficulty) convinced Meligraunce that he could attend to his own needs, and had become quite efficient at removing his own armor—though like anyone else he required some assistance getting back into harness in the morning. Since the night was so warm, he stripped off his shirt, his hose, and his breeches, and slipped between the rough linen sheets on his pallet of straw, with nothing but his skin between him and the bed. As usual, he had no difficulty falling asleep.

He woke in the middle of the night, with an eerie sensation that he was not alone, though the room appeared empty. Then something moved from the shadows into the moonlight, and he realized with a start that it was Gwenlliant standing there over his bed, clad only in her thin linen shift and a dull-colored cloak. Her face was wet with tears, and she pulled the cloak around her, as though conscious of some chill in the air that only she could detect.

It was all so familiar, he swiftly recovered from his initial surprise. He held up a blanket, inviting her into the bed, remembering another night, long past, when she had wandered sleepwalking into his chamber at Caer Ysgithr. "Is it the nightmares again, Dear Heart?"

"I cannot say," she replied tremulously. "I do not remember leaving my bed. But I woke in the yard, very cold and very frightened. Would you take me into your bed for comfort as you used to do?"

"I will and gladly," he answered, before he remembered that he was lying there naked under the covers, a fact which was likely to disconcert her as soon as she discovered it.

Yet before he could say anything she was lying beside him, and pressing her body up against his in a way that left no doubt of her intentions. This was no frightened child climbing into his bed, but a woman who was eager to receive his caresses. Her nightgown came off, and so did the silver chain, and before he knew it they were making love.

He covered her mouth with his, ran his hands over her body. Her breasts were full and heavy in the palms of his hands, there was nothing of the child left about her, yet the texture of her skin, the scent of her hair, the taste of her tongue were all familiar. When he grew too rough, bruising her nipples with his fingers, she cried out, but not in protest. When his hand slipped down between her thighs, her legs parted, and he found her damp and ready for him to enter.

"I love you," he said, against her skin. The words seemed so pale and so slight, so inadequate to describe the emotion surging inside him. "As God is my witness, there was never anyone but you in my heart."

Gwenlliant said nothing of love in return, but the way she was returning his kisses, moving herself against him, caressing him with her hands, no words were necessary.

He tried to be gentle, unwilling to hurt her, but as he thrust forward, so did she, and before he knew it he was deep inside her. Something at the back of his mind told him this was much too easy, that she was not a virgin, yet he was beyond caring, beyond thinking, caught up in the dizzying pleasure of fulfillment.

But just as the passion took him, even as she arched her back in ecstasy . . . one white hand crept out and grasped the silver spike still lying on the bed beside her . . . and with a movement that was faster than thought or reaction took the nail and plunged it into his chest.

It was more than pain, it was worse than dying—though he knew that he must be dying, with that spike impaling his heart. "Ah God . . . no," cried Tryffin in his agony, wounded in his soul as well as his body.

As he fell fainting on the bed, his last conscious sensations were an odor of graves and rotting bodies, and the soft cruel sound of a woman's laughter.

When Pellam had traveled some half league or more into the desert, he saw a black tower rising up out of a hollow valley of broken stones, and completely surrounding the tower and the rocks was a great wall of iron burning in the sun.

And beyond the valley of broken stones . . . he could hear lions roaring, and the voices of leopards crying out in the wilderness.

—*From* The Vision of St. Pellam

20.

The Cup of Sorrows

There was pain and there was darkness, then there was only darkness, long and deep. A long time after, there was a sound like steam escaping from a covered cauldron, and a warm savory odor like nettles boiling, and then a silver needle flashing in and out, in and out, a light tugging at the skin on his chest, and a woman's voice whispering . . . he was not certain what, but it was good to hear.

When he opened his eyes, he was lying alone on a wide bed, staring up at a beamed ceiling. He knew the place, though it was not the room that he slept in, yet he had certainly slept there before. He recognized the ceiling, the shape and the number of the windows, even the arch of the grey stone fireplace in the opposite wall. The shelves and cupboards that lined the walls between the windows, the black and green bottles, the silver mirror and glass baubles, wooden boxes, feathers, and bright pebbles, those he knew also, though they did not go with the room. On a chair beside the bed sat Meligraunce, and that was familiar, too.

"What is this place?" Tryffin asked weakly.

"Do you wish to know what room this is, or have you forgotten where we are?" asked Meligraunce, looking relieved to hear him speak.

"What room is this? I think we have been here before, but not recently."

The Captain nodded. "This is the Lady Guenwyn's stillroom. And though she has never admitted us before, yet we should know it."

When Tryffin tried to move, he realized that he was lying under a sheepskin covering, and that the place where a hole had been in his chest had closed. As he knew very well that he ought to be dead, he wondered why he was not.

"This," he said, "is Castell Ochren. Ochren . . . Charon, it is almost the same name. This is the shadow of Lord Cado's domain . . . no, Mahaffy's . . . just as Annwn is the shadow Gwyngelli."

The Captain moved his chair a little closer. "Yes, I realized that, too, as soon as I saw this room . . . one of the few rooms in Castell Ochren that either of us was likely to recognize, since practically everything else was in ruins when we paid our visit to the giant Pergrin. This was the room where you slept.

"Except, Your Grace," Meligraunce added, "it is not Ochren in quite the same way as Annwn is Gwyngelli. After I realized where we were, I made some inquiries—rather awkward, since a man feels a fool asking the year—and I discovered that this is Ochren as it was or might have been slightly more than two hundred years before our own time."

"When we were here before . . . the castle in ruins, the great river Acheron gone dry, and no sign of gardens or orchards, or the trees below the fortress . . . it was all very different," said Tryffin. "But if Mahaffy had been allowed to accompany us this time, he would no more have been fooled by a few appletrees, a muddy river, than I was by anything in Annwn. We would have known from the beginning that Dinas Garlon was Castell Ochren."

There was a long silence, then Meligraunce cleared his throat. "I wonder if you remember who it was that tried to kill you. I was the one who heard you cry out, and when I found you . . . there was some evidence that—that a woman had been in your bed."

The Governor shook his head. "There is no use pretending that you did not recognize the passion nail piercing my heart . . . or guess which woman I was likely to invite into my bed. But it was not Gwenlliant; it was the child-killer, the shapechanger. My cousin was never here at all, and it was my enemy wearing her face and her form all of this time. I only recognized her when I thought she had killed me."

He closed his eyes, overcome by a sudden weariness. "Where the creature is now, I do not know. Perhaps standing with statues somewhere in the castle. I am somewhat puzzled, however, as to why I am still alive. I felt the silver nail go into my heart."

"You will remember that King Avallach spoke of amazing powers granted to those who travel between the worlds; also, how swiftly your wounds healed in Annwn. It appears that we cannot be easily killed while we remain in the Shadow Lands . . . a fact which may have been known to Our Lady of the Living Statue, because the weapon she chose to murder you with so nearly accomplished it."

Tryffin opened his eyes, lay staring up at the oak beams again. "It was more than just the silver," he said at last. "It was also the cruelty of the attack and of all that went before, then the seeming reconciliation, followed by betrayal, all meant to destroy my desire to live. And . . . ach, what a fool I was! The iron cross was part of it as well."

Meligraunce shifted uneasily in his chair, took a long time shaping his thoughts before he spoke. "Are you certain, Lord Prince, that it was the creature pretending to be the Lady Gwenlliant . . . and not your lady—gone mad somehow—who was the quarry all along?"

"For one terrible moment I thought that she was," said Tryffin. He shuddered inwardly, remembering the soul-searing agony of that seeming betrayal. "It is true that the disguise was amazingly complete, yet I knew from the very first time that I spoke to her that something was wrong. I told myself it was only because she was so much older, had seen and experienced so much since last I saw her. I wanted to believe I had found Gwenlliant, Meligraunce, and so I aided the creature in her cruel deception.

"In truth," he added, with a sigh, "if Gwenlliant had changed so incredibly that she meant to destroy me, she could do so easily enough, without luring me into Anoeth and killing all those children. Besides that, there was the iron cross."

The Captain frowned. "You mentioned that cross before, but I did not understand what you meant."

"It was one of my geasa: never take iron from the dead. She offered me that cross, in order to entrap me, and like a fool I took it. But it never would have worked if she were not one of these ghosts herself." Tryffin put the back of his hand to his forehead.

"And that would explain her remarkable powers. She had no more business to be in our world than we have here in hers."

Meligraunce sat back in his chair, looking not entirely convinced. However, he seemed to think it was time for a tactful change of subject. "It was, of course, the Lady Guenwyn who ordered that you should be carried to this room to be healed. And there was something you might find of interest, about the way that she stopped the bleeding. It reminded me of something you once told me. When she sewed up the hole in your chest, she used a strand of her own hair."

The Governor began to laugh, and even though the laughing hurt so badly that it was difficult to breathe, he could not easily stop. "Mother of God," he said, when he was finally able to speak. "We have been tripping over our own footsteps all of this while. I thought there was something in the spell she used to heal the people that day, but I could not make the connection. Clan Guillyn, the Lords of Ochren . . . it would be very strange if one family produced two such extraordinary women. Guenwyn . . . Ceinwen. The names have a similar sound to them. It may be a difference in dialect, like Guenhumara and Gwynhwyfar, or merely a more ancient form of the same name."

He grew suddenly sober, as the full implications hit him. "But if that is so, the old woman I know is considerably more than two centuries old. She must be well over thirty now."

"Your Grace," said Meligraunce, with a shake of his head. "I can hardly believe that glorious woman and the ragged old crone I once met on the road could possibly be one and the same . . . even after two hundred years."

Tryffin's gaze traveled around the room. "But Captain, these are her things: the bottles, the boxes, the feathers, and glass balls. You were never there at her house on the Marches, but I was. There can be no doubt of it. Dame Ceinwen is Lady Guenwyn."

Though he soon felt well enough to dress and get out of bed, Guenwyn would not hear of him leaving the stillroom, for several days yet. "The men who carried you here knew you were practically dead. That you recovered so swiftly, even under my care, might cause some comment. And though it is generally safe to be a witch between the Mochdreffi Woods and the sea, yet this is not the best time to be known as such in Charon. Still, I think you might have trusted me with your secret . . . why did you not tell me you were a warlock?"

She was sitting on the chair that Meligraunce had recently occupied, with an inkhorn sitting on a small table at her elbow, and a book of receipts lying open in her lap, a goose-quill pen in one hand.

"Because," said Tryffin, who was pacing the floor, restless to be out and about, "I am not, in fact, a warlock . . . though certain gifts are strong in my family."

She studied his face for a moment, then went back to writing in her book. "I am amazed," she said, "that I never recognized your strong resemblance to your master, the King of Annwn."

Tryffin caught his breath, then released it slowly. "I was not born in Annwn. How could I be, and still pass your borders?"

"Very true," she said. "What a wicked young man this Avallach must have been, cavorting with foreign women when his poor lady was lying so ill after the birth of Prince Gruffydd. She must have died about the time you were born . . . or were you conceived when she was carrying the child?"

"As to that," said Tryffin, declining to enlighten her, "I am not quite certain, though I have my suspicions. But will you tell me this, Lady Guenwyn: Has Lord Garlon guessed why I am here? Has Lot of Caer Sant?"

She gave him an amused glance over her book. "That hardly seems likely, since neither one has ordered your imprisonment and execution. In truth, I doubt that either one has taken any special notice of you at all. But I hardly think that one of my brother's heavy fines would be quite sufficient if he knew you were after the chalice."

He sat down on a bench by a window. "Then why . . . " he began, before he caught himself.

"Why do I not have you thrown into a dungeon myself? Do you think it would pain me if the chalice were stolen? No, don't pretend to be surprised. I love my brother but I know what he is . . . and what he was before Lot gave him the cup. It is true what they say, that Garlon suffered greatly for the sake of the land and the people, and that now the people suffer on his account. My brother was dying when the chalice came, dying for his people, a noble sacrifice! Or so they tell the story. In truth, he was a young man with a great heart and good intentions, but he knew little of the mysteries in which he was dabbling, and the rite cost him more than he had expected. As did the healing he received from the chalice afterward . . . "

Tryffin sat staring down at the floor. "Then the cup has healing powers?"

"It can be used to heal, or to slay. I believe its powers may be more aptly used for the latter—and I fear that my brother has done so on several occasions," said Guenwyn. "But just as certain medicines become deadly poisons if improperly used, it was possible to use this deadly thing to bring healing. Though at the cost of my brother's peace of mind. He suffers great mental torments, as perhaps you have guessed, and these have changed him into the frightened and sometimes cruel man that he is today."

"How long," said the Governor, "have you known why my friend and I were here?"

Lady Guenwyn put her pen and her book aside, and closed the inkhorn. "I knew when you first arrived. I am, you know, gifted with the second sight, which is why some like to call me a prophetess. Yet I also liked what I saw, and had a presentiment that you would do me some good, render me some great service. Besides, it was of no consequence. I have said it would not cause me pain to see the thing gone. If I could destroy the cup, or conceal it where Garlon would never find it, if you could take the cursed chalice where my brother could not retrieve it, or the King of Annwn could hold it . . . so much the better. In fact, I would give it to you."

Tryffin thought that over. "Considering what you say of its effect on your brother, that would not be a very good thing for the people of Annwn."

"The King of the Fairies has no soul, and it would therefore be just as impossible for the chalice to corrupt him as it would be for any more beneficent influence to improve him morally," she said. "For better or worse he can never be anything other than what he is."

Tryffin nodded. What she said was not so different from what he had already concluded about Avallach and his sons. Being only shadows themselves, shaped by the expectations of living men, they could never rise above their essential nature.

But what of Garlon, Lot, and Guenwyn? What of everyone he met here in this Ochren-that-was? Were they equally soulless? They had once been real men and women . . . indeed, if what he had guessed about the Lady was true, she still lived and walked the earth, in full possession of soul and spirit. A soul could not reside in two different times and places—or could it?

He shook his head. These theological speculations were beyond him. Always before, the complexities of earthly existence had been quite enough to keep his busy mind occupied, and religion had been something more instinctive than conscious, a soothing set of rituals, a source of comfort during difficult times. Like most Gwyngellach, he had been happy to find that comfort when and how he could, and leave other men to do the same.

"And while I do not think it would be wise to give Avallach any more power than he already has, yet I think the cup would do less harm in his hands than it does in Garlon's," said Guenwyn, breaking into his thoughts. "That is, if he could hold the chalice, which he cannot. I wonder, young man, if King Avallach told you that he has already stolen the chalice twice and carried it into Annwn, and that in each case the cup was back in my brother's possession within the fortnight?"

"No," said Tryffin, conscious of a sudden desire to grind his teeth. "He neglected to tell me that."

"Well then," said Guenwyn, "now that you know . . . you see that I cannot imperil my position here by assisting you in another futile attempt. But neither will I betray you."

Tryffin stood up and began to pace again. "Lady, I believe that I have the means to take the cup out of this world entirely. Yet the King of Annwn holds members of my household hostage, and it would be hard for me to abandon them."

Guenwyn fixed him with her intense stare. "Then I will help you to steal it. Because once you have the chalice, you can easily recover your friends."

Tryffin drew in his breath. "By using the cup to murder Avallach . . . or by some other means that you are about to tell me?"

She rose from her chair and began to bustle about the room, putting things in place. "The chalice has various powers, most of them harmless enough, though even the most innocent might be twisted to suit the ends of wicked men. Many years ago, when we were young and reckless, Garlon and I explored those powers and properties together, and as you can see I took no harm from it. With the cup in your possession, if you knew how to use it, you would be a match for Avallach, with all his deceptions and illusions.

"Only," she added earnestly, "you must promise me that wherever you take it, you would never use the chalice as Garlon has done, to tamper with matters of life and death. Neither to kill nor to heal, no matter how great the need, or how compassion might prompt you."

Tryffin considered that carefully. "Lady Guenwyn, I do not pretend to be wiser than your brother was at my age, but I hope I am wise enough to profit by his unfortunate example. My one hope is to place the cup where it will do no harm to anyone ever again."

She stopped for a moment with a flask of medicine in her hand, studying his face. Then she nodded, and went back to her tidying. "You are a man who places great value on rational thought. You would not readily imperil your reason. Well, that will have to be good enough . . . that, and this presentiment of mine that you and your friend Brandegorias have come here to render me some service.

"The chalice resides in the same tower where my brother keeps his other treasures, but it is hidden away in a room of its own. In order to reach the chamber of the chalice, it is necessary to pass through seven locked doors, each divided from the others by a long corridor or staircase. Yet, though Lot would have it otherwise, my brother still trusts me to act as his Chatelaine, and I hold the keys to six of those doors. With my help, you can pass through all six unhindered, but the seventh presents a problem, because only my brother carries the key.

"However," she continued, in response to Tryffin's unspoken question, "there is another locked door to which I do have the key, and that door leads to a narrow staircase leading up to the roof. And from that roof, a man with a strong friend like your Brandegorias to help him might be lowered down from the parapet by means of a rope, to a certain window which opens on the room where the chalice is kept."

He shook his head. "But can it be that easy? Surely the window must be barred or shuttered."

"There are shutters made of iron," she said. "But I will find a way to leave them unlatched . . . most likely when the great cats are fed."

Tryffin stopped his pacing, in order to stare at her. "The great cats?" he asked, with a sinking sensation. "Does Lord Garlon keep lions in that tower?"

Guenwyn shook her head regretfully. "Not lions, but beasts even more terrible, for though they are smaller, they are considerably more fierce. Great desert cats which my brother had brought here from a foreign land, in order to guard the cup.

Leopards they are called, and you have probably never seen their like before."

Much to her surprise, he greeted this news with a wry smile. "Oh . . . but I have," said Tryffin. "And have the scars on one leg to remind me of that encounter." He wondered if there might be some connection between these leopards and the pair that the Princess Diaspad had kept. Perhaps Garlon's cats bred, and maintained the bloodline was maintained right up to Tryffin's own time.

"Well then," said Guenwyn, a little taken aback, "you know something about them, and having survived one such attack may be able to do so again. They are tame enough in my brother's presence, but the last man sent by King Avallach, two years since, a thief who was adept at picking locks, and so was able to get past all the doors, not being prepared to face the beasts when he entered the final chamber, was torn to pieces by them."

He considered a moment before he answered. "Well, it is a daunting prospect, that I will have to admit, but not so daunting that I am unwilling to make the attempt. But once I have dispatched the leopards, what then?"

"Then there is nothing to prevent you from taking the cup," replied Guenwyn, returning to her chair. "Except . . . the silver goblet with the smaller gems and the one great stone, which they display in the chapel from time to time, is no more than illusion. In order to remove the chalice from the place where it sits, you must make a picture in your mind, a picture of the cup as it is, not as it appears to be. But I will describe it to you, and all will be well."

The Governor concealed a smile. That part would be easier than she thought, since he had already pierced the illusion surrounding the vessel. In truth, it was the illusory cup that he could barely make out; the real one he had seen quite clearly. "But will you tell me this, Lady . . . why do they use the chalice in the church for Holy Communion? If what you say is true, it is not fit to be used in that manner."

Lady Guenwyn shrugged. "To conceal its true nature and purposes. Also, the glow is rather impressive, and Lot, God knows, would like to be known as a living saint."

This time, he did not trouble to conceal his smile. "I have been told there are people who would gladly hail *you* as such, with your Washing of Souls. And by all I hold sacred, it was truly amazing to see how you helped those people."

She sighed and shook her head. "I use the Earth magics to heal their minds and mend their broken hearts. After that, their souls take care of themselves."

He sat down on the bed, facing her across the room. "There is one thing we have not considered, and that is the risk to you. Your brother will wonder how the doors were opened, how the shutter came to be unlatched."

"There is some chance that I will be accused of helping you, but you must not regard it."

"But I do," he said, with a frown. "If you are planning to endanger yourself on my behalf, I must regard it."

"You are forgetting," she said, lifting her chin, and again he was aware of her remarkable self-possession, "that it is *you* who will be serving *me* by taking the chalice out of Charon. Whatever the consequences may be to me, I will accept them gladly for the sake of my land and my people. Do not condescend to me because I am 'only' a woman. Garlon made his sacrifice, and now, if it should be necessary, let me make mine.

"Also," she said, "Garlon will be so busy at first trying to recover his prize, I think that his anger may have cooled—and perhaps the evil influence of the cup may have faded—and perhaps he will remember that he loves his sister, when it comes time to punish her for stealing his treasure."

Tryffin remained doubtful, knowing that the cup was not the only evil influence over Lord Garlon, not while Lot of Caer Sant still lived. *Yet what right have I,* he asked himself, *to deny this brave woman—no, this great lady, who is so wise and so good—the chance to follow her heart and release her people from the grip of a tyrant?*

When Guenwyn had gone and Meligraunce returned, Tryffin related all that had passed between them. It was easy to see from the Captain's face as he listened that he was deeply disturbed by what he was hearing.

"Your Grace, it is for you and the Lady to decide, and for me to follow your wishes," he said stiffly. "But have you truly considered this plan and the peril to her?"

Tryffin sighed. "Meligraunce, think where we are and who she is. Here in this shadow of Ochren two centuries before our own time, what can we do to alter the past? Mahaffy told us that history will struggle to follow its accustomed course. If her part in stealing the chalice should become known, she may suffer imprisonment or physical hardship but she will not *die*. She is a person of considerable importance, and her fellow ghosts and shadows must preserve her existence."

The Captain shook his head. "If we cannot change the past, then why are we risking this? How can we take the chalice if it is meant to stay here?"

"I have thought about that," replied Tryffin, walking over to a window and gazing out, beyond the walls of the fortress to the countryside beyond and the muddy river Acheron, which stretched as far as the horizon. "She has a desire to be rid of the cup . . . and so must Dame Ceinwen have done in the true past. We can only hope that she eventually succeeded in sending the chalice out of Charon forever. If not, at least we may keep the cup just long enough to effect the rescue of our men in Annwn."

"So you are deceiving her," said Meligraunce, with a bleak look. "She does not really know who we are or where we are going. She has no idea that you are expecting to fail."

"I am not expecting to fail," said Tryffin, turning from the window. "In truth, I don't know what to expect. We know, with a fair amount of certainty, that the cup left Ochren, for it does not seem to be there in our own time . . . nor for eighty years before that. If Lord Cado had ever held the thing in his possession, the course of events would have been very different. The only question is *when* it was taken away. By God, I wish I knew more of the history of Ochren, but it never seemed important before this."

"Perhaps Mahaffy can tell us, when we have him and the others safe," said Meligraunce. "Aye . . . you have the right of it, Prince Tryffin. What choice do we have but to attempt this thing? But have you thought: Even if we do carry the cup into the lands we know, what do you intend to do with it then? The least of its powers, as the Lady has described them, make it dangerous. Too dangerous, indeed, to be disposed of lightly."

"I think," said Tryffin, with a faint smile, "I shall give it to the one person best able to recognize the danger, someone with wisdom and experience exceeding the Lady Guenwyn's, but with all of her honor and strength and courage."

"By my faith," said Meligraunce, with a dawning smile as the realization came over him. "You are going to give it to Dame Ceinwen, aren't you?"

The sudden disappearance of the Lady Gwenhwyach had already caused considerable comment throughout the fortress.

According to Meligraunce, who had spoken with the other guards, the blame had been variously assigned: There were some that said Lot of Caer Sant had made her a virgin sacrifice in some satanic ritual, and just as many who were firmly convinced that the Lady Guenwyn had spirited her away or somehow bewitched her to spite Brother Lot.

The talk soon died, however, and people found something else to whisper about. But Tryffin was left with an uneasy sense that the creature might still be lurking unrecognized somewhere in the castle, waiting until the night he made his attempt to steal the chalice to reveal herself.

When the night finally came, Tryffin donned his armor in the stillroom, while he and his confederates discussed their plan.

"Once you have it, you should experience no difficulty leaving the castle by way of the gate," said Guenwyn. "The guards will have no reason to stop you. But you must cross Charon as swiftly as possible, for there may be pursuit immediately afterward."

Meligraunce frowned, helping the Governor to strap on his vambraces. "But why should Lord Garlon even know it is gone before he goes looking for it?"

"He will know when it leaves the castle. He always has before, and that is one reason it has always been recovered so swiftly. He cannot endure being parted from the cup. Also . . . " She hesitated. "Also, my brother and Lot are men of power, each in his own way. Who can say they will not be aware of our movements, once we draw near the chalice?"

This sounded ominous . . . until Tryffin remembered an advantage they had, which Guenwyn did not know about. "Once we have it, we will not need to ride across Charon. We were told there is an archway down among the cellars and storerooms under the fortress, a break in the fabric of reality, which leads into Annwn."

"Yes, yes, I know of that," said Guenwyn, a little impatiently. "One may pass through in one direction only, from Charon to Annwn, but it is warded on the other side."

"King Avallach has said that his wards will not hold us," said Tryffin, declining to explain why that was.

He strapped on the shoulder harness Meligraunce had brought for his sword, so the blade would hang at his back and not impede his descent down the wall later. Meligraunce picked up the coil of rope that would be used to lower him. "You need only to guide us to the archway. And once we are through . . .

perhaps we will be able to rescue our friends and be out of Annwn before Garlon's men even cross the border."

They passed from the stillroom to the empty antechamber. The regular guards of the night watch outside the Lady's room had all been dismissed on one pretext or another, so that no suspicion should fall on any of them, if Guenwyn herself was implicated.

But for now, there was nothing suspicious, nothing at all remarkable, about the sight of the Lady Guenwyn taking an evening stroll through her brother's fortress: along an echoing torchlit corridor, down a winding staircase, and across a dark courtyard, with a sturdy guardsman striding along on either side of her—though some might wonder why the tall, fair Maelwas, so recently released from the sickroom, had already returned to his duties.

And as the nights were growing steadily cooler, there was nothing remarkable, either, in the fact that the Lady wore a long, concealing cloak.

They paused in the shadows at the foot of the tower, while Guenwyn sorted blindly through the keys she wore on her belt, and finally located the one that she wanted by its size and its shape. A moment later, Tryffin heard it turn in the lock, and the door creaked open.

Once inside, Guenwyn uncovered the lantern she had been carrying under her cloak. Tryffin and Meligraunce glanced cautiously around them. They stood in an empty corridor, at the foot of a narrow stone staircase leading up into darkness.

"There is no one here to see or hear us," said Guenwyn. "I would sense it if there were. So let us go swiftly."

In the absence of any need to go quietly, they hurried up the stairs to the next locked door, which the Lady opened, and then to the next, and the next . . . until finally they emerged on the roof. At once, Guenwyn covered her lantern.

The moon had already set an hour since, but the night was ablaze with stars. Enough light to guide him down the wall, Tryffin reckoned, as he removed his cloak, but not enough that he would be spotted from a distance in his dull dark armor.

"Here is the place," said Guenwyn, moving toward the parapet. "The window is immediately below."

Meligraunce brought out the rope and tied it into a noose, which he slipped over a merlon to anchor it. The Governor took the other end and fastened it around his waist. With only Meligraunce and the Lady to take the weight as he descended, it was some comfort to think of all the flesh he had lost during his recent convalescence, subsisting on nourishing broths and herbal drafts.

The descent was swift and uneventful, if a little dizzying, though his armor scraped softly against the wall more than once. He found the window ledge with no difficulty, and sat down, dangling his legs over the sixty-foot drop, while he unfastened the rope and pulled out his sword. The iron shutter, as promised, was unlatched and opened at his touch, allowing the faint glow provided by the chalice to spill out. Tryffin slipped through the window quickly, landing softly on his feet in the chamber beyond, and drawing the shutter closed behind him, lest the light draw any unwelcome attention.

He could smell the leopards, their rank, wild odor, before he saw them: the larger one sliding out of the shadows on the far side of the room, the smaller one hunched protectively over a pile of bloody bones, the remains of the goat they had torn to pieces earlier that day. Tryffin had entertained some hope that the cats would be lethargic, less inclined to attack so soon after one of their infrequent meals, but by the look of the snarling male it was immediately evident that hope had been a false one.

He had no more time than it took to draw out his dagger, before the first leopard came leaping to meet him. But expecting that sudden pouncing attack, Tryffin had his sword ready to thrust. The blade caught the cat in mid-leap, impaling the leopard but knocking Tryffin backward with the impact and wrenching the hilt out of his hand as the dying cat hurtled past him. He dropped to one knee to retain his balance and fumbled at his belt for the silver dagger.

He was crouched and ready with a dagger in each hand when the second leopard attacked. As the cat leaped, Tryffin sidestepped, aiming a slashing blow to the flank as the leopard passed him. The cat screamed, landed on four feet, and whirled to face him, drawing back its lips to show the vicious yellow fangs.

Belly low, the leopard crept forward, ready to spring again, but Tryffin inched backward, trying to maintain a safe distance. The cat pounced and the man sidestepped, but too late this time . . . the leopard managed to catch his left arm between its jaws, pulling him around and down to his knees.

As the cat chewed frantically at his iron vambrace, Tryffin was able to strike with the silver dagger, scoring a gash down the leopard's shoulder bone. He felt the hot blood spatter his face and hand, but the cat held on, chewing and clawing, its weight continuing to pull his arm down. His next stroke was better, passing between the leopard's shoulder blades but missing the heart.

With a desperate burst of strength, Tryffin yanked out the dagger and drove it in even further. He felt the jaws loosen as he struck the heart, then the cat spasmed once and died.

Tryffin knelt by the body of the leopard, his pulse pounding, a familiar crimson mist rising before his eyes. The battle madness—too late for the actual battle—was taking hold of him, nearly suffocating him with the force of the pressure building inside of him. What happened after that would be only a dim memory later, as he cleaned his sword and dagger on the leopard's fur, resheathed them, then strode across the room to the pedestal where the chalice rested. Reaching through the glow of the false chalice, he clasped the blood-red cup between both hands and lifted it into the air.

He slipped it into the velvet bag he had brought to carry it, quenching the glow, and tied the bag to his belt behind the silver dagger. Then, moving a bit uncertainly in the dark, he found his way back to the window and pushed open the shutters.

Once he had the rope in his hands, he scrambled up the wall like a cat, arriving unaided (and much to the surprise and consternation of the Captain and the Lady Guenwyn) on the flat tower roof only moments later. "Do not either of you touch me," he warned, waving a bloodstained hand as he leaned up against the rough stones of the parapet for support.

Now that the need for violent action was past, he was feeling the expected reaction: a trembling in the limbs, a gut-wrenching nausea, as the battle fury subsided. Yet he knew that it would not take much to make him lose control, to send him thoughtlessly and dangerously into action, striking out at whoever came near him, whether friend or foe.

"You are hurt," said the Lady, and would have approached him, heedless of the danger, had not Meligraunce gently restrained her.

"You cannot help him until the fit subsides, for he will not even be able to tell you if he is injured."

A short or a long time later, the mist cleared and his heart stopped racing, and Tryffin was able to reassure his companions that he had sustained nothing worse than a few bruises, where the leopard had gnawed on his plate-armored forearm.

"And you have the cup?" said Guenwyn. "Then, if you are able to walk now, we had better go as quickly as possible.

"Listen to me carefully," she went on breathlessly, as they entered the tower and moved swiftly down the staircase. "Whatever might happen along the way, do not attempt to use the magic of the chalice until after you arrive in Annwn. To do so would not only alert Garlon that the cup is no longer in his possession, but would probably lead him directly to you. In truth, if I did not fear just that, we could be using it now to aid your escape. And above all, do not *ever* use its power to heal or to kill, lest the cup exert its evil influence and so undo whatever good you might hope to accomplish."

They left the tower, crossed the grassy courtyard under the lemon trees, and entered the immense stone pile of the central building by way of a low door, heading for the stairs leading down to the cellars. They were walking down a flagstone-paved passageway, when they heard a great commotion, as of raised voices and slamming doors, filtering down from the floors above.

"He knows," said Guenwyn, the color draining from her face, as she unlocked the door at the end of the corridor.

The door swung open, and they started down the stairs, the Lady leading the way with the uncovered lantern. They were just past the first landing, when Tryffin heard the clatter of pursuing footsteps.

But of all the Principles and the Laws of Magic, the most potent of all is the Rule of Names.

—*From* The Three Parts of Wisdom

21.

Like a Rabbit in a Snare

Gwenlliant came back to the house when it was still dark and crept up the loft before any of the others returned. She sat on the side of the bed, staring guiltily down at the tousled little head on the pillow. She had been out most of the night, without any thought of Grifflet, without remembering once how easily she might lose him if the Mist started brewing and swept either one of them away. He opened his eyes and smiled drowsily. "Mama," he murmured. "Bedtime."

"I know," she whispered, and gathering him up in her arms, she sat there rocking him. He was still so small, so perfect. But what if she had gone wandering off in time and returned only to find him changed? He snuggled against her, safe and content, but a stab of fear went through her. He was going to grow up in any case. Some day he would be a big strong boy and she supposed that she would love him, perhaps even more than she did right now, but the little one that she held so tenderly, that lay so sweet and warm in her arms with his damp red hair against her shoulder, would be gone.

A painful lump rose in her throat. *Why do people have children, when they know they are only going to lose them?*

To soothe them both, she began to recite one of her stories under her breath: of the Princess Gwenlliant and her many beautiful children, and of Grifflet the eldest son, who was a most remarkable youth and the wonder of all his brothers and sisters.

After a time, she heard the women coming in down below, so she laid him back down on the bed and crawled in beside him, cuddling the little boy up against her while she still could. By the time that Maelinn and the rest came trailing up to the loft, Gwenlliant and Grifflet were both asleep.

In the morning, when she went out walking with Grifflet, it was all new, every twig, every stone, every cloud in the sky, because Gwenlliant saw everything with new eyes. On every tree there were tiny crystals of glittering ice—she saw them now, clear and distinct. The shapes and patterns of the dead leaves lying on the ground—she knew them one from the other, what tree each leaf had come from, despite its faded color, no matter its state of decomposition. Her other senses had heightened as well, scent, touch, and taste. Most peculiar of all was her sense of hearing.

Always before, Gwenlliant had been aware of the language of inanimate objects, trees and walls, cottages and castles—not true speech, really, only the echoes of men and women who had passed that way before—but now there was something entirely different carried on the wind. She heard blackbirds and sparrows chittering in the trees; she *knew* what they were saying. A wolf howled, thin and mournful in the distance; his language, too, she understood as though it were her own. Foxes, badgers, rabbits— Gwenlliant heard them whispering to their fellows, down in their dark, musty dens beneath the earth.

On a sudden impulse, she became a bridled badger, waddling along at Grifflet's side. A moment later, she was a sparrow, circling overhead, sweeping down to land on the little boy's shoulder. When they came to a stream winding through the forest, there was a flash of silver and a splash, as Gwenlliant turned into a fish and darted about in the shallows. Far from being frightened by these sudden transformations, Grifflet greeted each one with pure delight, and gurgled and clapped his hands like any small child who likes surprises.

It was an amazing day, and all the days that followed after were equally remarkable, as Gwenlliant explored the extent of her new powers, her deepening awareness of the wood and all the creatures who lived there.

But back in the house with the turf-thatched roof it was not so pleasant, because everyone there was tense and unhappy, dreading the day, which was rapidly approaching, when Tinne must go on to the other temple in the wood; swear the awful, irrevocable oath that would make her a priestess (and never speak another word afterward); and yield herself, body and soul, to the goddess Cerridwen . . . and to Gwythyr.

As for Tinne, she never complained, and she no longer wept. The time for tears was apparently past. Her greatest, and it often seemed her only, pleasure was caring for Grifflet when Gwenlliant was too busy to watch him. She would sit on the floor playing with him for hours, inventing new and ingenious amusements, or reciting songs and stories. As nothing else ever seemed to revive her flagging spirits, the others gave up trying to interest her in their own pursuits, and were happy enough to leave her to play with the little boy.

"He is a remarkably intelligent child," she told the others one day, "and the purest delight. But it is almost as though he were speaking two languages, because he babbles a good deal of nonsense and seems to be puzzled when no one answers. There is one word that he says again and again," Tinne added, with a wondering shake of her head, "as though it had some particular meaning. *Gwenlliant.* I wish I knew what he was trying to tell me."

Gwenlliant, who had been spinning yarn, looked up from her work. "As you say, it is a nonsense word; it doesn't mean anything," she said breathlessly, and hoped that none of the others had noticed the violent start which had nearly caused her to drop the spindle.

"But of course it means something," said Gleis, who sat on the bench beside her, winding yarn into a ball. "It is a woman's name, and one of the aspects of the Cailleach: Gwenlliant, the white flood. Yet we never speak it during any of our rituals, so where could he learn such a thing?"

Tinne took Grifflet into her lap, rumpled up his auburn curls. "He always looks over at his mother when he says it," she answered absently. Then she added, with a faint smile, "Perhaps your son thinks that you need a new name, Gwenhwyach. But what a strange thing, for a boy to name his own mother—they are usually more concerned to put a name to their fathers."

Everyone laughed and no more was said, but Gwenlliant had seen the sharp, inquiring glance that Maelinn gave her. She realized that it might have been a mistake telling Grifflet those stories, and she resolved to be more careful in the future.

The day finally came when Tinne was to move on. She stood by the door, pale and trembling in her squirrel-skin cloak (*like a rabbit in a snare,* thought Gwenlliant), clutching the chest containing the sidhe-stone vessel to her breast, as the other young women filed by, and each pressed a sorrowful kiss on her bloodless cheek.

"Good-bye, Tinne. We shall see you often, though it will never be exactly the same," Ettare whispered, in her ear. And everyone said the most comforting things they could think of to say, though it hardly seemed to do much good.

When the acolytes came to fetch her, Tinne took one last wistful glance over her shoulder, then sadly followed them down the forest path. It was not such a long way really—she would reach the other temple in less than a morning's walk—but the others could not help thinking it an immeasurable distance. Everyone who lived at the cloister in the wood had a future to look forward to, but Tinne was going to a life that she loathed, one from which she could never reasonably hope to escape.

"Well," said Maelinn, sounding relieved. "At least *that* is over and done with."

In the afternoon, Gwenlliant and Grifflet went out for their daily walk. Though it was still winter, there had been a brief thaw. The earth was dark and damp, the trees still bare, but the sap was just beginning to stir sluggishly, with the promise of spring soon to come.

Gwenlliant felt her own blood begin to tingle. She wanted to be a bird or a rabbit, yearned to take on feathers or fur and become part of the awakening forest. But she glanced down at Grifflet trudging along with his hand in hers. Ever since the day he had said her name aloud, she was afraid of how much he might reveal through his innocent babbling.

"I simply don't know," she told him. "You speak our language far better than you speak theirs . . . and besides that, children are always making up stories that no one believes. Would it really be so great a risk?"

She sat him down on a gnarled root, knelt on the ground beside him. "If only you were old enough that I could explain how important it is that you keep my secrets."

He smiled his sunny smile, reached out to pat her face with his chubby little hand. "Well," she said, "I suppose I can trust you this one last time. This one last time and then no more until you are older, or until we are somewhere I need not be so careful."

The only thing was, she thought sadly, that she could not really trust *herself* to keep that resolution.

She soared up into the air as a white raven, circled overhead for a short time, exulting in the freedom, the glory of flight. But caution soon drew her back to earth and back to her accustomed shape. She landed on her feet at the base of the tree, where Grifflet was still sitting on the root, happily playing with some sticks.

"So, Gwenhwyach, you have been deceiving and spying on us all of this time," said a cold voice, and Gwenlliant, after an initial start, turned to face Maelinn, who was staring at her with a hard glance.

Gwenlliant felt herself flushing. "I did not come to spy on you, and I am sorry if I lied to you. But Maelinn, I was afraid. You were all so powerful and I was a stranger."

"What reason had you to be afraid . . . when we were all so ready to befriend you?" the High Priestess said, with a contemptuous gesture. "When were we anything less than kind, anything less than generous?"

"I am sorry," said Gwenlliant again. At a moment like this, it was very hard to obey Dame Ceinwen's instructions. But once she gave Maelinn the dangerous knowledge, there was no telling what would happen. It was said to change them, these inhabitants of the Shadow Lands, learning they had power over someone from her world. To tell Maelinn the truth might destroy them both. "Once I began by deceiving you, it was hard to stop lying. Maelinn, forgive me. You have always been my friend, and I have always tried to be yours."

But Maelinn remained obdurate. "What kind of friend spies on her friends and steals their magic?" she asked, still with that cold, hard look.

Gwenlliant shook her head. "You know that nobody ever steals magic," she said softly. "You still have yours and I have mine . . . and I could never have worked any of your spells if I did not possess the gift to begin with."

As the High Priestess turned to walk away, Gwenlliant put a tentative hand on her arm to stop her. "Maelinn . . ." she asked breathlessly. "Are you going to tell the others what you saw here just now?"

Maelinn hesitated a moment before she answered. "I would appear a great fool if I did, since I was the one who insisted we take you in. How Caithne and Sceith would laugh if they knew," she said, with a bitter smile. "No Gwenhwyach, at least for now, your secret is safe with me."

There were visitors in the wood. Songbirds carried the news to the house of the twelve young priestesses, flying in through the window in the loft, delivering their message, and then leaving by way of the smokehole in the roof: Three men had come into the wildwood, and two of them had never been seen there before.

Maelinn looked up from the bread she was kneading. "Peth-boc, Ettare, and Gleis—you will accompany me to the visitor's hut," she said, pointedly ignoring Gwenlliant. But Gwenlliant decided to tag along anyway, without an invitation, knowing that the High Priestess, who was still keeping up the pretense of friendship for the benefit of the others, would not send her back.

It was not a long walk to the clearing with the hut, but since they had started late in the day, evening shadows were already gathering when they arrived. There they found Tadhg, Ma-bonograin, and a stranger with them: grey-eyed and brown-haired, his face painted with the spirals and patterns affected by the Hillfolk.

"We have come to speak with the Princess Tinne, if it is permitted," said Mabonograin, as the four women sat down on the hard earth floor of the hut. "I have come here in order to say farewell."

"The *Priestess* Tinne is no longer with us, so you will have to go on to the temple of Cerridwen," Maelinn replied coldly. "Permission to speak *to* her may be granted you, but you cannot speak *with* her, for she has already taken the vow of silence."

There was a painful pause, while Mabonograin struggled to conceal his disappointment. "I had hoped to hear her voice one last time. Yet that is not important, not if I can see her sweet face. I am going away, Maelinn." He indicated the other man in blue paint. "This is my kinsman Cassibellawn, who was sent by my father. I am returning home to the Hill Country, and I do not believe that I will ever visit Achren again."

At this, Maelinn softened considerably. "Ah, Mabonograin, you will be missed. Well, and if this is true that you are going away perhaps never to return, I feel certain Gwythyr will allow a last meeting with Tinne. And if he does not, if he decides to be stupid and stubborn, you must send word to me, and we will see what I can arrange."

All the time that Maelinn and Mabonograin were speaking, Gwenlliant was thinking her own thoughts. If Mabonograin was going away, she must ask his aid tonight, for there would never be another chance. But as it was already so late, whatever happened with Tinne at the other temple, the Prince and his companions would almost certainly sleep in the hut. She decided that the best thing would be to come back secretly later, and ask him to help her remove the ring.

And it was time, Gwenlliant realized with a mixture of relief and disappointment, for her to be returning home, too. She had learned the shapechanging magic, and as for the riddle of the past that she had been trying to solve . . .

I must have read too much into the things that I saw, imagined connections between things that were not really connected at all. Because if Mabonograin is going home now, it will all be ending, without any disaster. The feud may not start for another hundred years, and it was only a guess that Caerthinn and Cerddin were the same man.

And though it was discouraging to think that she had been wasting so much time, waiting for events that were not going to happen, at least it was over now. Once Gwenlliant was free of the ring, she and Grifflet could leave the wood, walk to the nearest village, beg or borrow or buy a pot and the right sort of herbs, then summon up the Mist. Somehow, she knew that it would come at her bidding now. Since the night of the Wolves and the Foxes, the night of the Shapechanger's Moon, she had grown into her power.

And perhaps it will not be necessary to go to Dame Ceinwen's old wizard at all, she thought, as she followed the path back to the house, hand in hand with her son. *Perhaps it will be time for Grifflet and me to go all the way home to Caer Ysgithr, where Tryffin will be waiting.*

Once she was back at the house, while the others were busy preparing supper, Gwenlliant went up to the loft and bundled her extra clothes and Grifflet's together, all the things she had made or been given since she first came to live at the cloister in the wildwood. She went to bed early, immediately after supper, in order to avoid arousing Maelinn's suspicions.

But when everyone else was asleep, Gwenlliant slipped quietly out of the feather bed, dressed in the dark, picked up Grifflet and her bundle, and awkwardly carried them down from the loft. It was no easy task descending the ladder with the little boy in her arms, but she somehow managed without waking him. She wondered, as she did so, how far she would be able to walk carrying Grifflet, now that he had grown so heavy.

With a sigh, she placed him gently on the floor by the hearth. Moving about the big room, by the light of the dying fire, she started to put together some bits and pieces of food to take on their journey.

"Gwenlliant," said a voice. And without even thinking she turned to answer.

"Maelinn, what are you . . ." Then she flushed, realizing her mistake.

"So the name was a lie, too. Even in so small a thing as that you have been sly and deceptive," said Maelinn, stepping out of the shadows at the foot of the ladder.

Gwenlliant bit her lip. How to explain when she could not tell any of the truth? "As you say, it was only a small thing. What could one name or the other possibly mean to you?"

"That," said the High Priestess, "is what I would like to know. What sort of creature are you, that has to conceal her name? Something strange and magical, I think."

Gliding across the floor, Maelinn kept her face half averted and mostly in shadow, so that it was difficult to read her expression. "I have heard of people not of this world, who can be commanded with a single word."

Gwenlliant took an involuntary step backward. This was beginning to be rather frightening. "Maelinn, I am going away tonight, so let us part friends, at least. If I am no longer here, how can I spy on you, or—or do anything else that you don't like? Once I am gone, you will have nothing to fear from me."

But Maelinn took another two steps in her direction, reaching out to grasp her by the hand. Without really knowing why, the girl shrank from her touch. "But no, you are not going anywhere. Not until you tell me all the things that I wish to know, not until I am ready to release you.

"By your name, Gwenlliant, I command you," said the High Priestess fiercely. "Speak now and tell me what sort of creature you are and what powers you possess."

The Lady Guenwyn stopped on the stairs leading down to the storerooms and cellars, listening to the footsteps of the men who came in pursuit. "Take the cup and this ring of keys and go swiftly," she said, detaching the keys from her belt and holding them out to Tryffin. "I will do what I may to delay the men up above, while you and Brandegorias escape."

"I will stay here and defend you," said Meligrance, drawing

his sword. An unprecedented defection, yet one that was not entirely unanticipated, his feelings toward the Lady being what they were.

"We will stand together." The Governor slipped his own sword out of the scabbard. He would be damned before he left Meligraunce behind. Always before, he had led while the Captain loyally followed; just this once he thought he would return the favor.

And by now it was too late to change his mind. Lot of Caer Sant, wearing dark armor under his priestly robes, and two of his militant Knights of Jerusalem came running down the steps, and the battle was soon engaged.

Tryffin, perforce, took the two men in the lead, leaving Meligraunce to draw his dagger, sidestep past the battle on the broad staircase, and challenge the far more dangerous Lot.

The Governor feinted, parried, slashed, and easily dispatched his first opponent, but the next was a bit more difficult, even though the man with his back to the top of the stairs could only cut down at his adversary's head and shoulders. Tryffin ducked, cut, stepped sideways, and parried another blow.

The warrior monk swung at his left side, but Tryffin avoided the blow by skipping up two steps. Their blades met, with no damage on either side. A moment later, Tryffin saw his opening: His sword swung up, around, and then the blade came down with deadly accuracy, a solid blow that nearly decapitated his opponent. The monk collapsed on the steps in a spreading pool of blood.

All this time, the Lady had been forced to stay out of the way, lest her interference prove more of a hindrance than a help. Now Tryffin had to stand helplessly at her side and watch Meligraunce's battle with Lot, because the steps were too narrow past the first landing for him to get by safely.

The Captain was fighting with sword and dagger, Lot with his sword only; they seemed to be evenly matched in terms of skill. But from the intent look on Guenwyn's face, Tryffin thought she was working some counterspell against whatever magic Lot was directing against the Captain.

Meligraunce swung, but Lot struck his sword aside. Both blades met with a clatter of steel, and the men struggled with their swords locked together. Then the Captain's arm came up, the dagger flashed, and the blade was suddenly buried up to the hilt in Lot's throat, just above his iron gorget. With a gasp, Lot staggered, then tumbled down the stairs, where he lay dead on the landing below.

"We must hurry before more men come," said Guenwyn, with a new urgency in her voice, as she stepped over the body.

They ran down the rest of the steps and through the cellars without anyone to hinder them, though twice the Lady had to bring out one of her keys and open a stout oak door. At last they arrived at the arch—which turned out not to be a work of craft, as Tryffin had envisioned, but a natural fissure in the rock.

"I expected a doorway fashioned by men," he said. "As it usually is with the pattern spells."

But this gave him something to think about, as he bade the Lady farewell and thanks, and passed through the arch.

When he came out on the other side, in the catacombs under Avallach's fortress, he had a clear idea in his head of how he might use what he had just learned to find his way through the Bearded Wood back to Anoeth.

But he waited a long, apprehensive moment before Meligraunce came through an invisible gap in the air, and was suddenly standing beside him. "My friend, you gave me a fright. I thought you had decided to stay behind."

The Captain shook his head. "It seems that we must have been *meant* to succeed. Or else why should Lot of Caer Sant have died?"

Tryffin nodded. "Undoubtedly he would have perished very soon anyway, but you should feel some satisfaction that yours was the hand that finished him—and that by doing so you may have spared Guenwyn much pain and grief."

He started down the passage lined with tombs and iron doors, Meligraunce panting behind him. It was the Captain's heavy breathing that finally alerted him, and he turned just in time to see Meligraunce stop with his back to the rough stone wall, and then slide in a slump to the ground.

"I am hurt, Your Grace. You will have to rescue the others without me . . . then return for me if you can," he gasped. And for the first time, Tryffin noticed the gap in his companion's mail shirt and the bright red blood running down Meligraunce's side.

He stopped to examine the wound, which appeared both deep and dangerous. "Do not delay for my sake," said the Captain. "Remember, we are not easily killed here in the Shadow Lands, and therefore, this cut is not likely to finish me. I may even be back on my feet before you return."

Tryffin nodded, seeing the sense in that. If a silver nail through his heart had not been sufficient to slay *him*, this lesser wound should not hinder Meligraunce long. Also, there was no way of knowing if King Avallach had become aware of their presence when they passed through his wards. Tryffin had to go swiftly, if he was going at all.

"Lord Prince . . . promise to go carefully," whispered Meligraunce. "The King knows *what* you are, and because of that he may also know some way to kill you."

The Governor put a hand on his shoulder. "I know that," he said. "And you need not worry that I will do anything reckless. That moment in Charon, when the nail pierced my heart, that banished forever any illusions I cherished of my own immortality."

Tryffin opened the bag in which he carried the cup and removed the crystal chalice, then proceeded down the long drafty passageway with the softly glowing vessel between his hands.

In truth, he told himself, the first part of his mission might take no more than a great deal of nerve, and an equal amount of luck. *"One of the more harmless gifts of the chalice is sleep,"* Lady Guenwyn had told him. *"If you should carry the goblet before you with this thought in your mind, those who pass within your sphere of influence—which is about two yards in every direction—will grow drowsy and almost immediately fall into a deep dreamless sleep. However, if they should suspect what you are about and resist, the cup will be useless, and the same would be true if your concentration should fail at any time."*

He was heading now toward the corridor outside the prison where his men were kept. When Tryffin had been there imprisoned with the others, there had never been more than three or four goblins standing guard outside their cell. He had to hope that would still be true, and that he would be able to approach all of the guards at once without alarming any of them. For this, he was depending on his resemblance to Prince Gruffydd, the dim light down in the passages, and the fact that he himself had been gone for so many weeks now that no one was accustomed to seeing the Prince's counterpart roaming about the castle.

With luck, it would not occur to anyone he met that the tall fair man was anyone other than the King's younger son, and so there would be no reason for a closer inspection. Any goblins that he could not deceive into an enchanted sleep, he would have to fight and disarm or kill, and that was something he hoped to avoid.

Peeking around the corner of a cross corridor, he saw that the first condition had been fulfilled. There were only four goblins guarding the prison, and they were all grouped together, kneeling on the ground by the door, apparently playing a game of knuckle-bones.

He rounded the corner and proceeded down the passageway treading softly, not wishing to attract their attention before he was almost upon them. He held the cup in front of him and a little to the side, as though it were one of the crystal lanterns, which it would resemble from a distance. His luck held: He was about twelve feet from the goblins before one of them looked up and hailed him as Prince Gruffydd. Two long strides, with his mind entirely focused on the idea of sleep, brought them all within the influence of the cup.

"If it please you, Lord Prince—" one of the guards began to say, with a gaping yawn, just before he tumbled to the floor. This might have aroused some fear and resistance in the others, were it not for the fact that their eyes were already closed. A moment later, they had all joined their fallen comrade, sleeping on the floor of the passageway.

Tryffin bent down to see which was wearing the key to the door. Once he had it, he fitted the key inside the lock, pushed the door open, and stepped inside.

Mahaffy and Conn, Garreg and Ciag, were gathered around a table eating their supper when the Governor came in. "Prince Gruffydd. We had not expected a visit so—" Mahaffy began, before it suddenly struck him who he was seeing, and his face lit up like a thousand candles. "Prince Tryffin. By God, you're a welcome sight, but what are you doing here?"

"Rescuing the lot of you, I sincerely hope," said Tryffin, closing the door behind him. "But we may not have much time. If anyone enters the passageway unexpectedly, and spots the sleeping goblins . . ."

The others were all up out of their seats in an instant, crowding around him. "Listen now, and we will greet each other later. This—as you may have guessed—is the magical chalice that King Avallach desires, but I do not wish him to have it. I hope instead to use the powers of the cup to spirit you out of the castle. But you must all do exactly as I say.

"This chalice," he went on, "gives the power of illusion. I am going to hand each one of you the cup in turn. When I do so, you must each pick one of the Sidhe that is known to you, and concentrate on assuming his face, making the image in your mind as vivid and exact as you possibly can. Then you must go from this place quickly, by ones or by twos, but *not* all four by the same way, and head first to the stable for a mount and then for the gates of the fortress. If the illusion holds long enough, and if the resemblance is strong enough, and if you don't meet the person that you are attempting to look like, you ought to ride through the gate with no questions asked. We will meet again at the foot of the hill . . . unless you should happen to hear an outcry behind you, which will mean that one of our number has been discovered and caught. Then you must ride as swiftly as you can and by whatever means possible to the ridge where we last saw the Bearded Wood. If the wood is there, let the horse loose and enter straight in, and try to find your way back to the clearing where we first arrived. There may be a place between two of the trees that will serve as the final portal in the pattern spell and take you back to Anoeth. If the wood is not there, then try to find a hiding place in the vicinity and wait there until the trees appear on the ridge."

The others listened carefully and promised to do exactly as he said. "You will each have to keep a cool head," Tryffin cautioned. "Act perfectly unconcerned as though nothing is wrong, and don't allow yourself to think like a man who is escaping."

He passed the chalice first to Mahaffy. The transformation was completed almost at once, for the young Lord of Ochren had a good imagination and the ability to concentrate on an image. Even though he was expecting to see a change, Tryffin blinked in astonishment, as the face and the figure of the half-goblin Dylan immediately replaced Mahaffy's.

"Go then, and safely," said the Governor, accepting the crystal goblet back again.

Conn was the next to take the chalice between his hands. He created an illusion almost as quickly as Mahaffy had done: white hair, silver eyes, the image of Brion. He relinquished the cup and followed his friend out of the door.

Garreg took the face of an elf lord named Nefn, and Ciag of another, named Siawn. Both were convincing, though the last was not a perfect likeness. Without a word, the men-at-arms left the room together.

Instead of following them immediately, Tryffin snatched up the cloak he had left behind when he was last in Annwn, the glittering cloak of Fairy silk, thinking he might use it to conceal the chalice at need. Then he headed back to the place where he had left Meligraunce.

The Captain was already on his feet, standing with his back to the wall for support, when Tryffin arrived. "I believe, Your Grace, that I am able to walk as far as the gate."

"You will go first, then, and I will follow after, close enough to keep an eye on you, in case you should have any difficulty. For the love of God," he added, when his henchman looked like protesting, "do not waste my time arguing about it. It is right that I should go last, because I will have the cup to aid me, should anything detain me."

Meligraunce took the chalice and worked the magic, transforming himself into an image of the goblin Dris. When Tryffin accepted the chalice back, a sudden revulsion at the thought of assuming the face and form of his elfin counterpart caused him to borrow the face of the King's *elder* son, the amiable Ffergus, instead. Then he put on the silvery cloak and concealed the cup inside its folds.

Outside, it was late morning, a piece of bad fortune, because Tryffin would have preferred dim light to assist the illusions created by the cup. However, he watched Meligraunce pass through the gate without any hindrance, which seemed a good indication that the others had already done the same before him. He kept the reins short and his horse standing for a moment in the courtyard, rather than follow too closely after the pretended goblin.

But that moment of hesitation was almost his undoing, because someone called out Prince Ffergus's name. Turning in the saddle, Tryffin saw young Brion approaching him across the yard . . . Brion, who so far as the gate guards were concerned had passed out of the fortress a quarter of an hour since. Be that as it may, he could only wait while the young elf approached and hope that the illusion would continue to last.

"Prince Ffergus, I was not aware you were to go out riding. I—" Brion stopped what he was saying, gave a self-deprecating laugh. "I didn't recognize you from a distance, Prince Gruffydd, and mistook you for your brother. Have you seen him this morning?"

The influence of the cup was already fading, and Tryffin had nothing to save him but his resemblance to Prince Gruffydd—which would hardly be sufficient in the pale light of morning, if anyone took a long, close look.

He would have liked to send Brion off in some other direction, with a false report of Prince Ffergus's whereabouts, but that would have required a lie, and that he was not willing to risk. "No," he said, "I have not seen my brother this morning. But if you will pardon me . . . ?"

"Yes, of course," said the silver-haired youth, taking a step backward. But then he remembered something else that he wanted to say and came back again. "The King said that he would go out hunting in another hour. Would you not prefer to wait and accompany him then?"

"Though it may seem both churlish and undutiful, I would not," replied Tryffin. He thought he would be able to go then, but Brion suddenly reached up, took the horse by the bridle, and stood staring up into the Governor's face with a thoughtful expression.

Then several things happened in swift succession. A spark of recognition, a dawning smile, and then a step backward, as he released the bridle. "Lord Prince, I think you should go as soon as you can. I hope you have a pleasant day's ride, and all of your companions as well."

"My thanks," said Tryffin, under his breath. "In truth, I have more than one reason to be grateful, Brion, and I will always remember that I left a good friend behind me in the land of Annwn."

The young elf responded with a wide grin as Tryffin took up the reins and rode through the gate.

He found his five fellow fugitives at the bottom of the hill. "Now we ride as swiftly as these horses can carry us," he said, by way of greeting. "And pray that the wood is waiting for us at the top of the ridge."

The Bearded Wood was not there when they first arrived, but shimmered into view at sunset, about the same time they first heard hoofbeats pounding up the path, as the host of the Sidhe came riding in pursuit.

"Into the trees at once," said Tryffin, drawing his sword. "That pathway over by the rock . . . I think that is the way we came. And let us hope that no one dares to follow us."

The wood was as dark and as close and as musty as ever, as they passed single file down the forest pathway. The oaks leaned in toward the path, as if scarcely able to bear the burden of so many tangled vines, so much drooping grey moss, but it was utterly, blessedly quiet, with no sound at all of men and horses coming after them.

"I hope to God," said Tryffin to Garreg, the tracker, "that after all of this time you remember which paths we followed before."

"Your Grace," said the guardsman, "what else have I had to do these last weeks while you and the Captain were in Charon, and the rest of us locked up under the hill, but retrace our path in my mind, over and over, until I was certain I would never forget?"

Their progress through the forest was slower than the Governor might have liked, because Meligraunce could not keep so swift a pace, with the wound in his side. Tryffin fought off the temptation to use the chalice to heal him. What use, he asked himself, was his promise to the Lady Guenwyn, if he cast it aside within hours of gaining the cup?

And even without stopping to heal Meligraunce, they eventually arrived at their destination, the clearing that would take them back to Anoeth, if Tryffin had guessed rightly about the portal between the trees.

"There, in that little space between the bushes. We will try that way first," he said, indicating a spot where the branches of trees on either side seemed to meet in a natural arch that was almost perfectly symmetrical.

He took the lead, pushing his way past the bushes. The dim green forest light seemed to waver for a moment, then went out like a windblown candle.

The crone sat in her chair of leafy branches, watching her guest eat his supper and contemplate the strange sequence of events which had brought him and his squires to her door.

"There is an ancient web of love and hate, kinship, murder, and betrayal that binds the men of your house and Corfil's closer than brothers for all their bitter enmity," she said. "It was to free you all that Calchas came into this world."

Her visitor took a bite of the hard bread she had offered him. "I reckon you did not know Calchas fab Corfil," Prince Tryffin replied. "He was not capable of any good thing."

Dame Ceinwen shrugged. "And so you are alive, while Calchas is dead. These destinies have a way of working themselves out. But after all, you must not consider yourself he victim of Fate . . . it was your deed, your slaughter of that poor, weak, wicked boy, that united your destiny and his for all time."

Tryffin felt his heart sink. He thought the witch might be swearing a destiny on him even as he sat there. And the last thing that he wanted—as hedged about by geasa and supernatural prohibitions as a Prince of Tir Gwyngelli was from the moment of his birth—was to inherit another man's geas as well.

22.

Between One World and the Next

It was dark in the crypt and it smelled of earth, with just a touch of smoke on the air, as though someone had come through recently with a torch. Tryffin took the cup out from under his cloak. By the soft moon-colored glow of the illusory chalice, he was able to make out the faces of his companions, as they appeared one by one in the darkness: Meligraunce, Conn, Mahaffy, Ciag, Garreg.

They glanced curiously around them . . . up at the vaulted

ceiling, across the chamber to the nearest archway and the steps leading up, at the massive pillars, stone coffins, and the marble slabs with the bones all neatly laid out. "We are back in Anoeth, then," said Conn, with a long sigh of relief.

"*Under* Anoeth, anyway, and likely to remain there for some time, if they have closed the crypt and if it is not possible for us to raise the stone from down below," Mahaffy admitted cautiously.

The Governor started moving toward the steps to the next level. "Someone has been here, not long since, and they are likely to return. We have apparently been gone so long, they are no longer keeping watch here, but perhaps they come down for a look every now and again. If we cannot raise the stone, we must hope they return soon. It would not be pleasant . . . nor would we be of much use to the people of Anoeth . . . if we were stranded down here for several days."

With the others trailing behind him, he passed through chamber after deserted chamber, until they reached the long flight of narrow stairs leading up to the ruined church. Much to his own relief, still more to that of his companions, they all saw a patch of blue sky at the top of the stairs. "They left the vault open, in case we should return," said the Governor. "That was sensible, anyway." And perhaps he and the others had not been in the otherworld so long as he feared.

After a long climb up the slippery stairs, he emerged in the ruined church. On the far side of the graveyard, leaning against a tomb, stood the Sergeant and two other men. The guards spotted Tryffin at the same time he saw them, and rushed over to greet him with glad exclamations.

"By my confession to God, Your Grace, we were beginning to think we had truly lost you," said the Sergeant. "It has been an entire fortnight. After three days had passed, we tried to follow you through the pattern spell, again and again, but perhaps we did not remember the figure correctly, or it was the wrong time of day, because we were never successful."

The Governor sat down on the crumbling altar steps in what remained of the sanctuary, and the others who had now come up from the crypt arranged themselves on the ground near his feet. It was a little dizzying to think that almost three months in the Shadow Lands had amounted to so little back in Mochdreff.

"You had better tell me, Sergeant, all that happened here while we were gone," said Tryffin, taking off his cloak, handing it and the chalice over to Conn, to be wrapped up and concealed. It was not the sort of object he could carry through the streets of Anoeth without exciting a great deal of comment. "You may begin by telling me if the child-killer ever returned."

"Two nights ago, another woman had the nightmare," said the Sergeant. "Several of us went to guard the house last evening— armed with silver daggers, provided by Dame Brangwaine. The shapechanger never came. We thought she might have sent the dream to flush you out, Prince Tryffin, if you were living in concealment somewhere in Anoeth. When *you* did not appear, neither did she."

Tryffin nodded, finding the conclusion perfectly logical. "And what of Lord Rhonabwy, Lord Cernach, and the other petty lords all of this time?"

"During the first week, they sent to the inn every day, asking where you were, when you were expected to return. After that, they gave it up." The Sergeant shrugged. "Naturally, everyone was concerned over your disappearance, and there have been a great many rumors . . . that you left the town secretly, and rode off to Cormelyn, or back to Caer Ysgithr. Or that you were dead, or the wise-women had put you under some spell. But as it had been so long since the last attack, and the appetite of the creature was apparently sated, the terror abated and everything was returning to the way that it was before the nightmares and the attacks began."

Tryffin smiled wryly. That was perfectly consistent with the stoical Mochdreffi character. "And the wise-women—Dame Brangwaine and Luned in particular?"

"Dame Brangwaine has insisted all along that you would soon return. The young lady did not appear so certain."

The Governor nodded, rising to his feet. "Those two should be told that I have returned. No one else. In truth, I do not intend to stay long, for I have most pressing business elsewhere." He turned to Mahaffy. "You and Meligrance must be in charge here, while I am gone. If I am not seen in the town, perhaps the shapechanger will continue to lie quietly in wait for me. If she should not, then continue to guard any house where the nightmare has been received as a warning. God knows, I would like to stay here and wage battle with the creature myself, but the sooner I carry the cup to Dame Ceinwen, the better for everyone, I think."

Meligraunce cleared his throat; a faint blush tinged his cheeks. "Prince Tryffin, I would like to accompany you, if I may."

Tryffin regarded him with compassionate eyes. "Ah, Meligraunce, I think that would be far too painful. She would not be at all the way we remember her . . . not only withered and aged, but a completely different woman after so many years. Nor would she remember meeting us both in Charon, because it never really happened."

He dropped a comforting hand on his henchman's shoulder. "You will be happier and a great deal more useful, I believe, right here in Anoeth."

The Captain looked unconvinced, but the habit of respectful obedience was strong. "Very well, Your Grace," he said softly. "It shall be as you wish."

Tryffin saddled up his roan gelding and rode south to Caer Ysgithr, where he was greeted many days later with joyful relief by the rest of his long-neglected household. He spent a single night under his own roof and then headed south again. On the second day out of Trewynyn, he turned west and set out across flat, boggy country. This was not precisely the way to Dame Ceinwen's house—he was well aware that remarkable house was not really located anyplace that he might reach by ordinary methods—but it was the only way he knew, having encountered the crone in that country twice before.

Toward nightfall, a mist came boiling up, seemingly out of nowhere, and he gave the gelding free rein, expecting that Roch could find the right path through the fog by instinct. If not, the crone would undoubtedly guide them, now they had come so close. Before long, the gelding was plodding along a narrow road on the edge of an unexpected cliff, and when the mist finally dissipated, he came out on a stretch of rocky moorland. On a rise stood the witch's cottage, exactly as Tryffin remembered it: white stone, honeysuckle, and a crooked chimney.

Dame Ceinwen was waiting on the threshold—gaunt and bony, windblown and ragged—when the Governor reached the top of the rise and dismounted.

"You have been a long time coming," she said, hobbling into the cottage. When he entered the house, she was already seated in her chair of woven branches.

Tryffin frowned, under the impression he was two months early. "I had no idea that I was wanted." Then he realized what she meant. "Ah God . . . Gwenlliant's not here. What has happened, and where has she gone?"

"She has gone into the Shadow Lands, where only you can fetch her back," said Ceinwen, glaring at him from under her shaggy white eyebrows.

Tryffin felt a pang in the region of his heart. What if he should be wrong about the shapechanger, and Meligraunce right after all? He crossed over to the hearth, where a cauldron was boiling, stripped his leather gauntlets off with fingers grown stiff from the chilly damp of the marshes, and held his hands out over the fire. He took a deep breath. "I have been in the Otherworld, too. In a shadow called Charon, where I met a woman wearing Gwenlliant's face."

He saw the flicker of interest in the witch's eyes, before she shook her head. "She is not in Charon, but in the forests of Achren, where she has been for many months, trapped by a curious ring that she wears on her hand. I cannot go there and help her myself, for I have been in that land before . . . and could not forbear to meddle with events so badly that the forces of nature—which in the Shadow Lands include history, custom, pattern, fate, and desire—banded together to cast me out. If I should try to return, I fear some cataclysm, or at least a meeting with the ghost of my younger interfering self. It can be painful, even dangerous, to meet your own shadow."

"Having done so myself," said Tryffin, "I bear witness it can be a most disconcerting and uncanny experience. But why does Gwenlliant need rescuing? You mentioned a ring."

He sat down on a stool at her feet. "Not a magical ring," she said, "not any more magical than any object made of the purest gold in the world, then wrought with exquisite craft by a man possessing deep and intimate knowledge of the qualities and attributes of metals."

A smile crept into his eyes. "In other words, a ring of Gwyngelli gold, shaped by a native craftsman."

The old woman nodded. "It holds Gwenlliant in the past, and it will not leave her hand. But the ring will obey you. Of that I am practically certain. In any case, it is just as well that you should go there, because your own quest would have led you into ancient Achren sooner or later."

"And that quest is?" asked Tryffin, certain that she did not mean his pursuit of the child-killer, but also suspecting that he already knew what she did mean.

"To go all the way back to the first cause of the feud between Gwyngelli and Mochdreff, uncover that first wrong, then return to the lands you know and attempt to right it," said the witch. "Last year, when you uncovered the perfidy of Lord Cado, when you followed the tangled skein of history back for nearly a century, and learned all the wrongs done by the clan of Corrig against your family, and by yours against Corrig and his descendants, you did not go back far enough. Now you must . . . indeed, it was that very necessity that drew Gwenlliant back into the past."

A sudden sense that something or someone was missing caused him to glance around the room. "Where is young Grifflet? Is he with Gwenlliant?" The old woman nodded. "Then the sooner you show me the way to find her, the sooner I will be off on that quest. But first . . . I have something to give you."

He rose to his feet and went out the door, unstrapped the leather saddlebag in which he had carried the chalice all the way from Anoeth. Back inside the cottage, he drew out the cup, knelt down at the old woman's feet, and placed the miraculous vessel between her suddenly shaking hands.

"So," she said, sounding mightily surprised. "Some things are more difficult to lose than one might think."

"Then you do know the cup?" he asked, though of course he already knew the answer.

She shot him a dark and piercing glance over the rim of the goblet. "Did you suppose I did not?"

He shook his head. "I was certain that you did. But did we really meet at Castell Ochren or Dinas Garlon as it then was, more than two hundred years ago . . . Lady Guenwyn?"

She was a long time answering him, staring absently down at the chalice, as though it held a great many memories, both good and evil. "No," she said at last. "I have no recollection of any such meeting, though I was certainly there at the time you mention, and the name I was christened by was Guenwyn Guillyn. An old-fashioned name," she added, with a hint of a smile, "which the people one meets today seem to find difficult to pronounce."

"Mahaffy said that you told him: Small events may be changed, the larger ones find a way to repeat themselves. Perhaps through those forces of history and fate you mentioned before? But if that is so, then you must have eventually found a way to hide or destroy the cup without my help, in the true past, or else I would never have succeeded in stealing it from Garlon in the Shadow Lands."

"I found a way to hide the cup where even I could not find it," she said, with a sigh. "Though I regretted it afterward and have been at some pains to recover it since. Now I will not have to—its shadow should serve my purposes just as well."

"Then you don't intend to destroy it?" said Tryffin.

"No," said the crone. "I believe I am old enough and wise enough to keep it now, without being tempted to use it in the wrong way. Also, I have an idea that it is going to be of use some day quite soon."

But about this idea, she seemed strangely reluctant to say any more, only mentioning that when the proper time came, she would tell him everything that he needed to know.

She is willing to keep the cup now, because she has grown so powerful, the chalice is hardly more than a plaything, he thought.

He told then of the shapechanger and the slaughtered infants in Anoeth, of his journey into the Shadow Lands, into Annwn and Charon. She listened carefully to all that he said, her head cocked to one side, her dark eyes studying his face as he spoke, and she asked many questions.

"Lady," he said, when he had finished his story, "I was fortunate to find my way out of the Shadow Lands before . . . if you send me there now, through the Bearded Wood or the Breathing Mist, how will Gwenlliant and I find our way back again without your help?"

"Gwenlliant knows how to summon the Mist herself. Once it surrounds you, there are landmarks along the way that she will see and sense—though all may be mist and darkness to you," said the crone. "As you draw near the Marches, I will be aware of your approach and will do my best to guide you the rest of the way."

He sat back on his heels, considering that. The passage of time in the Shadow Lands was still a mystery to him. The days and the seasons seemed to expand and contract in a manner he did not understand. And it was already April. If he and Gwenlliant did not spend a night together as man and wife, or if she did not sleep one night under his roof at Caer Ysgithr, instead, before her year and a day of absence was over, their marriage would be legally dissolved. "Then . . . even if there should be difficulties and delays after I find her, you and Gwenlliant between you can bring us back here, and from here to Mochdreff, in time for Midsummer?"

Dame Ceinwen shrugged. "From the Shadow Lands to here it is easy to make adjustments, forward or back in time, because it is such a great distance and the reality of those places is so fluid. But here on the Marches we are very near our own world, and between here and there I can twist time by a few weeks only. If you have some particular reason to reach Mochdreff by Midsummer, you cannot arrive here the first week in autumn."

He nodded and rose to his feet. But then he thought of a question that he wanted to ask her. "Avallach said that he could have commanded me to do anything he wished by the power of my name. I believe that the shapechanger is a creature of the Shadow Lands, yet she knew my name in Charon and never used it against me. Do you know any reason why that might be?"

"To enslave you by the power of your name," said the old woman, "she would have to be in her own time and place. Clearly, then, she was not a creature of Charon."

"But what," Tryffin persisted, "if Achren, where I am going now, should happen to be her own time and place? God knows, she must have met Gwenlliant somewhere: She knew so much about us both, and she was able to create such a convincing impersonation."

Dame Ceinwen considered. "If you should meet her and not recognize her, she will have the advantage. But if you meet her and know her, you must give her name back as soon as she invokes yours. There are matters of life and death between you. She took you to the brink of death in Anoeth, and yet you did not die: That gives you power over her. She did the same in Charon, and again you survived: That gives you considerable power over her. If you can learn her name as well, your power and hers should be evenly matched, though she stands in her own time and place. It will then come down to which of you has the stronger will to resist the other."

As Tryffin had already traveled far that day, Dame Ceinwen insisted that he eat supper and spend the night in her cottage. She gave him bread, and a stew made of onions and cabbages, then spread out a mat on the earthen floor for him to sleep upon.

At dawn, he was already awake and eager to begin his journey in quest of Gwenlliant. He had traveled light from Caer Ysgithr, in black riding leathers and his mail shirt, leaving the plate behind, but the crone said that he must not wear the mail, either. "They will have nothing of the sort in ancient Achren, so it will mark you as a stranger and may even make it difficult for you to approach Gwenlliant. She has been there almost a year of their time, and it is likely she has been accepted as one of their own."

So Tryffin set by his mail, and accepted her gift of a warm cloak of thick scarlet wool, to keep out the chill of the Mist.

After that, the old woman made herself busy, laying wood for the fire—holly, oak, and hazel—kindling a blaze, and setting the pot of herbs on to boil. Before very long, wisps of vapor began to swirl around the cottage, then to sail out through the chimney and under the hide hanging in the doorway. Outside, Tryffin could hear a creaking and a sighing, as the borders of reality began to shift.

"Now," said the witch, "you must go out the door and head straight down the path. Do not fear to make a wrong turn, for though you may not see me, I will walk with you as far as I dare, and I will be guiding you most of the way."

Tryffin nodded. Then, with a deep breath of the herb-scented air, he squared his shoulders and stepped over the threshold and into the clinging fog.

If the old woman was really with him, he was not aware of it. This mist was denser and more luminous than the one which had brought him to her cottage. It was also colder, chilling him all the way to the bone. And from the little that he could see, he seemed to be walking across flat, featureless country, devoid of the landmarks Dame Ceinwen had mentioned. There was nothing but the mist in his lungs and his eyes, the dampness creeping under his leathers and sliding across his skin, and the steady thud of his boots against the stony soil.

He did not know how long he had been walking, though it must have been many hours, when finally there was something else: a scent of woodsmoke and evergreen, violets and mulch. Tryffin realized he was now walking across a carpet of fallen leaves, and that the air was considerably warmer. When the fog finally dissipated, he saw that he was treading a narrow forest pathway, through the wildest and prettiest woodland he had ever seen.

There was a remarkable variety of growth: oak, hazel, elm, hornbeam, rowan, maple, crowding the path on either side, and holly, bramble, ivy, and briar-rose growing between the trees. Yet for all it was so wild, it seemed to be inhabited, because that hint of woodsmoke lingered on the air. But when he turned down a path, heading in the direction the smoke was coming from, he met a sudden resistance . . . not a barrier of air, precisely, but a strong sense of prohibition, a forbidding invisible presence that brought him up short, made him turn back and choose some other way. Whoever had set these wards was far more powerful than Avallach or his Fairy enchantments.

A little while later, when Tryffin had passed through a stand of pines and yew, and was trying to cross a bubbling spring, he met that prohibition again. Again, he turned back. He might have attempted to contest with the wards, but he had no idea whose purpose they served. This might be the guidance Dame Ceinwen had promised him, though that seemed doubtful . . . but it did not feel hostile in any case, and so far as he knew it was just as likely to lead him *to* Gwenlliant as to lead him away.

By following only those paths that were not forbidden, he eventually came to a small grassy clearing, with a beehive hut built of rough stones at the center of the open space. Crossing the clearing, he hailed anyone who might be inside the hut, then waited for a response. When none came, he ducked his head and peered cautiously into the dim interior. The place appeared to be deserted, so he went inside.

There were no furnishings or other signs of habitation, except for some stones that might be meant for a hearth. Neither were there cobwebs, or the droppings of animals, or scattered bones, to indicate that wild beasts had laired there—as they must have done if the hut had been deserted for any long period of time. Because of that, and because he had in some sense been led there, he thought this was probably a place set aside for travelers to rest. As the shadows of evening were already gathering in the forest, and he had certainly walked far enough for one day, Tryffin decided to accept the implied invitation.

He went outside, gathered some leafy branches to make a bed, laid them out on the floor of the hut, and spread his cloak across them. It was so warm, he had no need of a fire, having nothing to cook nor anything to eat, and he was much too tired to go out hunting or gathering. As soon as it was dark, he stretched out on his makeshift bed and fell almost instantly asleep.

He woke in the morning much later than he expected. A bright beam of sunlight was pouring into the hut through the smoke-hole, and he heard a sweet, girlish voice speaking outside.

"Pali and Tiffaine said there was someone wandering in the wood, but if they are here, they are remarkably quiet."

The words were oddly accented, but the voice was entirely familiar. He was up out of bed in an instant, and out through the door.

At the edge of the clearing stood a fair young woman in a grey linen gown and a stocky little boy with red hair.

"Gwenlliant," said Tryffin, under his breath, marveling that finding her should be so easy. And it was undoubtedly her. Indeed, it was so vividly and completely Gwenlliant, he could not understand how he had ever been fooled before, for all that the shapechanger had imitated so much more than her face and her form.

In two long strides he crossed the clearing, put his hands on her shoulders, and bent his head to kiss her. He was stopped by the startled look that she gave him, the complete lack of recognition in her wide violet eyes.

This was more painful, in its way, than his first encounter with her image in Charon. Because the woman there, for all she had been so cold and distant, had at least seemed to know him.

"Is it possible," he said, removing his hands from her shoulders, taking a backward step, "that you don't remember me?"

She smiled sadly, leaning down to draw the little boy against the skirt of her grey gown. "It is hardly surprising that I should not, for I was sick during the winter and spent many days wandering in my mind. Since then, I remember nothing that happened to me before, not anything about myself or my former life, only the things that Maelinn and the others have told me. Yet it seems very strange that you should think you know me, and then greet me by the wrong name."

Tryffin stood staring down into her face. He supposed that it made a certain amount of sense: The shapechanger had somehow stolen Gwenlliant's memories. That was how the creature had recognized him, known so many of the intimate details of their life, and been able to convince him that she *was* Gwenlliant.

But this turn of events, so completely unanticipated, left him undecided how to proceed. He certainly did not wish to frighten her, the more so because she might still be fragile after the illness she had mentioned. "I believe that we are acquainted. And your name—" He hesitated, uncertain whether to risk a wrong guess. "—your name is Gwenhwyach, I think."

Her face brightened. "Then you do know me. But why did you call me that other name before?"

Now that he was over his first surprise, he was beginning to realize a number of things he had barely noticed before. She was a little older than he had expected her to be, though not so old as she had seemed in Charon; she appeared to be about sixteen. Also, she was not speaking the High Celydonian, but an obscure dialect he had only encountered before in certain isolated villages in Tir Gwyngelli. Because he had some knowledge of that language, he had unthinkingly responded in the same tongue.

"Gwenlliant is the name you were called by when you were a small child," he answered truthfully. "I have known you since then, because we are cousins. But it has been a long time since our last meeting, and it is clear that much has happened to you in the meantime. Perhaps you will tell me what these friends of yours told you, about what you are doing here in Achren, and how you first came to this wood."

She nodded her agreement, took Grifflet by the hand, and led him over to a fallen log, where she sat down with the little boy beside her.

"I came with nothing but a bundle of clothing and a baby . . . my son, Grifflet. His father is dead, but he was apparently a wealthy and powerful man, because he gave me this bracelet with the twining dragons, and this sidhe-stone ring," she said, displaying both items for his inspection. "After my husband died, my father wished me to marry a man that I despised. A wicked man, very much older than I was, and one that I feared."

"Yes," said Tryffin encouragingly, "his name was Rhun of Yrgoll. He had already been widowed a number of times and he kept several mistresses."

She turned the name over in her mind, contemplating the sound of it, then shook her head. "Well, it may be as you say, though I have no memory of any such name. But however it was, I did not want to marry him, so I took my son and started a long journey to the place where one of my kinsmen lived, hoping that *he* would prevent the marriage. Only the Mist caught me and carried me here, where I was taken in by the Lady of the Wood and the Well, and treated as a sister by the twelve young priestesses, who all live together in a lovely little house, here in the wildwood."

Tryffin sat down on the log by her side, fighting back a powerful desire to take her into his arms, to cover her face with kisses—as if by taste, touch, and scent he could *make* her remember him. "I am the one who prevented your marriage to Rhun. And I may be the kinsman you were looking for, when you left home."

Gwenlliant smiled. "But how strange it is—we have been talking all of this time, and I never asked you your name."

He hesitated, doubting she would understand the necessity for keeping it secret. But how was he ever to help her remember him, if he gave her the wrong name? Also, since no one he met here would know where he came from—except for the shapechanger, who knew practically everything about him already—he decided the danger to him was so small, he was willing to risk it.

"My name is Tryffin fab Maelgwyn, and we are very nearly related. I have come all this way to take you home again."

But at that, her smile faded, her eyes went dark again, and she looked very troubled.

"I have no wish to be unkind," she said slowly. "But I lead a very pleasant life here, and I have many friends. For that reason, I am not so certain I would like to leave . . . especially with a man who says that he knows me, though I cannot remember anything about him. I am not even certain that I ought to believe what you tell me."

He was painfully disappointed, but he could hardly blame her for showing a certain reluctance, under the circumstances. And he remembered that Gwenlliant had been drawn into Achren to unravel the riddle of the past. Whatever she had learned, she had obviously forgotten, so it was now up to him to discover it all for himself. That meant he would have to spend some time in Achren, anyway.

"Supposing I stayed on here for several days—perhaps even a matter of weeks—so that we became reacquainted?" he asked. "In that way, you might learn to trust me. Would this be permitted by the people who live in the wood? You said there were twelve young priestesses . . . ?"

She considered briefly. "It is not really for me to say whether you can stay. That would usually fall to Maelinn, the High Priestess, who is not even here. Indeed, she has been exceedingly restless and wild all of this spring, and often takes journeys that last many days, which the other women say is completely unlike her. Still, if Caithne and the rest grant their permission, I see no reason why you should not remain at least until Maelinn returns."

Gwenlliant came back the next morning, with the news that Tryffin would be allowed to stay, unless the mysterious Maelinn returned and said otherwise. She brought several of the other priestesses with her, who were curious, they said, to meet the big golden man that she had described to them. The women carried with them a number of items to make living in the hut more comfortable: blankets for his bed, some old clay pots to cook in, a wooden cup and bowls, and a number of things to eat which he could not easily make for himself, oat cakes and cheese, barley bread, a jug of mead, and herbs and roots they had grown in their garden.

He generally made friends quite easily, and these women were no exception. Soon they were sitting with him on the floor of the hut—Gleis, Regan, Mai, Morfa, and Sceith—and telling him all about their house in the woods, where men were forbidden to go; the other house which was also a temple, but devoted to the goddess Cerridwen; the lives they had led before becoming priestesses; and of their High Prince, Caerthinn, who not only ruled in Achren, but was also the leader of a vast clan confederation, so that his influence extended over many different lands. "From the borders of the Hill Country in the south," said Regan, "to the Blue Lake in the north, and everything between the Great Woods and the sea."

For his part, Tryffin told them as little about himself as he could, listened quietly when any of them spoke, and asked a question every now and again, to draw them out.

Grifflet, who could hardly be expected to remember him after so much time, nevertheless took to him at once. The little boy soon crept into his lap and began to chatter of things he had seen in the forest that day: a rabbit, a fox, a squirrel, a hawk. The women shook their heads and smiled, taking it all for nonsense, not understanding a word that he said, but Tryffin felt a sudden rush of tenderness, a sort of wondering joy awaken inside him. This was the son that he had adopted, sitting in his lap and speaking to him in his own language.

"I do not know where he learned those words," said Gwenlliant, sitting cross-legged on the other side of the hut. "I believe that he made them up."

"You must have taught him before you became ill," said Tryffin. "It is the language of our people, which you have apparently forgotten."

Because no one else could understand what he said, he spoke to the little boy. "Do you know who I am, Grifflet Og?"

The child looked up into his face and smiled sunnily. "You are my father."

"That's God's own truth . . . but how did you know?" asked the Governor, around a sudden tightening in his throat.

"Tryffin fab Maelgwyn is my father's name. My mother told me," said Grifflet, snuggling up against his broad chest. "*And* I like you."

"And I," said Tryffin, dropping a kiss on his bright auburn curls, "love you and your mother with all of my heart."

He stayed many days in the hut in the wood, and the women came often to visit him, Gwenlliant among them, usually with Grifflet in tow, but she never again came to speak with him alone.

When he had no visitors, Tryffin explored the forest, those parts of the forest that were not forbidden him. He gathered what fruits and edible herbs he could—which were not very many this time of the year—and made snares to catch birds and small animals. *"You must kill them as swiftly and painlessly as you are able,"* Gwenlliant had admonished him. *"For this is a sacred wood, and the Green Lady will not allow her creatures to suffer needlessly."*

This meant that he had to stay close to his traps once he set them out, that he might instantly know when he caught a rabbit, a squirrel, or a bird, and put the creature out of its misery if his snare had failed to kill it at once. As he had always preferred to kill humanely, anyway, generally with a crossbow when he went hunting, he accepted the inconvenience without much grumbling.

One day when he went out for a stroll to stretch his legs, he met Gwenlliant and two of the others, Pethboc and Regan, who told him that they were walking to the temple of Cerridwen. "You may accompany us as far as the clearing, if you like," said Regan, "but no further than that, because you are not a priest or a woman."

This Tryffin was happy to do, since it gave him an opportunity to talk with Gwenlliant. "And what is your purpose in going?" he inquired, as he fell into step beside her.

"We are going to visit the Princess Tinne, who is a priestess at the temple. It will not be very amusing, I am afraid, because she is always so sad and so dull. But apparently she and I were friends last winter, and she seems to enjoy my company. It is difficult to tell, however, precisely what she feels or wants."

"And why is that?" said Tryffin, raising a sandy eyebrow. It was frustrating to be so close to her and unable to do so much as take her hand. When they had lived together at Caer Ysgithr, he had been in the habit of feeling ill used because he could never make love to her . . . yet for all that, there was always a great deal of innocent, affectionate touching. Now there was not even that.

"Because she has taken a vow of silence," Gwenlliant answered. "So whenever we go to visit her, *we* talk and *she* listens, and sometimes she makes little signs with her hands. But she is not very expressive that way. However, I think that Tinne is learning to speak the language of the birds—which she is permitted to do. And I saw her once, attaching a little bit of cloth with some writing on it to the leg of a blackbird. I believe she is exchanging messages with her brother, the High Prince. Or perhaps with Mabonograin, whom she meant to marry, before Gwythyr insisted that she enter the temple.

"Except that it is so far to the Hill Country, where Mabonograin lives," she added thoughtfully. "So I think she is probably only sending her birds to Caer Bannawg."

When they reached the edge of the clearing, Tryffin sat down on a stump to wait for them, and the women went over to a large wooden house, passing by several smaller buildings that surrounded it, and disappeared inside.

Merciful God, I am learning a great deal . . . but what does any of it mean? he asked himself. He waited patiently, reviewing it all in his mind, but never came any closer to a solution.

It was not very long before the women came out of the house, this time accompanied by a pale girl with long dark braids and a strutting little man with a neat black beard. Tryffin disliked the man on sight, even at a distance. The girl with the braids—apparently the Princess Tinne—was very young and she looked . . . not so much dull and sulky, as nervous and wary, flinching away when anyone even brushed against the skirt of her black linen gown.

When Gwenlliant and her friends rejoined him, they were speaking among themselves, in low, troubled voices. "It is making her ill," said Pethboc, as they returned by the path they had followed before. "This pining away over Mabonograin is simply destroying her."

Regan sniffed. "I think it is Gwythyr who is making her ill. If you want to know what I think, I think he is forcing her to sleep with him."

Gwenlliant appeared deeply shocked, but Pethboc only said, "Well . . . if he is, it is certainly unkind but you know it is nothing less than his right.

"Only," she added, with a sigh, "I would have thought he would wait awhile, until Tinne had conquered her grief and began to want him, too. After all, he has the other three women and they all seem eager enough to gain his favor."

Tryffin cleared his throat. "I think I may have misunderstood what you told me earlier. The Princess Tinne—she is the *wife* of this priest?"

Gwenlliant nodded. It was plain to Tryffin, if it had not been before, that she remembered nothing at all about her own past, her suffering at the hands of Calchas—or how could she speak of Tinne's plight with such detachment? "Yes. And while I do not really remember how things were done in the land where you and I come from, yet a priest with four wives does strike me as rather odd. Still, it is the custom here, and I suppose no one thinks it out of the ordinary."

"It is not really the custom," said Regan. "Or at least, it *is* the custom for the Priest of Cerridwen to marry again and again, if you can call anything about the swine cult customary, when everything they do is so out of the ordinary. Their rites are not like those of any other cult, and are often perfectly disgusting. In truth, I sometimes think that all these things come out of Gwythyr's head, and have nothing to do with the dreams that his goddess sends him."

Though Tryffin was more than slightly disgusted himself, he was also intrigued, remembering what the monk in Charon had told him, those rumors of an evil cult which had existed since pagan times, frequently taking a new name and a new form in order to disguise its previous history. "Then the cult of Cerridwen is a new religion?"

Pethboc shook her head. "It is just a new way of worshipping. And until quite recently, no one knew there was a separate goddess Cerridwen—it was just another name for the White Cailleach. But the boar is the sacred beast of Gwythyr's clan, and the goddess began sending visions to his great-uncle, just before he died, inspiring the old man and Gwythyr to create the rites and establish the temple between them."

Tryffin expelled a long breath. "And Gwythyr, I suppose, is the pompous little man that I saw with you earlier?"

At this, Pethboc and Regan both giggled. "He is not usually described that way . . . but yes," said Pethboc. "He is certainly very proud."

"And you think that he is forcing his attentions on that pale child back at the clearing?"

"In truth, I am convinced of it," said Regan. "And I suspect that her reluctance only makes him press his attentions even more urgently. Because he enjoys hurting people but especially women."

Tryffin ground his teeth, enraged by the situation, frustrated by his own helplessness. This Gwythyr was apparently raping a Mochdreffi woman, who had formerly been betrothed to a Prince of ancient Gwyngelli. All this was outrageous enough, in and of itself, but Tryffin thought that he recognized a familiar pattern forming.

But Dame Ceinwen had warned him against interference. If he tried to do anything to rescue Tinne, history would only find a way to embroil her in an equally heartbreaking situation. To make matters worse, by altering those things that he could, Tryffin would fail to learn *exactly* what had really happened— and perhaps fail in his quest because of that.

What he should do instead, he decided, was discover as much as he possibly could, in order to understand the situation completely.

"I think," he murmured, under his breath, "that I would like to learn a great deal more about this beast named Gwythyr and his equally beastly swine cult."

And when Pellam had finally accomplished these things, there was a harsh, bitter, burning light, the clamor of a mighty angelic host shouting in exaltation . . . and it seemed to him that he was finally permitted to gaze directly into the face of God.

And the splendor and the cruelty and the horror of that face was more than he could endure.

—From The Vision of St. Pellam

23.

The Cult of All Evil

In the morning, expecting no visit from Gwenlliant, Tryffin left the hut and walked purposefully through the wood in the direction of the temple of Cerridwen. It promised to be a fine day, for it was warm already, even under the shadow of the trees. This place was not, he was thinking, at all like the Bearded Wood, though many of the trees were the same, and the tangle of undergrowth just as impenetrable. But where the Bearded Wood was musty and elderly, everything here was young and alive.

When he reached the clearing, he sat down on the same stump he had occupied the day before, waiting for someone to come out of one of the buildings, someone he could hail and ask to carry a message. But the first person he saw, after about an hour of waiting, was Gwythyr himself. Catching sight of Tryffin there under the trees, the Priest of Cerridwen came over to speak with him.

"You are the foreigner the women speak of . . . the one who is wooing Gwenhwyach," said Gwythyr.

"I am the foreigner," said Tryffin. "But who told you that I came here hoping to marry my cousin?" Whatever Gwenlliant might have concluded from his offer to take her back home, he could not imagine her exchanging confidences with this fellow.

Gwythyr shrugged. "When a man, even a kinsman, comes so

far to find a woman, he must want something from her in return. If not marriage, then bedding. I hope you may find her worth your trouble."

There was something in the way that he smirked when he said that, the suggestive tone of his voice, which was indescribably obscene—and knowing what Tryffin did of the proclivities of the man made it even worse. In the long, long history of feuding and warfare between the Mochdreffi and the Gwyngellach, men had been cut into pieces and fed to the dogs for considerably less. This was not, however, an appropriate moment to imitate the barbarous ways of his ancestors—tempting though the prospect might be.

"Ah well," said Tryffin, "I've little doubt that she will satisfy me . . . one way or another."

The priest laughed heartily at this pleasantry, little guessing the murderous thoughts behind his visitor's amiably smiling face. "By the gods! You look like the man to see to it, too. But what brings you here to this part of the wood? If you are expecting to meet Gwenhwyach, she rarely comes this way."

"I am here," said Tryffin, "out of a desire to learn more about the worship of Cerridwen. Your goddess is unknown in the land of my fathers, yet I have heard much of her cult since I arrived in Achren, and I must admit that I find her mysteries intriguing."

Gwythyr studied his face carefully. "If you will pardon my saying so, you do not look to me like any sort of man with a religious vocation—nor a student of the mysteries," he replied bluntly.

Tryffin continued to smile. "Let us say that I am a man who knows the value of powerful friends, whether they should be men or gods. And I hear that the goddess Cerridwen can be amazingly generous."

Gwythyr continued to eye him speculatively. "She can be generous, but she can also be terrible. Whether she is willing to offer her patronage would depend on what you were able to offer her in return."

Tryffin lowered his voice. "I am a man who commands vast lands and wealth. Yet is any man ever satisfied with what he has? I believe I am meant to accomplish great things in my time, and those who assist me along the way will not go unrewarded. Even as I am now, I could give much gold, land for building a holy sanctuary . . . but how much more could I give, if I stood in my elder brother's place?"

Gwythyr nodded slowly, an avaricious gleam in his eye. He shifted excitedly from one foot to the other. No doubt he was seeing new possibilities, an opportunity to extend his influence into far countries, to see temples built and golden offerings collected. "And you think that the goddess Cerridwen could remove this obstacle, this elder brother of yours from your path?"

"Could she not?" asked Tryffin, avoiding the lie by giving the man his question right back again. "Or if it were done . . . by ordinary means, could it not later be proven to be the will of the goddess? Of course to do that, I would first have to establish her worship; the temple of Cerridwen and her priest would collect their reward in advance."

The little man was clearly dazzled. Along with his lust and ambition, he seemed to be venal as well, and that suited Tryffin's purposes precisely. Gwythyr took a deep breath before he spoke again. "Let me withdraw for a time to pray and meditate. It may well be that the mysteries of Cerridwen shall be opened to you, but for that I would need a sign from the goddess. Let us meet tomorrow in this same place and discuss the matter further."

Tryffin nodded, perfectly satisfied for now. Of course the priest was going to delay, attempting to strike the best bargain possible for himself and the temple. He would generally do everything in his power to acquire the upper hand in whatever dealings there might be between them. But there was little doubt in Tryffin's mind that Gwythyr would eventually tell him everything that he wanted to learn.

They met the next day, and the day after that, and while neither man committed himself to anything, Gwythyr dropped many dark hints about the powers of his goddess and the antiquity of her worship. "They say the cult of Cerridwen is a new thing, but this is not so. Her rituals have been practiced since the dawn of time; it is Cerridwen herself who changes, taking on a new aspect and a new name."

"And what does she require of her followers?" asked Tryffin, as he and the priest circled the temple clearing.

"Strength, power, ambition. She is no patron for the weak or timorous. Nor for the squeamish; her rituals require an enormous quantity of blood. She is not, in fact, precisely a she, as she exists beyond matters of gender," Gwythyr explained. "Yet she has adopted a feminine aspect at this time, because that seemed most likely to win her followers."

They stopped in the shade of a towering lime tree. "And that would be why her priest is so powerful, her priestesses so subservient," said Tryffin, lifting the damp blond hair off of his brow. "In the cult of a goddess, women would generally hold a higher status."

Gwythyr shrugged. "At the temple of Cerridwen, the women are not priestesses in the ordinary sense, they are only the priest's wives. In the distant past, they were known as the sacred concubines, but again, that would not be acceptable to the people of Achren, so we give them a name that vulgar folk may easily understand. Yet they do serve an important purpose, and for that are rewarded with some trivial arts, some minor tricks of power of their own."

"And that purpose is?" Tryffin asked—though he thought that he knew already.

Gwythyr leered up at him. "As Cerridwen has no gender, she cannot consort with the other gods and goddesses. Yet she desires to take part in the pleasures of the flesh. This she can only do through her priest, who—according to her requirements—must be a man of tremendous sexual appetites. Her enthusiasm for carnal pleasures is immense and her tastes can be . . . a little perverse."

Thinking of the four helpless, silent women that Gwythyr kept virtually in thrall, Tryffin felt his stomach lurch. For that reason, he decided to explore another line of inquiry, one that would not make him feel so sick and angry.

"What are the objects sacred to her worship?" he asked, leaning up against the trunk of the lime tree.

"These may change from time to time," said Gwythyr. "Yet blood, bone, dust, and ashes always play a part in the rituals."

And so, thought Tryffin, it was all true, everything Brother Airem had told him about "the cult of all evil." It had probably begun in biblical times and had continued from Gwythyr's day into the present, by way of the Knights of Jerusalem and the Order of St. Pellam, the Black Canons . . . and there was no guessing how many other twisted permutations of the Old Religion and the Christian Church.

"I recognize her now," he said out loud, suppressing with an effort his natural shudder of distaste. "She is *the terror by night, the pestilence that walks in darkness, and the destruction that withers at noonday."*

As he had expected, Gwythyr denied nothing, and actually seemed to take delight in this description. "In truth, she is all of those things," the priest said smugly, "and many, even more terrible, things besides."

Walking back toward the hut afterward, Tryffin was about to cross the gurgling brook where Gwythyr's acolytes went to fetch water each morning, when he noticed Gwenlliant kneeling on the ground further up the stream, gathering a feathery green moss off of the rocks. As she was alone, for once, without Grifflet or any of the priestesses in sight, Tryffin could not resist this rare opportunity for a private meeting.

She spotted him as soon as he left the path and began the short walk along the bank of the stream. But she gave him a troubled glance as he came up beside her. "So it is true. You have been meeting with Gwythyr—why else, indeed, would you be in this part of the wood?—and he has been initiating you into the mysteries of Cerridwen."

He hesitated a moment, wondering how much he could safely tell her. "I have been meeting with Gwythyr, in part to discover if the rumor was true: whether he mistreats the Princess Tinne, by forcing his attentions on her."

Gwenlliant put down her basket of moss, wiped her hands on her skirt, and rose to her feet. "Why should that matter to you?"

He shook his head. Even thinking about it made the edges of his vision turn red, the suffocating pressure, which always preceded the battle madness, begin to build in his chest. "How could it *not* matter? Do you think that all men are like Gwythyr? She is little more than a child, and children are far too precious to be mistreated in any way. And while a man may have certain rights over his wife, he also has certain duties . . . patience and kindness among them. Especially when he chooses to take so young a bride. In Tir Gwyngelli, where I was born, no decent man would even contemplate rape, whether he was married to the woman or not."

She nodded her agreement, though she continued to stare at him with wide, puzzled eyes. "But if you found out that he *was* ill-using her, what would you do about it?"

Tryffin sighed, sat down on the grassy verge of the stream. If this were Gwyngelli, he knew exactly what would happen. It would be bloody and prolonged, and no one would blame him afterward. But in Tir Gwyngelli no woman would be forced into a distasteful marriage in the first place. "There is nothing that I could do—not anything I might reasonably attempt, anyway. No, I was hoping to discover that it was all a mistake, that Tinne was perfectly safe. That would have set my mind at rest . . . and yours as well, I thought."

"And did you learn anything to ease our minds?" she asked wistfully.

"No," he said, "I did not. I wish it was possible to say that I had."

Gwenlliant nodded, went back to the business of gathering moss. "Maelinn seems to think that Tinne is weak because she shows her grief so visibly, but I think it very brave of her to endure so much for the sake of others. She only consented, you know, to turn aside the wrath of Cerridwen and prevent more people from dying as they did at Midwinter."

"The Midwinter Feast," he said with a thoughtful frown, because that had been mentioned before. "Do you know exactly what happened then?"

Gwenlliant shook her head. "It seems that I was there, but of course I don't remember it. They say there was a wild pig that ran through Prince Caerthinn's hall, slaying many people, and that other signs appeared as well. Only some of the women have questions as to why these things really happened. They should not say these things in front of me, of course, but sometimes they forget I do not belong here, they are so used to having me about."

She started to move further down the stream, in search of the bright green moss, and Tryffin sprang to his feet and followed after her. "If you made up your mind to return to our home, you would find many people there who love you dearly, and you might not have to wonder, then, about whether you belonged or not."

Gwenlliant stopped and glanced up at him. Though she was taller than he remembered, she still barely reached his chin. "I have been thinking of that. But there is something I would like to ask you, and I hope you will answer me truly."

"If I can," he said. "God knows, I would never wish to deceive you about my intentions where you are concerned."

She blushed and lowered her eyes. "Well then, I cannot help noticing how you look at me, and others have seen it as well. So

I want to ask . . . when you knew me before, were those intentions honorable, did you wish to marry me?"

"I did," he said heavily, not certain how she would receive the news.

"And now that we meet again," she went on, "do you—do you wish to marry me still?"

"I want very much for you to be my wife," he answered. "Does that distress you?"

She smiled and shook her head. "How can it distress me when you have been so gentle and courteous? The only thing is, I don't know yet if I wish to marry you. I like you very well, and I suspect that I might have liked you even better when we were better acquainted. Also . . ."

"Also . . . what?" he said softly. It seemed to him that she had been about to say something very important.

Gwenlliant blushed again and shook her head. "If I told you that, you might think me very bold," she whispered.

Tryffin felt his pulse begin to race. This was, he knew, a very delicate moment—and one that was full of possibilities. If she did not remember anything about him or their life together, neither did she remember Calchas or the vile spell he had once cast over her, or her own fear of intimacy which had resulted from that terrifying experience. If there was ever a time when it might be possible to approach her, without any of the old barriers standing between them . . .

"I have known you so long and so well," said Tryffin carefully, "that I don't think anything you might say would strike me as bold."

Gwenlliant took a deep breath, raised her eyes to his face. "Then . . . perhaps I can tell you, after all, that I am greatly attracted to you."

He felt himself acting without any conscious volition, reaching out for her, drawing her into his hungry embrace. She dropped the basket, put both of her arms around his neck, and stood on her toes to bring her face closer to his.

He held her so for a long delirious moment, the blood roaring in his ears, the pressure of her body against his almost unbearably sweet. When he finally kissed her, it lasted until both of them were weak and dizzy, and when it was over, Tryffin covered her face with short, breathless kisses. By the time they drew apart again, Gwenlliant was trembling.

"I begin to see that we were a great deal closer than I had imagined," she said, with a shaky little laugh.

He woke late the next morning in a hopeful frame of mind. Gwenlliant had agreed to meet him at noon, wanting time (she said) to think about all that had been said and done, before giving him her answer. Yet he was convinced that if her answer did not come today, it would nevertheless come soon, and it would serve as the beginning of a new life together.

As he was kneeling by the fire, attempting to heat up some oat cakes on the hot stones, he heard someone moving about in the clearing outside. A moment later, one of the little temple acolytes stuck his head in through the low doorway and delivered the message: "Lord Gwythyr has a desire to speak with you, and it is very urgent. Will you come with me now?"

Tryffin sighed. A meeting with the Priest of Cerridwen was just what he needed to cast a gloom over this bright new day—however, the boy was so flushed and excited, he thought it might be something important. So he finished dressing, picked up the oat cakes, still barely warm, and followed the acolyte through the wood, to the place near the temple clearing where he and Gwythyr usually met.

The priest was already there, white-faced and grim, pacing the ground with an impatient step. "Tinne has gone. An insult to me and an affront to the goddess Cerridwen. Of course this must not be allowed. I go to the court of the High Prince to demand justice. It is a journey of two days on horseback—I can demand horses of the villagers in Tremoc—and I would like you to accompany me. I fear there may be trouble along the way."

"I don't understand," said Tryffin, his brows coming together in a puzzled frown. "Are you certain she has really run off? Might she not be . . . wandering somewhere in the wood, seeking a little solitude?"

"She went out walking at dawn with two of the other women. At the edge of the wood, near the stone circle, she met a man on horseback, who apparently convinced her to ride away with him," said Gwythyr. "It is difficult, as you know, to communicate with any of my wives, for they only use signs and gestures instead of speech. However, by asking a great many questions I eventually learned that the man wore golden rings in his ears and blue paint on his face . . . it must have been Prince Mabonograin, come expressly to steal her away. She hardly seemed surprised to meet him, though the tryst could not have been specifically arranged—else why should she take the other women with her?"

Tryffin thought of what Gwenlliant had said about birds and messages. He guessed now that Tinne had not been sending those birds to her brother, but to her lover. He had come to the wood at her bidding, but they had met this morning by chance rather than design. "I suppose," he said, "that you cannot allow this insult to pass, the two of them to escape?"

Gwythyr ground his teeth audibly. "Could you—in my place?"

In fact, Tryffin was not so certain what he would have done, if Gwenlliant had run away with another man instead of the dwarf Brangwengwen. Almost, he felt a pang of sympathy for the man. "You said that you feared trouble along the way. Yet I would think that Tinne and this fellow Mabonograin would wish, above all, to avoid meeting you."

Gwythyr shrugged. "That may be so, but we have no way of knowing whether he came so far alone. He may have set men along the road to waylay me, and prevent me from reaching Caer Bannawg with the news."

That hardly seemed likely. From all that had been said of Mabonograin, he was not the sort to stoop to ambush and assassination. Besides, if he was truly Gwyngellach—and Tryffin was fairly certain that he must be—he would want to kill Gwythyr himself, and do it openly. That Mabonograin had chosen, instead, to take Tinne away in the manner he had, indicated a wish to travel quickly and secretly, and perhaps to meet up with his own men much later, once he was safely out of Caerthinn's territory.

In truth, thought Tryffin, *he sounds very much like a man who has been driven to take this desperate action in order to rescue the woman he loves from an intolerable situation—but who still seeks to prevent an armed confrontation that might lead to war.*

"Well," Gwythyr was saying impatiently, "will you come with me or not? I could use a strong man like you to defend me, but I cannot delay much longer."

As this looked so much like the beginning of those events he had come into the past to learn about, Tryffin was grateful for the invitation. Though if Gwythyr was right and an ambush had been arranged, he would be damned before he lifted a hand in the priest's defense.

Besides, Tryffin reminded himself with a grim smile, it was not his place to stand in the way of the course of history.

"I will ride with you," he said. "Only give me time to send word to my cousin, who expects to see me later in the day."

While Gwythyr went back to the temple to make some last arrangements for the journey, leaving the acolyte behind to carry Tryffin's message to Gwenlliant, the Governor wracked his brains for the right words. It would not do to give his cousin the false impression that he was going along in support of Gwythyr, but he must not say anything that the priest might hear and interpret to the contrary.

"Tell the Lady Gwenhwyach all that has happened," he said at last. "And say . . . say that I fear for the safety of the Princess Tinne."

It was sunset when the horsemen entered the wooden stockade at Caer Bannawg. All but foaming at the mouth with impatient frustration after the two-day journey, Gwythyr flung himself out of the saddle, strode across the torchlit yard and into the banquet hall, where he surprised Prince Caerthinn in the middle of a feast, and immediately launched into a long abusive tirade against Tinne and Mabonograin.

As for Tryffin, he silently followed the priest into the building, and stood with his arms folded across his chest and his back to one of the wooden pillars, listening while the others argued the fate of the unfortunate young lovers.

"I warn you, Caerthinn, if Tinne does not return to the temple, if this insult is not avenged, the wrath of Cerridwen will be terrible," Gwythyr concluded his account of Tinne's escape.

The High Prince appeared far more ill than angry . . . and very much as if he wished the matter had been brought to his attention privately, rather than before his entire court. "If she wished to elope with Mabonograin, why did she not do so before she went to the temple? What have you been doing, Gwythyr, to make her so desperate? I know your way with women, yet you promised me that you would be patient, and more gentle than was your custom. Have you broken that vow—was it your cruelty that drove her to such desperate actions?"

Gwythyr lowered his eyes. "She had no reason to complain of the treatment I gave her. And if I was cruel, why did she endure me so long?"

"And if she was frightened of Gwythyr, why did she not seek

the protection of the brother who loves her so dearly?" said a woman's voice, and a small-boned woman with a mane of glorious dark hair and a face of undeniable beauty stepped out of the shadows and into the torchlight. "Would you not have extended your protection . . . if she had asked for it?"

Prince Caerthinn nodded reluctantly. "You know very well, Maelinn, that I would have done so." A faint flush came into his cheeks. "They should have known that, too, Tinne and Mabonograin both. Why could he not do the honorable thing and bring her to me?"

"They have betrayed you," said Maelinn. "Your sister and the man who pretended to be your friend. Will men follow you, when your own sister flouts your authority? Will men respect you, when your friend takes your kinswoman away and sleeps with her unwed?"

There was a stir among the men and women assembled in the hall. "And what of the vow Tinne has broken?" said someone. He was a richly dressed man, who, judging by his resemblance to Gwythyr and Maelinn, must be the older brother, Lord Gereint. "How many of us shall suffer and die, because of what Tinne has done? If we ride out now and bring her back to be punished, if we kill Mabonograin, we may yet hope to avert the wrath of Cerridwen."

Many others murmured their agreement. But a handsome young warrior in leather armor stepped forward and spoke to the High Prince in a soothing voice. "We must certainly attempt to bring them back to account for what they have done, Lord Prince. But as for anything more than that . . . we do not even know for certain that he is sleeping with her. It may only be that he has removed her to some place of safety."

This time, the murmur of approval was muted. But Caerthinn seemed to take heart. "That is true, Tadhg. We must not judge them so swiftly and so harshly. Perhaps the matter is not so serious as we had thought."

There was much heated debate after that, in which practically everyone present took part, during which it became clear that few, if any, supported what Tadhg had said. And the High Prince began to look more and more hard-pressed, as though he realized he might be forced to take an action he might regret for the rest of his life, or else stand revealed as a coward and a man without honor.

But a man who was truly courageous and honorable would do

what he knew to be right, thought Tryffin. *Nor would he allow anyone to convince him to do otherwise.*

Glancing across the hall, his gaze chanced to fall on the woman in the scarlet gown, and Tryffin was astonished to receive, in return, an intense stare of sheer, venomous hatred. Could this possibly be meant for him, he wondered, when he and she had never even met?

Though she looked away quickly, an idea had already come into his head. This was the Maelinn that Gwenlliant and the other women spoke of, the High Priestess whose strange behavior and prolonged absences had begun at about the same time that Gwenlliant had lost her memories. And she *recognized* him; her animosity had been far too personal for there to be any mistake about that.

But now Prince Caerthinn was speaking again. "We will leave at first light tomorrow morning. We must go quickly, because Mabonograin may have an army waiting to meet him, and our own numbers will be few. But what happens when we overtake him and Tinne . . . that will depend on whether he had dishonored her or not."

Since the Princess was no longer a virgin in any case, that might not be so easy to prove one way or the other, and everyone knew it.

"But if he *has* dishonored your sister, and if it can be proven?" Lord Gereint persisted.

Prince Caerthinn passed a hand over his eyes. "If it can be proven, then I suppose that Mabonograin will have to die," he said bleakly. "And my sister . . . may the gods give me the strength to face her after I have condemned her lover . . . my sister must suffer as well."

They rode out the next morning, Caerthinn and his warband, Gwythyr, Lord Gereint and his men. And Tryffin was with them, still riding at Gwythyr's side. They covered a great deal of ground before noon, leaving Prince Caerthinn's personal holdings in tree-shaded Achren far behind, setting across a stretch of rugged moorland, though still remaining within the lands he governed as the High Prince. But even before they found Mabonograin's horse lying dead in the road, a leg broken, the throat mercifully cut, Tryffin knew that Tinne and her lover were doomed.

It required some final tragedy to set the feud in motion, lay waste to the land which would some day be Mochdreff. The swine cult, the Sons of the Boar, as Gwythyr and Gereint were known . . . that explained the mysterious matter of the wild pigs, which had apparently been the first cause. And Mabonograin was Tryffin's most famous ancestor, the legendary Mabon, whose foray into Mochdreff, much garbled with telling and retelling, had ended in disaster.

All that was required now, he thought with a heavy heart, was the shedding of blood.

Forced to go on foot, the lovers' tracks led across open country. They had left the road behind, hoping to get lost amidst the broom and the heather. Tryffin could imagine that desperate pair, grown weary at last, but continuing painfully on, hand in hand, knowing just as well as he did that they were doomed, but struggling on, each for the sake of the other.

I cannot prevent it, I may not even try, Tryffin told himself again and again. It was a stern test for a man who had spent his entire life meddling in the lives of others (*always for their own good, let God be my witness*), who could never forbear from influencing the people around him, if not with soothing, reasonable words, then with whatever action seemed necessary at the time. And now he could not even speak.

The Prince and his men, Lord Gereint and his, beat the heather all afternoon, and continued their search all through the long moonlit night. In the morning, just over the top of a rugged hill, Caerthinn, Gwythyr, and a party of half a dozen others found the sleeping lovers curled up together in a grassy hollow.

They had been weary, but not too weary for lovemaking. Their garments were in disarray, and Mabonograin slept with his head on Tinne's naked breast, his posture both possessive and defensive. As for the Princess, there were tearstains on her cheeks, but she was smiling in her sleep, and her dark hair, coming loose from its bindings, lay across her lover's eyes.

God knows, thought Tryffin, *it would take a heart of stone to disturb them, to wish to hurt them, after seeing them so.*

But Gwythyr, of course, had the requisite hardness of heart. "Now you have the proof that you wanted," he hissed. "Do as you have promised, Lord Prince. Kill Mabonograin."

And Caerthinn, a weak man, hard-pressed, knowing that he stood in danger of losing everything if he did not keep his word, took the coward's way out. Rather than face the reproachful eyes of his friend, he pulled out his dagger, bent down and rolled

Mabonograin off of Tinne . . . and just as the eyelids were fluttering open, slit his throat.

There was a gush of bright blood, a struggle for breath, and Mabonograin expired without ever knowing who had slain him. But the Princess awoke with a start, and seeing her lover lying dead beside her, her brother standing above with the blood on his blade, sprang to her feet and began to shriek and moan most piteously.

"Silence her," said Caerthinn, averting his eyes. "Somebody make her stop." He was so pale and sick and shaken, Tryffin might have spared a little pity even for him, if the man had been willing to comfort his sister . . . instead of allowing Gwythyr to lay rough hands on her.

"It is for me to chastise her," said the priest, pulling her to him in a cruel embrace. "She is consecrated to the goddess Cerridwen, and no other man may touch her."

Caerthinn nodded, still without looking—either at Mabonograin's body or at his half-naked, struggling sister.

But Tinne, with the strength of despair, managed to break loose and hurl herself in her brother's direction. Whether he acted instinctively or vindictively it was impossible to say, but his dagger flashed and then buried itself in her naked breast.

She was not long dying, for which Tryffin thanked God, as he stood with his hands clenched into fists, willing himself to control, battling with the fury that threatened to engulf him. He must not, must not, say or do anything that might alter the course of events in any way. Now that he had come this far, he was determined to know it all.

There was a long moment of silence, while the other men recovered from their shock, as the grim realization came over them. "You have killed a priestess," said one of the warriors, in a voice of superstitious dread. "And for that you are cursed."

The other warriors began to mutter and draw away, as if fearing to contract some contagion from the Prince's person. "If we burn her body," said Gwythyr, "we may avert the curse."

At this, there was a vast sigh of relief. Two of the men began cutting branches from the bushes on the hillside. Another took out flint and steel, made a little pile of sticks, and painstakingly kindled a fire behind a rock, out of the wind that was just coming up.

The men who were making the pyre were still piling dry

branches of heather and gorse over Tinne's body, when Tadhg rode up with another party of warriors.

"Prince Caerthinn, what . . ." Tadgh's dark, expressive eyes opened wide with shock, as he saw, first Mabonograin's corpse, then the pale figure of Tinne lying half covered with branches.

With an effort, he recovered enough to speak his news. "Lord Prince, we have seen men riding in the distance, under the dragon banner. We suspect it is Cassibellawn, coming to meet Mabonograin. As we will be greatly outnumbered, I would advise immediate flight."

"No," said Caerthinn, glancing up wild-eyed. "We will not flee. The wind is blowing in their direction. If we set fire to the heather, they will have to turn back."

Someone protested. "The wind is rising, the flames will run wild . . . the fire may burn unchecked all the way to the border."

So that was another thing, thought Tryffin, sick with horror. The Prince was ready to violate his sacred bond with the land, by setting his own fields aflame. Of all the enormities he had s :en today, Tryffin thought this one might be the worst. Accordir.g to the land-loving Gwyngellach, this was the equivalent of matricide.

The other men stood still, perhaps realizing this. Not one of them was willing to do as Prince Caerthinn commanded. Not even Gwythyr, not even Gereint. It was beyond even them.

But not beyond the High Prince, who by now had gone mad with anger, grief, and terror. He snatched up a branch of gorse from the funeral pyre to serve as a torch and plunged it into the fire. When it ignited, he started down the hill with the flaming brand held over his face.

Nobody stopped him. No one wanted to touch him, because his curse and his madness made him untouchable . . . even a momentary contact would spread the contagion. Caerthinn set fire to bushes all across the hillside, then stepped back to watch the flames spread, down the hill, across the fields below.

The wind continued to rise, whipping the fire into a tremendous blaze. Tryffin stood there with the smoke stinging his eyes and a pain in his heart, watching it all. On every side of him, he could hear the earth shuddering, crying out in agony, trees and bushes and grass dying, because the High Prince had broken his covenant with the land.

And when Cerddin died of the madness and the grief that was on him, no one could be found who was willing to prepare the corpse for burial, neither to bathe it, nor to embalm it with spices, nor to wrap it in fine linen, because he had died while under a curse and his body was considered unchancy and unclean.

So the lords of the realm found an old woman, who had been a midwife, and a witch, and one who lays out the dead, but had done murder and been condemned to die, and they promised her life and freedom if she would prepare the body for burial. And they summoned also a great number of outcasts and ragged beggars to carry Prince Cerddin to his grave, reasoning that the state of these folk was already so bad that nothing could be done to make it any worse. So all was done as the lords decreed.

But on the morning of the third day, the earth of the grave was found to be disturbed, and the corpse was discovered lying with its face toward the sky, about a dozen feet from the place it had been buried.

So they buried him again, in another spot, but again it happened exactly as before: Three days later the earth was found disturbed in the morning, and the body of the Prince was lying on a dungheap.

At this, the lords of the realm sent for the old woman who had been about to be hanged, and asked her what mischief and Black Magic she meant, to cast evil spells on the mortal remains of one who had been a prince, no matter how he had disgraced himself and his clan during his lifetime.

And the woman stepped forward boldly to speak. "This is no mischief and no magic of mine," said she. "But because of the wicked thing that Prince Cerddin did, the earth will not receive him, nor the honored dead accept him into their company."

—*From* The Nine Sorrowful Tales of
the Misfortunes of Mochdreff

24.

The Withering of Mochdreff

It was not the same forest by the time he went back for Gwenlliant three days later. The leaves were turning yellow, fruits had withered, nuts had rained from the trees to lie unripened on the ground. And the wood was so quiet, wrapped in an unnatural hush, the birds all flown, the foxes and the weasels, the rabbits and the deer, all fled.

Tryffin knew the forest would take many years dying, but the blight was there, it would die eventually. Other glades he had passed along the way appeared untouched, but this being a sacred wood and the heart of the land, it suffered first and worst. The others would feel the touch of this unnatural autumn soon enough.

He had returned the horse to the villagers in Tremoc, walked the rest of the way on foot, a longer walk than he remembered it, his steps slow and heavy. Even when he had been recovering from the wounds inflicted by the shapechanger, he had not felt this ill, this weary. *But I never knew before how cruel the world could be . . . I saw, but never believed.*

But when he came to the hut in the clearing, Gwenlliant was waiting for him, sitting in the grass by the door, watching Grifflet dig a trench in the earth with a stick. When Tryffin's shadow fell across her, she jumped to her feet, looked eagerly into his face . . . then, not finding the answer she wanted, put a hand to her heart.

"They are dead, then? Mabonograin and Tinne both?" she asked softly. "Was—was it very cruel, the way it was done?"

Tryffin shook his head. "Caerthinn killed Mabonograin sleeping. The Princess . . . the Princess did not live long after."

"And Caerthinn?" Gwenlliant asked wonderingly. "Could it be they allowed him to murder a defenseless man?"

"Since I didn't kill him, I suppose no one else will. Unless he should chance to take his own life."

She slipped her hand into his. "You are leaving something out. It must have been much worse than you say, to put that look in your eyes. Also . . ." She hesitated, uncertain whether he knew, not wanting to put a further burden on him. "Also, this forest is bleeding out its life. I think all of Achren is bleeding . . . perhaps all of Caerthinn's territories. What did he do?"

So Tryffin told her the entire story. Once he really began, it was impossible to stop, to withhold any of the details.

"What a terrible thing," Gwenlliant said, when he had finished. "And what a good man you must be to feel so much, when you scarcely knew any of the people."

He released a long sigh. "I need to go home, and you need to come with me. The life that you knew here, it will all be changed. And I . . . I cannot face the future without you and Grifflet beside me."

"Yes," she said softly, putting both her arms around him, leaning her head against his shoulder. "Of course we will go with you." Tryffin knew there was more pity than love in the gesture, but once he took her back to Dame Ceinwen, once the witch had restored her memory . . .

"Before we can go, you must let me remove the sidhe-stone ring that you wear on your right hand," he said. "It is the ring that brought you into Achren, when you were caught in the Breathing Mist, and it is the ring that keeps you here."

She held up her hand. "But it won't come off. I have tried to remove it a hundred times, because the stone is so large and it is always catching on things. In truth, I would gladly be rid—" Then she laughed in amazement as the heavy golden band slipped off of her finger, and lay in the palm of Tryffin's hand. "But how shall we return? Is it a very long way?"

"We have to return by the way we came," he said. "You were supposed to know the way, but since you have lost the spell along with your other memories—then we will have to rely on mine."

So he told her the herbs that he needed, and while she took Grifflet and went back to the house to get them, he built a fire on his hearth, filled his cooking pot with water, and set it on to boil. Gwenlliant and Grifflet returned sooner than he had expected, with all their things packed up and ready to go.

"You did not take long saying your good-byes," he commented, taking the bag of herbs she offered him.

"There was no need for explanations. I had already told everyone I would go as soon as you returned. And I . . . I don't know how it was, but I could not find a way to tell them about poor Tinne. Besides," she added, with a sudden spark of anger, "why should I spare Gwythyr from explaining it all himself?"

Tryffin nodded grimly. But the fact that Gwenlliant had been planning to go with him eased his pain a little. He dropped her herbs into the water, said the words he remembered Dame Ceinwen chanting, then waited for the steam to rise.

"Once the Mist gathers, we must remain close together," he told Gwenlliant. "And for the love of God, don't let go of the child for a single instant."

Gwenlliant nodded, took a firm grip on Grifflet's hand, and stepped closer. The water was soon boiling, the one-room hut filled with the scent of herbs. They all three went out the door together and watched the tendrils of mist come sailing out of the hut. "It may be difficult finding our way, since you don't remember, and I saw nothing," Tryffin said. "But perhaps between us—"

"Prince Tryffin," said a voice, interrupting him.

The woman stood at the edge of the clearing, exactly as he remembered meeting her in Charon, the same pale hair, the same heartbreaking face—Gwenlliant's face, but older and harder— the same black gown and trailing brown cloak. But the look in her eyes was different this time; it was the fierce glance of the woman at Caer Bannawg.

"Maelinn," he said, giving her name back. "You have no power over me in Achren."

Even as he spoke, she went through several transformations: Gwenlliant to Maelinn, Maelinn to an owl, the owl to an immense grey cat. But Tryffin had the silver-bladed dagger out of his belt, was already leaping to meet her attack.

She had chosen her shape wisely. The silver blade went in between the muscular shoulders, but not deep enough to kill. Yet the grey cat screamed, showed its dirty yellow teeth, and made a vicious swipe at him with one great paw, even as it collapsed on the ground.

Tryffin did not wait to retrieve the dagger, figuring it was likely to do the most harm where it was. And the Mist was growing thicker with every passing instant, the air was shuddering and whispering all around them. He turned, scooped up Grifflet in his arms, and caught Gwenlliant by the wrist, pulling her into the very densest part of the fog with him.

Just as Tryffin had feared, there were no landmarks along the way. When he asked Gwenlliant whether she saw anything, sensed anything, she shook her head and whispered no. But wherever they were going, wherever they ended up, it could not be a more terrible place than Achren had already become in his mind.

They walked for what might have been hours, what might have been days. Tryffin was aware of an ache in his right side, a spreading dampness where the grey cat had raked him with its claws, but gradually the pain subsided. He held Grifflet on his left side, trying to keep him as close and warm as possible. After what seemed an eternity, he felt Gwenlliant tugging at his sleeve. "I do begin to see some things," she whispered, "but what should I be looking for?"

"I hardly know . . . tell me what you see."

"There are reeds and cattails, a castle tower where ravens and blackbirds fly in and out, and a cottage built of stones," she said.

"We want to go toward the cottage," he replied. "Which way is that?"

Gwenlliant pointed the way, and they plodded on in that direction. After a little while longer, she said, "I smell summer, is that the way that we want to go?"

"Yes," he answered, thinking of Midsummer's Day. "That is the way that we want to go." So they moved in the direction of summer. In a little while, he could smell it, too.

They walked out of the Mist suddenly, and out onto the sun-drenched moors, about a hundred yards from the white stone cottage.

"I know this house," said Gwenlliant, staring at the reed-thatched roof, the crooked chimney. "I lived here once." Then she put a hand to her forehead, gone suddenly faint with the returning memories. "And I know you, Cousin . . . how did I ever forget?"

A short time later, they were sitting by the fire in the witch's house, exchanging stories, while the old woman cleaned and bandaged the wound in Tryffin's side. He had somehow bled all over Gwenlliant's gown as well as his own clothes, and he was feeling a bit light-headed after the loss of so much blood, the cold and exhaustion of their long walk.

Tryffin sat on a stool, Gwenlliant curled up on the floor at his feet. Grifflet had been put to bed in his own cradle, now barely large enough for him, and had instantly fallen asleep. The first thing Tryffin had asked of Dame Ceinwen was the month. *"There is no reckoning things by months here on the Marches,"* the crone had replied. *"But if there were . . . this would be the end of July."* He was only slowly allowing himself to realize that he and Gwenlliant were no longer married.

When she had finished dressing his wound, Ceinwen gave him a shirt and a tunic out of the mending basket she kept by her chair. It had always astounded him, the number of things she kept in that basket.

"So," said the old woman, when Tryffin and Gwenlliant had finished their stories, "it wās the Prince of Tir Gwyngelli, Mabonograin, who committed the first wrong, when he stole the Princess Tinne from her brother."

Tryffin sat up straighter, startled out of his haze of pain and exhaustion. "He stole her from Gwythyr, who was continually raping her," he protested.

"You are confusing the two different circumstances. Gwythyr did wrong, but that was a separate matter," said Dame Ceinwen. "It was one thing . . . and a fine and noble thing, at that . . . for Mabonograin to rescue her, another to take Tinne for himself, to lie with her and make her his mistress, who could never be his wife in honor because of the vows she had already taken. I wonder if he even offered to return her to her brother? And she . . . did Tinne even ask?"

"What they ought to have done," the old woman continued, leaning forward in her chair of woven branches, "was go before the High Prince to plead her wrongs. Had she behaved honorably, Prince Caerthinn, for all he was so weak, would have protected her from Gwythyr. But it is easy enough to see that she did not want her brother's protection. Tinne wanted Mabonograin, just as much as he wanted her. It is impossible not to sympathize with two such desperate young lovers, but one cannot deny the terrible consequences of what they did."

Tryffin considered that. It went against the grain, but he had to admit there was a certain amount of truth in what the old woman said. "Yet what Caerthinn did was far worse," he said. "It was his reckless and wicked act that brought the curse on Mochdreff."

"And that act must be atoned for," said Ceinwen, "or the blight on the land will continue, perhaps for another thousand years. It is Caerthinn's heir who must make that atonement and heal the land, as poor Garlon attempted but only partly succeeded. And you, because Mabonograin played his part in those terrible events, must bring these tidings to Caerthinn's heir and aid him in any way possible."

"But who *is* Caerthinn's heir, and how shall we find him?" asked Gwenlliant, leaving her seat to put more wood on the fire. "When you told me the story of Cerddin Wledig, you said nobody knew who his descendants were."

"Nor did anyone know when I told you that. But now I have learned the truth, and Prince Tryffin has as well . . . though he may have to give the matter a little thought," said Ceinwen.

Tryffin nodded his head. The different parts of the story were beginning to come together in a recognizable pattern. "When I was in the Shadow Lands, the Inner Celydonn, I always found myself in one of two places: Gwyngelli or Ochren. There must have been some binding or destiny involved that continually brought me back to the same place again and again. Also, there was Garlon's act of contrition, which brought water to the dying land . . . he could not have done that, were he not Caerthinn's heir. But you told me back in Charon that his ignorance of the mysteries proved dangerous—I suppose, really, his ignorance of the causes and the history of the blight was the reason that his suffering accomplished so little."

Tryffin moved his stool closer to the fire. "As for the Sons of the Boar, Gwythyr and Gereint, their descendants became Lords of Mochdreff. Corrig, Corfil, Goronwy, and Morcant, who ruled in Mochdreff, all came of that line, which had adopted the boar and the spear as their standard and their coat of arms. The Lady Essylt also came of that line, and therefore so does Grifflet. As Gereint, Gwythyr, and Maelinn gave bad council and brought Caerthinn to ruin, so it was a twist of destiny that brought Lord Cado of Ochren as councilor and secret enemy to their descendants. Before God, it has always been the same three families . . . I suspect that Lot must have somehow been connected with Corrig's line."

"He was," said Dame Ceinwen, "a distant relation."

And Tryffin thought of how the pattern of grief had repeated itself again and again: Tinne, Gwythyr, and Mabonograin. Diaspad, Manogan, and Corfil. Guenhumara, Menai, and Cado. And himself, Calchas, and Gwenlliant enacting the old tragedy in their own way. It even explained his own ill-conceived attraction to Dahaut and Essylt. "Lord Cado is dead, and his nephew Mahaffy is Lord of Ochren . . . that was once Charon, and before that Achren. Mother of God! That means that

Mahaffy is Caerthinn's heir, and he is the one who should make the atonement and become Lord of Mochdreff."

The full implications of that only gradually dawned on Tryffin, and when they did they were overwhelming. Until now, his task had been the *comparatively* easy one of bringing peace to Mochdreff, then installing one of Morcant's three heirs on the High Seat at Caer Ysgithr. "But to convince the petty lords and the clan chieftains to accept a fourth claimant . . . whose very claim was unknown until now . . . that is going to be difficult. As God is my witness, that is a task that could take me years to accomplish!"

"It may well do so," said Ceinwen. "But that is another task and another story. For now, you have only to bring Mahaffy to his act of contrition. I will describe to you how it must be done, for I remember how it happened in my brother's day. You must begin—as my brother did not do—with the reconsecration of the sidhe-stone chalice. That was meant to be the wedding cup at the marriage of Tinne and Mabonograin, and should have united their two lands in peace and prosperity for a millennium. Instead, it was consecrated to the so-called cult of Cerridwen, and its powers were corrupted in the very same instant they were fully revealed. The reconsecration will occur when members of all three houses drink from the cup together in the spirit of love and conciliation. You, Prince Tryffin, and Mahaffy . . . and since it is highly unlikely that we will convince young Math or Peredur, or the Lady Essylt . . . Grifflet must play his part. He will not understand the reasons, but he will feel the necessary good will. We must hope it will be enough. Then the ring shall pass from your hand to Mahaffy's, in token of the friendship between Mabonograin and Caerthinn, which should never have been broken. Finally, there is the act of contrition, for Caerthinn's crime against nature, which only Mahaffy can perform. With the weight of all those other ancestral sins removed, he should be successful."

The crone turned her intense dark gaze on Gwenlliant. "You shall guide him through it, child, for he will need a wise-woman to show him the way, and I shall be busy elsewhere. If Mahaffy refuses to bear the burden of his ancestry—and I hope that I raised him better than that—then there will be nothing that any of us can do."

"But I don't understand how Maelinn came to be the shapechanger," said Gwenlliant. "She did many things out of spite and ambition, when I knew her, and when she took my memories from me she was very cold and cruel, but slaughtering children . . . no, she was never so wicked as that."

"But we are not speaking of a living woman. The Maelinn you met was only a shadow," said Ceinwen. "They often go mad, you know, when they enter our world; that is why it is not good for them to do so. It must have been a great shock to Maelinn, arriving in our Mochdreff, to discover she was only a ghost . . . the ghost of a woman who had been dead for a thousand years. Then, too, she may have encountered her own image somewhere along the way, moving through time, and if it was not an imperfect copy, as Prince Tryffin met of himself in Annwn, that shock would have been considerable also."

"But for all that," breathed Gwenlliant, "why kill the children, why try to destroy Tryffin?"

The crone shrugged. "As you were the one who knew her, perhaps you can guess."

Gwenlliant considered for a time. "Well, perhaps I do see," she said, returning to her seat on the floor, staring into the fire. "Maelinn was ambitious. And I suppose . . . I suppose if she went mad and lost all sense of conscience, it might seem rather a grand thing that she and her brothers had accomplished: a curse that endured for a thousand years. She would not want anyone interfering with that, and she would consider Tryffin a threat, because of his efforts to bring peace and order to Mochdreff. And if she was really so proud of the terrible thing she had done—"

"That would explain why she did not seek to harm me at Caer Bannawg," said Tryffin. "Since I had come so close to the end of the tale, she wanted me to see it all, and marvel at the woman and her brothers who had accomplished so much. She knew I would be returning to the wood, anyway, and that is where she meant to confront and destroy me."

"The wound that you gave her with the silver-bladed dagger should hold her in the past for a time, and I can hold her a while longer," said Dame Ceinwen. "But eventually she must be destroyed."

"And so," said Tryffin, with a deep sigh, "I must do that with all the rest."

"No," Gwenlliant said quietly, "that must be my task, since it was I who gave her the power and the opportunity to escape the past. And . . . I am very much afraid that can only be done by meeting her in the Shadow Lands."

Tryffin opened his mouth to protest, but Dame Ceinwen stopped him. "She has the right of it, Prince Tryffin. It is her task and fairly so, nor will she lack the ability to perform it, once the magic she learned in Achren returns to her. But take heart: You and she will be together for a considerable period of time, because you have a very important task which you must accomplish first."

He still did not like it, but this was hardly the time for arguing. There was still so much to be done—and who knew how things would really stand afterward, anyway?

The old woman began to bustle about the cottage, fixing their supper. Gwenlliant would have helped, but Ceinwen told her to stay where she was. "You have traveled far this day, and you have a long journey ahead of you in the morning. Rest while you can."

And anyway, thought Gwenlliant, it was pleasant sitting down by the fire, soaking in the heat after the chill of the Mist . . . and Tryffin was so near she could reach out and touch him. Thinking of all the months when she had feared to return to the Marches too late, only to discover that he had lost patience waiting for her, it was a great relief to realize that he had never even considered abandoning her.

She reached up and slipped her hand into his big square one, felt the strong but careful grip in return. "It will be good to go home to Caer Ysgithr, however briefly."

A faint, sad smile crossed his face. "I hope that you truly mean that. But you should know: When we arrive in Mochdreff, we will no longer be married. You are free to go wherever you wish."

Gwenlliant caught her breath. "You sound . . . are you trying to tell me, Cousin, that you no longer *wish* to be married?"

Tryffin shook his head. "God knows, that is not what I wish at all. But I am trying to tell you that I did you a great wrong. The same wrong, maybe, that Mabonograin did Tinne. It was not really necessary for me to marry you in order to rescue you from Rhun of Yrgoll, though I told myself that it was at the time. Not even necessary for the sake of your good name, in spite of what your father said. We could have taken one of Rhun's women back to Caer Cadwy with us to keep things respectable along the way, and once you were safe in our cousin the High King's protection, you could have married me or not, just as you pleased. But the truth was, Cyndrywyn had frightened me with his damnable scheme, and I was so eager to hold you and keep you for myself, I wouldn't allow myself to think of any alternatives. So I let you believe you had to choose between Rhun and me."

She sat at his feet, thinking that over. She wondered if she had known these things all along, if she had been guilty of a similar self-deception. "It is true that I was afraid of my father, terrified of Rhun . . . and even after you arrived, I worried that my father would still take me away from you, if we did not do as he suggested. And I would have done anything you asked me, in order to show how grateful I was for being rescued, though I don't think I allowed myself to think what being your wife would *really* mean. But I do love you, and I know that I want to live with you, and try . . . try to put all the terrors of my past behind me and become your wife in very truth."

He gave a great sigh of relief. Yet the light was gone from his face, there was a defeated look in his eyes. "If that is how you really feel, I'd rather not take you back to Caer Ysgithr still unwed. It is true that I promised you a second, grander wedding in Tir Gwyngelli, a magnificent occasion with all my family looking on . . . and now I can only offer you another hurried, makeshift affair, no better than the first time."

She felt a tightness in her throat, tears stinging her eyes, to hear him sound so weary and self-reproachful. But she smiled and tried to sound cheerful. "I do like the idea of a wedding in Gwyngelli, and I shall almost certainly hold you to *that* promise. But in the meantime, I am willing to marry you as often as you please . . . and under practically any circumstances."

The meal was ready by now, so they ate black bread and toasted cheese, a stew made of nettles and sorrel, and finished it up with toasted apples. Afterward, they slept the sleep of the truly exhausted, curled up on the floor together, with their cloaks spread over them.

In the morning, they ate a quick breakfast and prepared to leave the cottage on the Marches. Grifflet, it had been decided, would remain with Dame Ceinwen for a short time, to be reclaimed as soon as certain arrangements had been made.

But before they left, the crone took Gwenlliant aside for a few final words. "Though he does not say so, it is easy to see that something has changed inside of him. The strength and self-confidence, so quiet and yet so evident always, it is all gone. He has many heavy responsibilities and he has suffered great pain and grief over this last year. Perhaps worst of all was the helplessness he felt watching the old tragedy repeat itself in Achren, for that great heart of his had never allowed him to spare any effort on behalf of others. In truth, he has suffered such blows that he may take a long time healing.

"In short," said Dame Ceinwen, "he needs all of the strength that you can give him. You have an important task to fulfill, one that may call for great dispatch and haste, because I cannot be certain how long I can hold Maelinn in the past. I fear that I am growing too old for these contests of will. But even if doing so should cause a brief delay along the road . . . I would advise you to wed Prince Tryffin as soon as you can."

"Yes," said Gwenlliant quietly. "I fully intend to do so."

I am generous, I give without stint
For I am the cauldron of plenty.
　　　　　　　—*From* The Song of the Lady Celedon

25.

The Vessel of Plenty

The witch sent them through the Bearded Wood, and they
came out of the ancient trees, the musty green darkness, on a
road near a village that Tryffin knew. It was located about five
miles distant from Anoeth. Sitting behind Tryffin on the gelding's broad back, Gwenlliant looked over his shoulder and
spotted a tiny white-washed church with a tree and a well, and an
even smaller house behind, which looked like an appropriate cell
for a monk.

They were married under the walnut tree, with the young and
exceptionally earnest brown friar officiating, and the whole
village looked curiously on. It was far more public than their last
wedding, and word was likely to spread, so at least there would
be no scandal when they started living together after more than
a year apart. They used the same rings they had used in Perfudd,
and exchanged the same chaste kiss, and though Tryffin held her
tightly afterward, and felt a slight easing of the pain in his heart,
he could see very well that it was going to be the same situation
all over again.

Gwenlliant had all her old memories and her old terrors back.
He was sick and wary, not trusting anything he had believed in
before, least of all himself. It was another hurried ceremony, and
a swift ride afterward, and too much to do once they reached
Anoeth to give them the time and the quiet they needed to
overcome any of these things.

But when they rode into the city and stopped at the inn, when
he reached up to help her down from the saddle and she slid

willingly into the circle of his arms, when they exchanged a long and lingering kiss right there in the street, he felt a little better. And when they went into the common room, and the guards (who had been living there so long it was beginning to feel like home) started up from the benches and greeted him with cries of surprise and delight, and Meligraunce and Conn, hearing the noise below, came clattering downstairs with their faces alight at the very sight of him, it was better still.

He gave his squire a rib-cracking hug and violated the Captain's dignity with another. Then Gwenlliant gave both of her hands to Conn to be kissed, which he did with a fervor that might have excited the Governor's jealousy under other circumstances, and she smiled at Meligraunce with tears in her eyes . . . and in spite of the fact that so many were missing—Cei, Elffin, and Garth back at Caer Ysgithr, Grifflet with the witch—they were *truly* a household for the very first time in over a year.

It took several minutes for Tryffin to realize that someone important was among the missing. "Jesus, Mary, and Joseph! Where is Mahaffy?"

The look that Conn and Meligraunce exchanged boded ill, until the Captain spoke. "He is improving more rapidly now . . . it is several weeks since the attack, and there is no doubt of his complete recovery. In truth, the wounds and the sprained wrist have already healed. It is just that he needs another week or two of rest."

"The shapechanger attacked him?" said Tryffin. At least it gave him some idea of what Maelinn had been doing during her long disappearance while he was in Achren.

"Your Grace, she did, and nearly had the life sucked out of him before Conn and Ciag came into the room and intervened."

"But where *is* Mahaffy?" asked Tryffin. They told him the young Lord of Ochren was under Dame Brangwaine's care and under her roof. "Then in God's name, let us go there and talk to him at once."

Mahaffy looked well, if a little thinner than the last time Tryffin saw him. Sitting in a chair in Dame Brangwaine's stifling solar, with dozens of candles blazing on every side of him, he insisted that he felt very nearly recovered and that his nurses were being overly cautious.

"The truth is," he said, "I feel most damnably embarrassed. She had been preying on infants and old, old people all of that while, and then she chose to attack me. What sort of weakling did she take me for?"

Tryffin suppressed a smile. "She attacked me, too, if you'll remember. What do you think she took *me* for?"

"That was different," said Mahaffy. "You were the one she wanted all along. You are the most important man in Mochdreff."

The Governor took a seat in a chair opposite him, and Gwenlliant stood behind with her hands resting on the back. "And she wanted you for the same reason," said Tryffin. "Because you were as great a threat to her ambition as I was."

"I?" said Mahaffy, sitting up straighter. "I think you must be joking. For all my blood is so old and so pure, for all I am inclined to give myself the most appalling airs on account of that fact, I am nothing. The lord of a great many barren acres . . . a man without kinsmen, allies, or influence . . . I threaten no one."

"You are wrong if you think that you have no allies," said Tryffin quietly. "For I am the first among them, and I hope to be of great use to you in the future." And because it seemed that the young knight was sufficiently recovered and strong enough to receive the information—at least as well as he was ever *likely* to receive it—the Governor proceeded to tell him the whole story, all of the parts he did not know already, and ended by explaining what was expected of Mahaffy now.

Mahaffy was stunned, although naturally he had seen the end coming even before Tryffin completed the story and went on to the explanations that followed. "I am the heir?" His face was white under the mop of shiny black curls. "Not Math or Peredur? Your Grace, I am hardly worthy. And truth to tell . . . I don't really know if I can even do what you wish me to do."

"I know," said Tryffin sympathetically, "that it sounds very painful and frightening. But you are the only one who can do it. God knows that I would take your place if I could. And you will have time to gather the strength and the courage you will need, because it will take a few weeks to gather the necessary assembly. Dame Ceinwen says we must arrange the act of contrition before we make any attempt to establish your claim, because the shapechanger may return and attempt to prevent it—perhaps by killing you. The men we gather together will not even understand what they are seeing, though we can hope the significance will come to them later, and convince them of your right to govern Mochdreff. Yet, you must do this difficult thing without any promise of a reward thereafter."

Mahaffy waved a hand, dismissing those words. "It is not the rite of atonement . . . I suppose I can steel myself to endure it with you and the Lady Gwenlliant by my side to encourage me. It is the part that comes after. Who is to say that I won't be as bad as my ancestors? They were all of them weak or wicked, and the recent ones, anyway, abominably arrogant."

Tryffin rose from his seat, crossed over, and put a comforting hand on the young man's shoulder. "The same may be said for the ancestors of Math and Peredur. By God, you have only to consider Peredur's mother! Corfil tormented his wife until she killed him with magic. Corrig fab Corrig had his own niece murdered, sent the girl to perish under a fall of rocks rather than allow her to marry my grandfather. Gwythyr and Gereint were purely evil. Goronwy was weak. And Lord Morcant was perhaps the best of the lot, but you know how cold a man he was.

"Besides," he added, "if it turns out that you are not fit to rule . . . then you *won't*. It is going to take many months, perhaps even years, to establish your claim. We are going to have to find allies, make new friends, and during that time you will have to travel at my side and practice considerable diplomacy. We may have to go to Caer Cadwy and convince the Emperor, who might not accept you on my word alone. Some may come over to our side because of what they see at the rite of atonement, some will understand that the healing of the land was your doing, but others will need *more*. And I wish to accomplish this with as little warfare as possible. In truth, you must behave as though you are a prince already, and win men over by your strength and wisdom. But you will have some time to learn these things as you go along. If you don't, and if no one is willing to support your claim . . . then politically, at least, Mochdreff will be no worse off than it is right now."

Mahaffy thought for a long time before he spoke again. "If you are willing to devote so much of your time and your efforts to this cause, then I suppose I would be a coward to do any less. And if I am to learn princely behavior—wisdom, strength, compassion, diplomacy—then God knows, I could not hope for a better example than the one you have provided these last two years."

He smiled wryly. "In truth, I believe I have profited by your example already, though there is still so much for me to learn."

"It is true," said Gwenlliant, speaking up for the first time. "Prince Tryffin has taught the Mochdreffi what their lord might be. They had ceased to expect that a man they could love would ever lead them, a man who would be as devoted to their best interests as they would be to his. Now they have seen the possibility, you have only to prove that you are that man and they will flock to your banner. It will not be easy proving that, of course, but you have this advantage over the other *supposed* heirs, that you will know better than they how such a prince thinks and behaves. Also, you are forgetting your own admirable qualities. Do you think that my lord, or I, or Dame Ceinwen would support you in this if we thought you unworthy?"

There was a sudden brightening in Mahaffy's eyes. "No," he said, with a dawning grin. "No, I do not. So I suppose I must trust in your sagacity, and accept that I am the man to do all these things. But Prince Tryffin . . . how are you going to manage to call together this great assembly you have mentioned, in a matter of weeks?"

"We may only be able to call together those who are our strongest allies already, as well as those who will come at *their* bidding," said Tryffin. He counted them over in his own mind before telling them off out loud. "Dame Brangwaine, I believe, will be with us, and most of her kin. Those who are under her influence and not Lord Cernach's. The three clans whose dispute you mediated so wisely will almost certainly come at your bidding. Teign of Peryf and his nephew Dywel of Oeth: Their clan has already shown its personal loyalty to me and may be expected to do so again. Clan Llyr, clan Glyn. The people in Ywerion, where we went hunting monsters last year. And that little village where you killed the two-headed talking boar, you and Garth between you: They have cause to feel grateful to you. With these allies, and such friends as they may gather, it should be enough. Perhaps a thousand witnesses to spread the word that a new age has come for Mochdreff, and that they were there to see it begin—and that the man who began it was Mahaffy Guillyn."

Mahaffy nodded. "It does seem as though these last two years have not been wasted, if we have made so many friends and allies between us. As though everything we have done in that time has been guided by . . . by a compelling destiny."

"Aye," said Tryffin, with the weariness returning. "But we were not the first ones to be so guided. Others had the same opportunities—perhaps even better opportunities—and yet they failed. We must strive very hard to make certain that we are not found similarly wanting."

∽∾∾∾∾

There were weeks of travel after that, while they carried the news from one end of Mochdreff to the other, because the Governor wished to speak personally to as many people as possible, and Meligraunce, Conn, and Mahaffy were sent out to places where they were nearly as well known as he was. Summer was past and autumn far advanced before they all met again, the night before the assigned day, at the place chosen for the assembly and the ritual.

They sat down together in a scarlet pavilion, part of a city of tents which had been pitched near a certain hill in Penafon, not far out of Ochren . . . not far, either, from the place where Tryffin had once taken a crossbow bolt in the shoulder . . . which the Governor was convinced was the same hill where Tinne and Mabonograin had died, and Caerthinn set fire to the heather.

Dame Brangwaine had arrived in a litter earlier that day, and had emerged from the purple and gold palanquin declaring that the journey had nearly killed her but she was not inclined to miss this occasion. She hoped that when she returned to Anoeth the springs of that city would have regained their ancient purity and all be producing sweet water—and perhaps the ceremony which healed the land would serve to revive her failing health as well. She brought her great-granddaughter with her, and the warlock page.

"It is the coming of the Millennium," she said, as she was carried in a chair into the tent. She fixed her eyes on Meligraunce. "It is a time for new men to assert themselves."

Tryffin was not quite certain that he knew everything that had happened in Anoeth during his time in Achren, but he had not failed to notice a new and interesting tension that existed between the Captain and Luned. And he wondered how much the ancient wise-woman had foreseen from their very first meeting.

Cei and Elffin, who had been Gwenlliant's pages, came from Caer Ysgithr to be reunited with her, and Conn's brother Garth, who appeared to be as devoted as ever. As they all sat down to supper in the pavilion, Dame Ceinwen made her entrance unannounced—but not unexpected—hobbling into the tent using her iron-shod staff for support, with a sleepy Grifflet tagging along at her side. She did not stay long, just long enough to embrace Mahaffy, turn the little boy over to his waiting parents, the chalice over to her former fosterling, and then disappeared into the night, to continue guarding the way between the worlds.

The hill was much eroded, but enough of its contours had remained for Tryffin to identify it. And there was quite appropriately a small stone church—of the orthodox sort and not connected with any of the more dangerous heresies—built at the base of the hill. There, Mahaffy went for his solitary vigil.

It was a long, restless night, filled with anticipation. At dawn, the Governor, Gwenlliant, and Grifflet went to the church to perform in private the first part of the ritual. The crone had removed the illusion surrounding the chalice, and now Gwenlliant filled the sidhe-stone cup with wine as red as the blood-red stone itself, and carried it to each one of the others, that he might drink in good fellowship: Tryffin for Gwyngelli, Mahaffy for Mochdreff and Ochren, and Grifflet for the Clan of the Boar. Gwenlliant made certain the child took only a little, and he did not seem to like it much, but drank his part manfully, then smiled his peculiarly winsome smile as the Governor swept him up into his arms and Mahaffy gave him a reassuring pat on the back.

"Is that all?" said Mahaffy, with a disappointed laugh. "I had thought there would be . . . something more to this part."

"Look," said Gwenlliant, and he saw that the chalice had changed color, to a luminous milky white crystal, more typical of sidhe-stone.

After that, Tryffin gave him the ring and they exchanged vows of eternal friendship. "And that friendship, God willing, shall extend beyond you and me and eventually encompass the people of Mochdreff and the folk of Gwyngelli as well," said the Governor. "For the oldest legends say that they lived together like brothers in the beginning, being of the same stock."

"Now," Gwenlliant said to Mahaffy, "comes the difficult part, but I shall be by your side every moment."

Mahaffy nodded grimly, gone suddenly pale. They left the church and climbed the little hill, around which the multitude had already assembled.

Tryffin stood a little apart, holding Grifflet in his arms, while Gwenlliant and the young Lord of Ochren took their place near the top of the hill at the rim of the grassy hollow where Tinne and Mabonograin had suffered their tragic fate. A light wind was blowing, and the sky was overcast. For all that, Tryffin could almost smell the morning sun on the heather, almost see the two young lovers lying together in the grass in such sweet abandon after their lovemaking. He must have shown something in his face, because the little boy slipped an arm around his neck as if to console him.

"Ah, Grifflet, it was a long time ago, and what right have I to mourn for that unhappy pair when I never really knew them . . . when I have a wife and a son and everything a man could want?"

On the rise above, Gwenlliant held the cup, and Mahaffy took out his dirk and swiftly and ruthlessly scored the backs of his hands, then held them so the blood might flow into the chalice. His jaw was set and his eyes dark with pain, though he never made a sound. Then he knelt on the ground and scooped up a handful of dirt which he kissed and dropped into the cup with his blood.

Tryffin knew instinctively that this was costing Mahaffy far more than the loss of blood. Even at a distance, the Governor could feel the Earth magic, a humming in his bones, a quicksilver fire in his blood. But for Caerthinn's heir it had to be far more intense: His whole body was shaking as if with ague, and not only his blood was burning but his flesh as well . . . Tryffin could see the glow, and Mahaffy writhed as one being consumed by flames, though his skin remained pale and unscorched. It was all his pride, all his arrogance, all his sins that were burning away, and along with them the multitudinous sins of his forefathers.

It was agony to watch, but it was soon over. The sky opened, and the rain came pelting down, filling the cup of earth and blood to overflowing, so that the mixture poured out onto the soil, while Gwenlliant and Mahaffy, drenched to the bone, stood like statues near the top of the hill and allowed the healing rain to wash over them.

The rain was over as quickly as it began, leaving the air so much fresher that the crowd—which ought to be feeling a bit disgruntled after its unexpected soaking—silently squelched off to change their clothes, looking rather more pleased with the course of events than otherwise.

But for Tryffin, standing motionless with Grifflet still in his arms, there was a great deal more than a refreshing breath of air. He could *feel* a stirring beneath the earth . . . sense seeds, long dormant, sending out roots . . . the paths of underground rivers, long dry, begin to fill with life-giving moisture. And not only was the land beginning to heal, but he was healing as well. He knew that he was going to find the strength and the courage for the long task ahead of him.

They met that night, under the stars, at the edge of a silvery little moonlit wood, about half a mile distant from the place where the tents were pitched. "I don't know why," said Gwenlliant, "but something seemed to be calling me out into the night, and I wanted to be where trees and bushes and grasses were growing."

"Yes," said Tryffin, gazing down at her, "it was the same for me. But if you don't want company . . ."

Gwenlliant shook her head. "I do want company. Your company, anyway. It is a perfectly remarkable night, you know. A fortunate night for those who were married this same day, and . . ." She blushed and looked away.

"Yes," he said, his voice shaking a little, "I had that feeling as well."

They found a place where the grass grew long, and Tryffin spread out his cloak. He drew her down to the ground, and held her in his arms, and kissed her long and deeply. Then there was a dizzying time of hands, mouths, tongues. And her gown came off, his shirt and tunic, until they were kneeling there half dressed, he in his linen breeches and she in her thin shift.

But when he put out a hand to cup her breast and feel its warmth and softness through the cloth, he realized that she was trembling, and her eyes were wide with fear instead of desire. "This still frightens you," he said, just above a whisper.

"I want this," she answered softly, "but it does still frighten me."

He took her hand and kissed the palm. "Then if you are afraid to let me make love to you . . . you must make love to me, and then there will be nothing for you to fear."

Gwenlliant gave a little breathy laugh. "I don't even know how," she whispered.

"I think that you do," he said. "You must just touch me in the same way that I have been touching you."

She put an uncertain hand on his chest. "The very same way?" The palm of her hand moved slowly down, then up again, leaving a trail of shivers across the skin. "I thought it would be different for you than for me."

It was difficult for him to keep from crushing her in his arms, covering her face and neck and breasts with kisses. "There is not . . ." he said, slowly and carefully, ". . . an inch of my skin that is not longing to feel you touch me. Begin anywhere that you like . . . and I am certain we will reach . . . the right places, eventually."

She ran her hands over the hard muscles on his arms, across his chest where she could feel his heart pounding strongly, down to the flat bands of muscles on his abdomen. His skin was smooth and warm, covered with tiny golden hairs, and his breathing was harsh and slow. When she kissed his neck, he began to tremble; when she put her mouth against his, a deep groan escaped him.

But eventually she did find all the right places, and losing her fear, because she was as eager as he was, allowed him to touch her as well. Their joining, when it finally came, was long and slow, and breathlessly sweet. Afterward, they lay exhausted but blissful in each other's arms.

In the morning, it was like waking to a new world. They dressed, helping each other with the buckles and lacings, and Tryffin insisted on braiding her hair for her.

"I thought," Gwenlliant said, with a smile, "that I had finished with ladies-in-waiting and tiring women, and was now quite capable of dressing my own hair."

"No," he said, kissing the winter-gold tresses he was weaving together. "I will wait on you whenever we are together after this, and you will wait on me . . . and we will banish all squires and waiting women who wish to interfere!"

As they walked back to the scarlet pavilion, the leaves were already turning a fresher green in the trees overhead, as though autumn had never arrived, the heather and the gorse were blooming in the fields, and armies of immense golden bees had arrived from somewhere, to hum among the blossoms.

"And it will be better each day for a long time to come, as the land continues to heal. I am afraid that the magic will no longer come so easily, while the wonder of this thing we are seeing now will gradually fade," she said.

"No matter," he answered, taking her into his arms. "We have the magic and the wonder today . . . and that is quite enough to satisfy me."